Scar Hill

ALAN TEMPERLEY

Alan Temperley.

Luath Press Limited

EDINBURGH

www.luath.co.uk

First published 2010

ISBN: 978-1-906307-52-3

The author's right to be identified as author of this book
under the Copyright, Designs and Patents Act 1988 has been asserted.

The publisher acknowledges the support of

 Scottish
Arts Council

towards the publication of this volume.

The paper used in this book is recyclable.
It is made from low-chlorine pulps produced
in a low-energy, low-emissions manner
from renewable forests.

Printed and bound by CPI Antony Rowe, Chippenham

Typeset in 10.8 point Sabon

Dedicated to my mother, my cousin Elizabeth
and my good friend Jean.

Acknowledgements

I wish to thank the following people for their friendship, kindness and help during the writing of this book: David Mackay, Nancy Fraser, Gordon and Margaret Mackay, David Banks, Elizabeth Jobling, Christina Mackay, Frank Gourlay (father and son), Becky Gallagher, Dolan and Moira Conway, Neil Macintyre, Jeanne Hughes, Patricia Niesen, John Miller, my many friends in the north, and most of all Jean Slaven for her constant help and encouragement.

Contents

I

Ben

THE BUS SLOWED as it neared the top of the Sandy Brae. Peter rose and swung his schoolbag to his shoulder. A friendly magazine batted him on the head as he made his way to the front.

'See you, Winnie.'

Peter Irwin, twelve years old. They had called him Winnie since primary school.

He bent to see through the windscreen. His dad's old van was not waiting at the gate. Peter hadn't expected it would be.

The bus crunched into the passing place and stopped. The door hissed open. Ignoring the driver, he descended to the verge and hitched his bag comfortable. The few children left aboard looked down as the bus pulled away. A six-year-old made a face. The bus drove on. A stink of diesel hung in the air as Peter crossed the road to the five-bar gate. It was broken, fuzzy with lichen.

Once there had been a sign, Scar Hill, the croft house where he lived with his father, but beetles and the years of wind and rain had worked their destruction and now not even the post remained.

There had been a second sign also, in better repair: Three Pines, the house of their nearest neighbour – indeed their only neighbour. But the woman who had moved in eighteen months earlier, Bunny Mason, liked privacy and had pulled it from the nail. Now nothing but two unmarked post boxes – the Irwins' falling apart, Bunny's stout and weatherproof – remained to indicate that somewhere out there in the rolling moor there existed two homes.

Peter's dog, Ben, stood waiting beyond the gate. He was a grey lurcher, like a skinny Irish wolfhound. On the days Peter's dad didn't drive down, Ben loped along the two and a half miles of track to meet him off the bus. As Peter drew close, the tall dog barked once, bouncing in welcome.

He went through and hooked the gate shut at his back. Impatiently Ben danced around him and jumped up to put his paws on Peter's shoulders. As he stood on his hind legs, his whiskery head was higher than the boy's.

Peter staggered to support him. 'Hello, Ben. Hello, lovely.' He buried his face in the dog's neck and felt Ben's bony skull against his own. Awkwardly the dog's tongue slopped his ear. 'Who's my *best* boy!'

Greetings concluded, he pushed Ben down, brushed the dirt from his jacket and started the walk home. Most days his dad drove him to the road in the morning and was there to pick him up after school. Sometimes Peter drove himself, in the old white van or on the tractor if his dad didn't need it, parked in the abandoned quarry, and drove back again at teatime. Occasionally he took his bike, bucking over the potholes.

It had been raining, the track was puddled. He scanned the sky; the clouds were opening. The bracken glowed red in a shaft of late afternoon sun.

A couple of hundred metres into the moor, a side track turned downhill between rocks and thickets of gorse. This was the road to Three Pines – though *two pines and a stump* would be more accurate, for in a great gale years before, the third tree had been snapped clean off. Bunny had planted a replacement, ringed by wire to protect it from deer and the goats and other animals which wandered round her cottage.

'Like a bloody gipsy encampment,' his dad had said not long after her arrival. 'Hens, cats, pony an' all the rest of it. What's she want all that lot for?'

'She's painting them,' Peter said. 'You know that fine. Supposed to be for a book.'

'A book, aye. Like Willie there, down by the shore. I'll

believe it when I see it.'

But Peter had been to the house and seen the paintings scattered around the kitchen where Bunny worked. For a children's book she said. He thought they were great. He had called just the once, to give her a lobster they'd caught in the boat, still cold from the sea.

Bunny couldn't accept it. 'Drop it into boiling water?' she had said, dog at her feet, cat in the chair. 'I just couldn't, Peter. It's very kind of you but sorry.'

Some weeks prior to this she had called at Scar Hill to introduce herself as their new neighbour. They had made her welcome and chatted by the fire with tea and cake, but Peter's father, Jim Irwin, was a private man and she seemed to understand that. She had not called again. In fact they rarely had a visitor, and neither did she as far as Peter knew, apart from a daughter who came to stay from time to time. Despite this, he liked Bunny Mason with her thick grey hair chopped short and her public school accent – more like Lord Rimsdale and the rich folk who came for the stalking and the fishing than people in the village.

Only the chimneys of Three Pines were visible from the track but Bunny appeared on the hill in her green anorak and knitted hat, calling 'Molly! Come on, Molly!' It was time to take the cow down for milking. Seeing Peter, she waved a vigorous arm and he waved back.

But Peter's thoughts that afternoon were elsewhere. What would he find when he got home? What state would his father be in? Had he spent the day at the Cod and Kipper, the shabby inn down by the jetty? That was his usual retreat when depression struck, when the black snakes, as Jim called them, came slithering from the drains and up through the floorboards to hang their heavy coils around his neck. Peter loved his dad, it wasn't his fault he was sick, but how drunk would he be tonight? How long would the mood last? It used to be two days but he seemed to be getting worse. How long this time before the snakes dropped from him and wriggled back the way they had come? It was Friday. The whole weekend lay ahead.

He took a deep breath as he walked and tried to be positive. There was football tomorrow and they were playing away. That would take up much of the day.

Ben put up a hare. Yelping with excitement, he shot off in pursuit. Ben was faster but the hare was more agile. Provided it made no mistakes, it would get away. If it did not, they might have hare casserole on Sunday.

If his dad was eating by then.

Peter walked on. In minutes the tarmacked road was hidden from view. Mile upon mile the ridged and rolling moor spread around him, right to the horizon. Familiar to Peter for most of his life, he hardly saw it: the long grasses bleaching with autumn, brown heather, red bracken, grey rock and white tufts of cotton grass bobbing in the wind. Far to the west a range of mountains, saw-toothed and hump-backed, formed a frieze against the sky. At his back, beyond the road and rugged headlands, lay the deep blue sea.

A distant scream made the hairs on his neck stand on end. He waited and after a minute or two Ben reappeared, trotting round the side of a hill. He looked pleased with himself.

'Come here.'

The big dog scrambled down some rocks and jumped a stream.

'Good boy.'

Ben was panting, his eyes bright, mouth flecked with foam. He trotted in a circle, too excited to stand still.

'Let's see you.' Peter caught him by the collar. 'What have you been up to?' Doggy breath hit him in the face. Peter wiped his muzzle with a hand. Mixed in with the saliva was a tiny tuft of grey-brown hairs, short hairs like a rabbit's. Ben had run down his hare. 'Good boy!' Peter clapped his muscular back. 'Go on, now, fetch.' He pushed Ben back the way he had come.

But Ben was not a retriever and he was not very well trained. Some words, like *come here ... good dog ... sit ... no ...* and his name, he understood perfectly. But *fetch*, when the object he had to fetch was half a mile away and out of sight, was beyond him. Knowing that something was required of him but not sure what, he looked around in confusion.

'Come on then.' Peter slipped his rucksack on to both shoulders and stepped from the track.

There had been a lot of rain in the past week and the ground was boggy. Though he stayed on rising ground and the sheep-nibbled grass as much as possible, for a hundred metres at a time he had to plough through drenched heather. Soon his grey school trousers were sodden to the knee. His foot sank in a hidden hollow. Icy water filled his shoe. Peter pulled it out and surveyed the clinging peat. 'Oh, shit!' he said. 'Bugger! Bloody dog!'

Ben realised where they were heading and bounded ahead over a rise. Peter followed. As he reached the crest, the wind that blows on the high moors hit him in the face, lifting his hair.

A short distance away, Ben was snuffling something on the grass by a big bank of gorse. It was the dead hare. He planted his feet and threw it in the air then danced all round.

'Ben, leave it!' Peter shouted. 'Leave it!'

Ben looked up. The turf was torn. This was where he had made his kill. The hare, confronted by the wall of thorns, had jinked sideways and in that split second the dog was on it, bowling it over, snatching a leg. It had squealed in terror.

'Good boy. Fetch. Fetch!'

At last Ben realised what was expected of him. Briefly he pushed the dead creature around then caught it across the back, settled his grip and bounced back to Peter, shaking his head as he ran.

It was a young hare, just fully grown. Ben had done well to run it down. Its head dangled on the broken neck. Its bright black eyes saw nothing.

'Give it here.' Peter took hold but Ben was reluctant to part with his prey. Peter made a fuss of him. 'Good boy. Let go now.' He pulled gently. 'Come on.'

Ben let him take it and looked up with eager eyes.

'Clever dog.' Peter praised him some more then turned his attention to the hare – its warm body, pink ears, big dirty feet. He was sorry it was dead, all that strength and vitality snuffed out in a moment. More to the point there was plenty of meat on it, it would be good eating. With luck his dad would be pleased, he liked the gamey taste of hare. Peter grasped the strong back legs in one hand. The hare's ears trailed on the ground. He shifted his grip. Red drips gathered at the hare's nose and fell to the grass. Ben sniffed at it then lifted his leg against a nearby rock and resumed hunting through the heather.

The hare was heavy. Shifting it from hand to hand and trying to keep the blood from his trousers, Peter started back to the track.

2

Scar Hill

PETER KNEW THINGS were bad even before he reached the house. The van had gone off the track and got bogged down in a peaty ditch. Hard revving had chewed the verge to mud. The front wheels were buried. It would take the tractor to drag it out.

The driver's door hung open. He looked inside. The passenger seat was wet, the air reeked of whisky. Otherwise all was the same as usual: the floor covered with grit, a few empty cans, torn wrappers, a sack of sheep nuts. His dad was gone so he must be OK. Able to walk, at least. Ragged handholds and a slither of knees in the ooze showed where he had clawed his way up the bank. Peter shut the door, banged it to make sure the lock engaged, and picked up the hare.

Ten minutes brought him to the cottage and cluster of outbuildings that had been his home for almost as long as he could remember. Scar Hill, as it was called, derived its name from a jagged outcrop of rock that ran down the face of a nearby hillside. A more fanciful claim was that centuries earlier, in the days of the clans, a battle had been fought on the spot, a battle with claymores and much mutilation. The river had run red. For a generation the men of the area had scarred faces and missing limbs. Jim had looked it up in ancient records and much to Peter's disappointment pronounced the story untrue. All the same, sometimes in the evening, when light was fading, he gazed at the surrounding slopes and imagined them echoing with the shouts and screams of warriors.

Nearer two centuries old than one, the cottage was built of grey stone and sat comfortably in the heart of the moors. It was a building that belonged. The roof, which originally had been turf, and then tin, was blue slate and covered with lichen and moss. Two dormer windows had been added, currently the bedrooms of Peter and his dad. The woodwork was green, the paint starting to curl. It gave the place a run-down appearance which was not improved by the earth yard, rusting shed roofs, oil drums which had been waiting five years to go to the dump, and shepherd's debris which lay on all sides. Despite this, Jim ensured the house was weather-tight against the gales and rainstorms that raged across the moor at any season of the year, and the blizzards of winter that cut them off for a week at a time. Peter liked those days, helping his dad to feed the snowed-in sheep, working until he could hardly stand, then retreating indoors to drink hot chocolate and scorch his face at the glowing peat fire.

As he reached the yard, Meg appeared in the doorway of the barn. She was a Border Collie, his father's working dog and inseparable companion. Meg adored his father and Jim loved her right back. One of Peter's earliest memories was a blazing row between his mother and father: 'You think more of that bloody dog than you do of me,' she had screeched.

'Aye, happen you're right,' he had replied.

At which she had snatched up a treasured photo of his parents and flung it at his head. His dad, usually a quiet man, knocked her to the floor.

Meg greeted Ben and sniffed the hare, then crept close to Peter and pressed her head against his knee. Jim's darkening moods distressed her. She thought she had done wrong but did not know what. She thought she was in disgrace. When his brows were drawn and in grim silence Jim set off for the Cod and Kipper, she shivered and whined.

Peter pulled her close. 'It's all right, beautiful,' he said comfortingly. 'There.'

The front door was shut but not locked, it was never locked. No light shone at the living-room window. No smoke blew from the chimney.

Jim had kicked his boots off outside, and when Peter went into the house his mud-caked trousers lay on the slabs in the hall. He dropped the hare beside them. Ben and Meg hovered at the entrance. He shut the door on them, hung his rucksack over the banisters and went through to the living room.

It was in gloom, the darkness of an October teatime. Breakfast dishes still lay on the table. His dad, in working jersey, underpants and socks, was stretched out on the settee. He was asleep, dead to the world and snoring softly in his throat. A scatter of cans and empty half-bottle of Bells lay on the carpet. A full-sized bottle, part drunk, was wedged at his side.

The room stank of spirits. Peter pushed up the window and covered his father's legs with a rug from the armchair. At the disturbance Jim coughed briefly, an arm fell towards the floor. He slept on. Peter lifted the arm across his chest and carried the debris into the kitchen.

He was a practical boy. Life with Jim had taught him to do most things. Cooking a meal, shearing a sheep, doing the family wash were commonplace tasks to twelve-year-old Peter. First thing he must do right now, while there was still light in the sky, was drag the van from the ditch and get it back to the house.

He wanted to show his dad the hare. Since he was asleep, Peter left it beside the sink in the kitchen and went upstairs to change into his working clothes.

The tractor stayed beneath a lean-to in the yard. Peter loved it, an old Massey Ferguson 35, rusty-red with no cab, a trusty workhorse. It would be years yet before he was allowed on the road, but it was perfectly legal for a boy of his age to drive up there on the moors. He had been driving down to the road and up into the hills since he was ten. Jim had lectured him sternly about safety, then taken the cushion off the cast-iron seat and made some adjustments so that he could reach the pedals.

The key was in the ignition. Rain had blown in. Peter scrubbed the seat dry and slung a coil of heavy rope over a bracket. As he reversed into the yard, Meg emerged from the barn to see what was happening and crossed to the door of the house. He climbed down, leaving the engine idling, and let her in to be near her sleeping master. Ben circled restlessly, eager to start, wherever they might be heading.

Peter set off down the potholed track. The steering wheel leaped in his hands, the big bucket seat bounced on its springs. A ragged skein of geese caught his eye, their cries inaudible above the roar of the engine.

It was less than a mile to the van. A broad moorland stream, splashing and full after the recent rain, ran parallel to the track. It was lucky his dad had swerved the other way, into the peaty ditch. The back of the van half blocked the track. Peter squeezed past on the tractor, big wheels clipping the bank of the stream, and stopped just beyond. He spread two plastic sacks on the churned ground and squirmed beneath the van to tie the rope to the chassis. Leaving a little slack, he attached the other end to the tow bar on the tractor.

In first gear he inched forward. The rope tightened and stretched. Peter watched over his shoulder and hoped it would not break. Slowly, with a suck and a lurch, the van skidded sideways. For a moment it nearly toppled over, then a wheel struck firm ground and it began to roll back to the track.

Soon it was up. He jumped down and crawled underneath to loosen the tow rope but the knot had jammed solid. His hands were filthy with grease and peat. He scrubbed off the worst with handfuls of moss and tackled the rope again but his fingers were just not strong enough. Reluctantly he pulled out his pocket knife and sliced the rope through.

There wasn't room for the two vehicles to pass. The van was nearer home and facing in the right direction. The keys, as always out there on the moor, were in the ignition. Peter slid the seat forward and Ben scrambled through to the back. Then Peter drove home to Scar Hill and parked in the yard. The wheels and grille were clotted with black peat. It could wait till the morning, he'd hose it off then.

The last streaks of daylight faded and stars were appearing

as he walked back with Ben to collect the tractor. The engine clattered into noisy life. Fumes puttered from the vertical exhaust pipe and were carried away by the wind. The best place to turn was half a mile further on where the track wound through a cluster of outcrops, little hills known locally as the Four Crowns. He switched on the headlights but discovered he could see better without them. A hunting owl, like a great white moth, flew past as he drove home with Ben loping alongside.

His dad was still asleep. The sacks had given Peter some protection but despite it he was filthy with peat. He cleaned the last of the grease from his hands with Swarfega and slung his clothes and his dad's dirty trousers into the washing machine. Jeans and a red sweatshirt lay crumpled in the drying cupboard. He pulled them on and smoothed the words on his chest: OK, PUNK, MAKE MY DAY.

The dogs were hungry. He mixed their food – boiled dog meat and dog biscuit – added a handful of treats, and carried the two bowls out to the shed where they spent the night. He switched on the light. Two naked bulbs on long flexes illuminated the interior: spider-web covered beams, sacks of sheep nuts, sheep drench, oil drums, disused feeding troughs, hay beds for the dogs, planks, ladders and much else.

Buster, Peter's polecat ferret, appeared at the door of his run. It was his feeding time too. Peter lifted him out and pressed his mouth to the soft fur, whispering endearments, letting Buster climb about his shoulders. But Buster was more interested in the smell of meat on Peter's fingers. He gave him a piece of raw heart and returned him to his run. Buster carried it off to a favourite corner, his eyes wild and teeth locked in the bloody prize.

It didn't take long to clear the dining table, clatter the dishes into the kitchen sink, put on the kettle, slap some rashers of bacon into the frying pan and empty a can of beans into a saucepan. The mouth-watering aromas of toast and bacon fat drove the whisky fumes from the window. Thursday's ash was shovelled into a bucket, and by the time his dinner was ready, peat flames were leaping up the chimney. Peter carried his plate into the living room and switched on the TV.

His dad stirred, rolled his head on the arm of the settee and swallowed. With bleary eyes he looked round the room.

'*Make my day, punk*,' he muttered. 'Suits me, chief.' He put a finger between his eyes. 'Right there. Any time you like.'

Peter munched a mouthful of fried bread and egg. 'Rough day?'

'You could say.' His dad shut his eyes again and covered them with the back of his hand.

Peter surfed the channels, one to four and back again. There was nothing worth watching. He slotted a smeary *Bugs Bunny* cassette into the video.

Jim bit back his anger. The volume was low but the screams and music cut into his hangover like a buzz saw. 'For God's sake, Pete! Have we got to have that on?'

Peter pressed the *mute* button but the damage was done. Heavily his dad sat up. The room spun. Vivid colours flashed across the TV screen, every one a stab at his eyeballs. He looked away. Night pressed against the windows.

Yesterday's *Guardian* lay on the table. It was the paper Jim liked best. Idly Peter pulled it towards him and packed his fork with bacon and beans.

Jim watched him, the son he loved so deeply it sometimes hurt, at times like this the only thing in his life worth living for. The whisky burned in his stomach, sharp as acid. Perhaps he had an ulcer in addition to everything else. It wouldn't be surprising. He pushed back the rug and saw that his legs were bare. Where were his trousers? He didn't remember. Making the effort, he swung his feet to the floor and sat up. The warmth of the fire hit him in the face. He hadn't lit that, he was sure, it must have been Peter. And he had cleared the table and cooked his own meal. A tidal wave of guilt engulfed him. He rose, steadying himself against the arm of the settee, and crossed to plant a hard kiss on top of his son's head.

'There was something …' He struggled to remember. 'Oh,

yes. I put the van off the road. We'll have to go along in the morning and ...'

Peter swallowed a half-chewed mouthful. 'It's OK, I did it.'

'Did what?'

'Pulled it out.' He mopped up some yolk.

'With the tractor?'

'Well I didn't use my teeth. Van's in the yard.'

His dad stared at him. His eyes, heavy with whisky, filled with tears and he stumbled into the kitchen. The cooking smells were strong. And the boy had got a hare. It lay beside the sink, eyes dulled, waiting to be gutted.

Jim's heart gave a lurch. He was not a strong man – or more precisely, was not a fit man. Something had happened to him in the army. He panted for breath. A spasm of pain hit him in the chest. He leaned against the draining board. The pain grew worse, like a fist tightening within his rib-cage. Grimacing, he pulled open a drawer and groped for his tablets. A little brown plastic bottle. Where was it? It should be here! He scattered the contents and found it. The bottle had a white safety cap. It didn't open. *Click – click – click*, the top spun round. He pressed harder, close to desperation. It opened. Tablets spilled across the table. Jim placed one beneath his tongue. For a minute, leaning on both hands, he stared into space. Slowly the pain eased, the room swam back into focus. He saw the cooker, the calendar, the black hairs on the back of his hands.

Peter stood in the doorway.

'That was a bad one.' Jim tried to belch but the wind wouldn't come. He forced a smile. 'Still, takes more than a little twinge to get a good ...' He tried to belch again. The panting returned. Sweat stood on his brow. 'Sorry, Pete. Better go outside, eh?'

Before Peter could move, his dad spun round and vomited into the sink. He hadn't eaten all day. There was a horrid, retching sound. A sour smell filled the kitchen.

Peter hesitated, torn between disgust and the feeling that he should do something to help. He had been sick himself, seen other children sick, but other people had always looked after it. And somehow a grown-up was worse. He turned away, leaving the rest of his dinner on the table, and went out into the yard.

Light spilled from the living-room window. A crescent moon was rising above the moors. He snorted the cold air to rid his nostrils of the smell.

Something touched his hand and made him jump. It was Ben, come from the shed. Peter rubbed his bony head. The tall dog stood close, keeping him company.

3

The Soldier

PETER LEANED ON the van roof. The crescent moon lay on its back with the dark side visible against the night sky. It reminded him of an old ballad they'd read recently in English:

> *I saw the new moon late yestr'een*
> *Wi' the auld moon in her arm ...*

Something like that. He liked poetry.

A drain gurgled. He turned to face the house. It was the outflow from the sink and went on for some time. Silence returned – the silence of the moor with a whisper of wind in the fences.

It was broken by a crash of china. His dad, he guessed, had knocked a plate to the floor. Then there was another crash – a tinkle – a loud smash. What was he doing? A shiver ran up Peter's back.

He waited a minute then started towards the house. Before he reached it his dad appeared in the doorway. A bin bag hung from one hand. In the other he carried the whisky bottle. He crossed to the wheelie bin. *Rattle! Smash!* In went the bag.

As he turned away he saw Peter in the darkness. 'Sorry, Pete.' He truly meant it. 'I've cleared up in the kitchen.'

Peter was shaken. 'Are you OK?'

'Me? Yeah, never better.' Jim started towards the byre then stopped. 'No, as a matter of fact I'm not, if you really want to know. I feel bloody awful.' He pushed back his hair. 'Nothing you can do about it though. Nothing anyone can do. So don't worry yourself. Be all right in the morning.' He set off again, a bit unsteadily. 'Think I'll just have a lie-down in …' he gestured with the bottle. 'Leave you with the telly. So's we'll not get in each other's hair. All right, son?'

'Yeah, OK.'

'Sleep well.'

'You too, Dad.'

Jim continued to the old stone byre that faced the house across the yard. Though Jim only farmed sheep, crofters in the past had run a few cattle as well. The entrance swallowed him up.

Peter's heart was thudding. The byre was his dad's escape route. He liked it out there, lying in the straw of an old cattle stall with the door open to the night moors. Mostly he just slept and sipped from the bottle, reliving old memories, but sometimes he sang snatches of hymns and old songs, soldiers' songs, and talked to himself. If it was summer and the swallows were nesting, he talked to them and they listened, looking down from the rafters. When Meg joined him, as she would in a few minutes, he talked to her. In the shed the demons which tormented him were less threatening, the memories less painful. The snakes slackened their coils. The peace was soothing, as were the creak of timbers in the wind and rattle of rain on the rusty roof. Away from the confines of the house he felt freer. And there in the darkness, with field mice and an occasional rat rustling about the walls, he would at last drink himself into oblivion.

He had spoken the truth. There was nothing Peter or anyone else could do about it. For years, aged eight, nine and ten, Peter had tried. To no avail. All he could do, he had discovered, was to trust his dad, leave him alone, and when he felt able to face the world again, to be there.

He made his way indoors. The living room was as he had left it, though the TV had been switched off and the fire banked high with fresh peats. The kitchen, however, all in a couple of minutes, was transformed. The sink gleamed and smelled strongly of bleach. The side tables and draining board had been cleared of dirty dishes and wiped clean. The unwashed pots on the cooker were gone.

He took the lamp which stood on the freezer and went out to the wheelie bin. It was half full. The black bin bag lay on top. He heaved it out and looked inside. There, in a mess of beans, grease and soggy cereals, lay the pans and broken crockery. In a sudden, drunken desire to help, Jim had rinsed away his sick and slung everything out.

Peter needed both hands and switched on the outside light. With the tips of his fingers he rescued the frying pan, saucepans, cutlery and those plates and cups that were not broken or too badly chipped.

'Let the bloody things be.' His dad's voice came from the byre. 'We'll get some new ones. Stop working, for God's sake. Finish your dinner. Watch the telly.'

'Right.' Peter returned the ruined china to the bin and gathered what was worth saving into two heaps. Grimacing at the slop on his fingers, he carried them indoors.

What was left of his dinner at the living room table had congealed on the plate. He scraped it into a newspaper.

Washing up didn't take long. The water was hot and soon the pots were back in the cupboard and the chipped china stacked on the shelves. To make a proper job of it, he mopped the floor and shook the mats in the yard.

He waited for a shout from the shed: 'Cor, make some lucky person a good wife, that's what you'll do.' But whether his dad heard or not, he passed no comment and Peter carried the mats indoors.

He hadn't stopped since he got off the bus. He opened a can of Irn-Bru and took a packet of biscuits to the fire. The peats glowed, flames licked up the chimney. He kicked off his shoes.

Ben lay on his crumpled day bed in the corner and crunched a handful of dog biscuits. Having snuffled up every last crumb, he came looking for more but no more were on offer. Idly Peter scratched the top of his head. Ben flopped on the rug and stretched his legs to the fire. He was so big there was no space left for Peter's feet. He trailed them over the dog's chest.

For half an hour they lay. Bart Simpson caused chaos on the screen but Peter scarcely saw him. His thoughts were out in the byre with his dad. He had seen him drunk many times but never sick like that. Never so desperate for that little white pill. It wasn't the effect of the whisky, he knew that, or not wholly the whisky. His dad's drinking was the *result* of what troubled him, not the cause. In a way the whisky was his medicine, not one recommended by the doctor but a medicine all the same. Peter wished he didn't drink but he didn't blame his dad for it. His dad was ill – and it wasn't his fault. Peter knew all about it.

When his dad was in the army and Peter was a little boy, so long ago he did not remember, he had been sent out to fight in the desert. At that time the army was frightened that the allied forces might be attacked by chemical or biological weapons, things like plague and anthrax, nerve gas or even uranium dust. For protection they were given pills and a series of injections before they set out, a very strong cocktail of drugs. In the event they were not attacked that way, but when the war was over, thousands of soldiers, British and American, complained of after-effects. Some, like Jim, who had seen his best friend killed when a tank went up in flames, had bad memories to contend with as well. Before Desert Storm, as the assault was called, these had been strong and healthy men. Now they suffered from a whole variety of illnesses: headaches and lack of energy, depression, sleeplessness, panic attacks, bad chests, forgetfulness, painful joints. And Peter's dad, along with others, developed a bad heart. Was it the result of those injections and the war? There was no proof. The army medics said it was not. The British government declared that Gulf War Syndrome, as it was called, did not exist; those who were ill would have been ill anyway.

Whatever the truth, the effect upon Jim Irwin and his family was catastrophic. Because of his lack of fitness and unpredictable mood swings he had to leave the army; and because the army claimed his illness had nothing to do with them, he did not receive a disability allowance. To make matters even worse, they had to leave the army house that was their home. All at once Sergeant Irwin, who was a career soldier and loved the army, found himself homeless, unemployed and, because his wife, Sharon, was an extravagant woman, three thousand pounds in debt. The television, washing machine, new three-piece suite and bedroom furniture were repossessed.

What were they to do: Jim, Sharon, their ten-year-old daughter Valerie, and three-year-old son Peter?

After a succession of shabby bedsits, they were housed by the social services. Home became a horrible damp flat in a decaying high-rise on the Salford side of Manchester. The toilet leaked, there was mould in the kitchen. Peter developed a cough which would not clear up. Valerie became bad-tempered and quarrelsome. Everyone hated it.

Peter never forgot those dark days: the smelly lift, playing on the cold graffiti-covered stairs, visits to the hospital, the big boys who pushed him over on the grass so that he became frightened to leave the house.

His mum and dad, the people who mattered most in his life, had blazing rows. For Sharon liked the good things in life: new clothes, twice-weekly visits to the hairdresser, taxis, dancing, holidays, nights out with girlfriends – and sometimes, when Jim was away on exercises or tours of duty overseas, nights out with boyfriends.

Valerie had been born just four months after they were married, when Sharon was seventeen and Jim two years older. For the first few weeks Sharon had rejoiced in her baby daughter, enjoyed the novelty, showed her around, liked dressing her up in frills and pretty hats like a dolly. But when Valerie cried at night it was Jim who got up to comfort her, change her nappy, give her a bottle, rock her in his arms until she fell asleep again. And all too soon Sharon, who was little more than a girl herself, came to resent the baby for her loss of freedom. Not only that, what little money they managed to scrape together – for at that time Jim was a young private – had to be spent on a cot and a pram, baby food, a playpen, locks for the windows, things for the bathroom, toys, shoes, a pushchair, Christmas, the list was endless. When she was teething she cried incessantly. She threw up her milk. She dirtied her clean nappies. She screamed until her face was scarlet. Nothing her mother could do would pacify her. Babies, as far as Sharon was concerned, were selfish, greedy, unappreciative monsters.

Despite Jim's longing for a son as well as a daughter, she refused point-blank to suffer the discomfort and ruin her figure for the birth of a second child. Despite this, somehow, seven years after Valerie, Peter was born and now here they were, broke, sick, unemployed and living in a cockroach-infested flat. Sharon wasn't prepared to put up with it. If her pathetic excuse for a husband – how could she have been so mad as to think he was fun – couldn't give her the life she wanted, there were plenty who could.

Jim needed to get himself together. He had grown up on a farm in Northumberland, the outdoor life suited him. So when his great-uncle Sandy died – Uncle Sandy whom he could hardly remember – and left him this croft at Tarridale, in the north of Scotland, Jim saw it as a gift from heaven. It was the very thing they needed: a house to go with it, plenty of space for the children to run around, a stress-free life, and work in the open air which might help him to get his strength back. Not only that, there was enough money to pay off their debts and a bit over. It would be a new start for Sharon and himself. He showed her the map.

Sharon was appalled. 'You're not serious! If you think I'm going up there to live in some godforsaken wilderness, you must be off your head.'

But Jim *was* serious. And Sharon's latest boyfriend, having tired of her empty head and expensive ways, had gone off with another girl, younger than Sharon, who had a well-paid job and her own flat. What else was she to do?

No one could say that Sharon lacked spirit. Looking on

the bright side, it occurred to her that among those lumpish Scotch countrywomen with their weather-beaten faces and headscarves, she'd be the belle of the village. And there were bound to be men around; those sturdy-legged young soldiers in the Highland regiments she'd seen on parade in their kilts, some of them must come from up that way. Maybe it wouldn't be too bad. In any case, she didn't intend to stay married to boring, sick Jim Irwin for the rest of her life.

So early one morning in March, Peter was bundled into the smelly lift for the last time, strapped into his dad's old blue Cortina, and off they set on the five hundred mile journey that would take them from the high-rise blocks and crowded streets of Manchester to the empty hills of the north.

4

The New Arrivals

FROM HIS FIRST glimpse of the moors and the sea, Jim loved it. He pulled up a few miles before Tarridale, which was to be their nearest village, stepped from the car and filled his lungs with the seaweed- and heather-impregnated air. Light-headed with happiness, he hitched four-year-old Peter into his arms and drew Valerie to his side. Jim felt he was coming home.

Peter always remembered that moment: his dad's big hug, the unfamiliar smells, the sudden blast of light and space all around him. A cold wind blew his hair. He had never known anything like it. He was wearing a blue jacket and saw it was the same colour as the sky between clouds. If this was to be his new home, he liked it.

Sharon felt differently. Long before they shut the door of the detested Manchester flat she'd had misgivings. And now, as she saw how Jim stood gazing ecstatically at the wild headlands and windswept moors, she felt in her bones that the venture was destined to failure. The closer they got to Tarridale the stronger grew her conviction. And when they turned off the road – a single tarmacked lane bordered by heather – on to the potholed track that led to Scar Hill, she knew it for certain. For Sharon, a girl from the city, the move to the Highlands was a disaster.

Peter was like Jim but Valerie was her mother's daughter. At the age of eleven the chief interests in her life were clothes, magazines, pop music, experimenting with make-up, comfort eating and older boys. Listening to all Sharon had said in the weeks before their departure, and seeing her mother's tight face as she looked out at the landscape, Valerie decided she felt the same. It was all right to hate their new life in Scotland. 'What are we going to do here?' she complained even before they had arrived. 'There's nothing but hills. It's boring.'

Uncle Sandy, a bachelor, had not lived on the croft for several years. At the age of seventy-three he had changed his lifestyle. A passion for Rangers Football Club, noisy pubs and a lively widow eight years younger, drew him down to Glasgow. There he had lived happily until his widow died, and shortly afterwards a surge of supporters outside a Rangers–Celtic match knocked him to the ground and left him so badly trampled that he died the following day in hospital.

In his absence the fields and hill grazing had been let to a crofter from the village, and the house rented to a succession of workmen. The last, a forestry worker barely out of his teens, had left the house a midden. It had been a meeting place for pals. Out there on the moor, safe from interruption, they had consumed crates of Export, watched videos, shouted at referees, fought, and slept in chairs. Bedding trailed on the floor, the carpets were filthy and chewed by mice, two windows were boarded over. The yard was a sea of mud.

Even Jim, when he saw the cottage that first afternoon, was shaken. Sharon refused to get out of the car. 'My God!' she said. 'You would bring us to a place like this? It's even worse than I expected. I've seen better caves. If you imagine in your wildest dreams, Jim Irwin, that I am going to live in that – that – filthy, sodden *dump,* you're off your head. I mean, look at it!'

It had come on to rain.

'I'm hungry, mum,' Valerie whined. 'I want the bathroom.'

'You hear?' With trembling fingers Sharon lit a cigarette. 'For God's sake let's get out of here and find this place we're going to stay. Though what *that's* going to be like I shudder to think.'

'There'll be a bathroom in the house, love,' Jim opened the door for his daughter. 'Come on, we'll find it together.'

'No.' She huddled back in a corner. 'I don't like it.'

'We'll just take a look anyway,' Jim said. 'Come on, Shar.'
Tight-lipped, she looked away and drew on her cigarette.

'Just you and me then, Peter.'

Happily Peter scrambled down and chased some jackdaws at the end of the yard. The house was dirty and in a mess but he liked it. From the upstairs windows he could see across the moor. In one direction, a mile below them, there was a shining silver loch. In the other direction, far away, a range of snow-capped hills.

'This will be your room,' Jim said. 'We'll give it a nice coat of paint and get you a new bed.' Peter looked all round. The ceiling sloped, the small-paned windows faced the yard. He thought it was lovely.

Peter was right, for despite the years of neglect, Scar Hill was a good house, the structure was sound. Jim spoke to Mr Fraser, of Simpson, Fraser and Cherriwick, the solicitors who handled Uncle Sandy's affairs. Grants were available, he was told, certainly for a young family like his, to improve the drainage, renew the wiring, replace rotted window frames, rip out the worm-eaten timbers, even have the damp walls dried out and replastered.

Teams of workmen arrived from the village. For weeks the air was loud with voices and the noise of hammering. Jim himself, with an unexpected surge of energy, decorated the rooms and painted the outside woodwork. With Sharon and the children he drove into Clashbay, the nearest town, to spend some of Uncle Sandy's money on carpets and curtains.

Peter loved those days, fetching for the workmen, stamping about the echoing rooms and listening to their funny accent. 'Funny accent,' they said as they sat around with cups of tea. 'You're a one to talk. What sort of accent's that you've got then?'

But carpets, curtains and a house of her own did not make Sharon happy. A house – even *that* house it appeared – could be fixed. The location could not. It was impossible! As she leaned on a fence, warming her hands round a mug of coffee and waiting for the van to deliver their first furniture, she had never imagined a place so lonely. Mile upon mile of empty moor, not a single cottage in sight, let alone the village or a shop. Even the bus stop was the best part of three miles down the track. One bus a day to Clashbay, a fishing port and the nearest town, thirty miles along the coast, and one to Tarridale, three miles in the opposite direction. To catch either, for Sharon did not drive, she needed Jim to take her to the road and pick her up on her return. Once they moved in and Jim was working, she would be a prisoner.

'We'll get rid of the old Cortina,' Jim offered. 'I need a tractor and we'll look for a little car so you can get about. I'll teach you to drive.'

Sharon grunted. She did not want a little car. She did not want to drive along a muddy, stony track to reach a deserted road three miles from a godforsaken village. What Sharon wanted was a big car, with a rich, sexy man beside her and a large vodka and tonic at the end of the journey.

For six weeks, while the house was being done up, they stayed with Mrs McKendrick, the widow of an offshore oil worker, who ran a bed and breakfast at the end of the village. Peter, interested in everything and happy to help, became a great favourite. Mrs McKendrick had a fifteen-year-old daughter named Mairi, a senior pupil at Tarridale High School. She and Peter – though not Valerie, who clung to her mother – soon became the best of friends. She took him paddling on the big white beaches and fished with worms in the River Teal which ran past the village. In the evenings she read him stories from books she borrowed from the infant class at school. Mairi had wiry blonde hair and blue eyes. Peter thought she was lovely.

5

The Village Shop

ON THE FIRST morning, while Jim drove into Clashbay to see the solicitor, Sharon dressed smartly to create an impression, made herself up carefully and set out for the village store. It was a walk of half a mile. Valerie held her mother's hand. Peter, who had wanted to stay with Mrs McKendrick and sweep the yard, trailed behind in his new jeans and anorak.

A strong wind from the north, straight from the Arctic, tumbled the sea into crested waves. Even though she pulled up her hood, Sharon's hair escaped and flapped in her eyes. The smoke from her cigarette whirled in every direction. By the time she arrived she was chilled to the bone. Valerie was whining.

The door bell jangled. A number of local women turned from their chat to survey the newcomer who had come among them. Word had gone round, they knew who she was. No detail was missed by their sharp eyes: her bleached hair, big earrings, pearl eye shadow, mascara, bangles and rings, false nails, and beneath the pink quilted parka her short tight skirt, plump knees and flimsy sling-backs.

For long moments nobody spoke, then a friendly middle-aged woman in an anorak and warm trousers took pity on her. 'Good morning, love. You look frozen. Come on over here by the stove.' She made room.

Sharon eased off her hood. 'No thanks.' She tucked back a lock of candy-floss hair and smiled. 'I'm fine.'

It was a rejection. But the woman was nosy. 'What about the lass then? Come on, sweetheart, you stand over here where it's warm while your mum does the shopping.'

Valerie drew back against her mother. At the age of eleven she showed little sign of the pretty teenager she was to become. Her cheeks were chubby, her knees fat. But she was learning about style. Her hair, a mousy brown, was streaked auburn and blonde. She wore lipstick and a trace of blue eye shadow. Enamelled pendants swung from her ears. Beneath a cream-coloured costume with fake fur collar she wore a bra. Her clumpy shoes were in all the magazines.

'What's your name?' the woman said. When Valerie failed to answer she went on, 'Valerie is it? Just moving into the old house up Scar Hill?'

Valerie rolled round to the far side of her mother.

Sharon answered for her. 'That's right. Irwin's the name. Staying down the road with Mrs McKendrick till we get the house done up. We want it nice. Last place down in Manchester was ever so smart, wasn't it, Valerie. Jacuzzi and everything.'

Valerie whispered, 'I'm cold, Mum.'

Sharon pushed her off. 'We'll be home in a bit, you can have a hot drink then. Stand up now and try to make a good impression.'

She looked around for Peter who had wandered off and stood examining some toy tractors and delivery vans. 'Peter,' she said sharply. 'Come over here. And don't be touching any of them mind.'

Ignoring her, he drifted on to a stand of magazines.

Valerie, needing something else to lean against, turned to the display cabinet by the till. Within lay chocolate, sweets and ice cream. She ran her fingers over the glass, smeary fingers with bitten nails and chipped red varnish. 'Can I have a KitKat – one of them big ones?'

'Not if you don't buck your ideas up.' Her mother poked her in the back. 'Come on, now.'

Valerie hit her on the arm. Sulkily she stared back at the women who were watching.

'Good morning.' The shopkeeper, a thickset, churchgoing man, came to serve them. His name was Mr McRobb.

'Have you got any Rothman 100?' Sharon asked.

'No call for them.' He looked at the cigarette shelf. 'Just the ordinary ones.'

Her lips showed irritation. 'I'll take sixty. And one of them lighters.'

He set them before her and jotted some figures on a bag.

'And a packet of biscuits. Them Belgian ones.' She scanned the shelves and spotted a small display of wine bottles. 'Got any champagne?'

The shop had two brands: Cava, which local people bought for a celebration, and a single bottle of Bollinger which had been ordered by a visitor who never returned to collect it.

'I'll take the Bolly,' Sharon said.

'Twenty-nine pound fifty,' the shopkeeper warned her.

Trailing a copy of the *Beano*, Peter emerged from the magazine stand and stood watching.

'That's all right,' Sharon said airily, observing the women from the corner of her eye and wondering what Jim would say if he found out.

Mr McRobb mounted the steps to fetch it.

She took out a small wad of notes and fluttered two twenties on the counter. 'No, that'll not be enough.' As if money were no object, she dropped a third.

The bell jangled and a man came into the shop. He was young and scruffy, in stained jeans and a torn sweater. Peter thought he looked nice.

The women greeted the newcomer.

'Hello, Billy. My God, you look a mess.'

'When did you get back?'

He ran fingers through a tangle of hair. 'Last night.'

'How's Angela?'

'Angela?' He seemed puzzled. 'Who's Angela? Never heard of her.'

The women laughed. 'Oh, you're wicked!'

'You want to watch yourself, Billy Josh. One of these days you'll get caught.'

He grinned, white teeth and three days' stubble. 'Aye, it happens to the best of us. But not just yet, eh.'

He wasn't Sharon's type. All the same, from the brief glance she allowed herself, he was certainly good-looking. And the way he was looking at her – cheeky beggar.

'Mum!' Valerie tugged her sleeve.

'Oh, yes,' Sharon said, 'and a KitKat. One of them long ones.' She looked round. 'What do you want, our Peter?'

But Peter wasn't listening. He was fascinated by a streak of fish scales, thick as paint, down the leg of Billy's jeans.

Billy saw him looking. 'Hello there, boy. And who are you?'

Peter looked up, shy at being addressed by this big stranger. 'Peter Irwin,' he whispered.

'His dad's just taken over Scar Hill,' one of the women told him.

'Sandy's nephew?' Billy said. 'That soldier he used to tell us about?' He looked back at Peter. 'Dad a soldier then, is he?'

Peter nodded.

'Must be quite a man to have a braw lad like you.'

Peter blushed with pleasure.

'Hey.' Billy glanced at Sharon. 'Your mum was asking if you want any sweeties. Best go and tell her. Soldiers' sons need their sweeties, eh?'

He ran across the shop. Sharon bought him the *Beano* and a tube of Smarties.

While the shopkeeper pressed keys on his old-fashioned till, she tucked the bulky cigarettes into her bag. Valerie tore open the KitKat and dropped the paper on the floor.

'Hey!' The shopkeeper saw her. 'Pick that up.'

It was a voice that allowed no argument. Valerie was startled.

'There's a bin over there.'

She did as she was told and returned to her mother.

Sharon was furious at being shown up. She shook her daughter by the shoulder: 'You know not to throw things down like that. How often have I told you.'

Valerie stared. She often dropped paper, spat chewing gum onto the pavement. Her mother took no notice.

'Come on then.' Sharon raked the change into her purse. 'Thank you,' she said coldly to Mr McRobb and turned to the door.

Billy opened it for her.

'Thank you,' she said again.

'We're all gentlemen here in Tarridale,' he said. 'See you up at the hotel maybe.'

Sharon swept past, ignoring him, and turned down the road.

Valerie, in her mother's wake, looked back.

He gave her a wink.

She smiled.

A red Mercedes two-seater stood opposite. Sharon was surprised. This year's plates. Not the sort of car she expected to see in Tarridale at all. Whose was it, she wondered. It hadn't been there when they went into the store. Surely it didn't belong to Billy Josh with his stubble and dirty jeans.

'Smart, eh?' he called after her.

For the car did belong to Billy who, contrary to appearances, was the best-paid man in the village. At the age of twenty-three he was part-owner and skipper of the *Silver Darling*, a successful trawler sailing out of Clashbay.

Sharon's heels click-clacked as she walked along the short stretch of pavement.

He returned into the shop. Already the others were talking about her.

'Doesn't half fancy herself.' A woman built like a bulldog struck a pose. 'I'll take the Bolly!'

'Jacuzzi and *everything* in our last house,' echoed another. 'Who does she think she's kidding, going out there to Scar Hill.'

'Tasty bit of jail-bait though.' Billy hitched up his jeans. 'Could do with a bit of new blood round here. What d'you reckon?'

'You behave yourself,' said the woman in the anorak. 'She's hardly arrived. Got that lassie and nice wee lad. You've got enough girls dangling there to keep you going the next ten years.'

'All right, all right.' He raised his hands in protest. 'I only asked. Anyway, it's you and me really, isn't it, Maggie.' He slipped an arm round her waist. 'Everyone knows that.'

'It'll be the day when you get me to join your harem,' she said stoutly.

He gave her a squeeze.

'Oh, you!' She slapped his shoulder.

Mr McRobb sipped his coffee and ran a duster over the counter.

As Sharon reached the corner the wind blew her sideways. It had started to rain, a grey squall that flattened the sea and hid the headlands. The drops hit her face like bullets. 'Here, carry this.' She thrust the champagne into her daughter's hands. 'Take care you don't drop it – and don't tell your father.' She turned a shoulder into the blast for protection.

'Bloody wilderness!' she muttered. If Jim thought she was going to live in a freezing, storm-battered backwater like this, he had another think coming.

Several metres behind her, Peter clutched his tube of Smarties and looked down at the windswept river and white sands. He didn't like the rain which was cold and made his eyes blurry. Apart from that he thought Tarridale was lovely.

6

The Good Dad

NO ONE WHO saw Jim and Peter would have taken them for father and son. Jim's hair was dark, his skin weather-beaten by exposure to the sun and wind. This October, as he lay in the byre struggling with his demons, he was thirty-eight years old, young to have a nineteen-year-old daughter. With his lean physique and soldier's bearing he would have been a handsome man, had not ill health hollowed his cheeks and robbed his eyes of their sparkle.

Peter, in contrast, was unremarkable to look at, though life at Scar Hill had made him stronger than one might guess. His hair was light brown, his skin fair, his eyes blue-grey. In the class photo Peter was a pleasant-looking boy of average build who did not stand out.

Except for a little scar through his right eyebrow, the result of a cut he had received at the age of six when an older boy stole a friend's mouth organ. Peter had gone to get it back and the older boy threw a sharp stone which hit him in the face. Crying and covered in blood, Peter had attacked him with his fists. The older boy dropped the mouth organ and ran away. The event was still remembered in school where the other children regarded him as a bit of a tough guy.

Peter never felt particularly tough. What he felt that Friday evening as he sprawled in his armchair, was worried about his dad and dog-tired. All he wanted to do was climb upstairs and fall into bed, but before he could do that there was the hare to clean. With a sigh he went through to the kitchen and took the big cook's knife from the drawer, its blade worn concave with years of whetting. It was a job he had done many times, though usually to rabbits he had netted with his ferret. As the knife slit open the hare's belly, the rank smell of entrails filtered through to the living room. It brought Ben to the doorway, slopping his jaws with a wet tongue.

The job didn't take long. First Peter pulled out the guts and dumped them on newspaper. Then he cut off the paws, setting one aside for luck. Starting at the rear end, he tore off the skin the length of its blue-pink body. Finally he sliced off the head and dropped it, still attached to the skin, on top of the guts. The liver, lights and heart appeared to be healthy. With red fingers he plucked them from the stomach cavity and chopped them up, setting two pieces aside for Meg and Buster. The rest he fed to Ben. Eagerly the big dog wolfed them down. Then Peter rinsed the carcass under the cold tap and jointed it – two back legs, two front legs, four sections of muscular back – and set them in a bowl of salt water. Finally he scrubbed the cutting board, washed his hands and carried the bloody newspaper out to the bin.

The clouds had rolled back. The crescent moon sailed higher, bright enough to throw shadows. Perhaps there would be a frost. He looked towards the open doorway of the byre and hesitated a moment, then returned into the house, making sure the door remained unlocked.

Normally Ben slept in the barn with Meg but this night Peter left him on his day bed in the living room. The water was gurgling in the hot tank, heated by the fire. He went upstairs to take a bath. Their water, peat-brown but pure, came from a filter a hundred metres up the stream. As he turned on the tap it spat and steamed, close to boiling. He ran in the cold. It was four days since he had taken a shower at school. Sometimes he went barefoot and his feet were dirty. His armpits smelled sweaty too. He reached for the shampoo and soap.

Ten minutes later, leaving the scummy water draining away and the wet bath mat crumpled on the floor, he padded along the landing to his bedroom and pulled on his pyjamas. It had been a long day. Almost before the duvet settled across his shoulders, Peter was asleep.

The minibus was picking him up at ten. He had twenty-five minutes to get to the road. Shovelling down a bowl of cereal, Peter crossed the yard. The sun shone slantingly into the byre where his dad lay sleeping. His legs were sprawled, his cheeks dark with stubble. Softly he snored through his nose. Meg looked up. Her tail stirred in greeting.

'Good girl,' he said softly. 'You keep him company, right?'

The tail wagged harder. Peter put down what was left of the cereal. Meg angled her black and white head and began to lap the milk. He stroked her ears. Briefly she licked his fingers then returned to the bowl.

His bike was kept in the shed and had a puncture; the track was hard on tyres. No time to fix it this morning. He returned into the house and collected his football kit from the drying cupboard. Jim would have given him pocket money. He took five pounds from his dad's wallet and left a note:

9.40. Hope your feeling better. I have taken a fiver and the tractor. I'll leave it at the quarry. Back around 4 or 5. Bike's got a puncture.

Love, Pete

Both dogs could be trusted near the sheep. Dogs that worried sheep were shot. He put out their breakfast and left them free to roam, then set off on the tractor.

The wind blew back his hair. There had been a brief deluge during the night and the giant wheels sprayed water from the potholes. The tractor didn't go fast, only thirty on the tarmacked road, on the track no more than fifteen or twenty.

In ten minutes he reached the abandoned quarry a hundred metres before the road and swung in beneath the rock face and scrubby vegetation. To ensure he didn't lose the key, he hid it beneath his usual flat stone. To protect the seat from the rain, he pulled a plastic sack over the top and tied it with a length of twine.

Rucksack slung over one shoulder, he let himself through the five-barred gate and stood at the roadside to wait for the bus.

It was a great day. They were playing against a school beyond Clashbay and won 5–3. Peter wasn't a particularly good player or mad about football like some of the boys, but he ran hard, tackled bravely, and this Saturday was rewarded by a fluky but spectacular goal, right into the top corner of the net.

Muddy from the wet pitch, they were taken to a rugby club for hot showers and lunch. In the afternoon the teacher who was driving the minibus let the boys loose for an hour to enjoy an autumn fair on the seafront at Clashbay – dodgems, rifle stalls, octopus, hot-dog stand – before driving back to Tarridale.

'Great goal, Winnie. See y'on Monday.' Friendly hands patted his arm as they stopped at the end of the track.

Daylight was fading. Roosting jackdaws had gathered on the walls of the quarry. As Peter walked to the tractor they took off with cries of alarm, crossing the sky like scraps of burned paper. He pulled the sack from the seat and jammed it between two struts. Bouncing on the springs as the tyres hit stones and potholes, he drove home.

Lights were on in the house. Smoke blew from the chimney. Ben and Meg heard the engine and ran to meet him in the yard. Wondering what he would find, Peter followed them into the house.

Jim was sobering up. He looked pale and haggard, but he had shaved and bathed and changed into clean clothes. A packet of paracetamol and a small glass containing the dregs of some white medicine stood on the table.

'Hello, Pete.' He blinked wearily and smiled. 'Got your message. Have a good day?'

He had made an effort. The room was tidy. The hearth was swept. A clean cloth covered the table.

'Yeah, it was great. I scored a goal.' Peter dropped his bag on the floor.

'Good for you. I like you to get out. Here, give me your things.' Jim rose unsteadily. 'I've left room in the washing machine. Then how about a cup of tea?'

'I'll make it.'

'No you'll not. You do more than your share. Give them here.'

Peter pulled out his muddy strip.

'What about your boots?'

They were in a poly bag, filthy and sodden.

'Go outside and scrape off the thick then I'll scrub them under the tap. Let them dry by the hearth. Give them a good oiling.' Jim belched and put a hand over his eyes.

'Look, I'll – '

'No you'll not, I've told you. Just don't argue. Give me the boots when you've done and sit down by the fire. I'm your father, for God's sake. *I'll* make the tea.'

'What about the sheep?'

'The sheep are all right. You went up yesterday, didn't you?'

Peter shook his head.

'I thought you did. Well you did something.'

'I fetched back the van.'

'The van?'

'You'd gone into the ditch.'

'What ditch?' Jim remembered. 'Oh, yeah.'

'I thought about the sheep, just going up for a quick look, but there wasn't time.'

His dad was silent then drew a deep breath. 'Well, we can't do anything now. We'll go in the morning, how about that? Take some sandwiches. Go up on to the hill.'

Peter loved these outings. 'Yeah, right,' he said and wondered if his dad would be fit enough by then.

A while later Jim made dinner: fish pie, chips and peas. It was excellent. Peter scooped up the last smears of sauce with a finger and picked chips from the plate his dad left almost untouched. For pudding he had banoffee tart with ice cream, while Jim made himself a coffee and foaming Alka-Seltzer.

By nine he was feeling a little better and turned the TV to a grisly murder mystery. It was good, Peter enjoyed it, but as the bodies began to mount up his dad fell fast asleep on the settee and began to snore. Rather than wake him, Peter switched off the set, made himself a hot chocolate and took a book up to bed.

When he woke next morning, Jim was already up and about. Ashamed of the past forty-eight hours, he had bacon and eggs ready to go in the frying pan, bread standing by the toaster and porridge plopping in the pot. A little colour had crept back into his cheeks. Purposefully he busied himself about the kitchen.

'One egg or two?' he said as Peter, still in pyjamas, appeared in the doorway.

Peter was surprised. He had come down to put on the kettle.

'Better make it two,' his dad said, 'if we're going out on the hill.' He dropped bacon into the sizzling fat. 'Just as well you rescued the frying pan.'

'Yeah.' Peter yawned and rubbed his hair. The floor was cold, he stood with one foot on top of the other. 'Want a hand?'

'No, I don't want a hand,' Jim said. 'I can manage bacon and eggs for God's sake. What I want is for you to go upstairs and get dressed, then come down and eat your porridge.'

'OK.' Peter blew his nose on a kitchen towel. 'What about the dogs?'

'The dogs are fine.'

'Tractor's low on diesel.'

'Give me a break! There's a full drum in the shed. Now away and get some clothes on.'

'I'm not cold.'

'Peter!'

'All right. Just trying to help.'

'I know you are.' Jim pushed back the frying pan. 'Come here.'

Jim gave his son a hard hug, trying to make up for the days of neglect. Peter hugged him back, feeling how bony his ribs and shoulder blades had become. He was getting thinner.

'You OK?'

'What do you mean? Course I am.' Jim returned to the stove. 'Come on, let's have breakfast and away out.'

Anxiously Peter went upstairs and pulled his jeans from the back of a chair.

7

Blae Fell

THE STONY TRACK from the road reached Scar Hill and continued up into the moors. Jim took the tractor, Peter and the dogs bouncing on a trailer behind. After two miles they reached a turning place, not the end of the track but a patch of rough ground bounded by heather, rocks and battered wooden sheep pens. Jim drew up alongside a rusty iron field gate. He hung his binoculars round his neck, picked up a small rucksack and jumped to the ground.

The gate screeched open. Beyond lay a broad marshy hollow. Preceded by the dogs, they splashed across and soon were on rising ground. After days of rain the clouds had blown away and the sky was blue with a few high wisps of cirrus. The air was so clear you could see for ever.

Blae Fell, five miles from home, stood on the edge of a great wilderness. Though not a mountain, it was a fine hill over four hundred metres in height. South and east, the rolling moors spread to the horizon. To the west the land descended into the broad glen of the River Teal, then rolled on to distant mountains where the snow clung to gullies right through the summer. To the north, beyond Scar Hill, lay the road, Tarridale village and the deep blue sea.

For most of the year Jim's sheep grazed on the southern slopes of Blae Fell. Every spring he burned off patches of gorse and heather to give them fresh green shoots. There were red deer on the hills as well, and grouse, and salmon in the river far below.

Half an hour after setting out they were high above the

surrounding moor. A burn rushed past, beer-brown and foaming. Peter spotted a big toad and crouched to catch it among the mossy roots. Jim waited, leaning on his shepherd's crook, while Peter examined it and set it on a stone in a pool. The toad sat still for several seconds, sides bulging, then crawled into the water and swam from sight beneath some overhanging ferns.

Ben, never happier than when he was out on the hill, came to see what was happening, decided it was of no interest, and bounded away through the long heather. Meg, well trained and eager to work, sat close to Jim and waited until they set off again.

There were two hundred ewes scattered across the hillside, white and long-legged from shearing. Rather than cut his flock's ears to distinguish them, Jim marked them on the shoulder with ruddle. The lambs had been separated two months earlier, taken down to the pens and herded aboard a sheep lorry for market.

Peter called Ben to heel and they walked among them. As they came close the sheep scampered away, tails swirling, then turned to stare at the dogs. One, which had been kneeling to eat, was lame in the forelegs.

'Footrot,' Jim said briefly. 'All this bloody wet weather. Wonder where she's been.'

Peter pointed to another which had escaped clipping. It was a scraggy creature. Half its fleece had dropped out, revealing the new wool underneath. What was left hung in rags. It had fled with the rest but there was something wrong for it stood twitching its dirty tail and turning to bite at its hindquarters. Abruptly it darted away in a skittering, zigzag run.

'Maggots?' he said.

'Bit late in the year.' Jim raised his binoculars and saw the patch of damp, discoloured wool on its rump. 'Looks like it though.'

'What we going to do?' Peter said. 'Drive them down?'

'Nah, it's only a couple of weeks till dipping.' Jim blew his nose. 'Let's take them round to the fank [pen] and have a look-see.'

He glanced down at Meg who stared fixedly at the sheep and then up into his face, eager for the word of command.

'Can I, Dad?' Peter said.

'You want to?' Jim said. 'OK.'

Peter had worked the sheep many times under his father's guidance, occasionally by himself. He walked a few paces off. 'Come on then, Meg.'

She was puzzled for a moment then shifted her gaze from father to son.

'Away, lass,' Peter said.

Meg tensed and hesitated, unsure if she was meant to respond to the son's command, then raced off to the right, fast and neat, circling the sheep anti-clockwise.

'Come by.' Peter's high, cracked voice rang across the moor.

Meg cut in to the left, separating a group of a dozen or so animals which included the two Jim wanted to examine. The other sheep scampered away, leaving the small flock isolated in the heather. One sheep bounded off in panic. Immediately Meg went after it, driving it back to the others.

'Good lass,' Peter called. Jim handed him the whistle and he blew it twice. 'Walk on.'

The sheep pen stood in a cleft of the hill, ten minutes beyond where they were standing. It was a circular, dry-stone structure with a rickety grey gate, a metal storage bin for sacks of sheep nuts, and an open lean-to with a rusty corrugated-iron roof where Jim sometimes stored bales of hay.

Meg was an intelligent dog and kept the sheep together, fifty metres ahead as they crossed the hillside. She understood where they were heading and needed no words of command. Soon the sheep pen came in sight, a little below them on the far side of the gully.

A stream splashed down from the moors. The sheep leaped across and in a couple of minutes they were there. Jim dragged the gate wide and ushered the sheep towards it as Peter and Meg walked them down.

Three times the flock escaped round the side; three times Meg fetched them back at Peter's command. The fourth time, hemmed in by the man at one side, the boy with his big grey dog at the other and the swift black sheepdog behind, they filed through the entrance. At once Jim heaved the gate shut and dropped the locking bar in place.

'Well done,' he said and rubbed his son's thick hair. Peter flushed with pleasure.

Tongue lolling, Meg flopped beside them.

Jim didn't feel too good, his energy had deserted him. Although he had taken one of the little white pills when they started climbing, his heart was playing up. Turning from Peter, he grimaced at a little spasm of pain.

'Which one first?' Peter took the crook.

'Mm?'

'What d'you want to do first, maggots or footrot?'

Jim shrugged. 'Whichever you like.'

The lame sheep was nearer. Peter ran after it, snatching with the crook. Twice he missed then hooked it round a leg and next moment his fingers were knotted in the wool. But Peter was not strong enough to wrestle the animal off its feet and got dragged to his knees on the nibbled grass, scattered with droppings. His dad came to help and expertly threw the sheep over on to its back.

Briefly it struggled and looked round with rolling eyes.

Jim drew a breath to steady his bumping heart and examined the two front feet. 'Aye, footrot,' he said.

Peter had seen it often enough. The horny part of both feet was deformed and rotten-looking. As Jim took it in his hands, a mattery discharge welled out and the sheep baaed with pain.

'Got to cut it away, old girl.' He pulled out his pocket knife and flicked up the sharp blade. Carefully he pared away the diseased tissue and tipped it into a paper to burn when they got home.

'It stinks!' Peter grimaced.

'How would you like that to happen to your feet?' Jim bowed over his work, cutting and scraping until the foot was as clean as he could make it. 'Must hurt like hell. Let's have the purple spray.'

Peter opened the rucksack and took out the can. Jim gave it a good shake and sprayed the foot from point-blank range. 'Kill the bacteria. Give it a chance to heal.'

He turned to the other foot and repeated the operation. Some fluid sprayed past and dyed the wool purple.

The front feet were finished. Jim checked the hind feet. They were not infected but he gave them a spray anyway. 'There you go.' He rolled the helpless ewe on to its side and slapped its flank.

The sheep scrambled to its feet. Limping on the raw wounds and baaing loudly, it ran to join the others which stood watching with alarm. 'See how she's doing when we bring them down for dipping,' he said. 'Put them through a couple of footbaths. Winter's tough enough with the cold and carrying a lamb, never mind having to cope with footrot as well.'

Then Jim caught hold of the ragged sheep. This time he kept the animal on its feet. It was strong and struggled while Peter pulled off the hanging tags of wool and clipped away the dirt round its bottom.

Jim was white. Peter saw he was sweating. 'Are you all right?'

'Don't worry about me.' He belched again. 'Just need my lunch.' He leaned past Peter to examine the infestation on the sheep's hindquarters. 'Ugh, will you look at that! Give me the willies.'

Peter snipped off the fleece round a raw patch the size of his hand. It was seething with blowfly maggots, big ones on top, so fat they seemed on the point of bursting, little ones underneath, like white seeds burrowed into the flesh.

'Why don't you do it.' Jim tightened his grip. 'I'll hold her.'

Peter swallowed. They disgusted him too. 'If you like.'

He took a white can from the rucksack and sprayed the moving mass. Instantly they convulsed. A few dropped off. He sprayed again and brushed away the maggots with the back of his fingernails. Twisting and writhing, they rattled to the turf.

Ben came to sniff. 'Get away.' Peter pushed him back with his boot and stamped the maggots into a paste.

The wound was clean, weeping red flesh, but the tiny maggots, from eggs laid later, were too deeply embedded to remove, and clusters of blowfly eggs, still unhatched, clung to the roots of the wool. Peter sprayed it again, a long burst. Unlike the foot spray, this was a clear fluid, a strong antiseptic, fly repellent and insecticide that would kill off the last of the infestation and give the skin a chance to heal. It burned like fire in the raw wound. The sheep baaed and struggled.

This patch was close to the sheep's bottom. There was another above its tail. Peter treated it the same way then Jim let the ewe go and she ran off, still ragged but looking better.

'Hope she's the only one,' he said.

Peter looked round the remaining animals. 'None here. Didn't see any others.'

'Bloody things.' Jim wiped a hand on his trousers and rubbed the sweat from his face. 'What's she doing with maggots in October? Climate's changing, that's what I reckon. Global warming.'

Peter opened the gate and the ewes ran out. Soon they would wander back and join the rest of the flock.

Part of the wall had fallen and been repaired with barbed wire. Jim sat on one of the stones and rolled a cigarette. Sheltered within the enclosure, the sun was warm. Peter lifted his face to the dazzle.

After a brief rest they climbed out of the gully and walked through the rest of the flock.

Jim looked at his watch. 'What say we have lunch?'

He hid his sickness so well that Peter said, 'Let's have it on the top.' He looked up at the crown of rocks and trig point that marked the summit of Blae Fell. 'Not that far. You be OK?'

'Why not?' If he'd been by himself, Jim would have lain back out of the wind and waited for the weakness to pass. With Peter watching, so young and enthusiastic, he did not like to give in. 'Away you go. Find a spot to eat – somewhere with a good view.'

'I'll take the rucksack,' Peter said. 'You've been carrying it all morning.'

Half angrily Jim pulled it back. 'Think I can't carry a bloody rucksack? Go on now, I'll be right behind you.'

It was no good arguing. After a brief hesitation Peter started straight up the hillside, pushing himself to see how fast he could go. He loved it, feeling the strength in his legs, the muscles in his back, the way his boots gripped the treacherous ground. Soon he was panting, his collar wet with sweat. A series of little cliffs rose before him. He climbed one and skirted round another.

Abruptly he came upon a big adder. It lay by a sun-warmed rock. If he had not spotted the creature he might have trodden on it. The snake felt his footsteps and raised its head with a warning hiss. Peter was fascinated and stepped closer, keeping just out of striking range. He had seen adders before, there were many out there in the wilderness. He liked them but they were scary and he was frightened that sometime Ben or Meg might get bitten, though it was unlikely to kill them. This snake was a female, light brown with a vivid zigzag pattern down its back. He pulled a stem of heather and tickled the back of its head. The adder reared higher and hissed again, then struck like lightning. Peter jumped back. Its mouth stayed wide, threatening. He saw the pink mouth-lining, two erect fangs.

'Dad.'

The snake sank to the ground and began to slither away. It didn't want trouble. Its flickering tongue smelled the air.

'Dad!' Peter looked back down the hill.

In a moment every thought of the adder was swept from his mind. His dad was slumped against a boulder. His head hung low, his knees were buckled. Clumsily he groped in his jacket pocket.

Peter ran back down the hillside, skidding on the peat, risking his ankles on stones. By the time he reached him, Jim had found the little brown bottle he was seeking and unscrewed the top. The blood had drained from his face. With shaking hands he tipped a scatter of small white pills into his palm and put one between his lips. It disappeared under his tongue. Carefully, like a drunk man, he poured the others back into the bottle and returned it to his pocket.

Peter faced him awkwardly. 'Is it bad?'

Jim looked at him with sick eyes and didn't reply.

After a while he sat on a rock. 'I'd rather have a night out with Sexy Sadie,' he said as the pill worked its magic.

Peter grinned with relief. 'Or a night in.'

'Yeah, or a night in.' His dad's colour was improving. 'Hey, you're only twelve years old. What do you know about these things?'

But Peter was serious. 'You should go to the doctor again.'

'I'm fed up going to the doctor,' Jim said. 'And the hospitals. They can't do anything.'

'You always say that but you haven't been for months.'

'Don't nag,' his father said. 'It was just a wee turn. I'm fine.'

'No you're not. You've told me, Dr Bryson said that –'

'All right, all right. If you want me to go to the doctor, I'll go to the doctor. Don't keep on about it.' Jim leaned forward and covered his eyes with a hand. 'It just won't do any good.'

'How can you know that if you never go?'

Jim didn't reply. Peter rested a hand on his dad's knee.

After a while he took two scraps of plastic sheet from the rucksack and spread them on the grass out of the wind. Jim joined him and Peter unpacked the sandwiches. He was hungry.

Jim could eat nothing but had a terrific thirst. By the time Peter had taken a couple of sips from his cup, the flask was empty.

8

The Hidden Photo

PETER BROUGHT BUSTER into the kitchen for a run around while he made the dinner. Jim had said he would do it, but when they got home he went to lie down for ten minutes and fell fast asleep. Peter didn't mind, he enjoyed cooking. Once you knew how to do a few basic things it was easy – for what he and his dad liked anyway.

There was too much meat on the hare to fit into the casserole dish so he gave Buster a front leg and put the excess into the deep freeze. What they needed for dinner he cut a bit smaller, rolled it in seasoned flour, browned it in the big frying pan and tipped it into the well-used dish. Next he fried the onions, sliced the carrots and added them to the meat, sprinkled on a little salt and pepper, just covered the mixture with boiling water, stirred in some gravy browning and put on the lid. The oven was hot. He set the dish on the middle shelf and shut the door. It would take an hour and a half, maybe two hours. In the meantime he scrubbed the potatoes and put them ready in the saucepan, then cored two big cooking apples for pudding and filled the middles with brown sugar and nutmeg. For good measure he studded the skins with cloves.

Living out there at Scar Hill, even though he was only twelve, Peter had learned how to do most things. Jim was determined to give his son a good start in life: plain food and plenty of exercise to make him strong, a good education, and the confidence to tackle whatever might come his way.

Buster had dragged his treasure into a corner. Peter picked

him up, needle teeth clamped on the bone, and carried him back to the shed.

Jim appeared at six, hair tousled and rubbing the sleep from his eyes. He looked better.

'Sorry, don't know what came over me.' He sniffed appreciatively. 'That smells good.'

'Will you be able to eat some?'

'Lead me to it. Had nothing since breakfast.'

'I'll put the tatties on.' Peter poured in boiling water. 'Baked apple for pud.'

Jim gave him one of his rough hugs and retreated to the living room. 'What about your homework?'

'Done it.'

'What was it?'

'Bit of maths and some geography. Had to read a chapter.'

'What's the book?'

'*The Midwich Cuckoos.* Finished it last week.'

'You read that a couple of years ago, it's on your shelf.'

'I know but now it's the class reader so I've read it again.' He added salt to the potatoes. 'It's good.'

Jim opened a beer and poured some for Peter. He reached for the chess set. In the dark evenings they often had a game.

'And you are going to the doctor, yeah?' Peter held out his fists, white pawn in one, black pawn in the other. 'That's twice this weekend.'

'Twice what?'

'You took a bad turn.'

'Ach, I told you, I'm sick of doctors.' Jim chose white and they set out the pieces. 'They've done all they can. I'll be OK, just have to take it easy for a bit.' He pushed up his king's pawn to start the game.

Peter countered. 'But you don't take it easy, do you?'

'Don't worry your head about it,' Jim said. 'You've got enough to contend with. We'll be fine, you'll see.'

They interrupted the game for dinner. The hare, smothered in rich gravy, was delicious. They ate the baked apples with ice cream. Afterwards, with mugs of coffee, they played to the finish. Jim won.

There were three rooms upstairs. At the top of the steep stairs, immediately on the right, was the bathroom. Next to it was Jim's bedroom. And to the left, at the end of the short landing, was Peter's room.

It was the room he had been given the day they arrived, with a dormer window, sloping ceiling and view across the yard. Black beams crossed the white ceiling. The walls were wooden, tongue-and-groove painted a soft green. In contrast, the duvet cover he had on at the moment was jazzy spaceships and planets, and the curtains, heavy material to keep out the winter cold and bright summer nights, were burnt orange with a pattern of leaves.

Peter brushed his teeth, changed into pyjamas and jumped into his cold bed. He usually read before going to sleep but this night he could not concentrate. After a time he swung his feet to the floor and padded to his chest of drawers. His socks and underclothes were in the second drawer down. He pushed them aside and pulled out a photo, about fifteen centimetres by ten, from under the lining paper. It was a picture of his mother, taken at a Sergeants' Mess party when his dad was in the army. She looked very pretty, he thought, in a sparkly off-the-shoulder dress with her hair piled high and a red silk rose above her ear. He went back to bed and propped the photo on his stomach.

Peter had only been four when she ran off so there wasn't much to remember, but a few images stood out from the fog of those early years: the rooms in Manchester with black mould on the walls and the doctor coming; his mum's lovely fat squashy hugs and smell of perfume; a hot day by the river where they had a picnic and he got sunburned; and that terrible fight when his dad knocked his mum to the floor and Peter ran away screaming, fell down the concrete stairs and had to be taken to hospital.

Apart from these and a scatter of half-memories, all he had to go on was what he had been told by Valerie. Jim, who had never criticised their mother, said little. Valerie, on the other hand, who adored her mother and hated her father, had filled in the blanks so thoroughly that sometimes Peter wasn't sure what he remembered and what he had been told. The scenes she described were as real to him now as what he had seen himself: lovely Christmases, parties, shopping trips, holidays and much more. It was Valerie who had told him, for example, how their mum was the toast of the mess and a sergeant had drunk vodka out of her shoe. And Valerie who had told him about jaunts in friends' cars, lovely cars with leather seats, when their dad was away on manoeuvres.

Peter himself remembered how his mother, looking pretty in a pale blue suit, had taken him to a café where they had tea with Uncle Tony. Peter didn't like Uncle Tony although he was jolly and bought him a cream doughnut. He didn't like the way Uncle Tony held his mummy's hand. He didn't tell his mummy this but just before they left the café and Uncle Tony had gone to the bathroom, she told him that his daddy didn't like him either because Uncle Tony owned a big garage and had lots of money so he wasn't to tell. When Peter asked what was wrong with owning a big garage and having lots of money, she yanked his arm and told him not to ask so many questions.

'She enjoyed life, she was fun,' Valerie had said one day when she was fourteen and Peter was seven. 'Mind you, even a dead sheep's fun compared with that miserable sick old bastard,' as she called their father. 'Always banging on about money and spoiling things. Taking us to that place in Manchester, and now this bloody awful house in the middle of the sodding moors. I don't blame her running off. Give us half a chance an' I'll be off myself.'

Sharon hadn't run off with Billy Josh, the handsome young trawler owner with the gorgeous red Merc, although it wasn't for want of trying because she had pursued him in her war-paint to dance and bar and quayside. But Billy, though tempted, had met Jim and Peter whom he liked. After a brief flirtation he sent her packing. So Sharon had to look elsewhere, and when she made her break for freedom it wasn't with Billy, or any of the other good-looking men from the village, but Morris Sinclair of all people, the chinless and ginger-haired brother of her hairdresser that everyone thought was gay.

Lying in bed Peter tried to imagine it – and failed. How could his mum betray his dad like that, chasing after other men, getting herself talked about? He had heard the stories, a spiteful girl at school had taunted him with them, making things up as she went along. When she wouldn't stop he had hit her and got into trouble. What she said about Billy Josh wasn't true, he knew that. Billy was a friend of his dad. He was married now with a big house and children of his own. Last summer holiday Jim had let Peter go off with Billy on his trawler, fishing round Iceland.

Peter had heard his mum's name linked with another man too, a bearded forestry manager who had long since moved to another part of the country. But there was no mystery why in the end she had chosen Morris Sinclair for her getaway, lanky Morris with his thinning hair and big Adam's apple, living off the Social, propping up the bar in his old jeans and sweater. For Morris had had a big win on the pools. All at once, no-account Morris had become a man with a new Volvo Estate and expensive leather jacket, buying drinks all round.

How could she have gone off with such a person, Peter wondered, deserting them even before they'd spent their first Christmas at Scar Hill? Did he, Valerie and their dad mean nothing to her? The affair hadn't lasted long, by all accounts. Within a few weeks Morris was back in the village, scuttling away like a frightened rabbit whenever his dad appeared.

And his mother, did she ever think of them? Did she have any regrets? She had never written or phoned, not even once. The last Peter had seen of her was that never-to-be-forgotten afternoon when she had rushed about the house packing her satin-lined suitcase, taking things from drawers, lifting them off shelves and throwing them hastily into the boot of the Volvo. 'Be good now,' she had said, giving first Peter then his sister one of her special big hugs. 'Look after your dad. Remember I love you.' Then she had stepped into the car and driven off down the track with Morris, leaving eleven-year-old Valerie to look after her broken-hearted and tearstained brother until their dad came back from the hill.

Like names pencilled lightly on paper, she had erased her husband, daughter and four-year-old son from her life. Despite this, sometimes Valerie had news, though only of the broadest kind. How she obtained it Peter never completely understood because he was only eight when Valerie herself left home, but a year or so after his mother's departure he learned that she was living in Leicester with a good friend, and later that she was living in Liverpool with another friend and calling herself Cynthia Talbot. She had found herself a part-time job in a cinema. The last he heard, in a letter from Valerie, was that their mother, though still legally married to their dad, had married again and emigrated to America where she was starting a new family.

One morning around the same time, Jim told him he was thinking about getting a divorce. 'Your mum and me, Pete, I don't think there's much chance of us getting together again. I'm sorry. Do you mind very much?'

Peter was ten. He knew what divorce was. The parents of Jo-Ann, a girl in his class, were newly divorced. But what did it mean to him? His parents lived apart already. He resented his missing mum. She had hurt his dad and Peter loved his dad.

All the same … He let the picture fall and looked up at the beams on his bedroom ceiling. His half-brothers or sisters, how old were they now? What were they like? And his stepfather? And his mother? Supposing she wanted to see him again sometime, did he want to see her? Peter thought about it.

No, he didn't.

Not really.

Not ever.

9

Stuff School

SUDDEN MUSIC CAME from downstairs. The Rolling Stones, his dad's favourite group. Peter listened: 'Jumpin' Jack Flash'. He'd heard it so often he knew the words by heart.

There was a chorus of barking from the dogs in the shed. It went on for some time. The front door opened beneath him and a slit of light appeared at a gap in the curtains. Peter threw back his duvet and crossed to the window.

His dad was in the yard. He called something to the dogs and opened the shed door. They came bounding out, Meg carrying something and Ben trying to get it. Meg shook whatever it was hard and turned away from him. As the light hit her, Peter saw something trailing from her jaws. It was a rat's tail. The unwary rodent had ventured into the dogs' sleeping quarters. His dad called her but Meg was too proud of her trophy to come at once. Tail high, she trotted round the yard, repeatedly shaking the rat hard, though it must be very dead by this time. Eventually she went to him, too excited to be patted and reluctant to part with her treasure. At length she let him have it and he straightened, holding the rat by the tail. 'Good girl,' he said, but both dogs were more interested in what he held in his hand. 'Go on then.' He threw it across the yard and they bounded in pursuit. This time Ben got there first and pranced away from Meg, holding the rat high above her head.

Jim saw the light at Peter's window and looked up.

Peter raised a hand and let the curtain fall back. The bedroom was cold. He pulled on his thick brown dressing gown and slippers and went downstairs. The dogs were still playing with the rat.

His dad looked round. 'Hello there, Pete. What you doing out here?'

'Couldn't sleep.'

'No? Not worrying about me, I hope. What happened this morning.'

'Not really.'

'Just a little turn, I'll be all right.'

They watched the dogs. 'I think that's enough, don't you,' Jim said. 'Much longer and they'll start to eat it. Ben!' he called. 'Come on now. Bring it here.'

Ben took no notice.

'Ben!' he said more sharply. 'Come here!'

Reluctantly Ben did as he was told and allowed Jim to take the rat from him. 'That's a good boy.'

'I'll get them a couple of biscuits.' Peter went into the kitchen and returned with two digestives and a handful of meaty chunks. He let the dogs sniff them and led the way into the shed. They knew the routine and flopped down happily on their beds. 'Good boy! Good girl!' he said and divided them equally. 'Night-night.' He gave each head a brief pat and switched off the light.

Jim had wrapped the soggy rat in newspaper and thrust it into the bin. Peter followed him into the house.

The Stones' CD was playing another track: '19th Nervous Breakdown'. His dad sang along as he straightened the living room.

'Right,' he said, turning to Peter. 'Can't get to sleep. How about if you go on up and I'll bring you a mug of hot chocolate with condensed milk?'

'Yeah, great!' The fire had burned low. Peter pulled the neck of his dressing gown close. 'And a couple of biscuits, those sultana ones.'

'No sooner said.' Jim nodded towards the stairs. 'I'll be up in a minute.'

They were delicious. Peter propped himself against the pillows and pulled the duvet to his throat. His thoughts returned to the rat. There weren't many but they were attracted by the sacks of grain and sheep nuts his dad kept for winter feed. He'd often thought of catching one and trying to tame it. Rats were intelligent, they made good pets.

Valerie hadn't agreed. He smiled, how his sister had hated them. Even the sight of a mouse, a harmless little field mouse at the end of the byre, was enough to make her scream. The thought of a rat made her go cold all over. When Peter wanted to torment her, he'd describe how a rat would come climbing up the bedclothes when she was asleep and creep around her neck, its skinny tail slithering over the pillow and its sharp little claws ... But by this time Valerie was shouting and hitting him to make him stop.

He missed her, even after all these years. When his mum went off, Valerie had taken her place. She was his big sister, lively, funny, who had hugged him, and smelled of sweat and scent, and told him secrets and had a total disregard for authority.

Her photo stood on his chest of drawers, indistinct in the night-time shadows.

What fights there had been with his father. One occasion he would never forget. It was a Saturday evening and Valerie was going off with Maureen Bates, a school friend, to a dance in the neighbouring village.

'Mind, I want you back by half past ten, not one o'clock like the last time,' his dad said. 'And not smelling like a cider barrel either.'

'Yes, Dad,' Valerie answered automatically.

'I mean it, Valerie.'

'I said OK, didn't I?'

'What a sight!' Her dad looked her over – the heavy make-up, streaked hair, skirt halfway up her thighs, blouse clinging to her ample young bosom. 'Is that what all the girls will be wearing?'

She rolled her eyes and didn't answer.

'Where did you get those shoes from anyway? I haven't seen them before.'

Valerie looked down at her chunky-heeled shoes in shiny red leather. 'I borrowed them from Maureen.'

'Is that right, Maureen?'

'Yes, Mr Irwin,' Maureen answered without missing a beat. 'We're the same size. I got them for my birthday.'

Which even at the age of seven Peter knew was a lie, because Valerie had stolen them from a shoe shop in Fortness one day when she and Maureen played truant. Ever since, they had stayed hidden beneath her wardrobe, right at the back where Jim would never find them.

In the event, Valerie and Maureen didn't go to the dance that night, had never intended to. Instead they went to a party at the house of Maureen's boyfriend, thirty miles away, where Valerie, on the vodka now, drank more than was good for her and fell asleep on the settee a bit after midnight. At two o'clock, as the party was breaking up, the boyfriend's father phoned Jim, explaining that his son, who had picked up the girls at Scar Hill, couldn't drive Valerie home because he'd had a couple of drinks – a gross understatement. Valerie was quite safe though, she was sharing a room with his daughter and they'd bring her back the next day. Jim wasn't happy about it and wanted to drive over and collect her right then, but Peter was too young to be left on his own.

It was early the next afternoon when Valerie, hung over and defiant, arrived home. The boy's father, seeing the expression on Jim's face, drove off quickly.

'By God, girl,' Jim said when they got indoors. She wore a silk scarf she had not been wearing the night before. He hooked it down with his finger and saw the love-bites on her neck. 'That's the last time you'll be going out for a while. You are not, repeat *not*, while you're living under this roof,' he drew a shaky breath, 'going the same way as your mother.'

His face was white. Peter and Valerie stared at him.

'Now away upstairs,' he said, 'and wash that muck off your

face. Have a bath. And then tidy your bedroom, it looks like a tart's boudoir. When you've done that you can help me put these sheep to the hill. I've lost the best part of a day with your shenanigans.'

Valerie was so sick and angry she couldn't speak and stormed away through the hall to her bedroom which was downstairs.

'I see you're still wearing Maureen's shoes,' he called after.

'What d'you expect?' she shouted back. 'Want me to come home barefoot? Yeah, you'd prob'ly like that, wouldn't you, mis'rable old sod! Tip some ashes over my head, shall I? Chuck out my clothes and wear an old sack?'

'I'd like it better than that you're wearing now, anyway.'

Peter, sitting on the settee, left off picking a scab from his elbow and stared from his dad to the door Valerie had slammed shut behind her.

After a while, when Jim had gone out to the sheds, Valerie crept down from the bathroom. She had changed into jeans and an anorak. Conspiratorially she looked at her young brother and put a finger to her lips then slipped away through the kitchen and out the back door. Peter watched from the kitchen window as she dropped into a nearby hollow of the moors.

When Jim came to look for her she had gone. 'That bloody girl! That *bloody* girl!' he stormed, hunting round the outbuildings, scanning the moors with binoculars. 'Which way'd she go, Pete?'

Peter was torn by conflicting loyalties. Wide-eyed he looked at his father and said nothing.

Later, when a cold wet dusk was falling and Valerie still hadn't returned, he was frightened and pointed across the heather.

Jim ran out, calling and searching every hiding place and dangerous spot for a mile around: peaty hollows, sheltered corners of dry-stone dykes, rocky overhangs. There was no trace of his fourteen-year-old daughter, not even a footprint. When it grew too dark to continue, he sat in the hall and phoned everyone he could think of: teachers, schoolfriends, people in the village, anyone with outbuildings. No one had seen her. Eventually, as midnight approached, he contacted the police, who came to the house.

He told them about the quarrel. They wanted to talk to Peter. Jim brought him down, dazed with sleep, but he could tell the police no more than he had told his dad. Searchers were summoned and went out into the moors with lights and loudhailers. Valerie did not respond. She was not to be found.

'Don't worry,' they reassured her distressed father. 'Teenagers do this sort of thing sometimes.'

'Not from this house they don't,' Jim said, his hair sleeked by rain that by this time was teeming from a black sky, slanting through the beams of the high-powered torches.

'Maybe she's found herself a warm bolt-hole,' they said. 'Anyway, there's no more anyone can do tonight. Leave it to us. We'll be out again first thing in the morning.'

And where was Valerie all this while? Keeping out of sight, she had made her way to the house of a girl in her class who lived just beyond the village. She was, Valerie knew, away with her parents for a few days. Valerie also knew, for she had seen the girl collect it, that a spare key was hidden beneath a watering can in the shed. And so, an hour after leaving Scar Hill, Valerie let herself into the house and locked the door behind her.

Looking through drawers in the kitchen, she came upon a scatter of money hidden beneath tablecloths. She counted it – just over forty-two pounds. How much could she safely take, Valerie wondered, and slipped a ten-pound note and a few coins into her pocket. Then, since the afternoon was cold, she made a cup of coffee, took some biscuits from the cupboard and settled down to watch a video.

Afterwards she carried a radio upstairs and sank into a jasmine-scented foam bath, which was not exactly the hardship her father was imagining.

It was a modern house built facing a panorama of sea and

headlands. The only habitation to be seen in that direction was a deserted holiday cottage. When darkness came, therefore, Valerie was able to close the blinds, draw the curtains and switch on the light with little chance of being spotted by inquisitive neighbours. A liquor cabinet contained vodka and there was orange in the fridge, so by the time bedtime arrived and Valerie climbed into her classmate's bed, her head was spinning for the second night in a row. She giggled to think of Jim searching for her. 'Serve him right,' she said aloud, 'miserable old git,' and pulled the frilly duvet to her chin. Tomorrow? Well, stuff school for a start. Tomorrow could take care of itself.

At eleven o'clock the next morning, having removed every trace of her presence as far as possible, Valerie let herself out of the house, replaced the key and walked the half mile into the village. On the way she shoved the wet bath towel, hidden in a poly bag, into the bottom of a rubbish bin. Then she bought a bar of chocolate in the shop and phoned her father.

That was the worst of her misdemeanours but there were others, many of them. She was her mother's daughter, just as Peter was his father's son, and relations with her dad were stormy. It was a battle which neither could win and in which neither would give way, not enough to bring a lasting peace.

In the end, a few months before her sixteenth birthday, Valerie ran away from home and never contacted her father again. Peter was devastated: first his mother and now his sister. Valerie wrote him a letter or card occasionally, and always, for the first two or three years, sent a birthday and Christmas present. So they knew Valerie was all right but not where she was, because the presents and cards came from different towns. This was puzzling, though it made perfect sense if you knew that Valerie was travelling with a third-rate boy band called Tinker's Cuss, whose single hit, a frenzy called 'Liquidise the Leaders', climbed to thirty-seven in the charts.

After eighteen months the band broke up and Valerie moved to Bristol with one of the other groupies. Little by little the cards and presents grew fewer, and for the past two years there had been no communication at all. The last Peter had heard, she was working in a hotel. The card was postmarked 'Bristol' but it was a pretty tourist scene so she might have been on holiday. In any case, by that time Valerie was seventeen and old enough to live as she chose. If she had wanted to hear from him she would have included her address.

The hot chocolate was finished. Peter slipped down the bed. His eyes were closing. The music had stopped and he heard Jim in the kitchen, clattering a few dishes and filling the kettle. His poor dad, Peter thought, one thing after another: he didn't choose to leave the army; he didn't want to lose his wife and daughter; he couldn't help being sick. It wasn't fair, he always tried so hard. Peter knew he should turn off the bedside light but his limbs were too heavy. And before he could do anything about it, he was asleep.

A while later Jim raked the fire, set their boots beside the hearth and came upstairs to bed. As he reached the landing he felt a bit light-headed. His heart was beating irregularly again. He gripped the banister rail to steady himself and swore under his breath.

Peter's light was still on. He crossed the landing and pushed the door wide. His son was dead to the world, breathing easily. A photo lay on the rug, face down. Jim picked it up. It was the picture of Sharon. He examined it. She was pretty, no doubt about it. He remembered the night he had taken it; remembered Sharon in their bedroom pinning the rose in her hair. With a sigh he slipped it back into the drawer beneath Peter's socks and T-shirts. Then he tucked his son's arm under the bedcover. Softly he kissed him on the brow, switched off the light and went from the room.

10

The Conger, the Cod and the Cumberland Sausage

AT QUARTER TO eight on Wednesday morning, as Peter was eating his cereal and revising for a history test that day, the telephone rang. They were surprised. Jim, unshaved and in his stocking feet, padded into the hall. It was Miss Berry, Peter's class and English teacher, a kindly woman known to generations of Tarridale children as the Goose. A digger had torn up a major electricity cable and half the village, including the school, was without power. No lighting, no heating, no lunch, which meant there could be no school that day. Peter, along with the other hundred and fifty pupils at Tarridale High, was delighted.

'That means I can come out with you in the boat,' he told Jim.

'Seems like it.' Jim poured himself another cup of tea and reached for the toast. 'Leave about ten, all right? Got a few jobs to do about the yard first.'

Peter loved going out with his dad. Their boat, an eighteen-foot, clinker-built, open boat with an eight-horsepower Yamaha outboard, rocked at its mooring in the little Tarridale harbour. Jim had painted it red and white for visibility when he bought it and renamed it the *Audrey*, in honour of Audrey Hepburn who was his favourite film star. The heavy outboard remained clamped to the stern, secured by a strong chain and protected by a canvas cover. The oars, fishing tackle and orange life jackets were locked in a stone shed against the harbour wall. They hung their oilskins and sou'westers in there too. On a day like today with little white crests on the waves, they were going to need them.

Peter untied the painter from a rusty iron ring and hauled the boat to the jetty. Grasping the handrail, he descended the slippery stone steps and went aboard. Jim handed him a half bucket of stinking mackerel which they would use as bait, and a tin squirming with lugworms which he'd dug at low water the previous day. The tide was three-quarters full. Looking down through four metres of water, Peter saw clumps of weed, stones, a few fish boxes and shoals of tiny fish swimming above the sand. Businesslike, he removed the engine cover and lowered the propeller into the water.

He exchanged places with his dad and pushed off, using the boathook to get clear of the harbour wall. Jim gripped the tiller with a bony hand and tugged the starting cord. The engine choked. He set his feet and tugged again. With a cloud of blue smoke it burst into exuberant life. Peter tidied the bottom of the boat and coiled ropes out of the way. Jim put the engine from *neutral* into *ahead* gear and eased open the twist-grip throttle. The powerful propeller churned the water into foam. Slowly they moved out into open water.

At once, as the *Audrey* rounded the breakwater, they were hit by the breeze and met the waves rolling in from the North Atlantic, or at least rolling in from the off-shore islands which gave the harbour some protection from the storms of winter. Broken water, bright in a shaft of sunlight, tumbled over the rocks. Beneath the keel the water was dark. Forests of tangle, five metres long and tough as belts, streamed and turned in the currents.

That October day Jim had thirty-two creels set round the islands, two and three miles off shore. They headed into the wind. Waves slapped the bow; spray rattled against their oilskins. Peter was caught unawares. He looked back at his dad and grinned, seawater trickling down his face. In twenty minutes they were in the lee of the islands.

The first float, looking like a bright orange football on the water, lay close to an outcrop known locally as the Red Rock.

Jim brought the *Audrey* alongside. Peter reached out with the boathook and grabbed the float, its long rope descending into the depths. Sometimes, in calm weather, Peter lifted the creels, but they were heavy for him. On a lively autumn day like today, with the boat tossing, he handled the engine while Jim hauled them up, hand over hand, from the weedy depths of the sea.

To Peter it was constantly exciting, watching the mesh frame, dim and wavering, rise through the water, never knowing what it might contain. Then a gush of water as it was heaved aboard and the discovery of their catch.

The first creel, that day, revealed nothing but two small starfish and a green shore crab that was no good for eating. Jim dropped them overboard and threw away the half-eaten bait which could act as ground bait. Then he re-baited the creel with a smelly half mackerel from the bucket at his feet and dropped the heavy frame into the water. Peter watched it sink from sight. Taking care that the rope did not tangle in the propeller, he opened the throttle and chugged on to the next float.

It took over three hours to lift them all, though midway they turned into a sheltered bay for lunch. The bows drove up onto a little white beach and Peter tilted the outboard to keep the propeller clear of the sand. Lounging against the gunwale, he helped himself to a cheese and pickle sandwich. Bright waves made the stern swing. The ebbing tide revealed colonies of mussels and vivid red sea anemones clinging to the rock walls.

'Good catch,' Peter said later when the last creel had been emptied and dropped back over the side.

Jim blew his nose and considered the seven fine lobsters and same number of edible crabs that crawled and clicked around in boxes on the bottom boards. Their powerful claws had been fastened by elastic bands to prevent them damaging each other. 'Not bad,' he said.

A brief excitement after lunch had been the capture of a conger eel a good metre and a half long. It had pursued a crab into the creel and been unable to escape. It writhed and twisted behind the mesh, thick as an arm, staring at them with wicked eyes, showing its terrifying teeth. The crab had been torn to pieces.

'What do you want to do, Pete?' his dad said. 'Let it go or chop its head off and take it home? Good eating, eels. Get a few tasty meals out of that.'

Peter wasn't squeamish but the thought of eating that ferocious blue-black creature did not appeal. He made a face. 'Let it go,' he said.

'Seems a waste, but if that's what you want.' Jim heaved the creel to the gunwale and unlaced the fastening. 'Might save a few fingers, I suppose.'

'Hang on a minute.' Peter left the outboard and clambered forward. It was a rare opportunity. He bent to examine the savage head and prodded its muscular side with the tips of his fingers.

'Strong, I'm telling you!' his dad said. 'Get one of those in the bottom of a boat and you'd better watch out.'

Peter gave it the handle of the boathook to bite on. The eel's jaws snapped shut, leaving deep tears in the wood.

Jim opened the creel wide and tipped it towards the sea. Everything slid out with a rush, but the eel's tail was caught in the netting. It hung in the air, lashing and furious, then slithered free and dropped into the waves. Fast as a whip it arrowed into the depths.

'Hey! Wow! I'm glad that didn't grab a hold of me.'

'You wouldn't be laughing if it did, I'm telling you.' Jim set the creel aside for repair. 'You know Murdo Sutherland, gamekeeper over the far side of Strath Teal? I have a drink with him sometimes.'

Peter nodded.

'One day he was out fishing – oh, years ago now – and *he* hooked a conger. Bigger than this one, close on fifty pound. Heaved it aboard and it went mad, lashing about in the bottom of the boat. Bit him the back of his leg, just below the knee. Didn't realise what had happened at first, just felt like a bash, so he killed it. Then he saw the bottom of the boat was red. Felt his foot all warm and soggy. It had bitten clean through an artery. His welly was full of blood. Pulled his pants down. The back of his leg was running like a tap. Managed to get a bit of rope round for a tourniquet. Felt himself slipping away. Nearly bled to death.' Jim grinned. 'Said the eel was a beauty. Got his old dad to take it to the smokehouse and they ate it when he got out of hospital.'

'Is that true?'

'Yeah, he showed me the scar.'

They went ashore on Bridget Mòr, the largest of the offshore islands, and walked about for fifteen minutes. Peter found a beautiful piece of driftwood on the dunes, white as bone and scoured smooth by the wind and tide. He thought it would look good in his bedroom and carried it back to the *Audrey*. Then Jim set off back to the mainland, heading for a dizzy crag white with bird droppings, while Peter prepared the fishing gear.

Gulls and fulmars wheeled overhead. They fished without rods, Jim at the stern and Peter at the bow so their lines did not become tangled. The water was deep, over thirty metres – nearly as deep beneath their keel as the crag was high overhead. Here, where the seabed was rocky and weedy, they fished with day-glo feathers and lugworm. Down went the lead weights, down and down, the line slipping through their fingers, slanting as the tide and breeze carried the boat sideways, then suddenly a slackening as the weight touched bottom.

Peter loved fishing and never more than today when not five minutes after the hooks went down he felt a tell-tale twitch, and a moment later another twitch on the line. He gave the fish, whatever it was, time to take the bait into its mouth then gave a swift tug. On the instant the line ripped away through his fingers. Peter knew he had caught something big.

'Dad!' he called. 'Dad! Come here! Quick!'

The pull was terrific. He let the fish run until the tension slackened then began to haul in. Jim fastened his line to a cleat and joined him in the bow.

It was a long struggle. Every minute Peter thought his line would break but he played it carefully and at length the grey, exhausted fish was brought to the surface. It was a fine cod, a fish that weighed in later at over seven pounds.

Jim took the gaff. 'Hold it there a minute, son, keep the line tight.' He leaned over the side, and as the fish swam close, rolling on its side, he gaffed it swiftly and hauled it into the boat. Two sharp blows on the head and it was dead.

'Well done, Pete. Well done, boy.' His dad put an arm round his shoulders and hugged him tight. 'A bonny fish. We'll get a few good meals out of that.'

Peter flushed with pleasure. 'Better than eel, anyway.'

'Could be right. Nothing tastier than a nice bit of cod.'

'With mashed tatties and peas,' Peter said, 'and parsley sauce.'

Which seemed remote from the silvery-grey fish with its rubbery lips and white barbel that lay on the sloshing boards at their feet.

In the space of an hour they caught two nice pollack and another conger eel, a much smaller one which had swallowed the hook, so they had to kill it and cut it open. Peter threw the remains over the side. Gulls dived and plunged and screamed, pushing each other right under the water in their frenzy to grab a beakful of the trailing innards.

Jim watched them. '*Nature red in tooth and claw*,' he said and gazed from the towering cliffs crowned with heather to the late afternoon sun streaked with cloud and sinking towards the sea. 'God! I love this place.'

They wound in their lines. Jim produced a couple of Mars Bars and rolled himself a skinny fag. They had drifted away from the protection of the islands and the swell rolled in from a thousand miles of open sea, heaping above the horizon as if it must overwhelm the little boat. There was no need to fear. Every time, without losing an inch of freeboard, the *Audrey* slid up the face of the long swell and dropped away behind, rocking companionably as they munched and chatted, and the breeze tossed the hair that escaped from their warm hats.

Then Jim sailed back towards Tarridale but cut the engine as they crossed Teal Bay, half a mile from shore. Here, where the water was shallower and the bottom mostly sand, they cast their lines for flat fish. Now they used a bright spoon baited with lugworm and tasty scraps of a little squid they had taken from the creels. They did not stay long but that day their luck was in. Jim caught a good-sized plaice with its red spots, and a small dab which he threw back. Peter caught a sole the colour of sand and pebbles.

As they returned to harbour he tossed the stinking mackerel over the side and rinsed out the bucket. It was needed to carry their fish. The lobsters and crabs they would cover with a layer of wet seaweed and leave in the boxes. Next morning Jim would send them off to market on the Clashbay bus.

'I can't be bothered cooking tonight,' he said to Peter. 'What say when we get back we look in at the Kipper and see what they're offering? Or do you fancy getting changed first and we'll go to the Tarry?'

There were two eating – or more commonly drinking – places in Tarridale: the Tarridale Arms, a smart Highland country hotel above the village, and the Cod and Kipper, a friendly but shabby howff close to the harbour, so called because of the old smokehouse which stood close by.

'The Kipper,' said Peter instantly. He loved the fuggy, fumy, low-lit, beer-smelling atmosphere of the squat little building with its open fire, and the chat of the village workmen who gathered there in the evening. Also, more often than not, the Kipper had Cumberland sausage on the menu. This was Peter's favourite meal in the whole world, a huge, golden-brown coil on a mountain of mashed potato, surrounded by a sea of onion gravy. And as if that were not enough, when there were no strangers about, the barman poured him a half glass of beer shandy.

'The Kipper it is.' Jim throttled back and turned neatly round the breakwater into the shelter of the friendly harbour.

11

Bunny and Doctor Bryson

JIM STAYED IN the van and Peter descended the short track that led down to Three Pines. He carried the plaice by three fingers through its gills. Stones turned beneath his feet and a chill rain began to fall. Bunny's animals were locked up for the night; only the tiny wild creatures that lurked in the heather and grasses were aware of his approach.

He did not know Bunny Mason well enough to go directly to the back door, so he opened the rickety gate and went to the front. It was bright blue. His torch picked out the big black knocker. BANG! BANG! He didn't knock hard but in the silence the noise was shocking. Within the house a dog began to bark. He heard a voice telling it to be quiet and the rattle of a bolt. The outside light came on.

'Good gracious! Hello, Peter.'

Bunny Mason stood in the entrance, square-faced and without make-up, her wild grey hair chopped short. She wore a thick cardigan and baggy jogging pants streaked with paint. The hall and stairs were lit by a warm apricot globe. An inquisitive Jack Russell terrier sniffed at the fish in Peter's hand.

He held it out. 'Dad thought you might like this.'

'How very kind.' She took it from him and stood back. 'Come on in.'

'No, I can't. He's waiting up in the van.'

'Come in out of the rain for a second anyway.'

Peter looked over his shoulder then stepped into the hall and scrubbed his shoes on the mat.

After the chill of the night the house was warm. Bunny

led the way into the kitchen. It was a large room, two rooms knocked into one like a farmhouse kitchen with an Aga cooker and big Welsh dresser. She had been working. A half-finished painting of two goats lay on the table. Other pictures were scattered about the room. She shifted some crockery and laid his fish on the draining board. 'Thank you so much. What a beautiful plaice.' She looked at it with an artist's eye. 'Have you just been out?'

'Yeah. Well, came back before it got dark. Dad took us to the Kipper for something to eat.' Peter liked Bunny well enough but he didn't want to be there, didn't want to linger. He eyed the spotted fish. 'He knows you don't like boiling lobsters so he told me to bring this down.'

'I'll clean it tonight and eat it tomorrow.' She smiled. 'With peas and a nice glass of Chablis.'

Although she scarcely knew Peter, their paths crossed from time to time. She liked him. He was well spoken of in the village.

Her terrier, with a brown patch over one eye and another on his back, looked up at the draining board. He adored raw fish. Slavers drooled to the floor. 'All right, Jasper.' She raised a warning finger. 'If you behave yourself you'll get a little bit. But not just now.'

Bunny had moved to Tarridale in the spring of the previous year. Her cottage, Three Pines, stood below the track, only a five minute walk from the road but hidden from it by the rolling moor. It was an old shepherd's cottage with two dormer windows, a yard and outbuildings, not unlike Scar Hill although the layout was quite different. In two other respects it was different also. Many years earlier an owner, having perhaps come into money, had roofed the house and outbuildings with red pantiles. They were unique in that part of the country, patched now with moss, but gave the place a jolly air. And Bunny, having no one to please but herself, had painted the woodwork and surrounding fences in cheerful colours, red and blue and green, even yellow in places. With the animals wandering around, it gave Three Pines, from a distance at least, a picture-book quality.

Closer at hand the image was more typical of life in the country. Rabbits dug under the fence and nibbled her garden to stalks. Attila, her tabby cat, killed things and left them on her bed. Damien, the smelliest of her goats, learned to unfasten the gate. Einstein, her much-loved pig, rooted in the flower beds until they resembled a ploughed field. And Molly, her red and white cow, stored up the vast quantities of hay, grass and wildflowers she consumed each day and dropped them in huge splats round the doorstep. Perhaps, Bunny tried to persuade herself, this was a mark of affection but it would be nice if Molly could find some other way of showing it.

This boisterous behaviour, undesirable to most people, turned out to have one big advantage, although for the first few months, as Bunny hosed her steps and chased goats from the kitchen, she would have been surprised to hear it. For Bunny Mason, whose public school accent and mysterious background made her an enigma to the people of Tarridale, had come north to write and illustrate children's books. And good books require characters and plots. She found these in her new life and the behaviour of her beautifully-drawn animals – real behaviour like the cow that pooped on doorsteps, the cat that crunched winkles, the parrot that was hooked on the sound of breaking ornaments, and the missing hen that emerged from the spare bedroom surrounded by a flock of cheeping chickens. Her first book was about to be published and another was in preparation.

'You're sure your dad wouldn't like to come down for a coffee?'

'No, he's wanting to get home.' Peter invented a lie. 'And I've got a bit of homework to do. Need a bath. Thanks all the same.'

'Oh, well. Another time maybe.'

'Yes.' He turned back through the hall.

'And you will tell him thank you so much for the fish.' She opened the door.

Peter nodded. The rain was heavier now, flashing through the circle of light. Beyond, all was dark, though Jim had driven down to the gate and turned. Peter zipped his jacket to the throat and tugged his woollen hat to his eyes. 'Night.'

'Goodnight, Peter.'

He ran down the path and shut the gate behind him. Jim opened the passenger door and he ducked in quickly. Bunny waited in the lamplit doorway. Peter raised his hand at the window and she waved back. Then Jim drew away and the light was switched off.

Peter reached for a tube of mints and passed one to his dad. They had been lucky with the weather. Now the wind was rising and rain battered on the roof. Small streams ran down the track and filled the already half-filled potholes to overflowing. The van dipped and lurched. Sheets of spray shot up. The creaking windscreen wipers did their best to cope.

As they swung into the yard the dogs ran out and gave them a big welcome. It was good to get into the house and switch on the kettle.

Dr Bryson had a cancelled appointment at two-thirty the next afternoon. Jim was pleased because it meant he could see the doctor, whose surgery was twelve miles away, and get back in time to watch Peter's football practice after school.

'Well, Jim.' The doctor gestured to a chair and pulled Jim's file towards him. 'What can I do for you this afternoon?'

Andy Bryson was a young man with a tangle of brown hair that fell over his forehead. He was popular with his patients, a member of the Scottish hockey squad and often seen out running on the moorland roads.

'Not much, I expect.' Jim knew the doctor well. 'Just I had a couple of ropy turns last weekend and I promised the boy I'd look in.'

Dr Bryson asked for details and rose. 'Pull up your shirt and I'll have a listen.'

The stethoscope was cold.

'Deep breath and hold it for a moment.' The doctor listened. 'Again.'

Jim did as he was told.

'Right, breathe normally.'

Despite his casual attitude Jim was scared. He did not like visiting the doctor. 'No change?' he said hopefully, tucking in his shirt a couple of minutes later.

'Tell me a bit more about these turns.' Dr Bryson returned to his desk. 'I mean the symptoms. Describe them to me exactly.'

So Jim went over it again: the black depression, the drinking, the savage pain in his chest, the vomiting. Then the second attack, two days later, on the hill.

The doctor took a deep breath and thought for a moment. 'Well, a little fluid on your lungs. I'll give you something for that. As for your heart – not in the best of shape but you know that. On the other hand, it seems no worse.' He sat back. 'You've been overdoing it again, of course. How often have I told you, plenty of rest and try to avoid stress. I mean, what *possessed* you to tell Peter you'd have lunch on the top of Blae Fell? He's how old – twelve or thirteen? At that age he can climb hills from dawn till dusk and come back ready for a game of football. But you're his dad, he knows you're not as fit as he is, you don't have to prove anything to him.' He toyed with his pen. 'And too much whisky doesn't help either, if you don't mind my saying. I was driving past the Cod and Kipper the other afternoon – Friday, was it? – and I saw you coming out.'

Jim looked out of the window. He'd heard the lecture before.

'Just as well I wasn't the police is all I can say. I've told you, couple of glasses of wine, fine, do you good. But stay off the whisky. And don't tell me you'd been on the beer, because you were carrying a couple of bottles – bottle and a half to be precise.'

'You forgot the fags.'

'Them too.'

'Yeah, you're right.' Jim shifted his legs. 'Things get me

down a bit sometimes, that's all.'

'I know, and it's not your fault, no one's blaming you for it. But you've got that boy of yours to think about as well.'

Jim's lips tightened. 'Think I'm not aware of that?' he said bitterly. 'Best lad ever walked on two legs, and that's official.'

Dr Bryson nodded. 'My sister's got a girl in the same class.' He looked at the screen beside him and pressed a few keys. 'Talks about him a lot, I'm told. Winnie this, Winnie that. Got a bit of a crush on him, I think.'

'That right?' Jim smiled. 'What's her name?'

'Becky Marshall.'

'He never said anything.'

'Well, boys don't, do they. Probably doesn't even realise.' Dr Bryson pulled the prescription from his computer. 'Come on through.'

The surgery was in the doctor's house, it went with the job. He led the way into a vestibule and unlocked the sturdy door of a room opposite. A small notice read *Dispensary*. In rural areas like Tarridale where the nearest pharmacist might be as much as fifty miles away, doctors kept a stock of the more commonly prescribed drugs on hand. The door was split horizontally like a stable door. Dr Bryson went through and shut the bottom half behind him. It was topped by a wooden shelf.

Jim stood in the hallway, jacket over his arm. 'Our Peter starting out with the girls, eh? Hope he doesn't give me the trouble his sister did.' He grinned. 'Come to think, he told me a bit of an iffy joke when we were out yesterday.'

'Out?'

'We went fishing. It's not bad actually, going the rounds in the school. Doctor and a trapeze artist.'

But Dr Bryson was concentrating on the prescription.

Shelves and cupboards were filled with jars, bottles and packets of medicine. A strong metal cabinet contained drugs that people might steal. The doctor screwed the top off a plastic container and tipped pills into a counting tray. 'Grow up fast these days.'

'Thirteen next month.' Jim made a wry face. 'Way things have worked out he's had to grow up faster than most.'

'Yes, I know.' Dr Bryson funnelled the pills into a little brown bottle, labelled it, then counted out a week's course of antibiotics. 'I'll give you these. There might be a bit of infection there. Anything else you're needing?'

Before he set out, Jim had checked the cocktail of pills he had to take each morning. 'No, I've got enough for the next couple of weeks. Rattling with the bloody things. I'll give you a ring nearer the time.'

Dr Bryson tidied the dispensary and switched off the light.

Jim dropped the pills into his pocket and shook the doctor's hand. 'Thanks, Andy. Look after yourself – who takes care of the physician, eh?'

'My wife,' said Dr Bryson and could have kicked himself. He liked Jim Irwin and knew how Sharon had gone off and left him with the children. In a village like Tarridale everybody knew. 'But it's not me we're talking about. Don't push yourself so hard.' He looked Jim in the eye. 'And keep off the demon drink.'

'Try my best.'

'I'm telling you. One day at a time.'

'What do you mean? I'm not an alkie, if you don't mind.'

'I know you're not, but the AA know what they're talking about. And you've got to look after that heart. We're not playing games here.'

Things were getting heavy. 'Yeah, yeah, I know.' Jim turned to go then looked back with a twinkle. 'Hey, d'you want to hear Pete's joke about the doctor and the trapeze artist?'

Doctor Bryson smiled. 'Don't you take anything seriously?'

'Not if I can help it. But listen, there was this trapeze artist. She had to be skinny, right, so her partner could catch her. But her boobs kept getting bigger. Dolly Parton wasn't in it. So she went to the doctor and he said …'

12

Goose Fair to Treasure Island

IT WAS A happy time of year in Tarridale. Everyone was busy. As the days shortened, one event crowded upon another in quick succession.

First there was the Goose Fair, a big autumn fête started by a couple who had moved north from Nottingham. Stalls for crafts, baking, toys, knitwear, vegetables, books and bric-a-brac were set up in the village hall. Awnings were erected for the sale of hens, guinea fowl, eggs, small livestock, and even one or two geese to be fattened for Christmas. Riders tethered their horses. Children showed their pets. There were games, competitions, raffles and lucky dips. In the late afternoon the tables were cleared for teas and in the evening there was dancing with a live band.

Peter played in a football match in the morning. In the afternoon he watched the men's game with friends then went to the Goose Fair and spent every last penny on games, sweets and an adventure story for his dad.

The clocks went back and then it was Hallowe'en. After an early tea, Peter dressed in black rags and a papier-mâché mask of a dog's head which he had made in the art class at school. Its eyes were wild, its teeth were savage, blood dripped from its jowls. Sharpened ice-lolly sticks, strapped to his fingers and painted red, made scary claws. A notice announced that he was *The Monster from the Moors*.

As a black night settled over the land, Jim drove him to the house of a friend in the village. The boys were joining some others to go guising. Jim had written a poem about worms and skeletons that Peter had learned by heart. Carrying a turnip lantern, he recited it from house to house. Steadily his trick-or-treat bag grew heavier.

Next, it was Guy Fawkes Day. Usually it rained, but this year the sky was starlit and cold. As Peter helped his dad after school, mist thickened above the moorland pools. A yellow moon hung over the islands, casting a track across the sea.

There was to be a firework display followed by a bonfire above the village. At half past six they locked the dogs in the shed, scraped the ice from the windscreen and set off.

Halfway down the Sandy Brae the headlights picked out a figure walking briskly. It was a young woman in jeans and a light-coloured parka.

'It's that girl staying with Bunny Mason, isn't it?' Jim said.

'Her daughter,' Peter said. 'Penny.'

'How d'you know that?'

'I met her when I was waiting for the bus.'

Jim flashed his lights and drew up ahead.

Peter called back: 'Penny, it's me, Peter Irwin. Me and dad.'

She stopped alongside. Jim leaned across: 'Can we offer you a lift?'

'We're going to the bonfire,' Peter said.

'Me too.' She pulled up her scarf. 'Mummy's coming along later. I fancied the walk – never saw so many stars.'

'Mebbe see the northern lights later on. Good night for it.'

'I hope so. Don't get skies like this in London.'

'I suppose not,' Jim said. 'Oh, well, enjoy your walk. Mebbe see you up at the fire.' He sat back.

'No, hang on.' She looked through Peter's window. 'Matter of fact I wouldn't mind a lift, it's further than I thought. Sure you've got room?'

Peter pushed the door wide and bunked across beside his dad.

'Thanks.'

It was a squeeze. Jim pushed Peter's leg off the gear lever. Penny's perfume mingled with the smells of oil and sheep drench.

'Nice and warm in here.' She pulled off her mittens and rubbed her hands. 'Beautiful out there but gosh, it's cold.'

'Great night for the bonfire.'

'Yes.'

There was a companionable silence until they reached the bottom of the hill. Peter wasn't used to the proximity of women, certainly not one as pretty as Penny.

'Staying a few days with your mother, Pete tells me,' Jim said.

'Longer than that, two or three weeks.' She saw their faces illuminated by the dials. 'Need a bit of a break. Get some fresh air.'

'Plenty of that up here.'

'Recharge the batteries.'

'Wouldn't mind some time off myself. Pete's always on at me.' He swept round a corner and braked hard as a tractor emerged from a field. 'Don't fancy London though. Had enough of cities one time we stayed in Manchester.'

'Some of us have to.'

'Yeah? What do you do in London then?'

'I'm a lawyer.'

'Lawyer, nice girl like you?' Jim didn't like lawyers. 'What kind of lawyer – solicitor?'

'No, I'm in chambers.'

'Barrister, no less.' Jim was impressed. 'Bit young for that, I'd have thought.'

'Ah, but it's dark in here, you can't see the wrinkles.' She laughed.

The tractor chugged up the hill to the village. There was no way past.

'Peter and me, we've been here – eight or nine years it must be.'

'Nice place to live. Mummy likes it anyway.'

'Yeah, I love it.' Jim glanced at his son. 'We both do, I think.'

The tractor swung off the road. Jim sped past and a few moments later turned into the car park of the Tarridale Arms, the smart Highland hotel that stood above the village. The van rocked as they got out. Peter collected his box of fireworks. He was meeting friends in the high field where the huge bonfire, topped by a Guy, was silhouetted against the stars.

Jim examined his watch in the light from a window. 'Quarter to seven,' he said. 'Firework display at half past – that gives us forty-five minutes.' He turned to Penny. 'I was going for a beer. Fancy coming, keep out the cold?'

'I didn't expect to be here this soon.' She hesitated. 'Yes, a half of lager would be nice. Thanks.'

'Be in the lounge bar, Pete,' Jim said. 'See you up by the fire, OK?'

It was a side of his dad Peter had never seen, taking an attractive young woman for a drink.

'No throwing those bangers mind.'

'I know, you told me.'

'As if you would.' Jim laughed. 'What's the fun having your own fireworks if your dad sets them off?' he said to Penny.

Peter watched as they vanished into the lobby with its little-paned windows that looked towards the sea. Briefly he stood, a solitary figure in the car park, then ran off up the lane to join his friends by the waiting bonfire.

The northern lights came early and from the high field, away from the streetlights of the village, they had a clear view, not the multicoloured display of the Arctic but green curtains flickering across the sky, and shifting searchlights from just above the sea to right overhead.

The fireworks stunned the night with explosions and filled the sky with cascading stars but the bonfire was even better. Peter tugged his hat to his eyes and pulled up his collar to protect his face from the roaring heat. The flames flashed up.

Sparks whirled thirty metres overhead. He singed his eyebrows running close to throw back branches. And when the fire died down he cooked sausages on bits of fence wire and buried potatoes in the ash.

The good times continued. Jim shaved carefully, put on his best jacket and took Penny to the Tarridale Arms a second time. They went a third time too, but it was as friends, not a couple. He told Peter this, told him that Penny had a boyfriend already, was as good as engaged, but Peter was not convinced. He liked to see his dad dressing smartly and going out with a stylish girl like Penny.

Then the boyfriend turned up, a balding young man called Marcus who worked in a bank and drove a Lotus. He was nice enough but not nearly as good looking as his dad. Jim took them out to the islands, and all five – Jim and Peter, Bunny, Penny and Marcus – went for a meal one evening. Marcus booked the best table in the Stag Restaurant at the Tarridale: crisp white linen spread with silver and three kinds of glasses, napkins folded like water-lilies, a wine-cooler, fresh flowers and candles. Peter wore his best trousers with a freshly-ironed shirt and tie. He enjoyed the evening very much.

Next morning, sadly, Penny and Marcus packed their suitcases into the boot of the Lotus and set off back to London.

On the twentieth of November Peter was thirteen. Sitting on his plate when he came down for breakfast he found a Game Boy, chocolates and a new pocket-knife with a brass-inlaid handle and two strong blades.

At school he was handed cards by two of his friends – and found three in his desk from girls, all drenched in the same perfume. At lunchtime a message appeared in coloured chalks on the blackboard: *Gillian Wood wants Winnie to kiss her.* Which Peter didn't.

And when he got home at four, Jock the postie had delivered

two more cards. One, which contained a ten-pound note, was from his dad. The other, with a picture of a footballer on it, was from Valerie. It read:

> *To Peter,*
> *HAPPY BIRTHDAY*
> *I have been thinking alot about*
> *you. Hope you have a nice time and*
> *are keeping well.*
> *Lot's of love,*
> *Val   xxxxx*

It was the first he had heard in two years.

'Lots of love, eh?' Jim handed the card back. 'What's the postmark this time?'

Peter examined the envelope. The ink was smudged. 'C – something.' He turned it round. 'Cand – lik?' His brow furrowed. 'No – Cardiff.'

'What the hell's she doing in Cardiff?' Jim said. 'What the hell's she doing anywhere, come to that?" He poured Peter a cup of tea and pushed a packet of biscuits towards him. 'I've booked the table for six o'clock. We'll leave about five, OK? Nothing for you to do, I've fed the ferret. We'll give the dogs something before we go.' Meg crossed the room and rested her head on his knee. 'Aye, you know when you're being talked about, don't you, girl.'

Ben lay on his rug in the corner, chin on his paws, watching beneath whiskery eyebrows. Peter fetched a couple of doggy bones from the kitchen. He didn't like his best pal to feel out of it. Ben heard the rattle of the packet and sat up, watching the door expectantly. Gently he took the biscuit from Peter's fingers. Peter gave the second one to Meg.

The Shangri La was a new restaurant in Clashbay. Peter wore his favourite jeans and OK, PUNK sweatshirt which Jim had washed and ironed. He liked Chinese – and enjoyed sipping lager from his dad's glass. Jim bought him an *as-much-*

as-you-can-eat-for-twelve-pounds birthday dinner. Having a competition who could burp louder, they walked through town to The Bay Cinema to watch *Screaming Calypso*, the new comic blockbuster that everyone was talking about.

And finally, just three and a bit weeks before Christmas, there was the St Andrew's Day ceilidh in the school hall. It was a popular event. People travelled miles to enjoy the Gaelic songs, jokes, pipes and accordions, dancers, choir, storyteller, young pop group, twenty minute play – and take tea in the dining hall afterwards.

The play, produced by Miss Berry and performed by one of her English classes, was a highlight. This year Peter's was the chosen class and he had been looking forward to it for weeks. He was playing Israel Hands, Long John Silver's second-in-command, in a scene from *Treasure Island*. It was a good part. Though normally a quiet boy, he played it dramatically with scarves tied round his head, blackened teeth, a scar on his cheek, a real-looking sword and rags that fluttered as he strode across the stage. He had practised his words at home, rehearsed it on stage, and couldn't wait to perform it before an audience.

But the good times could not last forever.

13

A Heavy Cold

IT WAS A long time, nearly two months, since Jim had last been assailed by depression, since the black snakes had come sliding from drains and cracks beneath the skirting boards to hang their heavy coils about his shoulders. Since that grim weekend of drunkenness and pains in his chest, he had felt fitter and more positive than for years. He and Peter were happy, the house and fences were in good repair, the flock had been dipped and served by the rams. It was as if some blockage had been cleared, like dirt in the fuel line of an engine, and he was free to move forward. But all at once, in the course of a late evening and wretched night, the sickness was back, the chasm reopened at his feet, his spirit was crushed. Whichever way he looked, everything seemed hopeless.

On the morning of the ceilidh, which was a Saturday, Peter slept late – late for him. At nine-fifteen, in crumpled pyjamas and rubbing the sleep from his eyes, he trailed downstairs for breakfast. The house was cold. No smell of toast or coffee greeted him as he went through to the living room. He was feeling cheerful, at least he would be feeling cheerful when he woke up properly. A good day lay ahead.

His heart sank at the scene that greeted him. The fire was dead. The remains of last night's supper lay on the table. Yesterday's *Guardian* was strewn on the carpet. Jim, in vest and work trousers, not even zipped up, sat on the edge of the settee. His feet were bare. He had pulled a rug round his shoulders for the cold.

'Dad?'

With difficulty Jim raised his eyes to his son and moistened dry lips. 'Sorry, Pete.'

Peter moved the whisky bottle and crouched by his knee. Both were silent then Peter said, 'Is there anything I can do?'

'Not really, son.'

'Have you taken your pills?'

Jim didn't answer.

Peter went to the drawer in the kitchen. He had a rough idea what his dad had to take. Carefully he read the prescriptions and dropped them, white pills, purple pills, red-and-yellow capsules, into the egg cup his dad used regularly and carried them with a glass of water into the living room.

'I don't want the bloody things.' Jim pushed his arm away.

Peter stood waiting.

'Got cloth ears?'

'Dad, come on.'

'They do no bloody good.'

'Don't be so stupid. If it wasn't for these you could be dead by this time.'

'I should be so lucky.'

'Oh, that's nice. Thanks.'

'I don't mean you, son. I don't mean you.'

'I know you don't. But you didn't feel like this yesterday. You didn't feel like this when we were out in the boat. It'll pass, it always does. So come on.' He thrust the egg cup towards him. 'Just swallow them.'

Jim belched and rested a hand on his arm. He had cut a knuckle and neglected it. The skin was inflamed. 'All right, give 'em here.' He tossed the pills into his mouth and washed them down.

'Good.' Peter stood back. 'What about breakfast? You'll not be wanting any, I suppose.'

'Who wants food when you can have pills?'

'OK.' Peter went back to the kitchen. The black frying pan stood on the stove. He smelled the savoury fat. 'I fancy a bacon sandwich. Sure I can't tempt you?'

'Trying to make me throw up?' Jim rose unsteadily. 'You be OK? Think I'll just go out to the byre for a bit.'

'Right, but leave the whisky. You know what Dr Bryson said.' He returned to the living room. 'Look, Dad, what if I – '

The front door shut. Tea towel in hand, Peter watched his father cross the yard. A scatter of rain hit the window. Jim's shoulders and arms were bare. He had pulled a jacket from the pegs in the hall; a corner of rug trailed on the wet ground. In one hand he clutched the sloshing bottle of Grant's, the cheapest whisky in the shop. From long experience he kept a bottle in case of emergencies. A glass wasn't essential.

The dogs were barking. They hadn't been let out. Jim unfastened the shed door. Ben rushed past and relieved himself endlessly against a stone corner. Meg squatted then followed her master into the byre.

The familiar pattern was established. For three days despair and drunkenness held Jim in a grip that he was powerless to break.

That first evening, the day of the ceilidh, Peter drove himself to the end of the track and was picked up by the parents of a friend who was also in the play. He threw himself into his pirate rôle with all the spirit he could muster. The audience applauded. Mrs Harle, the head teacher, rested a hand on his shoulder and told him that he had the makings of a real actor. But without his dad there, Peter's heart was sad.

At home he tidied the house, lit the fire, made his own meals. The ewes, in lamb now, had been brought down from the high moors to a pasture up the track where they could be looked after during the winter. Each morning, before it was light, he drove there with the trailer to fill the troughs with sheep nuts and the rack with hay. And when he came back from school he fed the dogs, gave Buster a run round the kitchen while he made dinner, did his homework and watched television.

Jim, meanwhile, moved like a tramp between the house and the byre. Sometimes he slept in the straw, sometimes on the settee, sometimes in his bed. His whiskers grew, his clothes started to smell. Risking the attention of the police, he drove to the Cod and Kipper and sat in the remotest corner, rejecting company, a beer and chaser on the ring-stained table before him. Visiting the shop he bought one, then a second bottle of Grant's, and some ready-cooked meals for Peter to put in the microwave.

Customers shook their heads: 'Dreadful ... let himself get into that state ... good-looking man if it wasn't for the drink ... clever too ... used to be a soldier, you know, in the desert ... it's that son of his I'm sorry for, such a nice lad ... the Social want to get themselves out there and see what the house is like ... must be a pig-sty.'

But Billy Josh, the trawler skipper, knew Jim better: 'Gossiping old women,' he said angrily. 'How do you know what he's been through? Poor man's not well. He's doing the best he can. Managing a lot better than I would in his circumstances, I'm telling you. All your churchgoing – hasn't taught you much about charity. Tearing a man to shreds behind his back. You make me sick!'

Whatever the talk in the village, no one mentioned it to Peter. He went to school as normal, worked at his lessons, played with his friends at lunchtime and protected his dad by keeping silent. Only the men who drank at the Cod and Kipper, as far as he was aware, had any reason to think his dad was going through a bad patch.

But what he did not know, what no one knew, was that twice Jim was hit by that savage pain in the chest that left him gasping and all but helpless. The first time it struck as he was lying in the straw; the second time as he was driving home from the pub, weaving from side to side of the narrow road. The attacks were, if anything, even worse than those he had experienced back in October. The little white pills he took everywhere with him worked their magic, though not quite as quickly and he was left shaken. A dozen times he recalled Dr Bryson's warnings, but his mind was so befuddled by whisky and despair there was no way he could do as the doctor advised.

Yet on Tuesday afternoon, as Peter rattled into the yard on the tractor, Jim was sufficiently recovered to greet him in the doorway with a wan smile. Light shone at the windows. A bitter easterly wind tore the smoke from the chimney. It was not yet four o'clock but already, in those first days of winter, darkness was settling over the moors. As they went indoors the house was, if not cosy, at least warmer than outside and the kettle was boiling.

The bad spell had lasted nearly four days.

'Sorry, Pete.' Jim rubbed his black stubble. 'I give you a bloody rough time sometimes, don't I? You OK?'

The drive had chilled Peter to the marrow. He nodded and blew on his fingers.

'I'll get a bath and have a shave later,' Jim said. 'Here, give us your jacket and sit down there by the fire. I'll make us a cup of tea.' He hung the jacket in the hall and went through to the kitchen.

Peter saw him massaging his arm and shoulder. 'What's up?' he called. 'Give yourself a knock?'

'God knows.' Jim eased his neck. 'Must have fallen or something. I can't remember.' He rummaged in the sink. 'Touch of rheumatics, maybe, lying out there in the byre. I'll have a look when I go upstairs.'

Working as hard as he did, Jim was always getting strains and bruises. Peter sneezed and shivered, crouching to the fire.

It was the start of a nasty cold which had been going about the village. Several girls and boys in Peter's class had caught it and been kept at home. On Wednesday, although he was slightly feverish, Jim allowed Peter to attend, driving him to school in the warm van and picking him up again in the afternoon. On Thursday, however, Peter was perspiring and had a hacking cough. His throat felt raw. When Jim went to his bedroom, he looked up with bleary eyes and croaked that he didn't want any breakfast.

'I'm afraid he's got that fluey cold that's going the rounds,' Jim told the head teacher over the phone. 'No, he'll not be in tomorrow, no chance. Maybe Monday, see how he gets on over the weekend ... What's that? ... Yes, he keeps pretty fit. I think it's the first time he's been off all year ... Pardon? ... Well, that's very kind of you. I think he's a fine boy myself, but then I'm biased.'

For most of that day Peter stayed in bed but on Friday he got up mid-morning and sat reading by a big fire, eating biscuits and drinking endless mugs of tea, coffee, hot orange and chocolate. Jim went down to the harbour to scrape and paint the *Audrey*, leaving him watching a video of *Space Rangers*, a sort of cowboy film set among the galaxies. When he came home at half past three, Peter had fallen asleep in his chair and the fire had burned low.

On Saturday he felt better. The coughing no longer made him sweat and when Jim produced bacon and scrambled eggs for a late breakfast, he polished off his plateful.

'Got to go up on the hill today,' his dad said, teacup in hand. 'What about you?'

Peter looked out of the window. A night of frost had turned the grass and fences white. The sun shone, low and dazzling, across the moor. 'Stay in for a bit. Might take the two-two out later. See if I can get a couple of rabbits.'

'Why not take your ferret? He's not seen the inside of a burrow for months.'

'Yeah, I could. Bit cold standing around.' Peter gave a racking cough, spat into a sheet of toilet paper and threw it into the fire.

'Wrap up warm anyway,' Jim said. 'And don't stay out too long. Don't want a relapse, specially with Christmas just round the corner.'

Jim pulled on his parka and hat and slung his small rucksack over one shoulder. 'Come on then, Meg. Back about three.' He rubbed his arm and grimaced. 'Bloody thing, don't know what's wrong with it. Anyway, plenty in the fridge for your lunch. I went to the shop yes'day, got some of that Cumberland sausage you like. We'll have that for tea.'

Peter stood at the window as his dad scraped ice from the van windscreen. After the cold night it was reluctant to start. At last, with a cloud of smoke, it stuttered into life. Jim grinned and gave a thumbs-up. Peter raised his hand and watched as he made a three-point turn and drove off towards the hills. *Toot-toot.* The end of the byre hid him from view. The sound of the engine faded.

14

Ferreting

PETER WASHED THE breakfast dishes then sat by the fire toasting his legs and looking through a book called *Weapons of the World*, an illustrated history he had borrowed from the travelling library. The low sun melted the frost, though in hollows and behind banks it remained white all day. Shortly before eleven, wearing his warmest jacket and pyjama trousers under his jeans, he went out to the shed and put Buster into his carrying box. The best rabbit warrens were at the Four Crowns, a cluster of small hills – remnants of the last ice age, Jim had told him – which stood midway between the house and the road. The track wound between them. Accompanied by Ben, he set off on the tractor.

There are several ways to go ferreting. The usual method is to spread nets over nearby holes before putting the ferret down; the fleeing rabbits run headlong into the mesh and are trapped by a drawcord fastened to a peg. A second way, if you are looking for sport, is to shoot them as they run off. A third way, if you have a good dog, is to let it chase the rabbits down.

Peter had Ben with him and Ben was fast, so he planned to try this method first. Sitting behind a gorse thicket out of the wind, he took Buster from his box. Buster could smell the rabbits and was eager, his black eyes fierce. Holding him round the chest, front legs between his fingers, Peter slipped on a muzzle and buckled it behind his ears to stop him killing and feeding underground. His stink was strong. When all was ready, Peter carried him to a gaping hole in the slope with a landslide of earth beneath it and a litter of rabbit droppings. Buster did not need urging. Without a backward glance he ambled downhill into the darkness.

Peter was racked by a spasm of coughing. He spat and waited. Ben, who had been ferreting before, was in a fever of excitement, spinning this way and that as he waited for the first rabbit to appear.

For half a minute all was silent then there was a thudding underground, a terrified squeal, and a big buck rabbit exploded from a burrow half a dozen paces away. At once Ben was on its tail. A second rabbit shot from the same hole, another from a hole at Peter's heels, and a fourth higher up the slope.

Ears flattened, Ben raced after his prey. The hillside was not open enough. Before he could reach top speed, the rabbit dived into a thicket of bramble. Ben hunted round the edge. From the corner of his eye he spotted another fleeing shape. He whirled round. Peter shouted and waved his arms. The rabbit jinked in mid-flight, saw that it was running directly towards the big grey dog and jinked again. It was too late. Ben pounced. His huge paws bowled the rabbit over and the next moment he had it in his jaws. A bite, a hard shake, and the rabbit's neck was broken. Delighted with himself, Ben shook it some more, danced in circles and threw it across the grass.

'Ben! Leave it.' Peter hurried forward. The rabbit's eyes were bright brown, its head dangling, warm fur streaked with Ben's saliva. He examined it for signs of myxomatosis. There were none. Ben circled round him, pushing to snuffle the dead rabbit. Some of its bones were broken, Peter felt them scrunch in his hand. It was a pity but Ben had done all that was asked of him, he hadn't been trained to do differently.

'Good boy.' Peter rubbed his ears. '*Good* boy!'

Rabbits have fleas. He jammed it in the fork of a hawthorn tree blown all one way by the wind.

Buster had not emerged from the warren. Peter knelt beside the big hole. 'Come on then,' he called enticingly. 'Buster!' There was no response.

He rubbed perspiration from his brow. He was not as well as he had thought. The wind was biting. He felt in his pocket for a chocolate biscuit and pulled his scarf to his mouth.

Another rabbit shot away, its feet thudding on the grass. Ben spun round but already the rabbit was gone.

Five minutes passed. Without warning, Buster appeared from a hole Peter had not seen a dozen metres away. Back humped like a weasel, he ran across the hillside. Peter caught him up. Briefly the ferret resisted, struggling to be free, then gave up and allowed himself to be carried. The tip of his tongue and a glimpse of white killing teeth appeared within the muzzle.

In the next thirty minutes Ben killed a second rabbit and Peter, having tethered him to a root, trapped three in the purse nets. Three were more than he wanted so he killed just one, that was healthy, and a second that was infected with myxomatosis. The third he let go. Its strong legs kicked against his chest as he untangled the mesh. A claw scratched the back of his hand. He licked away the red beads that instantly appeared, tasting the iron of his blood mixed with the animal scent of the rabbit. By the time it was free it had gone into a state of shock. Peter stroked it briefly and set it on the grass. The rabbit sat as if mesmerised then took a few uncertain hops. He coughed and spat. The rabbit crouched low to the ground then regained its addled senses and fled.

The rabbit swollen with myxomatosis was crawling with fleas. They swarmed in its ears. Peter wondered what to do with it. Eventually he dropped it into a poly bag, tied the neck tight and piled stones on top. The fleas that carried the horrible disease would die. It might help some poor rabbit to survive.

It had been a successful outing. Back at Scar Hill, Peter returned Buster to his run and gave him a piece of meat as a reward, then hung the rabbits, head down, on a barbed-wire fence and retreated indoors. Shivering, he piled peats on the fire and sat close, waiting for a blaze. The clock struck twelve-thirty. He put two slices of pizza in the microwave and made a mug of hot chocolate.

Ben ate a handful of treats on his day bed then crossed to Peter and stretched out before the fire. In moments he was asleep. His paws twitched as he chased rabbits across the hillsides of his dreams.

Peter shut his eyes but sleep wouldn't come, so he switched on a cop film. It wasn't very good but it would pass the time until his dad came home from the hill.

At about two o'clock, just as the story was getting into its stride, he was distracted by a sound from the yard, a soft whine and scratching at the front door. At once Ben scrambled to his feet. He gave an answering bark and trotted directly into the hall. Peter was sitting on the settee, his legs drawn up beneath him. Barefoot he followed and pulled the door wide.

Meg stood on the threshold. She was distressed. Peter looked round the yard. There was no sign of his dad.

15

Late Afternoon, Saturday, 7th December

THE VAN WAS parked in the turning place where Jim always left it when he went to the hill. Peter swung the tractor alongside and switched off the engine. As he jumped down, his boot caught behind the brake pedals and he stumbled to the ground. It was a jolt but he wasn't hurt. Scrubbing his hands on his jeans, he crossed to the van. The door was unlocked. There was no sign of his dad.

The keys hung in the ignition. He slid behind the wheel and turned the engine. It coughed into life. He reversed a few metres and drove back again. Nothing wrong with the van.

Where *was* his dad? The dogs stood waiting, not trotting around and marking the fence posts as usual. Meg never left his father's side but this time she had come home by herself. What had happened? Had his dad taken a bad turn? Had he had an accident? Ben knew that something was wrong. So did Peter.

He opened the gate beyond the wooden sheep fanks and followed the dogs along the path his dad always took through the bog. In places, where the reeds got no direct sunlight, they were still white with frost.

Soon they reached the rising ground. 'Which way, girl?' he said to Meg.

She looked up anxiously, unsure what was being asked of her.

Most of the flock were in lamb at that time of year and had been taken down to the lower pasture. Only the fifty or so eight-month-old lambs they were keeping and a few ewes which were not in lamb remained on the hill. Peter knew roughly where they would be grazing and which route his dad would have taken across the moor to reach them. 'All right,' he said to Meg, reassuring her. 'Come on then.'

He set off, climbing diagonally across the hillside towards the foot of Blae Fell. Meg trotted ahead eagerly, turning her head to see that he was following.

Peter's chest was tight. Long before he would normally have needed a breather he stopped, wheezing, and straightened up. His collar was wet with a cold sweat. His shirt had crawled from the waistband of his trousers. He loosened his belt to tuck it in and shivered as the icy wind struck his skin.

Meg stood waiting a dozen paces ahead. Peter shouted: 'Dad! ... Dad!' A grouse erupted from the heather and circled away. Silence returned.

He had crossed the hillside many times. Today, following Meg, he was lower than back in October when he and Jim had treated the sheep for maggots and footrot. A stranger might easily have lost his way in that great wilderness but Peter knew precisely where he was. Looking up, he recognised rocky outcrops and the rolling ridges of the moor. Yet everything was different. Now he was alone, his head spun with the effort of walking, and he was scared. The miles of russet bracken and red autumn grasses no longer welcomed him, were no longer beautiful. The whole landscape, from the rocks at his feet to the distant mountains and clear sky overhead, already in the mid-afternoon turning purple towards dusk, felt hostile and implacable. What happened to animals or people out there was irrelevant. Peter zipped the neck of his jacket as high as it would go and set off again.

Three-quarters of an hour after leaving the tractor he stood low on the southern slope of Blae Fell. Time and again he scanned the hillside and shaded his eyes from the westering sun to view the land beneath. In all that immensity of moorland, unchanged for thousands of years, where was his father?

Meg, zigzagging through the long heather, turned uphill

towards a ragged cliff. Had his dad fallen? Had he broken his leg? Peter halted again, hands on his knees, and looked in the direction she was heading. 'Dad!' His voice rang out, shockingly loud in his own ears. There was no reply. The endless wind whispered through the grasses.

When he had got his breath back, Peter climbed to the low crest where Meg stood waiting. As he reached her she looked up, trying to tell him something with her eyes. He patted her. She whined. 'Good girl, yes.'

A new stretch of hillside had come into view. He surveyed it and saw nothing. 'Da-a-ad!'

Ben joined them and touched noses with Meg. His sharp eyes spotted something. Peter followed his gaze and saw only heather and a few protruding rocks. Ben took a few paces and gave a soft '*wuff*' . Peter's skin prickled. Still he saw nothing.

Meg set off again, heading slightly downhill, Ben at her tail. Peter followed. After a hundred metres he saw that what he had taken to be a flat stone wasn't a stone at all.

'Dad!' Headlong he ran past the dogs.

Jim lay on his back, his head half-hidden by a clump of heather. His eyes were open. He was quite dead.

Peter had never seen a dead person before but from his first glance there was no doubt. His dad lay unmoving. His mouth was open, as if he had died struggling for breath. His dark eyes looked into the afternoon sky and saw nothing. Two fingers tugged at the neck of his jersey. The other hand, curled loosely around his pill bottle, was outflung in the heather. There had been a few spots of rain because his hair and the topmost folds of his jacket were wet. A scatter of pills lay on his chest and trousers, swollen with the damp and starting to fall apart.

'Dad,' Peter whispered. A terrible bumping was in his chest. He knelt close, frightened to touch him.

Delicately the dogs smelled Jim's clothes and fingers. After a while Peter touched the back of his hand. It was icy. His brow, too, was cold as a stone. The olive-green parka was half unzipped. Peter slipped a hand inside and felt a little warmth.

It was the worst thing that had ever happened to him. What should he do? There was no one to ask. 'Dad.' Something in his chest tore apart and he began to weep, terrible open-mouthed sobs that he could not control, did not try to control. It was a long time, years, since Peter had wept at all, and never like that.

Ben, distressed by his behaviour, raked at his arm with a wet paw.

The tears ran their course. He sat back on his heels, gulping air and scrubbing his eyes with his hand. What, he wondered again, was he to do?

There was only one answer, for there was little he could do right there. He had to get back home and telephone for help.

But although Peter had never seen a dead man before, he was well acquainted with death. Just a few hours earlier he had killed two rabbits, one with his hand, the other with a stick. When they were out in the boat they killed fish, sometimes big fish. Dead seals and seabirds washed up on the tide, and once a school of pilot whales, twenty feet long, had swum ashore and died slowly. He had seen his dad shoot sick and injured sheep; they came upon dead sheep on the hill. The first thing that happened was that birds – crows and gulls and ravens – flew in from afar and pecked out their eyes with cruel beaks. Sometimes they blinded lambs as they were being born. This must not happen to his dad.

He looked for something to cover Jim's head while he went for help. It seemed terrible to leave him lying on the open moor but there was nothing else he could do. Perhaps he could pull off his dad's jacket and cover him with that. But when he moved Jim's outflung arm, he found it growing stiff and had to pull quite hard. The thought of rolling his dad's heavy body around while he tugged at his clothes was too awful to contemplate. He looked in the rucksack, hoping there might be a scarf but there was not, nothing but shepherding gear and his dad's lunch in a red and white supermarket bag. There seemed only his own clothes and already he was shivering. It didn't matter, his dad's face had to be protected. Peter peeled off his jersey. The December wind bit through his polo shirt. Quickly he pulled his jacket back on and zipped it to the throat.

With the tip of a finger he closed his dad's brown eyes. They half opened again. He held them till they stayed shut. Then he lifted Jim's head to wrap the jersey around it. It was awkward and heavier than he had expected but at last the job was done. It was a small relief to think of his dad's face protected by the warm wool of his jersey. It was a fisherman's jersey, dark blue. Unaccountably he remembered buying it at the ships' chandler's in Clashbay and his dad paying the young assistant. Who could have guessed it would be put to such a use?

Peter brushed off the crumbling pills and fastened his dad's jacket across the chest. He shivered again and coughed. There would be hot tea in the thermos but somehow he did not want it.

How could he remember the spot? Had it not been for the dogs, he might have spent days searching. He looked all round. A group of sheep stood watching from a safe distance. Directly above them, halfway up the fell, was a little cliff with a crack running down it. Closer at hand and directly in line, a tumble of boulders emerged from the heather. Peter thought for a moment. If he weighted down the rucksack with peat or some small stones and stood it on the boulders, he should be able to find the place easily enough. If he tied the bright supermarket bag to the top that would make it easy to spot.

He looked down, finding it hard to come away. 'You'll be all right, Dad,' he said awkwardly. 'I'll come back as soon as I can.' He hesitated. What was the proper thing to do? 'God bless you.' The words were embarrassing. What a queer thing to say to his dad, they never spoke like that. He went on his knees in the heather: 'Our Father, which art in heaven ...' He said the prayer to the end and when he had finished went on, 'Please, God, look after my dad wherever he's gone. He was a good man and it's not fair everything that's happened to him – my mum and the army and his health and everything. And keep him safe here and away from the foxes and birds and everything until I come back. And the insects.' He pressed his hands together and squeezed his eyes tight, trying to force God to listen. Then he said, 'Amen,' and a while later rose to his feet.

Time and again, as he walked away, Peter looked back. It was past four o'clock, the last daylight was fading. Jim's body was soon hidden by the heather, but Peter knew where he lay and the bright poly bag fluttered in the breeze. Meg touched his hand with her nose and he stooped to comfort her. Then the hillside intervened and his dad was gone.

A scatter of raindrops hit him in the face. Peter coughed and spat into the heather. Heavily he trudged back across the moor. By the time he reached the van and the cold, exposed tractor it was dark. Despite the walking, he was frozen. He let the dogs into the van – Ben in the back and Meg in the passenger seat as usual – then got in himself. The driver's seat was pushed back for Jim. Never again would his dad sit there, Peter realised, never hold the steering wheel in his thin brown hands as Peter was doing now. His presence was everywhere: an empty packet of tobacco, throat lozenges, a crumpled woollen hat, fingermarks, an empty half-bottle of Red Label, a letter from the income tax. Peter tightened his lips and slid the seat forward.

As he drove home his headlights picked out a small group of red deer. Elegantly they leaped over the ditch that ran alongside the track and disappeared into the dark moor. It was a sight that always gave him pleasure. Today he barely registered it.

A few minutes brought him to the house. The yard felt different. In three hours everything had changed.

The cold had got into his bones. His stomach cramped. The fire was almost out. He stirred it into life and threw on some broken black peats from the bucket. Then he filled the kettle, set a mug on the kitchen table and went to the phone in the hallway.

The Tarridale Police Station, which was also the constable's home, stood in a row of council houses with a rarely-used cell in the garden. Peter knew Constable Taylor, he was a kind man with three children. The oldest, a twin boy and girl, were in the year behind Peter at school. He found the number in the telephone directory and dialled. There was no reply. That afternoon Mrs Taylor had taken the children to their gran's for tea, and Constable Taylor, who was off duty, was drinking a can of lager and watching the end of a rugby match on TV. He couldn't be bothered answering the phone.

Peter replaced the receiver. He was taken aback, he had imagined there would always be someone on call at a police station. Who else could he ring? There were several people: his class teacher, the minister, Bunny Mason and one or two others. But somehow he did not want to tell any of them. Apart from Constable Taylor, whose job it was, the only person he would have liked to come to the house was Billy Josh. He liked Billy. He was a friend of his dad. Peter flipped through the directory and found his number.

Again there was no reply. That morning Billy had taken his children, aged five, four and two, to Santa's grotto in Clashbay, then on to have lunch and spend the afternoon with his mother. The voice mail invited Peter to leave a message. He didn't want to leave a message, he wanted to speak to Billy.

At least he had thought he wanted to speak to Billy but in a way it was a relief that Billy wasn't there. For as Peter returned across the moor, a frightening thought had stopped him in his tracks. His dad was dead, nothing could be worse than that – but what about himself? What would become of him now? He couldn't stay on at Scar Hill, not alone, people wouldn't let him. He would be sent away – but where to? And what about Ben and Meg? And the croft? It was the only home they all knew.

Peter put the phone down.

His hands were red and shook with the cold. He sneezed and coughed. Coughed and coughed.

The kettle had boiled but he needed more heat than could

be provided by a cup of tea. Instead he went upstairs, switched on the bathroom heater and ran a scalding bath.

Slowly the ice left his bones. But with comfort came the full realisation of what he had lost. It was unbearable. For the second time that day, with the water sloshing about his chest, Peter's heart broke and he gave way to tears.

16

The Body in Denmark

PETER DIDN'T PHONE again that evening, not Constable Taylor or Billy Josh or any of the other kind people in the village who might have helped. After a long soak in the bath he went to the drying cupboard and pulled on clean underwear, jeans and a warm jersey, as if by a change of clothes he could distance himself from what had happened.

He fed the dogs and wondered about dinner. The Cumberland sausage Jim had intended to cook that evening lay on a shelf in the fridge. Peter looked at it until his eyes started to prick then pushed it to the back of the shelf and shut the fridge door. But that seemed like getting rid of his dad, so he returned it to the front. Cooking it was beyond him, so he took a chicken pie from the deep freeze and put it in the oven. Without considering if he would eat them, he peeled potatoes and carrots and set them to boil, then sat down by the fire with a cup of tea.

As he waited for his meal to cook the benefits of the hot bath ebbed away, and by the time savoury aromas reached him from the kitchen, what little appetite he had was gone. The thought of sitting down to a steaming plateful made him feel sick. He switched off the oven, tipped the vegetables into a sieve and left the golden-brown pie congealing beside the sink.

The dogs ate in the shed but usually spent the evening in the house. Needing their company, Peter went to fetch them. As he crossed the lamplit yard his eye was caught by the rabbits. Heads down and dry blood at their mouths, they hung from the fence. While he was ferreting – the thought kept recurring – his dad had been struggling for life out there on the moor. He hadn't known, there was nothing he could have done in any case, but that didn't take away the distress. As for the dead rabbits – he felt sorry for them, wished he had not killed them, could not think of cleaning them. Maybe a fox would discover them, he hoped so. At least they would not have died in vain.

The dogs stretched out by the fire, Peter on the settee, all close together. He switched on the TV. They didn't have satellite television, Jim couldn't afford it, and reception was often poor. Peter surfed the channels, one to four and back again: a game show, a soap, a cookery programme, the local news. Nothing held his interest. He switched off the sound and shut his eyes.

It was Ben who woke him, raking at his knee with a big paw. He wanted out. Peter blinked. The fire was low, the clock showed twenty to nine. His head throbbed. He let the dogs into the yard and returned to the settee. An old *Inspector Morse* had started and he switched on the sound. Familiar music and comfortable voices filled the silence. Morse's maroon Jaguar purred to a halt. He descended to a riverbank. Police let him through. A body lay in the shallows. Morse took a look and turned away; the chief inspector didn't like bodies. Normally Peter loved them. Not today. It wasn't the dead victim he saw but the body of his dad on the hillside. Like a film on a loop, the events of the afternoon played over and over in his thoughts.

As he let the dogs in again, a bright moon lit the yard and the roofs of the outbuildings. The same hard moon looked down on his father. His jacket and trousers would be crusted with frost. Were rats or beetles burrowing beneath?

Peter returned to the living room. What was he to do? Phone Constable Taylor and seal his fate? Ensure by doing so that he could no longer live at Scar Hill? Be sent to a foster home or children's home, maybe in some rundown area like the flat they had all hated on the outskirts of Manchester? Abandon Ben and Meg?

He needed time to think.

Peter coughed hard. A gob of phlegm filled his throat. He spat into the back of the fire. The phlegm sizzled.

Inspector Morse and his sidekick, Sergeant Lewis, had gone to the mortuary. The corpse lay naked on a steel table. Forensic instruments lay alongside. A pathologist in a stained apron was explaining the cause of death. Peter didn't want to know. He switched off the TV and lay back. His limbs were heavy. He felt himself drifting away.

The clock woke him by striking ten. He shivered, the room was cold. The peat bucket was empty. It was time to go to bed.

He trailed across the yard to lock the dogs up for the night – then decided he wanted them nearby and led the greatly-wondering Ben and Meg back to the house. He made a fuss of each, particularly Meg, and gave them their bedtime treats on their day beds. Then he switched off the lights and climbed upstairs.

Some time in the middle of the night Peter woke with a start. Something was wrong. He sat up. Abruptly he realised he was going to be sick. Just in time he reached the bathroom and fell to his knees, retching into the toilet bowl. A cold sweat stood on his brow and made his hair prickle. When the spasm was over he pressed the flush and sat back on his heels, spitting and scrubbing his lips with lavatory paper. As he stood up he felt dizzy. The light hurt his eyes. He rinsed his mouth at the washbasin.

Ben had come up to see what was wrong. In mute sympathy he stood on the landing. Meg waited behind him in the shadows. 'It's all right,' Peter said wretchedly. 'Good boy. Good girl.'

The clock by his bed said quarter to two. His pyjamas were wet with perspiration; he threw them into a corner. Rather than go downstairs for a dry set, he pulled on his T-shirt and underpants and crawled back into bed. His pillow was wet too. He turned it over, reversed the duvet top to bottom and pulled it to his ears. The room swam. Ben stood by the bed, just touching it with his whiskery chin, then flopped to the rug alongside. Peter trailed a hand from the bedclothes, feeling for his friendly head.

Five minutes later he was asleep.

Alone in the house Peter passed a bad night, tossing and turning and beset by fevered dreams. He thought he was going to be sick again and lay awake in the darkness, wrestling with the loss of his father. Although he'd been sweating he felt cold and went downstairs for a hot-water bottle and a towel to cover the damp pillow. Then he slept again and by dawn his sleep was calmer. Some time later the dogs, who could wait no longer to go outside, woke him with their whining. Peter let them out and returned to bed.

It was midday when he woke finally. Limply he lay and gazed at the ceiling. He felt washed out but better than he had done in the middle of the night. His headache had lifted. The bedclothes had dried.

Briefly he worried about school then remembered that today was Sunday.

Sunday, and his dad had been dead for a day. A whole day, lying out there on the wintry hillside. By this time, following the cloudless night, his body would be as hard and cold as the earth itself.

He didn't want to think about it and swung his legs to the floor. As he stood up he felt light-headed. He drew back the curtains, letting a shaft of brilliant December sunshine into his room. The roof of the byre, directly opposite, was still white with frost. So was most of the yard. A shadow line, straight as a ruler, divided it from the part that had thawed.

The house was cold. Heavy-limbed, he lit the fire, gave the dogs their breakfast and sat down with a cup of tea.

His problems would not go away, they had to be confronted. What was he to do about his dad? There was no one to ask, he was on his own. Plainly he had to inform Constable Taylor. Perhaps he had committed a crime by not reporting the death already. But if he phoned right now, as he should, what would be the outcome? His dad would be picked up by an Argocat or helicopter. And he himself would be taken to – well, wherever they took homeless boys. They wouldn't leave him at Scar Hill, anyway, that was for sure. And what about Ben and Meg, out in the yard? Would they be taken to some dog pound? And later, if nobody offered them a home, would they be given a lethal injection? It was unthinkable.

What could he do? There must be something, he thought, *some* plan he could work out before making the fateful call.

He needed more time. It would be dark in an hour or two. If his dad had been safe at the foot of Blae Fell until now, it was going to make little difference if he was left there until the morning. This gave him the rest of the day and another night to think about it. If people wanted to know why he hadn't phoned before, he could say truthfully that he *had* phoned but nobody was in. He'd been sick.

For the rest of that short day Peter stayed warm by the fire and switched on the TV for company. His headache returned and he took a couple of paracetamol. It was twenty-four hours since he had eaten and his stomach was empty. He went to the kitchen and spread two slices of bread with peanut butter. Later he divided yesterday's pie between the dogs who scoffed it up as an unexpected treat, then he opened a tin of soup for an early tea. By the evening, though his chest was bad, Peter was feeling a little better.

The weather was changing as the met office had forecast. A northwesterly wind blew rain clouds in from the Atlantic. The temperature rose a few degrees but it felt colder.

At nine he went to bed and slept more soundly. During the night he woke needing to go to the bathroom and padded barefoot along the landing, trying not to wake his dad. His dad's bedroom door was open wide. The memory hit him like a blow and he clung to the banister. Beneath him gaped the cold, black well of the stairs. From happiness to despair was as fast as the flick of a switch. Tears brought on an attack of coughing. Scarcely able to see, Peter groped his way to the toilet and back to bed. Even though the bed was warm, he found himself shivering and made another hot-water bottle. Lying in the darkness he heard the downstairs clock strike once, then once again, then twice, before he was claimed by sleep.

At seven-thirty he let the dogs out into the wet, black yard and returned to bed, but he did not sleep and an hour later trailed downstairs in his dressing gown and slippers. Gusts of wind rushed about the windows. He made a mug of tea and switched on the rusty electric fire. One bar didn't work; it gave out little heat. He wrapped a rug round his legs and cupped the mug in both hands.

It was Monday. A day and a night had brought no answers but matters could be put off no longer. A decision had to be made, and right then, that morning. His dad could not be left out on the hill indefinitely, like a dead sheep. Peter had seen countless dead sheep: rotting carcases, gaping mouths, scattered bones. He wouldn't let himself think about it.

The phone was in the hall. He could pick it up right then and speak to Constable Taylor, or if he wasn't there, to his head teacher, or the minister, or the parents of a friend – though not to Billy Josh, for by this time on a Monday morning Billy was away on his trawler. He longed for someone else to take the decisions, shoulder the responsibility, but still there was no one. Ben stood by his knee and looked at him with trustful eyes.

And Peter's long hours of wakefulness had produced other thoughts:

His dad was dead, nothing could change that awful fact, but did that mean Scar Hill belonged to him now – even though he was only thirteen? And whatever money his dad had, was that his too? Or was it Valerie's? Or did everything belong to his mum, wherever she was? Had his dad made a will?

But that was for the future. Peter had had an idea. Well a sort of idea, not a plan exactly, it was too shocking for that, but something to consider. Probably it was a crime, something that would get him into *serious* trouble. He stared into the dead grate. It wasn't something he could actually do, surely not. And yet ... It would certainly give him more time. A week maybe? Two weeks? Long enough, anyway, to make some enquiries.

He pulled the dressing gown across his chest and turned up the collar. Some months earlier, he and Jim had watched a science programme about a prehistoric man in Denmark who had been buried in the peat moss thousands of years ago. When he was discovered and dug up, his body was perfectly preserved. You could see what he had looked like, enough to recognise him. Archaeologists had even taken his fingerprints. He had been sacrificed, they said. And he wasn't the only one, there were hundreds of them, all over northern Europe, including Scotland. They were called bog people. The peat preserved their bodies.

And peat was something Peter knew about. Every day he burned peat on the fire and smelled the fragrant smoke as he came home from school. When he walked on the moor he walked on peat and avoided the deep black pools they called dhu bogs. For years he had gone peat cutting with his dad, Jim digging out the wet black slabs with his tusker-spade and Peter stacking them on the moor to dry. He knew how soft and spongy it was, how easy to cut once you got past the tough roots of heather.

If he were to bury his dad out there on the moor, Peter thought, he could easily dig a hole deep enough. Provided there weren't any rocks, of course, and maybe not six feet, but enough to bury his dad properly. It might take a long time but he was sure he could do it.

And he knew, he was positive, that his dad wouldn't mind. He'd probably have laughed and told him to go ahead. 'Take off my watch mind,' he'd have said. 'It's a good watch that.' He loved the hills, they were his favourite place in the whole world and he'd been all over in the army. He'd often said so and Peter thought it would be a nice place to be buried, much better than a graveyard, even the one in Tarridale with dry-stone dykes and a view of the sea. It would be a bit lonely maybe, but then his dad was a bit of a loner. He'd like it out there with the wind blowing and the moon shining down.

The clock struck nine. He took down a photo from the mantelpiece. It showed his dad and himself standing on the ramparts of Edinburgh Castle. He remembered how Jim had asked a French tourist to take it. His dad was laughing. Peter examined him, from his off-white jeans to the sparkle in his eyes. It had been a great holiday.

'Is it OK?' he said to the man with an arm round his shoulders.

The man laughed back

'Don't take things too seriously.' It had been one of his dad's favourite bits of advice. 'Nothing matters that much. When in doubt go ahead – unless it's drugs and that. It's the things in life you don't do that you regret. Just so long as you don't hurt anybody.'

Well, Peter thought, this wasn't going to hurt anybody. Apart from his dad and himself there was no one to *be* hurt.

And it wasn't as if he was going to be left there for ever, just for a few days until he got things sorted out in his head. Just to keep his dad safe. Then they could dig him up again and bury him properly, with flowers and a church service and everything.

He had almost talked himself into it. Still, actually to bury his dad out there on the hillside ...

He mixed the dogs' food and fetched Buster into the house for a run around while he made some toast. As he crossed the yard, still wearing his dressing gown, the wet air brought on his cough. He felt far from well.

But by the time he had picked the last crumbs from his plate and finished his second cup of tea, Peter's mind was made up. The idea terrified him but he would do it. Whatever the outcome, it was a relief to have made at least some sort of decision.

He returned Buster to his run in the shed and collected a spade from the corner, then went upstairs to change.

17

The Lonely Peat Moss

THE HALL WAS cold and it was by pure chance that when the head teacher picked up the phone Peter was convulsed by a coughing fit.

'Hello? ... Hello?'

'I'm sorry, Mrs Harle, it's – ' Cough, cough, cough.

'Who is that speaking? Just take your time.'

'It's me, Mrs Harle.' He caught his breath. 'Peter Irwin.'

'Good morning, Peter. That's a nasty cough you've got there.'

'Yes, that's why I'm phoning.'

'Sounds as if you should be in your bed.'

'No, I'm,' he took a steadying breath, 'much better now thanks. But my dad had to go off to the sheep and he said I should give you a call to let you know I'll not be in today.'

Mrs Harle liked Jim Irwin. He had his faults but most of the time he was a good, hardworking father who took Peter's education seriously. She liked Peter too, a straightforward, reliable boy. On the rare occasions he missed a day's schooling there was always a good reason.

'Yes, he rang me last week,' she said. 'You look after yourself, Peter, get good and fit before you return to the fray.'

'That's what dad says. Thanks, Mrs Harle.'

'Bad luck it has to be just now, you'll be missing some of the run-up to Christmas.'

'Yes.'

'You'll be back in time for the party, I hope.'

It was more than a week away. Peter had been looking

forward to it. Now it seemed so unimportant he was surprised to hear her mention it. 'Yes, I expect so.'

'Good. Well, give your father my best wishes. It must be cold out there on the hills this time of year.'

'Yes, it is. I mean, I will.'

'All right then, Peter. Look after that cough. Be sure you keep nice and warm, plenty of hot drinks. Thank you for ringing.'

'Bye then, Mrs Harle.'

'Bye-bye, Peter.'

The phone went dead.

'Bye,' he said forlornly and put down the receiver.

Mrs Harle was right, it *was* cold on the hill in December. She was right, too, that Peter should have stayed warm indoors until he got his strength back. Unfortunately it was not possible.

As he tramped through the wet heather he wheezed and sweated and tucked the scarf round his throat. The cloud cover had thickened during the night and it had rained. Watery ice covered the moorland pools. A strengthening wind, moisture-laden and just a degree or two above freezing, blew into his face from the north-west.

His progress was slow. He wore gloves, an old pair of Jim's with the fingers cut off, and shifted the spade from hand to hand as he climbed. On his back he carried his schoolbag with a thermos and sandwiches in it and two short planks sticking out of the top. It took an hour and a half to cover the two and a bit miles from the parking place to the shoulder of Blae Fell. As he topped a low ridge his dad's rucksack came into sight with the remains of the red and white poly bag fluttering from the top. He looked past it and saw the hump in the heather that two days earlier he had thought was a protruding rock.

His heart thudded, from fear as much as the climb. Peter did not want to do what he was planning. He wished the next hour or two were past and he was on his way home. The dogs sensed it and stood close by. He touched Ben's head. 'Come on then.'

Jim lay as Peter had left him, although his clothes and the navy-blue jersey that swathed his head were sodden. He dropped the spade and took off his schoolbag. With relief he saw that his dad's body was untouched. All the same, he refrained from unwrapping the jersey. He wanted to remember his dad as he had been, not as he might look two days after death, encased in ice-cold saturated wool.

As he crossed the moor, Peter had planned what he must do. His first task was to go through his dad's pockets. His wallet would be there, his credit cards, maybe letters or papers that should be taken home. He pulled off the clumsy gloves.

Jim wore his old, olive-green parka. One or two heart pills had dissolved into white stains. The pockets had flaps and studs but they were not fastened. Peter slipped his hand inside. Everything was cold and stuck together with the wet. His fingers encountered slippery peppermints, his dad's pocket knife, a dirty handkerchief, his plastic wallet of tobacco, a cheap lighter, a biro, an empty envelope, a seashell and a pebble with nice markings. One at a time he laid them on a bright green patch of moss.

His dad's hand, outflung in the heather, still grasped the little pill bottle, part full of water now. Peter prised it loose. His gold watch, bought in the back streets of Cairo when he was a soldier, ticked on bravely, counting the hours of his death as it had counted the hours of his life. Peter removed it from his wrist, feeling how icy the skin was, and added it to the pile.

The jacket had a storm flap. It opened with a rip of Velcro. There was an internal zip. Peter pulled at the tab with numb fingers. It jammed. He jiggled it and tugged harder. It would not budge. He took a better grip and wrenched it up and down. The body rocked. The zip slid to the bottom. He pushed the jacket wide and was confronted by the Shetland pullover his dad wore most of the time. It was his favourite and brought back memories. Peter swallowed a lump in his throat. He had promised himself, whatever might happen, he would not cry.

There was no wallet, there were no credit cards. They must be in another jacket or a drawer back at the house, maybe Jim's private drawer in his bedroom. Methodically Peter went through the inner pockets of his jacket then turned to his trouser pockets. This was worst of all. His dad's legs were rigid. First he searched the side pockets then, exerting all his strength, turned him over to reach the back pockets. There was little of value in any of them, at least little to a thief: a ten-pound note, a few coins, a list of items he needed from the farm store in Clashbay, a card from church giving details of the Christmas services – and a little holder containing two photos of Peter.

He stared at it. It was too much to bear. Peter wept for his loss.

The wet wind struck through his clothes. He looked for a sheltered spot and carried his schoolbag to the lee of some rocks. The scrap of plastic sheet that he always took to the hill gave him a dry seat on the grass. The dogs waited expectantly. He gave a biscuit bone to each and opened his thermos. It was something he had done a hundred times and it always brought pleasure, a hot cup of tea with the breeze blowing his hair and the wild land stretching before him as far as the eye could see. Not today. Today was different. Today there was no dad to share a joke with. Today his dad lay forty metres away with a spade at his feet.

He scanned the moor for sign of any shepherd or dogs. There was none, the sheep grazed peacefully. That far out, certainly on a bleak day in December, they rarely saw another figure, and never anyone to speak to.

The tea did him good but Peter was far from well. He felt dizzy and when he coughed his lungs smelled dirty like bad breath. The sooner he got home to a warm fireside or his bed, as Mrs Harle had told him, the better.

He packed away the unopened sandwiches and returned to his dad. Taking the spade, he tested the ground for the best place to start digging. There was unlimited choice. He selected a spot close-by where, in his imagination, the earth looked kinder. Exerting his strength, he tore up as many stalks of heather as he could, then took the spade and started to dig.

It was work of the hardest sort. From the first pitch of the spade he was sweating. The peat itself was soft, but before he could get into it he had to chop through a mat of tough and tangled roots. He used the spade like an axe, jabbing it down vertically, jumping on the blade and ripping up the roots with his hands. They were hard to break. Even a strand as thick as string resisted his tug. It was a nightmare.

Once the roots were cleared it was plain digging, but every spadeful of the waterlogged peat had to be thrown up to the ground above. The deeper he went, the higher grew the mounds on three sides.

Peter was coughing constantly. His head throbbed. The clothes clung to his back. He threw off his woollen hat. At once the cold wind struck through his hair. He wiped his brow with a filthy, frozen hand.

Near the surface the peat, the rotted moss and heather of centuries, was earth-brown. As he dug deeper it turned darker. Black gobbets fell from the spade, hit his legs and dropped back into the hole. It was wetter than in June when the peats were cut for fuel. In the trampled ooze his boots were scarcely visible.

Peter scrubbed his hands on a patch of fresh green moss, so different from what lay below, and pulled off his jacket. The wind cut through his jersey. He had a choice, to freeze or sweat like a horse. For the moment he needed to freeze.

The grave had become a ragged hole roughly two metres long and a bit less than a metre wide. Every few spadefuls he stopped to straighten his back. He had thrown down the clumsy gloves. With black fingernails he scratched off the dirt to examine his blisters. One had burst. He spat on it and scrubbed it clean against his jeans.

Slowly the hole deepened. At last Peter judged it was deep

enough. If it wasn't – well, it would just have to be. He could do no more. The surrounding moor was level with his hips. The wind had strengthened, flapping his wet hair. He scraped the bottom of the hole until it was roughly flat and heaved himself up to the heather. The warmth of his jacket and hat were welcome.

He had brought with him with two pieces of wood, a hammer and nails, a small Bible, and a jam jar with a tight lid containing a piece of paper on which he had written his dad's name and address, and a brief account of what had happened. Peter had taken great care with this, writing it in rough then copying it out in his best handwriting and signing it.

For ten minutes he rested in the shelter of the rock. Now came the worst part of all, the part he had been dreading. The hole was about four metres from Jim's body. 'Sorry, Dad.' He grasped the bottom of Jim's trousers and swung his legs towards the grave. They were very heavy. He took hold of his jacket. For a minute he couldn't move the rigid body at all. It clung to the ground. He shifted his grip and lifted again. The body moved a few centimetres.

At last his dad lay on the brink of the hole, the near side that was not piled high with peat. Peter turned him on his front so that when he fell it would not be face-down. He had brought a sheet from home. Trying not to look, he unwrapped his jersey and bound Jim's head in the clean white cotton. Then, gritting his teeth, he rolled him into the grave.

He landed with a thud that made Peter wince. To his relief his dad had fallen as he hoped, on his back with his head straight and one arm at his side. When the hole was filled, he saw, the outflung arm would be well covered. He clambered down, standing astride, and straightened his dad's jacket. Carefully he placed the jam jar by his shoulder and climbed out again.

A hidden stream tumbled down the hillside. The splash of a small waterfall reached his ears. He rinsed his hands in the icy water and dried them on his trousers. It did not occur to him to rinse his face which was also filthy. He took the black Bible from his schoolbag. With no minister in attendance, Peter had planned what he would read and had written a prayer on a sheet of lined writing paper. The prayer marked the page.

He looked behind him. The dogs lay in the heather. 'Ben,' he called. 'Meg. Come here. No, round this side. Good girl. Sit.'

Obediently, though puzzled and not entirely happy, they did as they were told. Meg looked up and whined. He stroked her black and white head.

Standing beside the grave, Peter read Psalm 121 aloud. They were words that Jim had liked and sometimes quoted:

> *I will lift up mine eyes unto the hills*
> *From whence cometh my help;*
> *My help cometh from the Lord*
> *Which made heaven and earth ...*

Before he had finished, the writing grew blurred and he had to blink away his tears.

Then he said the Lord's Prayer and read his own prayer, saying what a good man his dad had been and asking God to look after him.

Not knowing what to do next, he stood for a long time with his eyes sometimes shut and sometimes open. Where was his dad, he wondered for the hundredth time. Had he just gone, like the rabbits he killed ferreting? Was that it? Or was he really up there somewhere? He raised his eyes to the slate-grey clouds. They had not been great churchgoers but he hoped so. Would he be pleased with what he was doing? Peter thought he would.

The dogs moved away and at last he began to fill in the grave, it couldn't be put off forever. As the black peat thudded down, Peter felt each blow as if it struck his own body. Worst was his dad's face, bound in the white sheet. But little by little the hole filled up, covering his legs, his stomach, his chest, until nothing was left but a hand-sized glimpse of olive-green jacket.

He threw down a last spadeful.

His dad was gone.

Peter's head swam. He retreated to his seat by the rocks. Although the body was covered, the grave was only half filled, there was over half a metre to go. He thought he could never finish the job. His stomach heaved and he brought up his tea. It made him feel briefly better and after a short rest, planning to do just a little more, he returned to the spade. And somehow, with repeated breaks, he kept going until at last, well into the afternoon, the grave was filled to the level of the surrounding moor. He would have liked it to be a mound like new graves in the cemetery, but the last of the peat was scattered among the heather and it was not possible. He could do no more.

Then Peter took the two pieces of wood he had brought and nailed them together in the form of a rough, untreated cross. Using the flat of the spade, he battered it into the moor behind his dad's head. On the crosspiece, using paint that would merge into the background, he had written his dad's name, James Allan Irwin, and the years of his birth and death. Less than a metre high, the cross was almost hidden by the surrounding heather. In an attempt to camouflage the grave and trampled black peat that surrounded it, he scattered the ground with the stalks he had pulled earlier.

Peter had finished what he set out to do. Clearing up did not take long. Wearily he tipped out the dregs of his thermos, ate a mouthful of his sandwiches and gave the rest to the dogs. Before he started digging he had put Jim's possessions into a plastic bag and tucked it away in his schoolbag. The sheet of plastic went in too. The rest could stay. He never wanted to see his jersey again and threw it into a dhu bog, using the spade to push it beneath the surface, then hid the spade and his dad's rucksack under a whin bush.

His emotions were all used up. With a last, 'Bye, Dad. It won't be for long, just a few days,' he turned away and began the long trek across the hillside.

He was so tired his legs would scarcely go where he wanted

them. As he reached the crest he looked back and saw the black scar among the greens and reds and golds and browns of the moor. The scattered stems of heather did not conceal it very well. If anyone chanced upon it during the next few days, which was unlikely – well, it couldn't be helped. A good downpour would start the healing process by rinsing the leaves and washing the loose peat down into the roots.

Right on cue the rain, which had held off all day, flung a scatter of drops into his face. Dark cloud, so low you'd think you could hit it with a stone, hid the summit of Blae Fell. The way ahead was shrouded by a heavy squall. Peter coughed and spat. Summoning the last of his strength, he tugged his hat to his eyebrows and resumed walking.

Ben and Meg, blinking as the rain grew heavier, followed at his heels. Behind them the grave of his dad was lost in the advancing dusk.

18

Asleep at his Desk

PETER WAS WET to the skin; the cold had got into his bones. Clumsily he opened the van door. Ben shook himself in a whirlwind and scrambled through to the back. Meg followed, taking her privileged seat in the front. Peter fell into the driver's seat and pulled the door shut behind him.

Rain blurred the windows and drummed on the roof. For a full minute, hardly knowing where he was, he stared at the windscreen. It was Ben, scratching the back of the seat, who roused him to start the engine and drive home through the near dark.

For a long time Peter soaked in a hot bath. He was shivering and dizzy when he stepped into the water, he was boiled and dizzy when he stepped out. Dutifully he tended to the animals, made himself a hot water bottle and crawled into bed.

For two days he hardly stirred. There was some old cough medicine in the bathroom cabinet and half a box of paracetamol. He dosed himself with these, drank endless cups of tea and hot orange, and did his best to keep the house warm. Again he vomited and twice had to change the bedclothes because they were wet with perspiration. It was a testament to his health and strength that he did not develop pneumonia.

By Thursday the worst of the fever was past and Peter sat listlessly on the settee, picking at a bowl of cornflakes and watching daytime television. His cough had broken. He blew his nose into sheets of toilet paper and threw them into the flames.

He telephoned school to say he'd been laid up in bed and it would be Monday before he returned. But he saw no solution to the greater problem. It never went away, though now Jim was buried there was less urgency. People rarely called at the house and if anyone did come knocking, Peter thought, he could always tell them his dad was out on the hill. It might even be possible, if he could head off awkward questions and somehow look after the sheep, to live on at Scar Hill for weeks.

But could he?

Jim had died on Saturday. He counted on his fingers – five days. It was hard to believe. Wherever he went around the house and outbuildings there was a void, his dad wasn't there. He wasn't doing jobs in the yard; he wasn't lolling in his chair with a can of lager; he wasn't asleep in the byre; he wasn't making dinner in the kitchen. His bed, made as always with military precision, had not been slept in. His jacket was missing from its peg in the hall. There was no need to make a second mug of tea. There was no one to talk to.

The house was on edge with his absence.

The dogs hung about the yard with their tails down. Were they missing Jim too, or simply responding to his own mood?

Peter sniffed his cornflakes and decided the milk was going off. The last thing he needed was to upset his stomach with sour milk. He tipped them into the sink and ran the tap, squashing them down the plughole with a finger. Half a litre of milk remained, he had forgotten to put it back in the fridge when he was ill. Reluctantly he tipped it after the cornflakes and found some evaporated in the cupboard. It tasted horrible in tea but was good with cereal. He punched a couple of holes and made himself a fresh bowlful.

Afterwards he looked for a biscuit. Only two were left in the packet. The bread was stale. The dogs' food was getting low. He had thrown out the Cumberland sausage and a pack of stewing steak. Even if they'd not gone off, the idea of meat and gravy turned his stomach.

He needed to go to the shop. There was plenty of money, he had the ten pounds from his dad's pocket and another forty from his wallet in the bedroom. Jim's credit cards were also in his wallet. There were two, his Visa and a cash card for which Peter knew the PIN number. Jim hadn't kept it secret, not from Peter. 'Hop along and get us fifty quid, Pete,' he would say, passing him the card when they were out shopping in Clashbay. 'I'll see you in the Co-op.'

And until the Social Security learned about his dad's death, the money would keep coming – at least he thought so. A hundred and twenty pounds a week, straight into his bank account. Jim was a proud man and had hated it, hated living on hand-outs, but the income from a flock of sheep and a few lobsters was not enough to pay the bills and provide a proper home for his son. Perhaps some day, Peter thought, a form would arrive for his dad to fill in, a letter requesting him to appear at the Social Security Office. He didn't know. For the time being, however, although there was little food in the house there was no shortage of money.

If he had been four years older with a driving licence and insurance, he could have driven into the village that afternoon. Feeling weak wasn't a reason to go hungry. As it was, he would have to attend school tomorrow, Friday, and get his messages at lunchtime. Otherwise it would mean waiting until Monday.

Peter slumped on the settee. He could manage for one day. What he had to do now was rest and get as fit as possible for the next morning so he could tackle his lessons and not get sent home. Sent home? Who could fetch him with his dad buried out there on the moor? Maybe Mrs Harle or one of the teachers would insist on driving him. He tried not to think about it.

Buster had been shut in his run for days. Peter fetched him into the living room for a run around. The dogs, particularly Ben, didn't like Buster too much although they worked well out of doors. There was nothing would have pleased Ben better than to pounce on the ferocious little ferret and kill him with a snap and a good shake like the stuffed sock that was his favourite toy. This was absolutely forbidden and Ben knew it but that didn't take away his longing. Buster understood the situation perfectly but it wasn't in his nature to be afraid.

Careless of the danger, he ambled round the room and it was Ben who watched uneasily and curled his grey paws out of the way.

Peter watched them and smiled. The fire slumped with a shower of sparks. His eyes closed. The afternoon slipped away.

At eight-forty next morning the school bus picked him up at the roadside. Peter felt a little better but even driving the van to the end of the track had raised a perspiration. His face was white. There were dark circles like bruise marks beneath his eyes. In his schoolbag he carried a thick wad of toilet paper for use when he coughed.

The bus was full of noise. 'Hey, Winnie, how you doing?'

'You don't look too good.'

'Should you not still be in bed?'

When they saw how rotten he felt they left him alone.

He had been absent for eleven days. Now the classroom was decorated with streamers, a Christmas tree, Santas, a crib, tinsel, cards and an Advent calendar.

'My dad wanted me to stay at home,' he told Miss Berry, who was his class teacher as well as his English teacher. 'But Mrs Harle said how everyone's getting ready for Christmas. I didn't want to miss it.'

Miss Berry, a tiny old lady, had taught English at Tarridale High School for as long as anyone could remember. She was popular with the children. Half their mothers and fathers had been taught by her.

'Well, if you're sure, Peter,' she said. 'Stay quiet then and don't do too much.'

'Thanks, Miss.' He forced a cheerful smile. 'I'll be fine.'

'I don't like to seem uncaring,' she added, 'but do try not to give it to the others. There were eight off on Tuesday. Go on like this, there'll be no one left.'

Friday started with double Physics and Geography. At break time he sat in the cloakroom. Then it was double English.

The bustle of the classroom in the run up to Christmas,

which Peter had never noticed before, was exhausting. Miss Berry set them to write a seasonal story to be gathered into a book and passed around the class. A girl raised her hand.

Miss Berry looked up from her marking.

The girl pointed silently. Head on his desk, Peter was sound asleep.

'Yes, I know,' said Miss Berry. 'Let him sleep. He's not well. How's your story coming along?'

'I've finished,' she mouthed silently. 'I'm just doing the drawing.'

'I look forward to seeing it,' the teacher said.

The girl gave her a smile and pushed back her hair, lowering her head above a scene of reindeer flying above snowy trees.

Peter had been looking forward to Christmas for ages. He loved everything about it, not just at school but at home where, even though they lived in the heart of the moors and there were just the two of them, they decorated the house with streamers and evergreen. Every year a sparkling tree stood in its blue tub in the corner. Jim bought a cake which Peter covered in marzipan and icing sugar with Santa's red sleigh, the same one they used every year, dashing across the surface. He hung up his stocking and Santa filled it while he was asleep. On Christmas Day they roasted a turkey, steamed a pudding and pulled crackers, sat by a roaring fire to watch the big Christmas film, filled themselves with nuts and chocolates, and played with Peter's new games. Before this, around the start of December, Jim gave him twenty pounds to buy presents and cards. Others he made at the living-room table. Those were the ones his dad liked best.

It was a happy time. Christmas was special.

Not this year. As Peter saw his classmates rushing round with cards and talking excitedly about the presents they would be getting, he felt cut off from them, separated by a thick sheet of glass. Christmas was irrelevant, another world, somewhere he did not belong. In the last week, Peter felt, he had aged twenty years. Fifty years. Grown up.

He looked around the room. When the others found out what he had done, when the news reached Miss Berry and the other teachers, they wouldn't believe it. They would be horrified. Look at him as if he were some sort of monster.

But when he thought about his dad who had loved him so much, and Ben, and their life at Scar Hill, he didn't feel like a monster at all.

At lunchtime, with an effort, he managed to eat half his excellent mince and potatoes, and some of his sticky toffee pudding with hot custard. Afterwards, his nose streaming in a wind that blew the sea into crested waves, he took the short cut above the football pitch to the village shop. There he bought milk, bread, dog food, some ready-made meals, cough mixture, paper hankies and a few other things.

Mr McRobb, the shopkeeper, stood by the till. Over the years he had grown fleshier and freer with his opinions. He enjoyed his days at the hub of village gossip.

'Not like your dad to make you do the family shopping.' He totted up the bill and took the two ten-pound notes that Peter handed him.

'He didn't make me,' Peter said, 'I told him I would. He's been having a bit of trouble with the van.' He had prepared his excuses in advance. 'The bus will drop me off at the gate. Dad'll take us home on the tractor.'

Mr McRobb saw Jim Irwin as a village character. A bit of a chancer, a drunk. 'Best not take it on the road too often eh?' He winked conspiratorially.

There were others in the shop. Peter flushed. 'Do you mean he hasn't got it taxed?' he said plainly.

Mr McRobb was taken aback.

'He doesn't need to tax it,' Peter said hotly. This was none of Mr McRobb's business. 'He never takes it on the road, he only uses it round the house and on the hill.'

It was Mr McRobb's turn to go red. He was not accustomed to being chastised by a thirteen-year-old. 'Makes sense, I suppose.' He handed Peter his change. 'No point wasting money.'

Peter was outraged. His dad always doing his best and lying dead out there on the hill. He knew he should ignore what the shopkeeper said but couldn't control his tongue. 'How dare you say things like that about my dad.' A coughing fit caught him unawares and he pulled toilet paper from his pocket.

Mr McRobb was a father himself. He checked an angry retort and looked at the white-faced boy across the counter. 'You OK, son? You don't look too hot.'

'I'm fine.' Peter wiped his lips. 'Thank you.'

A lady held the door open. He went through and lugged his messages back to school. The bus stood at the end of the playground. It was unlocked and cooler than indoors. He left his messages on a seat.

In the afternoon they had French, Maths and History, but at half past two the choir was summoned to the hall to rehearse a couple of pieces they were to sing in church at the end-of-term service. Peter was in the choir and went with the rest. The music teacher was a thick-set, bearded man with hairy fingers that crashed down on the piano keyboard. He was famous among the children for his sudden explosions of rage. Despite this, or perhaps because of it, they liked him, and when the bell went an hour later he told them their singing was dreadful, the performance would be a complete disaster, but he hoped they would have a happy weekend anyway.

A cold wind blew round the corners. Mrs Harle stood with Miss Berry and watched the children troop out of school. Two seventeen-year-olds ran whooping past. A small girl dropped a drawing and scrambled to retrieve it. Peter was among them

'How did he get on?' Mrs Harle pulled up her collar. 'He doesn't look at all well.'

'He isn't,' said Miss Berry. 'I'm surprised his father let him come. But you know what they're like up there at Scar Hill, a hardy pair. Didn't want to miss out on the run-up to Christmas. He'll be all right.'

'So long as you haven't caught anything yourself,' said Mrs Harle. 'If you took ill just now I don't know how I'd cope.'

The teachers waved as the bus drew away. A score of hands waved back. Peter sat by himself. His tired fingers appeared at the bottom of the window.

19

Lights in the Window

BEN WAS WAITING at the five-bar gate, bouncing on his front paws and jumping up to lick Peter's face. They made their way to the van, hidden in its usual spot in the quarry. Peter let Ben in ahead of him, dumped his shopping on the passenger seat and drove home.

He failed to see Bunny in an old tweed coat, standing on a crest above Three Pines. Her iron-grey hair tossed in the wind. An impatient nanny goat tugged at the carrot in her hand. Absently Bunny tightened her grip. She had often seen Peter driving, usually the tractor. Now it was the van and he was doing the shopping. And from the way his shoulders drooped he wasn't at all well. What was up, she wondered. Was his father going through one of his drunken spells? Poor boy. Poor man. What a rotten thing to have to contend with.

'Ow!' She pulled back her hand. Frustrated at being denied the rest of the carrot, the goat had given her a nip. Bunny examined her finger. 'Bad girl, Lucy. That was sore. No, you can't have the carrot, you'll have to wait.' She pushed off her yellow-eyed companion and watched the departing van. It rocked on the rough ground. Water sprayed from a pothole. A bend in the track took it from sight.

Thoughtfully she walked down the hill to her cottage. The goat trotted alongside, butting her legs in a not altogether friendly manner. 'Stop it, Lucy. Stop it or you'll make me fall.' She relinquished the half carrot. 'How would I get on out here with a broken leg? Who'd look after you then?'

Lucy gambolled ahead with her prize.

With blue eyes sharp as a camera – snap! snap! snap! – Bunny watched the goat's victorious run and filed it away for reference.

Her kitchen was littered with books and papers. The house needed tidying. She made a mug of coffee and carried it to her rocking chair beside the stove. Throwing over the pages of her current sketch book, she picked through the charcoal in a filthy saucer and began to draw.

There was no fire at Scar Hill. The house was cold and gathering dust. Peter shovelled yesterday's ashes into a bucket and went to the peat stack. A couple of firelighters, a match, a few broken bits, and soon the smoky flames were licking up the chimney. The dogs had been on their own all day. He gave them a handful of treats as he put the shopping away then carried a mug of tea – his dad's mug with a leaping salmon on the side – to the hearth and waited for the fire to generate heat.

Somehow he had got through the day and now that he was home, now there was food in the house, now he didn't have to talk to people and pretend everything was all right, he felt able to relax.

That evening, after half a quiche with peas and a slice of strawberry cheesecake for dinner, Peter went to bed at nine and fell at once into a deep and, as far as he could remember, dreamless sleep which lasted until the dogs woke him twelve hours later. It was the rest his body had been craving. A rough wind buffeted the house and flung rain at the windows but he felt better, still weak but on the mend.

It was Saturday. Peter hardly left the house, even though by mid-afternoon the storm had passed and the clouds were opening to a washed blue sky. Instead he sat by the fire and read, watched TV, did a little cleaning, and put his wet clothes and towels which had lain for days and were starting to smell, into the washing machine.

Sunday broke clear and bright. In the late morning Peter

drove up into the moors. A mile beyond the sheep fanks where he parked going to the hill, the track came to an end. He swung in a semi-circle and stepped from the van. It was a wild and pretty spot, deep in heather and stunted bushes, where the stream came tumbling down a series of waterfalls. The pools weren't big enough to swim in but sometimes on a hot summer's day he bathed there.

The December sunshine struck warm on his cheek. A broad grassy hillside was dotted with sheep, well over a hundred. This was the lower pasture, south-facing and sheltered from the north and east winds, where they brought the lambing ewes to be cared for during the winter. Already Jim had started feeding them hay and sheep nuts but it was not strictly necessary. For the present there was still plenty of grass and in the summer he had planted a few acres of swedes adjacent to the pasture which the sheep could nibble well into February.

Peter leaned on the gate and surveyed the flock. They looked well enough, none were dead, none limping, none attacked, none scouring, none escaped on to the nearby hillsides, all grazing or lying contentedly. It was a relief, for in the week since his dad died they had been totally neglected.

He took a toffee from his pocket. Ben looked up with interest. 'Not for you,' Peter said and stroked his bony head.

'Good gracious.' Miss Berry looked up from her desk. 'I didn't expect to see you here today, Peter.'

'I'm better, Miss, thanks,' he said.

'The way you looked on Friday, I wondered if you'd be back this term.'

He smiled.

'A tough lot, you Irwins,' she said. 'What's the secret?'

'I don't know, Miss.'

'I hope you've not passed it on to your dad.'

'No, he's fine,' Peter said.

'Well, that's good news. So you'll be here for the party after all. And the play, of course.'

The children enjoyed acting and Miss Berry always put on a short Christmas play with her form class, just for the school. It had become a small tradition. This year it was to be *A Christmas Carol*. Following his success as Israel Hands, Peter had been given the rôle of the Ghost of Christmas Past.

'I'm afraid I've had to give your part to Charlie,' she said apologetically. 'Mrs Harle said you sounded so poorly we didn't know if you'd be back in time. I'm sure we'll be able to find you something though.'

Normally it would have been a big disappointment but now it came as a relief. 'That's all right, Miss. Charlie'll be good.'

Peter headed for his desk. It was good to be back among friends and he enjoyed the rest of the day, at least enjoyed it as much as any boy could who carried such a burden of guilty secrets and wasn't fully recovered from illness.

As always, Ben was waiting at the gate. Peter hugged him round the neck. 'Come on then.' He let him into the van and started homeward along the track.

But as Scar Hill came into view across the darkening moor, Peter's heart gave a jump. He jammed the foot brake to the floor. The van bounced off the verge and skidded to a halt. There were lights in the windows. He was sure he had not left them on. Smoke blew from the chimney. He switched off the headlights.

There was somebody in the house.

20

Bottle Blonde

PETER DROVE ON and drew up behind a patch of whins nearer the house. He got out of the van and peered round the spiky branches. The curtains were open. Nothing moved. Only the lighted windows and a trail of smoke told him the house was not empty.

'Stay by me,' he told Ben firmly and started walking.

'Who could it be, he wondered. Someone looking for his dad? A lost hillwalker? A tramp? Anyone opening the door would see the house was occupied; the family might return any minute. Yet the intruder had not only gone in but lit the fire. For a gruesome moment he imagined it might be his dad, not dead at all and returned from the moor.

Peter was glad he had Ben with him. As they entered the yard, Ben moved a step ahead. A ridge of hair rose on his neck. His lip lifted in a silent snarl. Peter crept to the living-room window.

A woman sat facing the fire. She was reading a magazine. Her hair, bottle blonde, straggled over the back of the settee.

Peter saw her from the back. Who was she? No one he recognised. His stomach turned over; maybe it was his mother, come back from America after all these years. She turned a page. He saw friendship bracelets and a couple of chunky silver rings.

Ben jumped up, his big forepaws on the windowsill. Meg, who lay by the fire, scrambled to her feet. Alertly she stared towards the window.

The woman swung round. It wasn't his mother, she was too

young, not much more than a girl. There was something about her that Peter recognised. Next second she also was on her feet, gripping the arm of the settee because she was very fat.

'Pete!' Her eyes lit up. With a waddling gait she ran into the hall.

At that moment he recognised her. 'Val!' Silently his mouth formed the word.

He was still standing there as she appeared in the doorway.

'Hello, Pete.' She looked around fearfully. 'Is dad with you?'

He shook his head.

'Thank God for that anyway.'

Ben stood between them. *Grrr! Rowf! Rowf!* His bark was savage, warning off, protecting Peter. He snarled, long wolfhound teeth, right to the gum.

Valerie drew back. 'What bloody dog's that you've got with you?'

'That's Ben. He's mine.' Peter crouched to pacify the friend he loved best in the world. 'All right. That's a good boy. She won't harm you. Ssshhh!'

But Ben wasn't ready to be pacified. His muscles were rigid.

'He only bloody bit me when I first come.' She pulled up a trouser leg and showed him the marks. A puncture had been bleeding. A dry trickle ran down to her pink and white sock.

'He was only doing his job,' Peter said defensively. 'He doesn't know you. He was guarding the house.'

'My God, it could only be here,' she said. 'He ought to be put down. He will be, too, if I report him. Savage brute.'

'He's all right.' Peter looked up, his arm round Ben's shoulder. 'Don't you dare say anything.'

Ben permitted himself to be held but all his attention was on the intruder. Peter took him by the collar. 'Come and say hello,' he said to Valerie.

'Not on your life. He's stronger than you are, he'll go for me again.'

'No he won't. Come on. You didn't used to be that soft.' Holding tight, he led Ben forward.

Tentatively Valerie reached down. Ben didn't like her. Again that warning growl, the teeth, the hair on his neck.

'He's not normally like this,' Peter said. 'I'll put him in the shed. He'll come round.' He dragged Ben away. 'Silly sausage,' he said. 'That's Valerie.'

Ben resisted, twisting to look behind. He did not like being led away. Peter, whom he tried to protect, had abandoned him in favour of this stranger. Peter shut the shed door. Deep barks and the sound of raking claws followed him across the yard.

Meg, who had known Valerie in the past, left the house and communed with Ben through a crack in the boards.

Now the coast was clear, Valerie ran to meet him in her stocking feet. 'God, give him a chance and he'd have my throat out.' She wrapped Peter in a tight, sisterly embrace. She needed a bath. He smelled sweat and sickly perfume. Her belly pressed hard against him.

'Where's the old man?' She broke free and looked along the track.

Peter hesitated. 'I expect he's out with the sheep.'

'Ask a silly question.' She made a face. 'He got my letter, yeah?'

'Letter?'

'I wrote to him.'

'You never write to him.'

'Well I did this time. Gave him the news. Told him I'd be coming home.'

'How long ago?'

'Bit over a week. Gave him my address and everything but he never replied. Don't tell me he never got the letter.'

Peter hadn't looked in the mail box. 'I don't think so.'

'Oh, bloody hell! That means I've got to tell him to his face. Just what I need.' She sighed. 'Oh well! What's he like these days anyway? Still hitting the bottle?'

Peter nodded. 'Sometimes.'

'Surprised he's lasted this long, the way he was carrying on.'

'He was sick.' Peter slipped into the past tense.

'If you say so.' Valerie didn't notice. 'Bad-tempered old sod the best of times.'

The clouds were shot with crimson.

'He can't be much longer, it'll be dark soon.' A thought struck her. 'You just back from school?'

'Where d'you think I've been?'

'Only asking. Whose class are you in now, Mr Macleod's?'

'That was primary. I'm in secondary now.'

'Secondary! Blimey, you were just a little kid when I left. How old are you now, twelve?'

'Thirteen.'

'Thirteen? My little brother? Give me a break. You'll be six foot tall next and chasing after the girls.'

Peter shrugged.

'Who's your class teacher then?'

'Miss Berry.'

'The old Goose? She still on the go? God, I thought she'd be pushing up the daisies by this time. I couldn't stand her.' She glanced at her watch. 'How'd you get home by this time anyway? Saw your bike in the shed, thought the old man must've taken you.'

'No, I, er – ' She caught him unprepared. 'Well – '

'What's the mystery?' She let it pass and stood back to look at him properly. 'Our Peter! You've grown but I recognised you straight away.' She smiled and put her head on one side. 'Not bad actually. Know who you look like? You look like our mum. You've got her hair an' the same eyes.'

He was taken aback. It had never occurred to him. If Valerie spotted it, his dad must have seen it too. He'd never said.

''Cept you're a bloke, o' course.' She twined her fingers in his and started back to the house.

'You've changed.' Peter took in her bleached hair, smudged make-up and big hoop earrings. She had let herself go. Her shoulders and chin were turning to fat. He glanced beneath and saw her heavy breasts and enormous stomach beneath a patterned nylon jumper.

He stopped in his tracks.

'What?'

Peter was staring. It wasn't just fat, his sister was pregnant.

'Oh, yeah. That's the news. Top marks for observation.' She turned to face him and pulled the jumper tight. Her belly was round and hard as a beach ball. 'Knocked up, that's me. In the club. Got one in the oven. How d'you feel about being an uncle?'

Peter was shocked. Out of his depth. Didn't know how to respond to such momentous news. His cheeks burned with embarrassment.

Valerie took it more matter-of-factly: 'To save you the trouble of asking, no, I'm not.'

He was lost. She wasn't what?

'Married,' she said. 'And I'm not living with Moses no more neither.'

He got the story in fragments:

Four years had passed since Valerie ran away from Scar Hill. As Peter understood it, the first of those years she had spent travelling the country with Tinker's Cuss, the boy band whose single hit had crawled into the top fifty and stayed there for six undistinguished weeks. At the start, especially after life in Tarridale, it had been thrilling: the blast of sound, screaming teenagers, parties every night, sneering at authority. The excitement didn't last. As Valerie put it, 'Only thing they cared about were theirselves, third-rate load of tossers.'

When everything turned sour and the band broke up, she had moved to Bristol with a friend called Zoë, another of the groupies, and rented a tatty basement flat. It was all they could afford, but after they had cleaned it up and put a few posters on the wall, it wasn't too bad. They were looking for a good time. She showed Peter photos: there was Valerie on her birthday, plump and pretty, glass in hand, surrounded by a laughing crowd. There she was at the zoo, at the seaside, coming out of a nightclub. It was fun at the beginning but sadly, like so much else at that time, things didn't work out. Zoë got heavily into drugs and Valerie left the flat to move in with the first of a long series of boyfriends.

They were young and carefree, none had a proper job, most were unemployed. Kashif worked on the fish dock. Chris, when he wasn't sleeping, played the tin whistle in an under-pass. Harold sold dodgy CDs in the market. And Phil, a drop-out student who got drunk every night, turned out to be gay. The best of them was Moses from Cardiff who was studying with the Open University and sold the *Big Issue* outside Sainsbury's, but when it turned out that she was pregnant, and not by him, he threw her out the bedsit.

For much of this time, to her credit, Valerie had kept her job in a back-street chippie, which was why she was getting fat. But now her baby was due in a few weeks, the owner had replaced her with his niece whom the customers liked better and Valerie, permanently tired and sick of the life she had made for herself, had returned to the only real home she had known.

It had not been an easy decision. Valerie didn't lack courage – with Sharon and Jim for parents this was not surprising. But after all that had happened, she did not look forward to asking her dad for help.

That first evening, as they sat with tea and biscuits and the last of the daylight faded to darkness, she said, 'How come he never got that bloody letter? What's he going to say, me coming home like this and the baby and everything? Is he going to go mental, sling me out like Moses did? Mind you, in a way I can't say I'd blame him.' Like a beached whale she lay on the settee. 'Miserable old bastard.'

Peter said, 'You're not to talk like that about my dad.'

'No, you and him were always close. You were his favourite.'

He couldn't deny it. 'But that's only 'cause you set out to

annoy him. You can't wonder he got angry.'

'A bit maybe.' She plucked at her clothes. Whatever she wore these days it was uncomfortable. 'He was just so bloody authoritarian: don't do this, don't do that, do what I tell you.'

'That's not fair.' Peter thought about it. 'Anyway, he had good reason, you were thieving all the time.'

'He didn't know that.'

'Maybe not, but you were. All them tops an' bits of jewellery an' stuff you used to hide under the wardrobe. He didn't want you staying out all night, that's all. He got sick of the shouting matches. He didn't like you going around with that horrible Maureen Bates an' getting into trouble.'

'Well, I've got into trouble all by myself now, haven't I?' She was a good mimic and put on Jim's voice: '*I knew it would come to this one day, Valerie. Swan off looking for the good life and come crawling back here expecting me to look after you.* Is that what it's going to be like?'

He shook his head.

'Well what? You're not saying he'll welcome me back like the Prodigal Son? That'll be the day.'

'No.'

'What *are* you saying then? Anyway, where is he? You said he was out to the sheep. That can't be right 'cause Meg's here. Got one of his precious moods has he? Away down the Kipper, drinking himself blind?'

'I wish he was.'

'Pardon?'

Peter found it difficult. The words stuck in his throat. He heard a voice say, 'Dad's dead.'

Valerie stared. 'What do you mean?'

He didn't reply.

'Dad's dead?' The words hung in the air. 'What are you talking about? How's he dead?'

Peter gave an awkward shrug. 'He just is.' His face told her it was the truth.

'Good God! What happened?' She struggled to the edge of

the settee. 'Are you all right?'

'Yeah, I reckon.'

'But I phoned Maureen just last week and she'd seen him in the shop. He was all right then.'

'Not last week he wasn't.'

'Was it an accident or something?'

'Not exactly.'

'Well how long ago?'

He didn't need to count: 'Ten days.'

'Ten days? Bloody hell, Pete.' She thought for a moment. 'What are you doing here then?'

21

Money and Lies

'GOT ANY MONEY? I'm needing fags.'

Valerie, who had a driving licence but no insurance, was taking the van to the village to collect the suitcase and assorted cardboard boxes that had accompanied her from Bristol. They contained all her worldly goods.

Peter went to the sideboard, keeping his back turned, and took a ten-pound note from Jim's wallet. Valerie saw his secretive manner and pushed past. 'That dad's? How much we got?' She plucked the wallet from his hand. 'Forty quid? I'll take twenty.' She tucked it into her purse. 'That the lot? Not got any stashed away in that drawer in his bedroom?'

He shook his head.

'You looked?'

'That's where he kept the wallet.'

'Well, this'll not last long will it? I'm going to need stuff for the baby apart from anything else.' She thought about it. 'Suppose that means I'll have to go to the Social.'

'But you can't, they'll find out –'

''Bout dad an' what you done an' everything? Could do, I s'pose. But they've got to find out some time, haven't they? I mean, you can't go on living like this forever.' She looked him in the eyes, her young brother who'd always been so quiet, burying their dad like that. And she'd thought some of the people she mixed with in Bristol were wild. 'I still can't hardly believe it.'

'But you *can't* tell them,' he said. 'You can't tell anybody. That's the whole point. That's why I did it, I told you, 'cause of the dogs an' the house an' everything. To give me time.'

'Well we need money, I need money anyway, and I don't know how else to get it.' She looked at her watch, sparkly pink plastic and big as her wrist. Her boyfriend Harold, two before Moses, had nicked it from the market. 'We'll talk about it later. If I don't go now they'll be shut.' She headed for the door, leaning backwards to balance her bulge.

'Dad's prob'ly got some money in the bank,' Peter said desperately. Valerie had a loose tongue, it was all he could think of to stop her talking.

She turned. 'Bully for him but what good's that to us? You got to have a PIN number.'

He lowered his eyes.

'You know his PIN number?'

It was the last thing he wanted to tell her. 'Yeah.'

'God, you're some boy. How'd you find that out?'

'I used to pick up money for him.'

'He never bloody asked me to pick up money for him. How much has he got?'

'I'm not sure – a few hundred?'

'What, two hundred? Nine hundred? I bet the old skinflint had a bit tucked away.'

'I don't know, honestly. A thousand maybe.'

'A thousand!' She thought about it. 'And there'll be his money from the Social coming in every week, that gets paid straight into the bank. And his tax credits. And his child benefit for you.' Valerie knew her way round the system. 'What's that add up to?'

Peter shrugged.

'Must be five hundred a month,' Valerie said. 'Mebbe a bit more. Better than I'd get for Maternity anyway. Bloody hell, Pete, we're rolling in it.'

Her enthusiasm made him feel sick. 'As long as you don't tell anybody,' he said.

'You're right there. Mum's the word.'

'Not *anybody*,' he said. 'Ever. Specially not that Maureen Bates.'

'Silent as the grave,' she said and suddenly giggled. 'Silent as the grave.'

It didn't seem funny to Peter. 'You'd better not get caught driving,' he said. 'The police'll be round here wanting to talk to dad.'

'You seem to have thought of everything,' she said.

'I've been thinking about nothing else for days.'

'Where's his cards anyway?'

He didn't want to say.

'In his wallet?' She found them. 'What's the PIN number?'

Peter pretended not to hear.

'Come on, Pete.' As she turned she bumped into the back of a chair. The baby protested. Valerie stopped in her tracks, holding her belly with both hands. 'It's going to be a boy, I'm sure of it. Got a kick like a bloody mule.' The baby settled down and her face cleared.

Peter pointed to the clock. 'Fifteen minutes and they'll be shut.' He put more peats on the fire.

For the moment, at least, the matter of the PIN number was forgotten.

When she had gone Peter slumped at the table. He picked up some cake crumbs on the tip of a finger. It had been a stressful hour. Valerie had made coffee while Peter put biscuits and the last of a cherry cake on a plate. Then, tight-chested and eyes pricking, he had told his sister the whole story: how Meg came home by herself, how he had found their dad dead on the hillside, and buried him two days later, and been ill, and gone back to school, and lied to the teachers. 'And that's … what happened,' he said at last and drew a deep breath. 'If I tell anyone … they'll make me go away. And now you're here. And I don't know what to do.'

He had needed to tell someone, and although Peter did not realise it, it was the start of healing.

'Good God, Pete. What a terrible thing.' Valerie reached across the table and caught him by the fingers. 'But listen, darling, you're not in any trouble. No one's going to blame you for anything. You did what you thought was right. Dad would understand. And the dogs'll be OK. No one's going to put them down, I'm sure they won't. They'll go to different homes, that's all.' She brushed his knuckles with a thumb. 'But you can't stay on here by yourself, you know you can't. I'm sure the Social Services or the Children's Panel or whoever it is, will find somewhere nice for you. With foster parents or in a children's home or somewhere. Just until they organise something more permanent.'

'Where?' Peter sniffed and swallowed.

'Well, I don't know, love.'

'Tarridale?'

'You'd know that better than me. Are there any foster children in Tarridale?'

'I don't think so.'

'Maybe not Tarridale then, but Clashbay perhaps, or Inverness. Somewhere nice anyway.'

It was not what Peter needed to hear. He drew his hand away on the pretext of looking for his handkerchief and blew his nose hard. His face was white. Suddenly, even though flames were leaping in the hearth, the room felt cold.

Valerie returned with her boxes, cigarettes, shampoo, moisturiser, chocolates and one or two other things. While she took a bath Peter fed the dogs, tipped out some frozen peas and put a cottage pie in the oven. For pudding they had ice cream with some expensive out-of-season strawberries she had found in the shop. Afterwards she helped clear the table.

'Leave the washing-up till the morning. Don't mind if I go out, do you, Pete? Thought I'd look in at the hotel an' find out what's been going on.' She pulled on a squashy hat and lime-green jacket with fur trimming. 'I'll not be late, promise.'

Peter stood in the doorway and watched her drive off. There was a knack to driving the van. The sound of the engine and crashing gears faded. He let Ben from the shed and made a fuss of him to make up for what had happened earlier, then went back to the house and did the washing-up.

Struck by a thought, he went to the sideboard drawer. A handful of loose change lay at the front. The twenty-pound note had gone from his dad's wallet. Peter took the bank cards for safe keeping and looked for a hiding place. He had recently seen a film in which a key was hidden under the edge of a stair carpet. It seemed as good a place as any so that's where he put them, nine treads up on the left. Valerie was not to be trusted with money. Once she got her hands on the cash-card and wormed the PIN number out of him, his dad's savings would be gone like snow in summer.

She wasn't back by ten-thirty. She wasn't back by eleven-thirty. At a little before midnight Peter went up to bed. As he came out of the bathroom, tasting toothpaste and smelling of soap, he looked in his dad's bedroom. For as long as he could remember it had been a man's room, a soldier's room, tidy and formal. In thirty minutes Valerie, who preferred it to her old room downstairs, had transformed it. The bed was crumpled and strewn with women's clothes: jeans, tops, pants, bras, tights, slippers. Boxes and other clothes littered the floor. The air was heavy with the scents of perfumes and creams. Framed photos which had stood on the dressing table, precious to Jim, were gone. In their place lay a scatter of bottles, tubes, pots, lipsticks, make-up brushes and eyebrow pencils. Peter hated it. From here, too, his dad was gone.

It was two o'clock when Valerie returned. Although her baby was due in a matter of weeks, she had been drinking. Alcohol was a no-no, they had told her that at the clinic in Bristol. But what harm could there be in a couple of vodkas, she felt, sitting in the lounge bar with friends and having a reunion? She did not intend to take more, but when people kept putting them down in front of her – well, she could hardly pour them down the loo.

For Peter's sake – and maybe out of habit at Scar Hill – she tried not to make a noise. She was too drunk to succeed. In the kitchen she knocked over a chair; on the stairs she stumbled; and in the bathroom her sturdy constitution, more mindful of the baby than Valerie herself, rejected the vodkas and she was sick. On the landing she paused but no sound came from Peter's room although he was wide awake. She continued to her own bedroom and shut the door. The air was cold. The unremitting wind blew through cracks and stirred the curtain. Heavily Valerie swept her clothes to the carpet and crawled into her father's bed. Two minutes later she was asleep.

The next morning, as Peter got ready for school, she did not appear. He let the dogs out, made himself some breakfast and tapped lightly on her door. There was no response. He eased it open. The room might have been hit by a whirlwind. Clothes everywhere. Valerie lay on her back in the middle of the double bed, her mouth open, belly a mound, blonde hair tangled on the pillows.

'I'm just off,' he whispered, feeling he should say something.

For answer she grunted and slept on.

He left a note in the kitchen:

> *I am taking the tractor to the road. The van needs petrol soon. Ben will be alright if you leave him alone. Peter*

Valerie did not appear as the tractor clattered into life beneath her window and roared away across the yard. Only the dogs stood watching as Peter grew smaller down the track that led to school.

There wasn't a bank in the village. Twice a week a junior manager and a cashier came from head office in Clashbay and conducted business from a room in a sandstone house adjoining the store. There was a cash machine in the wall.

At lunchtime Peter walked over from school. When the road was clear and he was sure he was not being watched, he slotted Jim's silver cash card into the machine and typed in the four-figure PIN number. At once a big blue menu appeared. He examined the choices and pressed the button for *mini-statement*. After a few seconds the card reappeared and the printed details slid out. There was, Peter saw, a balance of £1384.16 in the account. Two recent deposits, dated seven days apart, were for £134.56. He guessed they were the Social Security payments. A note at the foot of the statement informed him: *You can withdraw £300.00*. This was his dad's daily maximum.

He thought for a moment. Valerie needed money, she had to buy things for the baby and there were other expenses too. But she couldn't have it all, he needed to keep some for himself in case she went away again. He examined the figures; another payment was due in a couple of days. That made over fifteen hundred pounds. How much could he reasonably keep? Six hundred seemed fair. Then he could give her the card and the PIN number. Valerie would get the remaining nine hundred, and the money from the Social would keep coming, a hundred and thirty-four pounds every week. She would get most of that too.

A woman had emerged from the shop and stood waiting. He moved aside to let her use the cash machine. It was Mrs McKendrick, the lady they had stayed with when they first came to Tarridale.

'Hello, Peter,' she said. 'Getting your finances sorted out?'

He smiled. 'Yeah, dad's busy. He asked me to pick up some cash.'

'Good for you,' she said. 'I'm afraid not every boy and girl these days could be trusted with a job like that.'

Nerves made him chatter on. 'I'll have to be careful I don't lose it when I go back to school.'

'You certainly will.' She glanced at the cash machine. 'Have you finished?'

'Not quite. But you go ahead, Mrs McKendrick.'

'Well thank you.' She liked Peter, he was one of those straightforward boys. Always polite. You knew where you were with Peter. 'Here, you left your card in the machine.'

He took it from her. 'Thanks, Mrs McKendrick.'

She was soon finished and put the money away in her bag. 'Bye-bye, then, Peter. Give my regards to your father.'

'Yes, I will. Bye, Mrs McKendrick.'

When she had gone, he checked up and down the road and withdrew the whole three hundred pounds: fourteen twenty-pound notes and two tens. Carefully he folded everything together, money, cash card and statement, and buttoned them away in the back pocket of his grey school trousers.

During the afternoon, as he carried out a chemistry experiment and wrote up the results, then went to the hall for rehearsals of *A Christmas Carol*, he felt the wad of money pressing against his bottom. Having lost his part as the Ghost of Christmas Past, Peter had been asked to play Mr Fezziwig, Scrooge's kind-hearted employer, which meant he had to dance a polka all round the stage. It was embarrassing at first, dancing with the Goose and then one of the girls, but once he'd got used to it he enjoyed it.

Valerie was in the house when he got home. She had had a busy day. First she had been to the ante-natal clinic in Clashbay where the nurse had given her a thorough examination and pronounced her fit as a flea. Then she had gone for lunch and afterwards visited a store to look at cots, clothes, nappies, bottles, sterilisers and all the other things she was going to need for the baby.

'A woman at Oxfam said she knows where she can get us a pram cheap,' she told Peter, 'you know, with one of them detachable carrycots. It's all going to cost a fortune. I looked for dad's credit cards but you must have taken them. Did you find out how much he's got?'

'Didn't have a chance,' he said. 'The Goose kept us in all lunchtime rehearsing. I'll go tomorrow.'

'No need, I can go myself.' She held out a hand. 'Let's have the card. What's his PIN number?'

Peter made a pretence of searching through his pockets. 'Give us a minute, I've got it here somewhere.' The card wasn't to be found.

'Don't tell me you've lost it.'

'No, I … Oh, I remember, I hid it in my desk in case it fell out when we were playing.'

'You mean it's at school?'

'Yeah, don't worry though. It's quite safe.'

'And here's me thinking you were the careful one.' She poured boiling water on a couple of teabags and opened a packet of Jaffa Cakes. 'Well don't forget tomorrow, our Peter. I'm needing that money. There's a lot to do before the baby arrives.'

'OK.' He went to the fridge for milk.

'Hey, come here.' She pushed her hair back and turned her neck for him to smell. 'Blue Grotto, they had a special offer, eight quid off. Maureen give us a loan. What do you think?'

22

The Christmas Tree

IN TARRIDALE HIGH School there was so much excitement about Christmas that even Peter was affected by it. Several times, during those last few days before the holiday, he forgot the lie he was living for a whole hour at a time.

On the Wednesday, he withdrew another three hundred pounds and spent ten pounds of it on presents for school friends and a cake to take to the party. He had dressed in his best trousers and shirt because the party was that same afternoon.

On the Thursday, the school kitchen produced a delicious Christmas lunch with turkey, plum pudding and crackers. In the afternoon Peter's class performed their play before the whole school and were cheered to the ceiling.

On the Friday, lessons were abandoned in favour of games and in the late morning, class by class, they walked to the ancient village church of St Andrew's. Streamers hung across the windows. A tall tree glowed with lights and shimmered with tinsel in the draughts. There were carols and readings. Accompanied by the organ instead of the school piano, the choir sang their pieces. And during the prayers Peter shut his eyes tight and thought about his father.

There was no lunch that day and at one o'clock, after Mrs Harle had wished everyone a happy Christmas and reminded them what day to come back, the buses whisked them away home to start the holiday.

The children chattered like magpies. A friend had given Peter a tin kaleidoscope. As the bus descended to the dunes and started up the long Sandy Brae, he shook it and looked happily at the bright patterns. But as they drew closer to the point where he must dismount, his happiness began to ebb.

Valerie had not forgiven him for lying to her, drawing out the six hundred pounds and hiding it away – behind a roof beam in the byre, to be precise, folded into an old tobacco tin to keep it safe from the mice.

'But I'm your sister, for God's sake!' she had cried. 'How are we going to get along if we can't trust each other?'

'Well are you going to stay on here?' Peter had shouted back. 'How long for? You've always hated it. What am I supposed to live on if you suddenly push off again – assuming they haven't found dad by that time? What if I come back one day and find there's no one here but me and the dogs?'

'Leave you by yourself? What do you think I am? I'd never do that to you.'

'You did to dad. And never wrote to him once.'

'But I wouldn't to you.'

'Maybe not without telling me, but you'll go when you get fed up.' His face was red. 'And you're so extravagant.'

'Extravagant!'

'You know you are. You've only got to see something and you want it, you've got to have it. How long's the money going to last the way you go on? I mean, look at your hair for a start. How much did that cost? Twenty quid? More?'

Tired of her blonde locks and dark roots, Valerie had indulged herself at the hairdresser. Her thick hair, now glossy red with two-tone highlights, curled fashionably about her neck and forehead. It had, in fact, cost sixty-five pounds, a figure she would never admit to Peter. A manicure and facial – work in the chip shop had not been kind to her hands and complexion – had cost another forty-five. In addition Valerie had treated herself to a silk scarf, a maternity top and new shoes. As if to demonstrate that she was being practical, two giant packets of disposable nappies (two for the price of one) stood on the floor at the end of the settee.

'Oh, you!' she said, for she had wanted Peter to admire the

new Valerie. 'What do you know about it anyway? Bloody men! You're as bad as dad.'

In the end they had formed an uneasy truce, but of all the Tarridale pupils heading home that afternoon, Peter was the most troubled.

'See ya, Winnie … Merry Christmas! … Give you a ring.' Voices pursued him down the aisle. 'Coming to the match tomorrow?'

'Not sure. I might.'

'Come on, man, there's teas after. Tell your dad we're all looking for you. Give him a kick up the jacksie.'

The bus crunched to a halt. The doors hissed open.

'Tell your dad Happy Christmas, Peter.'

Startled, he looked round and met the driver's big smiling face. 'Thanks, Robbie, I'll tell him. You too.' His heart was thudding.

A black bin bag was tucked into a space behind the driver's seat. The top had come open revealing a corner of red Santa costume and curl of white whiskers. Robbie saw Peter's glance and turned. 'Oh-oh!' He tucked them out of sight. 'Don't tell the little ones, eh?'

He had been distributing presents to the children in the primary school. Everyone knew that Robbie Duncan played Santa Claus. He had been Santa for the last twenty years, it was a village tradition. 'I won't,' Peter assured him and stepped down.

The bus drew away. He stood at the roadside.

The Christmas holiday had begun.

Snow had been forecast. The sky was leaden grey. As Peter bucked and bumped his way home on the tractor, his cheeks stung and his eyes watered with the cold.

The dogs gave him a big welcome, circling the tractor as it roared into the yard. The van wasn't there. The house was empty. Valerie, who didn't like being on her own, had left him a note:

Don't worry Iv'e not gone shopping. I am not being EXTRAVAGENT! I'm going to visit Maureen. Back around five. I'll make dinner.

Luv, Val   xxxxx

PS We'll go shopping tomorrow for the baby. Then you can see for yourself how much it cost's.

He missed her in a way but it was nice having the house to himself. He threw his school clothes on his bed and pulled on the jeans and sweater he wore round the house.

It was time to put up the Christmas decorations. They were stored in a cardboard box at the back of the cupboard under the stairs. He tipped them onto the carpet and added a bag of paper chains the class had made and were being thrown out. Now he needed to find a tree.

The moors were carpeted with moss, grasses, heather, bracken, wildflowers and bog cotton, nothing bigger than gorse bushes and a few stunted alders. A mile beyond Scar Hill, however, there was a stand of Scots pines. Many of these noble trees were over twenty metres tall and when the gales blew they swayed and roared like an ocean storm. Around them, particularly on the more sheltered slope, grew a profusion of saplings. This was where Jim had always cut the Christmas tree and Peter planned to do the same.

After some beans on toast and a mug of hot chocolate, he collected the bushman saw and a pair of loppers, called the dogs and set off with the trailer.

The stand of trees was a few hundred metres above the track. Peter crossed a boggy ditch and was starting up the hillside when he spotted a group of stags, several with fine antlers. They had stopped feeding and stood with raised heads, watching the intruders. Ben froze, staring towards them intently, then decided they were too far off to be worth chasing and resumed his zigzag path through the heather.

The traditional Christmas tree is a spruce. These were pines with tufty branches like bottle brushes. Jim thought the young trees were prettier than spruce and that is what he had taken home for as long as Peter could remember.

After a brief search he selected a tree a bit less than two metres tall and kicked back the undergrowth. Branches grew close to the ground. He lopped them off, ignoring the needles that pricked his hands and poked him in the face. Half a metre of trunk was exposed. He was sorry to destroy such a fine young tree even though dozens were growing around it. A minute's sawing brought it toppling sideways, bouncing on the springy branches.

As he worked it began to snow. He blinked up at the dancing flakes, dark overhead and white against the pine trees. Small and unmelting, they settled on his shoulders.

It was awkward to carry the tree and tools at the same time. He half-dragged, half-carried the tree down to the track and heaved it on to the trailer then returned for the loppers and saw.

'Meg, Ben, come on.' The dogs jumped aboard.

The snow had thickened, tickling his eyelashes and turning the folds of his jacket white. A ghostly half-white was settling over the landscape.

Cutting the tree was always a great thing to do, one of the fixed moments of Christmas. As he drove home, exposed on the high seat of the tractor, Peter was quite proud of himself because he thought his dad would have been pleased.

The tyres left tracks but by the time he drove into the yard the snow had stopped. Daylight was fading. Cracks of cold sky appeared between the clouds.

Valerie had phoned and left a message:

'Hello, Peter, love. Val here. Look, I'm not going to be back in time to make dinner. Sorry. But listen, there's a pizza in the deep freeze and a sticky toffee pudding in the fridge. You can heat them up OK, yeah? I'll not be late, promise.
Lots of love. Bye.'

Peter knew about the pizza and the pudding. He had put them there.

The cold had penetrated to his skin. He shovelled out yesterday's ash and lit the fire, then helped himself to a couple of chocolates from the box in Valerie's bedroom.

By mid-evening the house had taken on a festive air. Multicoloured streamers crossed the walls. Trails of ivy from the back of the byre were coiled round the beams. Ropes of glitter hung over the pictures. In pride of place the pine tree, clamped in its blue bucket and smelling of resin, sparkled like fairyland with the big Christmas star at the top.

A few cans of beer were gathering dust on top of the fridge. Peter didn't like beer much but was pleased when Jim gave him a mouthful in the bottom of a glass. By way of celebration, he popped one open and took it to the fire with a packet of crisps.

It was a nice thing to do and there was a good cartoon on TV, but the beer tasted even worse than usual. By the time it was half drunk he felt his head start to spin. With a belch he tipped the rest down the sink. 'Sorry, Dad,' he said and filled a glass to the brim with water. Ice-cold and brown from the peaty stream which was its source, it tasted much better than the beer.

By ten, when Valerie returned, the alcohol hadn't left his system and Peter was grumpy. His head ached. She had seen the decorations through the window and came straight into the living room.

'Peter, love, that's beautiful!' She leaned over the settee and planted a kiss on his hair. 'Did you go out and cut the tree all by yourself?'

'No,' he said, making her pay for being late. 'Santa Claus come over and give me a hand. Who d'you think cut it? I'm not a baby, you know.'

'You don't have to tell me that, darling. But if you'd left it till tomorrow we could have done it together.'

'You'd have to get out of bed first,' he said. 'And up the hill? I don't think so.'

'Maybe not up the hill, no, but here in the house.' She looked round, unbuttoning her coat. 'It's really beautiful anyway.'

'I'm glad you like it.'

'What do you have to be so cross for? Like I said, if you'd waited I would have helped you.'

'Wait for *you*, I'd be waiting till doomsday.'

'Is it 'cause I wasn't here to make the dinner? I left a message, I did say sorry.'

'Yeah, sorry, big deal. You *never* do what you say you will. You've been back four days now an' you're never even here, you're always out shopping an' drinking an' visiting people.'

'Well, if you're determined to be disagreeable there's nothing I can do about it. It's no mystery who you get that from.' She threw her coat on the settee and went into the kitchen. 'I'll be here tomorrow night, anyway, 'cause I've invited Maureen and some of the others over.' Her head appeared round the door. 'An' I'd say it's going to be really nice, you having the house all decorated and everything, but you'd only snap my head off so I'll not bother.' She disappeared again and there was a sound of cups clattering. 'Do you want a coffee?'

'No,' he said. Then, 'Yes, tea.' He pursued her to the kitchen doorway. 'But if they come tomorrow they'll see dad's not here.'

'Ee, so they will,' she said as if she wasn't quite the full quid. 'I never thought of that.'

'Well they're going to start asking questions and – '

'Oh, give us credit for a *bit* of nous, our Peter. Of course they're going to see dad's not here. We'd hardly be having a party if he was. I've told them he's gone down to visit his brother in Newcastle. Just had a heart bypass. I'll be looking after you for a few days.'

Peter thought about this imaginary relative. 'What's his name?'

'Who?'

'Uncle – whoever he is.'

'Never thought about it. What do you fancy? Jimmy?'

'Don't be stupid, that's dad's name. What about ... Frank? Uncle Frank.'

'If you like.'

'Uncle Frank,' he said again. 'Yeah.'

It had a nice ring to it. To a boy with no relations apart from an absent mother and a pregnant sister he hadn't seen for years, Uncle Frank was a welcome addition to the family.

23

The Party

PETER HATED IT. From the early afternoon people had been arriving. Cars filled the yard and lined the side of the track. The house was full of bodies – living room, kitchen, hall, stairs. Only Peter's bedroom was unoccupied. Football was on the TV and a few boys tried to watch, even though heavy rock drowned out the commentary. The air was thick with the smells of beer, sweat, perfume and cigarette smoke.

Some of the cigarettes had a funny smell. Peter watched a girl rolling one, crumbling something from a scrap of paper into the tobacco. He'd seen her somewhere before, her name was Julie – a thin, dark girl with purple lipstick. She lit up and drew the smoke deeply into her lungs, tilting her head back and shutting her eyes. When she saw him watching she laughed and held out the skinny cigarette.

'Come on, you'll never know if you don't give it a try.'

Peter gave her a look of disgust and moved away.

'Ah, mama's baby,' she called after him.

Food and spills were being trodden into the carpet. People were kissing, eating, drinking from bottles, cans, glasses, paper cups. Trailing arms around shoulders. Shouting to make themselves heard. A new smell, burning burgers, came from the crowded kitchen.

Deirdre and Malcolm, school friends Valerie hadn't seen for years, lay glued together on the settee, jammed in by others. Malcolm rolled aside for a moment. 'Hey, Valerie. Val!' He raised questioning eyes to the ceiling, meaning upstairs. She saw Peter watching and shook her head. Malcolm followed her glance and scowled. 'Why don't you just piss off,' he said to the tense, thirteen-year-old boy whose home this was.

Peter had had enough. None too gently he tugged the rug from the back of the settee, collected the torch from the top of the deep freeze and went out into the yard. The bitter wind cut through his party shirt. It had started snowing again. To escape the crush, a few people were sitting in cars, drinking, kissing, talking. Engines were running to operate the heaters. Clouds of exhaust, illuminated by the outside lamp, rose into the night.

Ben and Meg had been locked in the shed. Peter joined them and shut the door behind him. After the hubbub of the house it was a haven of peace. The dogs had never known such an invasion and pressed close to be reassured.

'That's all right,' Peter told them softly. 'Good boy! Good girl! Yes, it's much nicer in here.'

Buster came to the door of his run to see what was going on. Peter stroked him through the wire mesh.

The shed was used as a store: tins and sacks, timber, wire, tools, small pieces of machinery. A kind of shallow box was built into the corner, filled with straw and a couple of blankets to make a warm bed for the dogs. There was nothing to make a bed for Peter.

'Come on then,' he said. 'Let's go to the byre.'

They crossed between the cars and went into the old stone building. He pulled the twisted door shut behind them. A couple of wall lights strapped with iron provided illumination. One end of the byre was filled to the rafters with bales. Broken bales and loose hay were heaped in the back of the crumbling cattle stalls. Peter chose the second stall from the end, not the one where his dad used to sleep but the one adjoining. He pulled down some armfuls of hay and kicked it around to make a bed, then switched off the light and wrapped himself in the warm rug. The dogs settled nearby, Ben so close that Peter could reach out in the darkness and touch him. He shone his torch about the ancient walls, picking out the cobwebbed harness that hung from nails, finding patterns in the twisted timbers, winkling the beam into black corners.

Throbbing music came from the house, mingled with the clamour of a party in full swing. Peter tucked an arm beneath his head. The comfortable darkness closed about him. After a while, like his two companions, he fell asleep.

He might have slept the whole night through but was disturbed a while later by the sound of revving engines and raised voices in the yard. Momentarily he was confused; where was he? What was happening? What was this prickly stuff under his hands? Abruptly he remembered.

'You'll be fine, it's not that deep yet.' Valerie was calling to friends. 'Wouldn't waste any time though.'

'Bad for drifts?'

'Can be. Dad has to put a snowplough on the tractor sometimes, dig us out.'

'Thanks for the party, Val.'

'Yeah, it was great.'

'Sorry it had to end so soon.'

'Happy Christmas.'

'God, I can hardly see straight. Geoff, you'll have to drive.'

'Me? You've got to be kidding.'

More engines starting up. The noise of over-revving. A crash of metal and a loud swear.

Laughter.

Voices.

Gradually the sounds faded. The last car drew away. No sound but the moan of the wind. The door of the house banged shut. Peter lay in the darkness, nothing to see but streaks of light around the byre door. They disappeared as the yard lamp was switched off.

He lay still, warm and comfortable. Had everyone gone home or were some of them staying the night? He hoped not. Minutes passed. Meg gave a little whine in her sleep. Peter felt himself drifting.

Abruptly the peace was shattered. 'Pete?' Valerie was shouting. 'Pete! Are you out there somewhere?'

The light reappeared.

'Where the hell are you?'

He waited to be found.

'Pete!' There was a sound of footsteps in the snow. The byre door was flung wide. Valerie stood silhouetted in the entrance. She peered into the darkness. 'Are you in there?'

The dogs were on their feet. She groped for the switch and turned on the lights. Peter shaded his eyes against the glare. His sister stood staring.

'My God!' she said at length. 'It's bloody dad all over again.'

He sat up, the air icy against his warm neck.

'What are you doing out here?' She was cross, concerned. 'It wasn't that bad, surely? It was a *party*, for heaven's sake. You know half the people who were there. Tony, Marina, Brendan, you *know* them. You didn't have to run away out here.'

'It was horrible. Everybody drunk and snogging. Dropping stuff all over the floor.' He pulled the rug round his shoulders. 'What time is it?'

'I don't know. Half eleven, bit after.'

His eyes felt full of sand.

'Dear God, Pete, you didn't have to come out into the byre.'

'It's nice out here,' he said. 'Better than all that … in there.'

'It was a party,' she said again. 'That's what people do at parties, let their hair down.'

'And be disgusting in other people's houses,' he said. 'And take drugs.'

'Who was taking drugs?'

'That skinny girl, Julie something. She tried to get me to do it. And there was a guy fiddling with a wee cardboard box went into the bathroom.'

'Mark?'

'Don't ask me. A blond guy with tattoos on his neck.'

'Yeah, that's Mark, he's going back into rehab.'

'Oh, well, that makes it OK,' Peter said drily. He fished a stalk of hay from his collar. 'Neat, though, Dad just dead an' you filling the house with drunks and drug addicts.'

She didn't reply.

'Everybody gone home?' he said after a while.

'Yeah. Before the drifts start building up.'

'No one staying the night?'

'Just you and me.'

'Good.'

She stood aside. 'You're a right miserable sod sometimes aren't you.'

He squeezed past her into the yard. Two inches of snow had fallen and it was still snowing hard. The ground and roofs of the outbuildings were bright as day in the lamplight. The van was covered. Rectangles where the cars had stood were already whitened over. As Peter looked around the familiar scene, so suddenly transformed, his spirits rose. The snowflakes tickled his cheeks, the swirling wind nipped his ears. This, he felt with a sudden keenness, was his home, this was where he wanted to be. Always. Perhaps, the thought returned, Scar Hill even belonged to him now. Within the bright living room, windows banked with snow, he saw the Christmas decorations. The intruders were gone. In a few hours all trace of them would be washed and swept away. He turned to his sister, blinking the flakes from his eyelashes, and smiled. 'I love the snow.'

Meg and Ben emerged from the byre. He kicked the snow in their faces, making them bark and dance in excitement.

Valerie bent with difficulty. A snowball burst on Peter's shoulder. Instantly he retaliated. The snow was crumbly. She screamed as one after another they exploded on her anorak.

'No! Pete! Stop it! It's bad for the baby.'

He let her go and she fled back to the house. But when his back was turned she made a second snowball and flung it with deadly accuracy. It hit him smack on the side of the head. With a shriek of triumph she vanished into the hall and slammed the door shut.

Peter saw her grinning through the window and threw the snowball in his hand. Her face was obliterated. Hooking the snow from his ear and clutching the rug close, he walked to the end of the byre. Sheltered from the wind, he watched the grey blizzard sweeping across the moor.

24

Christmas is Coming

VALERIE SURVEYED THE aftermath of the party. 'Oh, I can't look at this tonight, we'll do it in the morning. Fancy a cup of tea?'

'Yeah, thanks.' Peter wondered why 'we' should do the clearing up. It wasn't his party; they weren't his friends. Would Valerie even be out of her bed before midday?

The house smelled bad and looked worse: food and fag ash trodden into the carpets, spills of beer, empty cans, furniture pulled askew, cigarette burn on the mantelpiece, frying pan burn on the worktop, spilled grease, hearth full of debris, the stink of smoke and blackened burgers. When Peter went to the bathroom there was a smell of sick, though the basin and lavatory were clean. He opened the window, preferring snowflakes to the smell. And when he went into his bedroom the duvet was crumpled. Who had been in there, he wondered, and hoped it wasn't Malcolm and Deirdre. Whoever it had been, he put on fresh covers and stuffed the others into the washing machine.

'Bit of a mess.' Valerie handed him his tea and took some salted biscuits from a plate. 'I'm off anyway. Don't worry, tomorrow we'll have the place looking like new. Night-night.'

She was gone, labouring up the stairs. Peter looked around, hating it, and thought about making a start. Then he said aloud, *Why should I?* and took the dogs out to the shed. Eagerly they scoffed some half-eaten burgers.

He locked the front door and took his tea up to bed.

During the night the blizzard ceased and the clouds rolled back. When Peter woke at nine it was to dazzling sunshine and a world made new.

In contrast to the fairyland outside, the house was a slum. He was disgusted by it, especially because his dad had always kept the place respectable, if not a hundred percent dust-free. Angrily he cleared a space to make tea and toast for breakfast. Afterwards he washed the dishes he had used and left a note for Valerie:

> *Gone to feed the sheep and see their OK.*
> *Leave you to clear up here. It was your party.*
> *Pete*

It was great to be out of the house. Every day since Jim died and Peter had recovered from his illness, he had loaded the trailer and driven up the track to feed the sheep in the lower pasture. On school days there was little time. This morning, since the grass and swedes were covered by ten centimetres of snow, he planned to scrape out the feeding troughs, fill them with sheep nuts and fill the wooden hay racks to the top.

The hard-packed bales of hay were too heavy for him to hoist into the trailer. So were the sacks of sheep nuts. He had worked out a way to deal with this. When he cut the twine the bales broke apart into compressed slabs. These he could load with no difficulty. And each time he opened a new sack of sheep nuts he tipped half into an empty sack. These, too, he could handle easily. To prevent the hay blowing to the four winds as he drove to the feeding place, he laid a ladder on top.

If the blizzard had continued for two more hours, he might have needed to attach the snowplough. As it was, the worst drift was only sixty or seventy centimetres deep and the tractor forced a way through.

The sheep were hungry and huddled for warmth in the lee of a dyke, their breath clouding in the frosty air. As Peter approached they baaed and jostled towards the empty feeders. They knew the tractor and recognised the dogs as they leaped from the trailer. He lugged the first sack of nuts through the gate. The eager ewes pressed about his legs, desperate to be first at the trough. He pushed them aside and tipped the heavy trough on its face, banged it on the ground and kicked it to get rid of the snow. Some had frozen and he scraped it out with a small spade. Then he trailed the sack of nuts from end to end. The moment they rattled down the sheep were feeding, closing in at his heels like the Red Sea behind Moses.

There were four troughs. When he had filled them all, Peter turned to the wooden hay racks. What fodder remained was blanketed in snow. He brushed it off and filled the racks from the trailer, shredding the hay to make it more palatable.

When all was done he counted the sheep, and counted them again because they kept moving. Ninety-six, as far as he could tell. He hoped so anyway.

A tributary stream, overhung with grasses and rimmed with ice, ran down through the pasture. Peter leaned on the gate and took in the wintry scene. The saw-toothed mountains to the west were hidden but the white summit of Blae Fell rose above the surrounding slopes. He thought of his dad out there in his grave beneath the pure snow.

On the way home he lingered to let Valerie finish cleaning the house. The red deer stags, a herd of twenty or more this time, were back by the stand of pines. He crossed half a mile of moor to test the ice on a loch where he went fishing. A deep gully was fringed with icicles, some longer than himself. As he tramped back to the tractor a pair of golden eagles soared high overhead against the blue. His eyes ached with the dazzle of the sun on snow.

Peter drove into the yard ready for a stand-up row but the van had gone, leaving a dark rectangle and tracks through a drift. Valerie had straightened the house after a fashion and done the washing-up. She had left two messages. The first, which was scribbled out, read:

Thanks a bunch!
Val

Beneath she had written:

House is driving me bloody nuts.
Gone to pub. V.

Thirty-two Christmas cards stood about the room. Half were Peter's from school, some were Jim's, the rest Valerie's. Idly he read a few and went into the kitchen. The vinyl, which Valerie had not washed properly, was sticky beneath his boots. As he lifted his feet they made a tiny *tik* sound.

Peter switched on the immersion and set to with cloths and soapy water. He opened the windows, letting the icy breeze carry away the smells of fags and booze and squashed food. For an hour he laboured, tipping the dirty water down the drain in the yard, sponging the chairs, wiping the tops, repairing the Christmas decorations with Sellotape and drawing pins.

At last the house was presentable. With relief he shut the windows, banked up the fire and flopped on the settee. Ben and Meg retired to their day beds while Buster explored the unfamiliar smells and clawed his way up beside Peter to amble across his chest and face. Peter lifted him away, dangling heavily from his fingers, and looked into his wild, unafraid eyes.

'See you,' he said. 'You're wicked, so you are. What are you? Wicked. Yes, wicked!'

He shook the ferret teasingly and set him back on the settee. Buster shook his fur comfortable and resumed his circuit of the room.

Peter sighed contentedly and wondered what was on TV.

That was Sunday.

On Monday the frost held.

On Tuesday, Christmas Eve, there was a thaw – temporary according to the weather forecast – and the track turned to mud. That afternoon Peter and Valerie put presents beneath the tree. At teatime they sat with plates on their laps and watched the Festival of Nine Lessons and Carols from King's College,

Cambridge. In the evening they watched more TV and opened the Christmas nuts and chocolates. And at quarter to eleven Valerie drove through floods and puddles to the Watch Night service at St Andrew's, where Jim had taken Peter every year for as long as he could remember.

Like cutting the tree, the Watch Night service was one of their Christmas rituals. First there was tea and mince pies in the church hall, then they moved into the candle-lit church for carols, prayers and Christmas readings with the huge tree shimmering beside the organ. Peter knew a lot of the congregation and spotted two of his classmates sitting with their parents. At midnight, as the church bell rang out over the village, the minister proclaimed: 'Christmas Day is upon us. The Christ Child is born. Peace be with you all.' Then came the moment Peter found embarrassing as he was forced to turn this way and that, shaking hands and wishing everyone 'Happy Christmas'. One was Bunny Mason. Another was his class teacher, Miss Berry. A third was a whiskery old lady from the village who to his horror clutched his shoulders and kissed him on the cheek. Finally, after a prayer which Peter spent with his eyes tight shut and his thoughts with his dad, they sang 'O Come All Ye Faithful' and filed out through the porch.

The minister greeted him cheerfully at the door. 'Dad not with you this year, Peter?'

'No.' Peter had prepared his lie. 'He had to go down to Newcastle and see his brother.'

'Not home for Christmas?'

'Oh, yes.' He amended the lie quickly. 'But he got a bad chest down there. Didn't want to come out.'

'Not a nice night. I hope he's better soon. Anyway, Happy Christmas. God be with you.'

'You too,' Peter mumbled, his blushes hidden by the darkness.

Valerie, who was right behind Peter, introduced herself as his sister.

The minister welcomed her, his eyes slipping to her belly

and then her hand, looking for a wedding ring. Valerie smiled and looked him in the eye.

Then they were walking through a sea drizzle to the van. Valerie heaved herself into the driver's seat and squeezed behind the wheel. 'Well, that's Jesus born,' she panted, meaning no offence. 'One down, one to go. I'll be glad when this baby's born an' all, I can tell you that.' She reached for the seat belt.

'Two weeks to go,' Peter said.

Valerie did the sum in her head. 'Two weeks and two days. God, I'm going to burst! I hope it's bloody on time.' She followed the line of cars into the road.

'It'll be nice,' he said.

'Nice!' Valerie swerved with shock. 'What are you talking about? It's going to be hell on earth. I hate babies.'

'A bit late to think of that now,' Peter said.

'Tell me about it. I've got friends down in Bristol driven half off their nuts. Bloody babies crying all the time. Wah-wah-wah! Nappies, feeding, bathing, shopping, walking up and down half the night. Lost their figures. Boyfriends walking out. It's going to be a nightmare.'

Peter refrained from saying that she didn't have a boyfriend to walk out on her.

'Thirteen years old anyway,' she said. 'Living here with dad. What do you know about it?'

Peter watched the wipers clear the windscreen. 'Not much,' he admitted. 'A baby in the house though. I just think it'll be nice, that's all.'

25

The Snowplough

FOR AS LONG as he could remember Christmas Day had followed the same pattern: a roaring fire, playing with his new toys, mouth-watering smells from the kitchen, a huge turkey and trifle dinner, cuddling up beside his dad to watch TV. It was a magical day.

So it seemed wrong at eleven forty-five to be washing his face, dressing in his best trousers and jersey, and setting off with Valerie in the van.

'There is no way,' she had said a few days earlier, 'when I'm lugging this brat around inside me, I am going to flog myself to death in a hot kitchen making Christmas dinner. You can forget that. I've booked a table at the Bridge Inn for one o'clock. I tried to get the Stag but they were booked solid. The Bridge will be fine.' She misinterpreted his surprise. 'Don't worry, you'll love it. At least you'd better love it, the amount it's costing.'

So they went to the Bridge in Fortness, a pretty village a dozen miles away, and although it wasn't Christmas dinner like at home, Peter enjoyed it enormously: the sparkling table, the big tree, the crooked beams hung with decorations, the choice of dishes, second helpings, Christmas music, mulled wine, the festive atmosphere. As they left the table to have coffee and mince pies in the lounge, a fat woman who had drunk more than her fill called out to Valerie:

'By gum, lass, what's that, triplets? I hope you make it home in time.' As she roared with laughter her eyes fell on Peter. 'Ee, your 'usband's a bit on the young side in't he?'

'Not a bit,' Valerie said coolly. 'Got two more at home, haven't we, Pete.' She let him pass ahead of her. 'Come on, big boy.'

They were back at four. The waiter had given Peter a huge doggy bag. Ben and Meg – it was their Christmas too – wolfed down the turkey bits and sausage-meat stuffing he fed them with his fingers.

Valerie went to bed for a couple of hours, leaving Peter to enjoy his presents. The best was a red 'Hardrock' mountain bike with knobbly tyres. Jim had taken him to buy it in Clashbay at the beginning of December. It was the biggest present he'd ever been given and very expensive, but his dad felt Peter needed something sturdy and reliable to get about and visit his friends. Now he spent an hour racing along the track, getting used to the gears and practising wheelies. It was brilliant.

When Valerie came down they made tea and cut the Christmas cake.

A while later she said, 'You won't mind if I go out for a bit will you, Pete?'

'Course not.' It was disappointing but there was no way he was going to complain. 'Where you going, as if I didn't know?'

'Well, there'll be some of the crowd there,' she said. 'Have a laugh. If you were a bit older we could go together, have a few beers.'

A few beers at the pub, Peter thought, were what you had on a Saturday not Christmas night. 'Cold weather's coming back,' he said. 'Better watch the roads, they'll be like a bottle.'

'Gritters will be out I expect.' She smiled. 'Promise I'll be careful.'

'Heavy snow too. Coming in from Europe.'

'You old fusspot.' She pulled on her coat. 'Stop worrying.'

'I'm not worrying, I'm just telling you.' He took a chocolate. 'It was on the telly 'cept you didn't see it 'cause you were in your pit.'

'I hope that's not a criticism.' She headed for the door. 'Size

I am, it's a miracle I'm ever out of it these days. Anyway, have a nice time. Ring round some of your friends, see what they got for Christmas. Don't expect I'll be late. Bye.'

She was gone. Peter pulled the door open in her wake. A hand fluttered as she drove away.

The clock struck eight. He was just in time to catch the start of a *Star Wars* movie he had been looking forward to for weeks. Juice at his feet, walnuts at his side, he sank back on the settee. But something was wrong. No sooner had the credits faded and the adventure started than he didn't want to watch any more. The joys of Christmas and the exploits of Luke Skywalker and Obi-Wan Kenobi were swamped by a sudden flood of loneliness. He tried to concentrate but it was no use, the film meant nothing to him, less than nothing. Switching off the sound, he wandered into the kitchen then upstairs to his bedroom, sat on his bed for a while, came down again and stood in the doorway looking out on the yard. The wind had fallen. The sky was clear. As if to cheer him up, the stars sparkled and the northern lights had returned. He switched off the lights and went outside. Green curtains shifted and gleamed, searchlights shone high overhead. It was a fine display. Beyond them he picked out the Great Bear, pointing one way to the Pole Star, the other way to Arcturus, a much brighter star, although at this time of year it was hidden below the horizon. He turned and looked south at Orion, the great hunter, with his belt and sword, blazing against the backdrop of a million smaller stars. They weren't really smaller, Peter knew, just smaller to him looking from the Earth. Some, like Betelgeuse at Orion's right shoulder, were supergiants, eight hundred times the diameter and fifty thousand times brighter than our sun. Others weren't individual stars at all but nebulae and distant galaxies like our own Milky Way.

He wore no jacket. The night air fingered through his clothes, icy against his warm skin. He shivered and welcomed it. Reluctant to go back indoors he stood a while longer, arms wrapped across his chest, then returned to the house and switched on the kettle. Perhaps, he thought, his spirits lifted by the wonders he had seen outside, he would give *Star Wars* another shot.

The snow didn't come that night but when it did, drifting from a mantle of cloud at eleven o'clock next morning, the ground was frozen to receive it. By the time Valerie rose from her big bed, the yard was three centimetres deep; the piebald remains of the last snowfall merged into the whitening moors. By one o'clock it was building up in gateways. Sculptured drifts were gathering at corners. By three it was falling more thickly then ever, clinging to posts and cables, obliterating the lower half of the windows. A severe weather warning on TV informed viewers that blizzard conditions were affecting roads across the country. Snowploughs were out on the motorways. Minor roads in the north were becoming impassable.

'So where does that leave us?' Valerie warmed her hands round her coffee mug. 'If dad was here he'd have the snowplough on the tractor by this time, keep the track open.'

'I can do it,' Peter said. 'At least I can try. It's not as if you need to be strong to drive the tractor.'

'You?' Valerie said.

'Well what do you want to do, drive it yourself? I'm happy to stay here as long as it lasts. You're the one always needs to get into the village.' He rubbed the condensation from the window. 'There's no way you'd get through now, look at it.'

The snow swept past, blanketing the wall of the barn.

'Our little Pete,' Valerie said after a while. 'Do you really think you can? Fit the snowplough, I mean, keep the track open?'

'I've no idea. Who else are you going to ask?'

'I don't want you to take any chances.'

'You mean just wait till the thaw comes? Let the sheep go hungry?'

'I'd rather they starved to death than you came to any harm.'

'I'll be careful. It'll be an adventure.'

He pulled on wellies and his wet-weather parka, tightening the cord round his face until all that could be seen was a pair of eyes. As he opened the door a drift fell into the hall. The second he walked outside the blizzard had him in its grip. It was one thing to plan, quite another to put that plan into action. The tractor was covered. He brushed off the snow and scratched the ice from the bucket seat and the controls. In such bitter conditions the diesel needed warming. He turned the key halfway to activate the glowplug. After thirty seconds or so it gave a little *pop,* indicating it was ready. Peter turned the key the rest of the way. The engine coughed but did not start. He turned it again, and then again, hammering the frozen machinery until at last it clattered and shuddered into life. Smoke belched from the overhead exhaust and was torn away by the gale. Gradually the faithful old engine settled down. As he put it into gear the wheels and brakes broke free. He circled the yard and drew up with the nose of the tractor close to the shed door.

The snowplough lay in a corner. It was a discarded plough from the county lorries which Jim had adapted to bolt to the front frame and power-lift of his tractor. Peter dragged aside some sacks and drums. The curved ploughshare was smeared with grease. He scrubbed it with an old meal sack, revealing the silky-smooth blades beneath. The frame to which it was welded was red with rust. He grasped a projecting arm. It was heavy. Exerting all his strength he dragged it a couple of metres. Struts dug into the crumbling concrete floor. He pulled from a different angle. Half a metre at a time, the snowplough skidded forward.

Movement in the doorway made him look up. Valerie had come to see how he was getting along.

'Here, let me give you a hand.'

'No, not in your state. I'll manage.'

'Don't be stupid, I'm not made of china. You'll strain your back. Here, give us a hold of that thingy over there.'

Peter wiped his brow.

'It's all right,' she said, 'I'll be careful. I'm not suddenly going to give birth on the floor of the shed here.'

Peter giggled. 'Like a pea-shooter.'

She stuck a finger in her mouth: *POP!*

They rolled about laughing.

'Vulgar child,' Valerie recovered first. 'I wish it *was* that easy. Here, you take hold of that bit with a hole in it. Right, on three: one, two – *pull!*'

The snowplough slid a metre forward, screeching on the concrete.

'Again,' she said, settling her strong legs. 'One, two and – '

Soon they had dragged it to the door and out into the snow. The shed gave them protection from the worst of the blizzard but their heads and shoulders were soon covered. With difficulty they manoeuvred the snowplough into position and Peter lowered the hydraulic arms to twenty centimetres. Fitting the bolts was the most difficult part and took all his strength. He heaved the ploughshare a centimetre this way, a centimetre that, all the while keeping it square to the tractor and supporting the struts at the right height. Abruptly it skidded and the heavy frame toppled on to his foot.

'Ah! Ah!' He hopped in agony until the pain went away.

Valerie said, 'Here, give it to me.' A snowy lock of hair flopped in her eyes. 'You grab that bit at the end and get ready to drop in the bolt. Now – lift!' With a little grunt of effort she straightened her legs.

The snowplough angled from the ground. The metal arms slid together. For a second the holes were lined up. Peter thrust in the bolt. Momentarily it jammed. He banged it with the heel of his hand.

'Oh!' Valerie gave a little cry and straightened, hands on her belly.

Peter stared. 'You OK?'

She bit her lip uncertainly. The stab of pain had gone away. 'Yeah. Yeah, I think so. Better not try that again though.'

She had no need. Now the first bolt was in place the second went in more easily. So did the third and the fourth. Covered like snowmen, they retreated into the shed.

Peter loosened his hood. His cheeks were aflame. 'I can manage the rest. Just got to tighten the nuts. Sure you're all right?'

'Don't know what it was. Gave me a turn there for a moment. Yeah, no problem.' She gave a happy smile. She had enjoyed working with her brother. 'Us Irwins are a tough lot.'

'That's what the Goose said.' He smiled in return. 'Listen, you go on back to the house. I've just got to get the shifting spanner. Be there in ten minutes.'

Valerie beat the snow from her clothes. 'I'll put on the kettle. Cup of tea and a slice of Christmas cake.'

'Lovely,' he said.

She disappeared across the yard.

Reception wasn't good. The driving snow clung to the aerial and made the picture flicker. Valerie liked the film better than Peter, so shortly before six he went through to the kitchen and made a big fry-up for dinner with microwaved treacle pudding and custard to follow.

'That was great!' Valerie wiped her lips on the paper towel that served for a napkin. 'After the snow, perfect.'

Peter rose to clear away.

'No,' she said. 'You made it, I'll clear up.'

'OK.' He piled peats on the fire, fell into an armchair and flicked through the TV guide. Nothing worth watching for an hour. He threw it aside and propped his stocking feet in the hearth.

Valerie was clattering dishes in the kitchen. He heard her fill the kettle. For a moment there was silence then a small startled cry: 'Oh! Ohh!'

Peter sat up. 'What is it?'

There was no reply.

'Val?'

Still silence.

He ran to the kitchen door.

Valerie stood by the table. With one hand she gripped the back of a chair. Her knuckles were white.

'Val, what is it?'

Then Peter saw that a wet patch, not a spill from the washing-up, was spreading down her legs. He stared then looked up into her face.

'What is it?' he said again. 'What's happened? Have you wet yourself?'

'I wish.' She gave a gasping laugh. 'No, my waters have broken.'

'What?' It sounded terrible. 'I don't know what you mean.'

'It's all right, there's nothing wrong.' But Valerie was frightened. 'It's just the first thing that happens.'

'Happens?'

'Oh, God!'

The wet patch was almost to her knee, creeping down and down.

'Happens when?'

'When d'you think, you bloody fool?' she said. 'I'm having a baby, aren't I?'

A fierce gust made the window rattle.

26

Headlights on the Snow

'PHONE THE DOCTOR,' she said. 'No, make it the hospital.'

Peter had never in his life phoned either. 'Tell them what?' he said.

'Martians have landed – what do you think? Tell them what I told you. My waters have broken, the baby's started. Ask them what we do now. Find out when the midwife can come.'

'The midwife!' Peter glanced at the snowed-up window. 'How's she going to get here?'

'How would I know? Maybe she'll follow a snowplough. Come in a helicopter. Just give them the bloody message.'

The phone was in the hall. He hunted in the battered address book but the hospital wasn't there. He couldn't find it in the directory either.

Valerie pushed past clutching a towel and climbed the stairs. 'No, hang on.' Her voice came from the bathroom. 'They give me a special number. God knows where I put it. Have a look on the dresser.'

Ten minutes later, swathed in Jim's dressing gown, she came down holding a blue leaflet. 'It was in my bag. Tells us what to do.' She sat on the hall chair and scanned the pages. 'Here we are, *Important Numbers*.'

Peter stood by the banisters as she punched in the number and pressed the receiver to her ear. There was no dialling tone. She rattled the rest and listened intently. The phone was dead. 'Oh, God! Don't tell me!' A look of panic came into her eyes. She held the rest down firmly, let it go and tried again.

Silence.

Her fear passed to Peter.

'What is it?' he said.

'The lines are down.' She clattered the handpiece into its cradle. 'Wouldn't you know it. Wouldn't you bloody just know it! What am I doing here? I must have been mad. How can anyone live in this godforsaken dump?'

He didn't reply.

'Baby on its way and just the two of us. Talk about a nightmare. If it wasn't so scary it would be almost funny.' She gripped the hall table and stood up. 'How'd you get on in your midwife classes?'

Peter stared.

'All right, just a joke.' She waddled into the living room. 'For God's sake get me a drink. A whisky, good strong one. Then we'll try and work out what to do.'

The blizzard continued.

'Does it hurt?' Peter said much later.

'Not too bad, just can't get comfortable.' She had tried half a dozen positions: lying on her side, kneeling, flat on her back. The right position at that particular moment was sitting on the rug with her legs straight out and her back against the settee.

They had talked about Peter cutting a path to the road when the snow eased off and phoning from Bunny's. Or if her line was down as well, heading on into the village.

'How long's it going to be?' he said.

'Till the baby comes?' Valerie shrugged her fat shoulders. 'You tell me. Four hours? Forty? Sooner the better, far as I'm concerned.'

'Are you going to be OK?'

'I sincerely hope so. Assuming nothing goes wrong. Assuming I don't *die*.' She hitched herself to one side. 'All right, don't look so scared, it's not going to happen. They said I'm a *strong, healthy young woman*. Sounds a bit like a cow.' She smiled wryly. 'Anyway, women in China and India have their babies without doctors all the time. Pop off under a hedge for an hour, have the kid, wrap it up in a shawl and back to work.'

'Is that right?'

'God knows but I read about it a couple of times. If they can, why not me?'

But Valerie wasn't feeling so confident.

''Sides, if I do pop my clogs,' she tried to make a joke of it, 'you're the chap knows what to do, aren't you? Quick trip out to the moors, couple of holes an' Bob's your uncle.'

'Shut up,' Peter said. 'Stop it.'

Snow on the aerial had made it impossible to watch television. Abruptly he realised a silence had fallen on the room. The wind had ceased its rushing and whining. He rubbed the steamed-up window. It had stopped snowing.

'Just going to look outside,' he said.

Valerie didn't reply. Her contractions were coming more frequently, every fifteen minutes or so. They weren't painful yet, at least not really painful, but as Peter spoke the spasm had her in its grip.

He went through the hall and switched on the outside light. As he opened the door, a fresh avalanche tumbled into the house. After nine hours of blizzard the yard was deeply covered – thirty centimetres at least. Walls and posts were plastered. Big cornices hung from the roofs. Around corners and gateways the swirling wind had piled the snow into elegant drifts, some waist-deep. One side of the van was buried. So were the snowplough and front wheels of the tractor.

Peter wondered if the engine would start; if the rear wheels with their deep tread would be powerful enough to cut a path to the road. When the snow was bad at Scar Hill, it was even worse on the open moor. And if he did manage to reach the road and had to continue to the village, would the county snowploughs have kept the road open? His dad had often dug them out but never at night, as far as he could remember.

A few flakes drifted through the light. But what if there was more snow on the way, heavy snow? What if it arrived when he was midway and couldn't turn back? What if he couldn't follow the track and drove into a ditch? He shivered and returned to the living room.

Valerie stood by the table. The contraction had passed and she was calm again. 'They're getting stronger,' she said. 'Ask me, the little bugger's going to be born tonight.'

'How soon?' Peter said.

'God, *I* don't know.'

'The snow's stopped.' He drew a deep breath. 'I can try and cut a way through now if you like.'

Valerie looked at him. 'I need a doctor or a midwife or somebody. I don't know anyone that's given birth all by herself.'

'Apart from those Indian women.'

'Apart from them, yeah. And you read about people giving birth in taxis and stuff. Mind, I don't want you going out there and getting stuck. There'd be no one at all then.'

'I can give it a try. If it's too deep or it starts to snow again I'll just have to come back.'

Valerie watched as he pulled on over-trousers and boots, parka, scarf, hat and gloves. He went into the kitchen and took the torch from the charger. As he came back she was struck by another contraction.

'Oh! Ohh!' Her brow furrowed, her eyes filled with pain. 'Ohhh!' With both hands she clutched the bump that was her baby. The contraction passed. Her face shone with perspiration. 'That was a big one.'

'Anything I can do before I go?'

She shook her head. 'Just make sure there's a midwife handy when your own girlfriend's having her baby.'

There seemed no answer to this. 'Sure you don't want me to stay?'

'Just go,' she said. 'Be as quick as you can. And come back safely.'

The engine of the old Massey Ferguson was packed with snow. Peter scraped it out and went through the starting procedure.

At the second attempt, in the hour of need, it clattered into boisterous life, sending clouds of exhaust into the bitter air. With a gloved hand he swept the snow from the seat and controls.

The tractor stood nose to the shed door as they had left it. He backed round the yard, smashing through deep drifts, and lifted the snowplough on its hydraulic ram to thirty centimetres above ground level to avoid catching on the rough track. A covering of snow dimmed the headlamps and he jumped down to clear them. Valerie stood watching at the window. He raised a hand, opened the throttle and started round the end of the byre.

The residue of grease made snow stick to the ploughshare. He returned to the shed for a piece of wood and a rag to scrape it away. After a while the bright blades stayed clean.

He drove slowly, though fast would have been better, cleaving a path through the drifts like the prow of a ship. For Peter this was impossible because the track was hard to see, especially in darkness with the headlights casting shadows. Time and again, long snow wreaths and levelled-out hollows hid it completely.

The night-white moors spread around him on every side, mile upon mile, vanishing into the dim distance. It was beautiful, wild and very lonely. Also, although this was a track he had travelled a thousand times, on that December night it was unfamiliar and scary. Only the tractor with its glowing dials and headlamps offered any sign of life in the frozen land. It was a countryside where living things went to sleep and did not wake up. The engine roared, but in the silence beyond there was an air of expectancy. Before long, Peter guessed, it was going to start snowing again.

Perched high on the iron seat he was unprotected and very cold. The light breeze froze his cheeks. His stomach cramped. He could hardly feel his feet. Repeatedly he took a hand from the wheel and beat his thigh to warm his stiffening fingers.

Despite this, he made good progress. Ahead lay the unbroken

snow, behind him a tumbled wake imprinted with chevron-shaped tyre tracks. It was a pity, Peter thought, to spoil the perfection. For the twentieth time he twisted to look back. He chose a bad moment for just then, beneath its white mantle, the track swung left. The tractor lurched as the front wheel slithered sideways into a treacherous ditch. Peter clung to the steering wheel to avoid being dumped on the ground.

The engine stalled. Cross with himself, he swung down to inspect the damage. Nothing seemed to be broken but the tractor had come to rest at a steep angle. The snowplough had dug into the far bank, but the rear wheels seemed to be on reasonably firm ground. With luck, Peter thought, he should be able to back out.

The engine started first turn of the key. He hoisted the snowplough and put the engine into reverse. The big wheels skidded, throwing up a spray of snow and dirt that hit him in the face. He tried a second time. The wheels spun then gripped for a moment, spun and gripped again. Slowly the tractor dragged its nose out of the ditch.

Peter wiped his face. A mile and a half to go. A short distance ahead lay the Four Crowns, the cluster of small hills where he went ferreting. It was here the drifts were likely to be deepest. Wondering how Valerie was faring, he dropped the snowplough and set off again.

He had become aware of a slight headache and a feeling in his guts as if he needed the lavatory. He'd had a fright. He was alone out there. If anything went wrong there was no one to help. There would be no one for days. And any number of things could go wrong: the engine might pack up; he could skid off the track and get stuck this time; the Sandy Brae, which was notorious for getting blocked, might be impassable; it was going to start snowing again soon, and until he was past the Four Crowns there was no place to turn. He had a choice: to drive on as planned and try to get the help Valerie needed, or abandon the tractor and start walking back to the house.

He drove on, his eyes watering with the cold. The snow was

treacherous, shadows played tricks with the light. The humps of the Four Crowns rose to meet him. As he followed the twisting track between them he was several metres off course. Tussocks of grass lay before him. One was not so innocent, for at the foot of the snowy plumes lay a large boulder. The snowplough skimmed the top but the front wheel struck it a jarring thump. The steering wheel leaped in Peter's hands and the tractor veered violently to one side. Half-frozen and slow to react, he was pitched headlong to the ground. A drift broke his fall but as he tumbled his right boot caught behind the brake pedals. His weight wrenched it free.

With the throttle open the tractor kept going. Peter saw the great back wheel bearing down upon him. He flung himself aside. It missed him by less than a centimetre, crunching past his head so close that the tyre brushed his hair.

The tractor roared on, leaving him behind. For forty metres it continued, weaving as the wheels hit hidden bumps, then swung into a thicket of whins and buried its nose in a bank. For a few seconds the tyres churned then the engine stalled.

Peter lay on his side, shaken by his fall and what had so nearly happened. Silence had returned to the moor, a silence that was total except for occasional creaks from the hot engine. He pulled himself into a sitting position, testing his limbs for damage. Apart from his right ankle he seemed to be whole – but the ankle was sore! Hot fires had started up deep inside and already it was swelling, pressing against the leather of his boot. He pulled off his gloves and probed inside his sock. What was normally sinew and bone felt puffy.

He needed the torch to examine it, not that it made much difference. He had given his ankle a nasty sprain or maybe worse. The torch was on a shelf beneath the dashboard. With difficulty he stood, but the second he put any weight on his foot the pain made him cry out. He couldn't walk. He could scarcely hobble. Even hopping made it hurt.

The seriousness of the situation burst upon him. He was a good mile and a half from home. How was he to get back? It might not be too difficult, from what he could see, to reverse the tractor out of the thorns – at least, not if he could drive. But with a foot that couldn't operate the brakes, driving was impossible.

The headlights shone in the midst of the whin bushes. Hopping at first, then crawling on hands and knees, he followed the tractor's tumbled track through the snow and pulled himself upright by the linkage system between the rear wheels. He squeezed round the side, trying to avoid the thorns. As he leaned forward, groping beneath the steering wheel for the torch, the first snowflakes drifted from the sky.

27

A Night to Remember

PETER THOUGHT HE could go no further. Three hours had passed since he left the tractor, two since the torch battery ran out, and he was still half a mile from home.

The blizzard had not ceased, closing his world to a circle of whirling flakes. Only the splashing black stream and broken snow of his outward journey, rapidly disappearing beneath the fresh snowfall, kept him on the right path. Only a few features that he knew well – a three-metre boulder, a bridge, a small ravine – recorded his progress.

At the start there had been a whiff of adventure – almost fun – about his journey, despite its serious purpose. A rock beneath the snow had changed all that. The only thing that mattered now was getting home – surviving even. At first he had tried limping and hopping but the snow was too deep, the pain too great and he kept falling. Then he tried crawling on his hands and knees, and for most of the way had continued in that manner. The driving snow whirled about him. For a while he had sheltered beneath a thorn bush, but the snow filtered through and the wind chilled him so much that he was forced to move on.

He had never imagined being so tired. Every muscle cried out for him to lie down in the snow, close his stinging eyes and go to sleep. It would have been the easiest thing in the world. But anyone who did that, as he well knew, would not wake up again, and Peter had no intention of dying that night, not while one raw knee could crawl in front of the other. The next few metres, from what he could see, appeared a little easier. He tugged the snow-caked gloves up his wrists and shuffled forward.

No one in trouble should look to nature for help: good things may happen, bad things may happen, that is all. In Peter's case it was a good thing. His reserves of strength were fast running out when, raising his head, he realised that the snow was easing. The flakes were smaller. He could see ten metres. Then fifty. Within a few minutes the snow had stopped altogether. And there, just come into sight beyond a ridge of the dim white moor, were the lights of Scar Hill. He sank to his elbows, head on his wrist. Something like a sob came into the rasping breaths in his throat.

There was no sound but a whisper of wind in the grasses.

'Help! Val!' He stood to shout. 'He-e-elp!'

From far away there came a scatter of barks. The dogs had heard him but from the house there was no response. No curtain moved. No fresh light appeared. He examined his watch, holding it to what luminescence came from the snow, and could just distinguish the hands: ten past one. Four hours since he had set off from home. Now he could see the buildings Peter knew that he was going to be safe. But it was a long way on hands and knees and by the time he reached the familiar byre, the hands of his watch had crept past two o'clock.

'Val!' he called for the twentieth time. 'Va-a-lerie! It's me! Peter!'

Surely she must have heard but there was still no movement within the house. Then there came an answering cry, almost a scream. It was a cry of pain, a long drawn out, 'Aa-hhh!' And then a moment later, 'Aaa-hhhh!'

Peter was shocked. 'Valerie? Val? What is it?' He tried to limp across the yard but even that short distance was too much. Falling to his hands and knees, he crawled through the deep snow. The door was plastered to half its height. Peter groped for the handle. Amid a white avalanche, he fell into the hall.

The fire had burned out but coming in from the night a rush of warmth hit him in the face. 'Val! I'm home!' he called and threw the door shut. Compacted snow stopped it from closing and it bounced back. He scraped the snow away and shut it again.

The welcoming walls closed around him. He sank to the floor, legs buckled beneath him.

A voice called from upstairs. 'Yeah,' he replied, beyond caring what it said. The words were repeated.

He did not respond.

Valerie, whose state was as bad or even worse than his own, came to the landing. She wore Jim's towelling dressing gown. Her brother was slumped at the bottom of the stairs. Thick snow covered his clothes. He looked half dead.

'Pete?' Her voice was anxious.

He did not move.

Her body was gripped by another contraction – they were coming more frequently now, every five or ten minutes. She squatted to ease the pain and clenched her teeth, trying not to cry out. Deep breathing was supposed to help but despite her best efforts she could not suppress a sob.

The contraction passed. Clutching the stair rail, she descended laboriously to the hall.

'Pete?'

'Hi.' He looked up and gave a wan smile. 'Couldn't get to a phone. Sorry.'

He had pulled off his gloves. Valerie saw that his palms and knuckles were bleeding.

'You're home now,' she said. 'You'll be all right.'

He nodded. 'What about you?'

She had been counting on Peter getting help. The thought of being alone as the pain got worse and maybe something went wrong terrified her. But selfish, irresponsible Valerie had a tough streak. What could be gained by frightening her young brother who had apparently nearly killed himself trying to help her? 'I'll be OK.' She smiled back. 'Bloody agony though. In a hospital they'd be giving me something for it.'

'Not if you were one of them Chinese women.'

'I suppose not. Or some poor kid on the street who daren't tell her family.'

Peter straightened his legs. 'What can I do?'

'Not much, darling. Get yourself warmed up and into some dry clothes. Just be there if I need you. Might want you to fetch me something.'

'Like what?'

'Towels, scissors, cotton wool, that sort of thing. Stuff I've bought's in a bag in my bedroom. Make sure everything's really clean. Boil the kettle and a few saucepans – least that's what they always do in the films.' She tugged the dressing gown, trying to keep herself covered. 'What happened to you then?'

So Peter told her about the accident and pulled up the leg of his over-trousers and jeans. For nearly four hours he had dragged his trailing foot through the snow. His knee was raw but that would soon scab over. More importantly, his ankle was badly swollen and purple as a grape. Shortly after he set off from the tractor he had slackened his bootlace to ease the pressure. The knot had jammed. Valerie fetched a knife and cut the lace. Peter gasped as she began to ease off his boot.

'No, leave it. Leave it!' He pushed her hands away. 'I'll do it.'

The pain was excruciating but a minute later his foot was free. He peeled off his sock. The ankle did not seem to be broken although the bruising extended almost to his toes and up the lower part of his leg. Cautiously he flexed his foot up and down and from side to side. It hurt but there was no agony of grating bones and nothing seemed to be out of place.

'A nasty sprain,' pronounced Valerie who was addicted to hospital dramas and had learned more about childbirth from TV than at her ante-natal classes. 'Needs a cold compress. Soak it in iced water.'

'Iced water! You've got to be joking. I'm freezing!'

Valerie was seized by another contraction. 'Oh, no! Ah! Aahh!' She squatted again and tried to bear the terrible pressure that was forcing her baby to be born.

Her muscles relaxed. The pain passed. Glistening with

sweat, she looked up with desperate eyes. 'Oh, bugger!' she said. 'Sorry, Pete, but it's sore! If you bloody men had to put up with it maybe you'd take a bit ...' She began to haul herself back up the stairs.

Peter called, 'Hey, it's got nothing to do with me.'

'Not yet,' she said and disappeared into the bedroom.

He sat a while longer then rose and began to strip off his clothes. Too tired to care, he left them in a melting heap on the floor. Reduced to underpants, he hopped and crawled upstairs to the bathroom. The water in the tank was boiling. He ran a deep bath, poured in a capful of Valerie's hibiscus-scented bath oil and subsided into the steam.

His hands and knees burned like fire in the hot water. The pain subsided to a tingle and he rinsed them gently with the tips of his fingers. His ankle was soothed until the throb was no more than a pulse.

Slowly the ice melted from his bones. After his struggle in the snow the peace would have been perfect had not Valerie, in the adjoining room, suffered two more contractions and sworn loudly at the mounting pain.

Some time after three, when he had dressed and bound his ankle with an old elastic bandage, Peter went to her room. Valerie lay in the big bed, propped up on pillows. She looked dreadful, her hair tangled, face greasy and eyes full of pain. He stayed by the door, trying not to look at her fat knees, wide-spread and protruding from the crumpled duvet.

'I just wondered if there was, you know, anything you wanted.'

'I could murder a cup of coffee, thanks. And if you'd pass me that box of skin fresheners on the dressing table. I feel like hell. Oh, and my hairbrush. And maybe a dab of Miss Dior.'

Somehow he carried the coffee upstairs without spilling it. Thick snow whirled beyond the window. An electric fire blazed by the wardrobe. The room smelled of sweat, cigarettes and a spring-like perfume.

Valerie smiled gratefully. 'You're a good lad. We'll get

through it somehow. Don't think it'll be too long now.'

'Do you want me to stay for a while?'

'If you were my boyfriend, too bloody right.' She sipped her coffee. 'But since you're my thirteen-year-old brother, no, I'll be fine. Thanks all the same.'

Greatly relieved, he left her looking better and hopped back downstairs to make himself a mug of tea and several rounds of toast. As he did so he thought of Ben and Meg out in the shed. It would be nice to have them in the house but there was no way he was venturing back into the blizzard. They had been fed, they would be fine until the morning. It would be good to have the fire going too, but he was too tired even to think about it and pulled the rug round his shoulders like a shawl. He carried his tea and toast to the living room and slumped on the settee. They tasted good but after the hardships of the night his eyes were closing. And before he knew it, the slice of toast he was eating fell butter-side down in his lap and Peter was conquered by sleep.

It was a sleep so profound that for two hours he did not stir. Even Valerie's shouts, as the waves of pain came faster and faster until it was all one continuous agony and she tried to push her baby out into the world, barely reached him.

But at last, a little after five o'clock, a cry so loud and long it might have woken their father out there on the snowy moor, made him sit up with a start. For a moment he was dazed. A sickening jolt to his ankle brought him back to the present. Something had woken him. What was it? A movement at the window caught his eye. It was still snowing. He sat still and listened. From upstairs there was no sound at all.

'Val? … Val?' He called loudly but there was no reply. 'Valerie, is everything OK? Are you all right?'

The house remained silent. Then there was a sound. A thin, coughing cry like a mewling cat.

Peter felt the hair prickle on the back of his neck.

The crying grew louder.

He threw back the rug and hopped towards the stairs.

28

Daisy

PETER STOOD OUTSIDE the bedroom door. All was silent but for the rush of wind in the skylight and the sound of a baby crying. He tapped and waited, scared what he might discover if he just walked in. There was no reply. He tapped again, harder.

'All right, all right, I can hear you.' Valerie sounded different.

'Can I come in?'

'You'll have to speak up. I can't hear you above this bloody noise.'

'I said, is it OK for me to come in?'

'Give us a few minutes. And bring some clean towels. And a whisky, for God's sake.'

He waited a little longer. 'What is it?'

'It's a panda, what do you think?'

'I mean is it a boy or a girl?'

'Pete, I'm just too tired.'

Five minutes later, clutching an armful of towels and trying not to spill the drink, he hopped back up the stairs. The baby had stopped crying. He heard Valerie whispering, 'There! Sshhh!'

When he knocked she was ready for him. 'OK, come on in.'

He pushed the door wide.

Valerie sat up against the pillows. She looked in a state of shock. Her face was white, her hands and wrists streaked with blood. On a towel in her lap, the first thing he saw, lay a newborn baby. It was a tiny girl. Her face was crumpled, her skin red and blotchy. Valerie had cleaned her eyes, mouth and nose but the rest of her was streaked with blood and some sort of creamy white stuff. An ugly twisted cord, about two centimetres in diameter and pulsing with blood, ran from her belly and disappeared beneath the duvet.

Peter stared in amazement. Ever since Valerie came home her belly had been enormous, like a beach ball. Out of it, all at once, had come this perfect little girl, messy in a way he had not imagined but absolutely complete: two skinny legs and feet fringed with ten toes, two arms and tiny fingers clenched into fists, lots of dark hair, slitty eyes, a button nose and pretty red lips. It was a miracle.

He set the drink on the sea-chest Jim had used as a bedside table. 'Can I touch her?'

'Well, she's not going to break.' Valerie reached for the glass. After what she had been through over the past few hours she thought she deserved it, never mind what they'd told them about alcohol at the clinic. 'In fact you can do better than that. Which is the softest of them towels?'

Peter felt them and handed her a pink one.

'Yeah, that'll do.' She passed it back. 'Wipe off some of the gunge will you. Give her a bit of a clean up.'

He was taken aback. 'What about – ?' He indicated the umbilical cord.

'Oh, yeah. That's got to be cut.' She thought for a moment. 'Did you boil up the kettle and a couple of saucepans like I told you?'

'I fell asleep but they're on now.'

'Right.' She shut her eyes. 'God, I feel washed out. What you've got to do's give the kitchen scissors a good wipe then drop them in the boiling water. And we've got to tie it off. I've been thinking what we can use. Is the ribbon still round that box of chocolates – the big one you give me for Christmas?'

'I think so.'

'Well give it a rinse-out and drop that in too.'

'The saucepan?'

'Well not the waste bucket.'

'How long for?'

'I don't know. Five minutes?'

Peter couldn't take his eyes from the baby and stroked her cheek with the back of a finger. Her skin was warm and unbelievably soft. Momentarily the crying stopped. Her eyes cracked open, dark blue and out of focus, a little squint. He touched her fist and the fingers opened halfway. He shuffled his finger into her palm and her fingers closed around it.

'She's gorgeous.'

'Gorgeous?' Valerie was surprised. 'I don't know if that's the word I'd use.'

'She is,' he said and leaned down to plant a kiss on her blotchy forehead.

The baby also seemed surprised. At point-blank range she looked into his face then turned her head aside and gazed across the room.

Peter smiled and stood back. He had forgotten his ankle. The sudden pain made him cry out and he fell against the bed.

'You OK?' Valerie was concerned.

'Give us a minute.' The pain ebbed. 'Scissors and ribbon. Anything else?'

'Yeah,' she said. 'A lifetime's supply of the pill. I'm not going through this lot again, I'll tell you flat.' She looked down with neither love nor the lack of it at the baby in her lap and took another sip of whisky.

'Have you thought what you might call her?'

'Not really. I thought she'd be a boy. I was going to call him Paul.' She thought for a moment. 'Could call her Paula, I suppose.'

'Paula? Paula Irwin? It sounds terrible.'

'Pauline then. I don't know. I'm too tired, Pete. And it bloody well hurts. We'll talk about it later, OK?' She slumped back on the pillows.

The saucepans were boiling hard, filling the kitchen with

steam. Carefully he wiped the scissors from the drawer, untied the knots in the red Christmas ribbon and dropped them into the bubbling water.

Pauline Irwin? It sounded all right but there was a girl at school called Pauline. No one liked her much because she was always telling tales. He sat at the table to wait five minutes. Mary Irwin? Barbara – hopeless. Alison? Louise? Jennie, that was nice – Jennie Irwin. Peter was a great reader, he liked names. Rachel, that was nice too. Sharon, after their mother – no! Kylie? Becky? There was a pen on the table. He ran through the names of some other girls in his class and wrote them on the back of an envelope: Marie ... Hazel ... Adrienne ... Jacqui ... None seemed right. Rose? That was nice – Rose Irwin. He underlined it. What about other flowers: Heather? Buttercup? Dandelion? Daisy? Daisy Irwin. He pictured the tiny girl upstairs. Daisy. Yes, Daisy was just right. He wrote it in his best handwriting. Then printed it in capitals. Daisy Irwin. His niece Daisy.

He had forgotten the time. Ten minutes had passed. Condensation dripped from the cooker hood. He turned down the heat and took a fork from the drawer. Carefully he fished the scissors and ribbon from the saucepan, dried them on a clean towel and set them on a plate.

Valerie had wrapped the baby in the pink towel. The thick umbilical cord had stopped pulsing. She seemed content.

'Did you wash your hands?'

He nodded.

'Right.' Valerie opened the towel. 'About five centimetres from her belly button. Cut off a bit of the ribbon and tie it round the cord. Quite tight. Don't worry, it won't hurt her.'

Peter did as he was told. The ribbon, boiled to a pale pink, gripped tight and he fastened it in a reef knot.

'Now another one a bit further along.'

'Here?'

'That's fine.'

He tied it and snipped the ends of ribbon short.

'Now cut the cord between the two.'

'Are you sure?'

'Well she can't stay joined to me for the rest of her life.'

So Peter took the big scissors and cut through the cord. It was tough and he had to press quite hard. There was little blood, just a couple of drops on the towel.

'God, that's a relief.' Valerie puffed out her cheeks. 'No longer attached to the little bloodsucker. Maybe start getting back to normal now.'

The stub of cord stuck out from the baby's belly. 'What'll happen to it?' he said.

'Drop off in a few days. Got to keep it clean and dry that's all.' She folded the baby in the pink towel. 'Could you give her that wipe now, Pete?'

'Yeah, if you like.'

'Sit on the bed then.'

He made himself comfortable.

'Be sure you support her head that's all.' Valerie lifted the bundle into his arms.

Very carefully Peter cradled the baby against his chest. She sneezed and turned red. 'Is the room warm enough?'

'Warm enough! Heater's been on all night, it's like a bloody oven.'

For five minutes he cuddled his tiny niece, examined her long fingernails, pressed his cheek against the smeary top of her head. Then he set her on the duvet and unfolded the towel. 'What do I clean her with?'

'Just use the end of the towel, it's nice and soft. Don't need to be too fussy, I'll give her a wash later.'

Very gently Peter wiped the baby's face and head, her chest and back and arms and legs. She didn't like it and began to wail.

He was wrapping her in a fresh towel when Valerie grimaced. Although the baby was born, her contractions were not quite finished. She nodded towards a carrycot which lay at the bedside among bloody tissues, sweet wrappers, magazines and other debris. 'Put her in there would you, Pete. Afraid you'll have to leave for a few minutes.'

He looked at her anxiously.

'No, I'm OK. It's just the afterbirth. You don't want to know, I'm telling you. Come back when I call.'

Supporting the baby's head carefully, Peter laid her on the soft blanket which lined the carrycot and covered her with another.

Valerie was watching. 'You'll make a good dad one day,' she said.

He gathered up the rubbish and hopped to the door.

'Fetch us a couple of things when you come back,' she said. 'Do you mind? A facecloth and some warm water – drop of Dettol.' She winced again. 'An' a decent-sized poly bag – one of them Co-op bags.'

He asked her again: 'Have you thought of a name?'

'When you come back,' she said. 'Go now.'

The clock struck six. Peter sat doodling names at the table. His eyes were closing. He pushed back his chair and rested his head on his arms.

Valerie's voice reached him from a great distance. Hardly knowing where he was, he sat up. Half an hour had passed.

'Ready when you are,' she called.

'Coming.' Wearily he pushed himself to his feet. He ached all over. His hands hurt. He turned them to the light. His palms and knuckles, raw with crawling, were covered by a thin scab. He pulled up the legs of his jeans and saw that his knees, too, which had been red and weeping, were mostly dry.

The things Valerie had asked for lay on a chair. It was difficult to carry water in the washing-up bowl, so he had cleaned a small red bucket that stood beneath the sink. Carrying it in one hand and stuffing the bag into a pocket, he limped through the house and climbed the stairs yet again.

She heard his footsteps. 'All clear, sweetheart. Come on in.'

No one could accuse Valerie of lacking guts or spirit. Just

an hour after giving birth, she had tidied the bed, combed her hair and now sat up against the pillows feeding the baby at her breast. In the days and weeks that followed, breast-feeding became routine and neither she nor Peter thought anything about it, but that first time both were shy and she kept herself covered.

'She was just lying there, little thing,' Valerie explained. 'I thought she might be hungry. Didn't know what else to do.'

Peter looked away.

Two towels, one containing something and wrapped in the other, lay on the floor. 'Don't look. Don't even ask,' Valerie said. 'It's the afterbirth. Just put it in the poly bag, tie the handles and drop it in the dustbin.'

Peter carried it out to the landing.

'Thanks,' Valerie said. 'If you hadn't been here I don't know how I'd have managed.'

The baby made a face and a small slather of milk ran down into the bed.

'Oh, my God!' Valerie mopped it up with the towel. 'When she's finished I'll give myself a wipe down. And then, if you'd be an angel, I could kill a cup of coffee and a handful of biscuits. Have a bath later.' She hesitated. 'And when I get up do you think you could change the bed and put all the sheets and stuff in the wash?'

Peter could hardly keep his eyes open. 'Course,' he said and nodded towards the baby who seemed to have fallen asleep. 'What does it feel like? It must be queer.'

'Feeding her, you mean? Bit sore. No earth-mother stuff about bonding with your baby like it says in the magazines, I'll tell you that for nothing. Not for me anyway.' She hitched the baby comfortable. 'But that's the worst over, thank God. We've been lucky. Never again though. That is it! I'm telling you.'

Peter pulled the envelope from his pocket and sat on the bed. 'Have you thought what you might call her?'

'Not really. Like I said, I thought she was going to be a boy.'

'I made a list when I was downstairs. Do you want to hear it?'

'Why not?' She blinked wearily. 'It's not as if I'm going out or anything.'

Peter read her the names he liked best.

'I like Jennie,' she agreed. 'Jennie Irwin, that's nice.'

'Short for Jennifer,' Peter said.

'Oh, I don't like Jennifer so much. Maybe I could just call her Jennie. And did you say Rosie? That's nice too. What about Lee-Ann? I had a friend called Lee-Ann once. And Kelly.' She listened to the sound of the names and looked down at the blotchy baby on her breast. 'Kelly Irwin, what do you think?'

'Can I tell you my favourite,' he said. 'Daisy.'

'Daisy,' Valerie said. 'Like daisies in a field. Daisy May.'

'I think it sounds just right for her,' he said. 'Daisy Irwin.'

'Yes, I like that too,' she said. 'You're good with names. Daisy May Irwin. It's got a ring to it. Specially if her hair turns blonde. It might do as well, her dad was fair. He had a blond ponytail.'

'Was that the one called Chris? Him that played the tin whistle? The busker?'

'With his dog, yeah. Least I reckon it was Chris.'

She had been thinking about him recently, remembering his wispy beard and easygoing blue eyes. Lying against his long lean body in bed – at least on the mattress, they didn't have a bed. A good-looking man if he'd taken the trouble. Clever, too, all those books he used to read. They'd had some good times together: nights at the pub, bonfire parties on the beach, going with the crowd to Glastonbury and the folk festivals. Of course it was the dog he had loved really, the only thing he loved when it came down to it, but she had understood that from the start. All the same, when they broke up it had hurt, although at that time she didn't realise she was pregnant.

'I did tell him, you know.' She looked Peter in the eye. 'Went back to the flat but he wasn't interested. Didn't even get up from the settee. 'So what do you expect me to do about it?' he says. Scared stiff I might come after him for money. Money! Him! That's a laugh. Got himself fixed up with another girl by that time anyway. Useless bloody article.'

Peter stood silent. He had heard most of it before, this life Valerie had made for herself down in Bristol, and before that travelling the country with Tinker's Cuss. It didn't seem much to leave home for – but none of that mattered now. The only thing that did matter, not that he could see much of her at that moment, was the little girl in his sister's arms. The rest was history.

She tidied a curl of her baby's hair with a red fingernail. 'You Chris's daughter then, are you? Eh? Daisy Irwin? Is that who you are?' She pushed back a corner of the duvet. 'This is your Uncle Peter.'

Peter was startled. Uncle Peter? How could he be Uncle Peter? He hadn't even had a sister for the last four years. He was only thirteen.

29

New Year's Day: Saving the Sheep

FOR FOUR DAYS the north-east wind held the country in its icy grip. Pipes froze. Train services were disrupted. Cars were buried beneath drifts. In the beleaguered towns and cities, heaps of dirty snow blocked the pavements. Out in the countryside, woods stood dark in a landscape that was white from horizon to horizon.

On the fifth day the wind backed into the southwest and rain blew in from the Atlantic. The snow melted and swollen rivers burst their banks. Cattle drowned. Houses built on low-lying ground were flooded.

On the moors which surrounded Scar Hill, the heather shed its heavy load and sprang upright. Slabs of wet snow slid from the roof and landed *crump* beneath the windows. Peter's snowballs became dripping balls of ice.

By this time he could put weight on his ankle and hobbled about the house with the aid of a walking stick that had belonged to Jim's father. If the ankle was strapped tightly, he thought, he might be able to operate the foot brake on the tractor.

Hogmanay, the last day of the old year, passed with lashing rain and the yard turned to a quagmire of slush. But New Year's Day broke fair, and when Peter went out to release the dogs, he saw that three-quarters of the snow had vanished from the track. For ten metres at a stretch the dark earth showed through. The deep drift at the end of the byre had melted to a wet white strip.

'Val.' He tapped at his sister's door and went in.

Though Peter gave Daisy a bottle and changed her nappies as often as his sister, that night the baby had been restless and Valerie had had little sleep. As he drew back the curtains, admitting a dazzle of winter sunshine, and announced that the track was open again, all she could manage was a muffled, 'Go away.'

'Come on,' he said. 'Get up. The track's passable I reckon. We can go into the village and phone the nurse. Knock up old Robbie and get him to sell us some bread and milk and stuff.'

'You go.'

'How can I go?' he said. 'I can't drive on the road. They'll want to know where dad is and everything. Come on, I'll make you a coffee.'

Daisy, whose blotchy skin was turning to roses and cream, was sound asleep in her carrycot. Peter brushed her cheek with his knuckles and headed downstairs.

Although Daisy had been given a feed at five she had to be fed again and changed. Then Valerie took for ever getting ready so it was well after eleven before they could set off. Peter drove the van while Valerie, who had not yet bought a car seat for the baby, nursed Daisy at his side.

Swollen by the melting snow the stream rushed alongside, spilling onto the track. The slush was treacherous. Progress was slow. Every metre of the way, Peter recalled his nightmarish crawl a few nights earlier. As the track wound through the Four Crowns the tractor came into view, cleared of snow by the heavy rain. He saw the rock he had hit, clearly visible now, with tall plumes of grass nodding above. The tractor stood as he had left it, snowplough buried in the thorny bank.

He drew up. 'What do you think?' he asked Valerie. 'Shall I see if it'll start? Lead the way?'

'And I drive the van you mean?' she said. 'What about the baby?'

'Oh, yeah.' It hadn't occurred to him.

'Leave it,' she said. 'It'll be there tomorrow. We're doing fine, let's get on into the village.'

Two drifts brought them to a halt. Peter dug out the slush banked up beneath the wheels and in a few minutes they were on their way again. Slewing and slithering, they reached the road without further difficulty. As he got out to open the gate, Bunny Mason was leading Molly, her red and white cow, across the side of the hill.

'Hello there, Peter. Happy New Year!' She waved a cheery arm. 'I've been wondering how you and your dad are coping out there on the moors. And your sister too, of course.'

'OK,' he shouted back. 'The phone line's been down. We're just heading into the village.'

'Yes, everyone this side's been cut off. Hope to have us reconnected sometime tomorrow. Robbie's had a delivery though and he's staying open till four. Wouldn't waste any time. The rate people are stocking up you'd think there was an ice age coming.'

'Thanks.'

'How's your dad keeping? Haven't seen him around for a while.'

'Busy with the sheep.' His heart thudded. 'Had to dig some of them out.'

'No wonder after a blizzard like that. Poor things, did he lose any?'

'One or two I think.'

'Oh dear! Well tell him to look in for his New Year when he's got the time. You too, of course. And your sister. What's her name again?'

'Valerie.'

'Valerie, that's right. How does she enjoy being back home?'

'Not much. She's had her baby though. Five days ago.'

'What! In all that snow?'

'Yeah.'

'By herself? Oh, my goodness! How is she?'

'She's all right.'

'And the baby?'

'A little girl. She's all right too. We're just going to phone the nurse.' He dragged the gate wide.

'Just a minute. Don't rush away.' Bunny tied the cow to a strand of fence wire and trudged across the hillside. She wore thick trousers, a quilted green anorak and a bright knitted hat from which her grey hair escaped in disarray.

Valerie wound down the window.

'Hello, dear.' Bunny leaned forward to see Daisy, sleeping quietly and wrapped in a chequered baby blanket. 'Oh, what a beautiful little girl.' She moved a fold to see better. 'What are you calling her?'

'Daisy,' Valerie said. 'Daisy May.'

'Oh, she's just lovely,' Bunny said. 'And you there all by yourself.'

'Not quite. I had dad – and Peter of course.'

'Well yes, I know. But it's not the same as being in a hospital is it?'

'I suppose not,' Valerie said briefly. 'I've never had a baby before. We managed anyway.'

'Just heroic if you ask me.' Bunny smiled. 'And you're looking so well. How does your dad like being a grandfather?'

'All right, I suppose. I never asked him.' Though the woman was nice, Valerie did not appreciate so many questions.

Bunny sensed it and stood back. 'Well I think it's just lovely, a new baby and the family all together. If there's anything I can do to help, you out there with your dad so busy and your brother going back to school in a few days, don't hesitate to ask. I've had three of my own and I know what it can be like.'

'Thanks.'

Valerie and Peter swapped places.

Bunny shut the gate as they drove off. 'Happy New Year,' she called again to the open window.

'You too,' Peter called back. 'Happy New Year.'

Snow was banked high at both sides of the Sandy Brae but the gritting lorries had been out and the road was clear.

'Nosy old bat,' Valerie said as she changed gear.

'No she's not, she's nice.' Peter made Daisy comfortable on his lap. 'Asking us in for the New Year though. What are we going to do?'

'Nothing,' Valerie said. 'Forget it. If she asks again, say dad's too busy or he's in bed with bronchitis or something.'

They went to the shop first. Peter stayed in the van with Daisy to avoid unwanted attention while Valerie crossed the road with her purse. A number of women noticed that she walked gingerly and was no longer pregnant but Valerie's bold stare prevented them from asking questions. The bread was nearly finished but Mr McRobb, who didn't like the Irwins much, let her have a couple of loaves, a two-litre carton of milk and a few other things to keep them going until the end of the holiday. As Valerie left, the tongues began wagging.

She rang the district nurse from the red phone box up the road. After such severe weather the nurse was run off her feet but promised to look in that afternoon. Since she drove a Land Rover for her work, the track would be no problem. She would, she said, arrange for Valerie and Daisy to be examined at the post-natal department of the Royal Infirmary in Clashbay the following day.

After lunch, leaving Daisy asleep in her carrycot for a few minutes, Valerie drove Peter to the Four Crowns to collect the tractor. Then, while she waited for the nurse, he drove to the lower pasture with a load of hay and sheep nuts to see how the ewes had fared in the bad weather. During the blizzard they had huddled in several groups in the lee of a drystone dyke and been covered over. Their breath and the warmth of their bodies had melted the snow around them so that they lay in a number of caves, the walls thin enough to provide oxygen. The thaw had released them.

As Peter drove up the track, the snowplough clearing the last of the drifts and the trailer bouncing behind, they gathered at the gate, clamouring for food. Ben and Meg stood watching as Peter forced the gate open and carried the first shoulder of hay to the racks. The sheep pressed around his legs, baaing loudly. The second he tossed in the hay and pulled some through the bars, they began tearing at it ravenously. The troughs were full of snow. He knocked it out and filled them to the brim with high-energy sheep nuts. There was no shortage of water; fifty metres away the burn gushed from the moor. The sheep were more in danger of being swept downstream than suffering from thirst.

Five had not survived the blizzard. Peter dragged them from the remains of the drifts, their fleece sodden and yellow against the snow. It wasn't possible to tow the trailer up the hillside, so he disengaged it and drove up on the tractor. It took all his strength to hoist the dead animals on top of the snowplough. One at a time he carried them down and loaded them aboard the trailer. Then he drove to a rocky outcrop well away from the pasture and dumped them in the open where crows and other scavengers would reduce them to fleece and bones, and what remained would rot away quickly.

Five ewes, each carrying one or two lambs, meant a loss of about thirteen animals. It could have been worse, much worse, and as Peter drove home his mood was one of relief. His fears since the snowfall had been laid to rest and although his ankle hurt, it had not prevented him from driving the tractor. The sheep had been fed and he had dealt with the carcases. His dad, he thought, would have been proud of him.

30

Valerie Goes to a Dance

THE NEW YEAR gathered pace.

The blizzard was past and though hard frosts and more snow were yet to come, they were nothing compared with what had gone before.

Valerie presented Daisy and herself at the maternity unit and both were found to be in excellent good health, although blood tests and nicotine-stained fingers revealed her smoking and drinking habits. 'It's not good for your baby, Valerie,' the nurse told her. 'I know, you're quite right, I am trying to cut down,' said Valerie, hoping they wouldn't keep her much longer because she was desperate for a fag and due to meet Maureen Bates at the Stag and Hound in fifteen minutes.

By the time school started on Monday, January the sixth, Peter's ankle was so much recovered that with an effort he could walk without a limp, though running was mostly a matter of hopping, and football was out of the question. 'I fell on the ice,' he told friends and teachers. 'It's getting better.'

Valerie ran into Bunny at a coffee shop in Clashbay. 'Your dad's all right, is he?' Bunny said. 'I don't mean to be inquisitive, but I often used to see him at the gate, you know. I haven't seen him for ages.' Valerie, her hair freshly shampooed and set, explained that Jim had been called south again to visit his sick brother in Newcastle. Peter was looking after the sheep in the meantime. No, there was nothing they needed, thanks all the same. She wasn't sure when her dad would be returning.

Imperceptibly the days lengthened. In the third week of January, storm-force winds heaped the sea to a fury and blew spray high above the headlands. Valerie drove Peter to the harbour to check that the *Audrey*, turned upside down above the shingle, was safe from the tumult.

A few days later, his sprain no more than an occasional twinge, he walked across the hill with the dogs to visit Jim's grave. Some of the stalks with which he had covered it had blown away, the rest lay sodden on the peat. A few blades of grass, the first signs of healing, had sprouted round the edges. Now he was there Peter wondered what to do. For a while he stood remembering and trying not to think of his dad down there in the wet earth. Briefly he went on his knees but no words came and the ice-cold moss soaked through his jeans. So he stood and told Jim about Valerie, and Daisy, and the dead sheep, and his crawl through the snow. Then he asked God to look after his dad and all of them. The cross was lopsided. He straightened it and waited a few minutes longer then walked on to cast an eye over the hill-wintering sheep.

Week by week, regular as clockwork, Jim's Social Security benefits went into the bank. Valerie bought a car seat for the baby and filled her days by driving out to see friends. In other people's kitchens and living rooms she drank coffee and wine, listened to their tales of clubs, bars and boyfriends, and moaned that because of Daisy her life wasn't her own any more. Never again, she said, and bored them with tales of dirty nappies, milky vomit and sleepless nights. People cooed over the beautiful baby, kissed her curls and rocked her in sympathetic arms when she cried. Valerie was happy for them to do so. 'Just for God's sake keep taking the pill,' she told her girlfriends, secretly hoping they might get caught out too. 'I got careless and look where it landed me. Bloody men, what do they care?' She was never unkind to Daisy but like her mother, who had been even younger when she was born, Valerie was resentful and longed for the day when she could leave the baby with Peter and go out for a night to enjoy herself.

What she failed to tell her friends was that in the evenings and at weekends it was Peter as often as herself who bathed his little niece and made her bottle and nursed her when she was fretful. For whatever reason, perhaps her inner turmoil, when Valerie tried to quieten Daisy she was often unsuccessful, whilst there was something in Peter to which the tiny girl responded and within a few minutes her wailing subsided to hiccups and shortly afterwards contentment and sleep.

It was strange. Before Valerie came home Peter had never given a thought to babies, no more than any boy who encountered them in shops or at a friend's house and saw how annoying they could be with their crying and constant demand for attention. What was a baby to a boy whose days were crowded and all life's excitements lay waiting to be explored? But now, when Peter sat on the settee with Daisy, he felt as he sometimes did with Ben, and as he had felt sitting there with his dad's arm around him. It was a warm feeling, something deep inside. Ben was his best pal in all the world. With his dad he had felt safe and protected. And now, though Peter never thought about it that way, he wanted to do the same for the helpless little scrap on his knee.

He took a twenty-pound note from the tin in the byre and bought an expensive book on baby care from the shop in Clashbay. Then he took a ten-pound note and bought a CD of nursery songs which he sang to Daisy in his cracked voice.

Valerie saw how often the baby looked up into his face and gave her gummy smile. 'What have you got that I haven't?' she said crossly. 'You're a boy, for God's sake. You should be out playing football and getting into trouble, not nursing babies. You're meant to find babies boring.'

'Do you want me to stop then?' he said.

'No, I don't,' she exclaimed. 'It's just not normal, that's all.'

Peter shrugged. 'Who says?' He rocked Daisy a little longer then set her down on her back and pulled the blanket to her chin. Ben put his head into the carrycot and sniffed briefly then looked up with tawny eyes. 'Who's my good boy!' Peter patted him and took the dogs outside while he prepared the hay and sheep nuts for the next day.

January slipped into February and one Friday, when Daisy was six weeks old, Valerie announced that if Peter would look after her for the evening, she would like to go with Maureen and some others to a dance in the nearby village of Brathy. There was to be a live band. She had got him some cans and crisps and a couple of videos from the library van.

'What time will you be home?' he said.

'Not be that late, it finishes at midnight.'

'So you'll be back by one.'

'Before that, I expect,' she said. 'Too cold to hang about.'

Peter wasn't going anywhere. He often looked after Daisy in the evening. 'OK,' he said, remembering the dance nights when Valerie was fifteen. 'If you promise.'

'I said so, didn't I? Blimey, you're getting as bad as dad.'

At eight o'clock, bathed, perfumed, made-up and wearing – although her figure had not recovered yet – a clinging silver top and red matador pants, she pulled on Jim's warm overcoat and set off to meet the others in the lounge bar of the Tarridale before going on to the dance.

It was the first dance she'd been to since she came home – in fact the first dance she'd been to for a couple of years. Her earrings swung. Beyond the mascara her eyes shone with excitement. Peter and Daisy went to the door to see her off. One of the rear lights on the van was broken. 'Bye. Hope the videos are good. I'll not be late.' A hand with red and silver nails fluttered from the window. *Toot-toot!* She drove off towards the village.

But Valerie *was* late. She wasn't home by one o'clock. She wasn't home by breakfast time. She wasn't even home by midday.

And when she did finally turn up at four o'clock in the afternoon, she wasn't alone.

31

Matt

HIS NAME WAS Matt and he was an HGV lorry driver. The previous day he had driven a load of fertiliser 250 miles from Glasgow and delivered it along the coast. It was dark by the time he finished so he had left his vehicle, an eighteen-wheel, forty-four ton articulated lorry, on a patch of ground the far side of Tarridale and gone to the pub for a drink. A couple of lads had invited him along to the dance at Brathy.

Eighteen hours later, as the old white van swung into the yard that Saturday afternoon, it was Valerie who was driving. Peter could not see the man beside her, but as they stopped he pulled her close and gave her a kiss. Briefly she responded then pushed him away and looked towards the window where Peter stood watching.

Daisy was awake, her carrycot on the settee. He was standing beside it as they came into the room.

Valerie did not run to her baby, she introduced her friend. 'Matt, this is my brother Peter I was telling you about. Peter, this is Matt. I met him at the dance.'

Peter nodded watchfully. For a night and a day Valerie had abandoned him without a word. He was deeply angry. He did not like her bringing her boyfriend home, the boyfriend she'd so obviously spent the night with, not after they'd been going out for a while but straight after meeting him.

Matt held out his hand, a big hand roughened with work and spotted with freckles. 'Hi there, Peter. Hope you don't mind your sister bringing me back to the house. She's quite a girl.'

He was a rangy man, close on six feet, with blue eyes, ginger curls and two days' growth of stubble. He had not changed to go to the dance and still wore his work clothes, jeans and a shapeless sweater. His age, Peter discovered later, was twenty-five and he was due back in Glasgow with the lorry that same afternoon. Instead, he had followed Valerie up the Sandy Brae and parked in the old quarry where his huge vehicle was hidden from the road.

'Boss is going to be bloody angry,' he said. 'Get my cards most like, but hey, worth it to meet a girl like your sister here.' At which he smiled, showing a missing tooth, and rested a familiar hand on her neck.

'Sorry I didn't ring, Pete,' she said. 'I tried to, but the batteries were out on his mobile.'

'Couldn't you have phoned from the village?'

'Well, I suppose but it was lashing and we were in the lorry.' At last she crossed to Daisy. 'She didn't give you any trouble, I hope.'

He was tempted to say, 'Yeah, she cried all night, hardly slept a wink,' but a glance at the contented baby made him change his mind. 'No problem. Wanted a feed at two and I had to change her, then another feed at eight. Good as gold.'

'This yours then, the one you were telling me about?' Matt was looking over Valerie's shoulder. 'What did you call her – Buttercup or something?'

'Daisy,' she said.

'That's right. Pretty little thing.'

She looked round. 'You got any children, Matt?'

'Yeah, two. Boy and a girl. Live with my wife – my ex-wife that is, like I told you. Don't see them very often.'

'How old are they?'

'Boy was two when I went inside. That means they'll be,' he worked it out, 'six and seven. Stay with Suzy and her partner down in Liverpool.' He saw Peter looking at him. 'What's up? Me being in the slammer?'

Peter was silent.

'Nothing so very terrible. Nicked a few cars, that's all. Needed the cash, got in with a bad crowd. Couple of months in Barlinnie. Did me no harm.' He pulled Valerie to his side. 'All that's behind me now.'

She looked up at him. 'I hope so, Matt.' Shrugging free of his arm, she lifted Daisy and cuddled her against a shoulder. The baby did not like being disturbed. Her face crumpled and she started to cry.

'For goodness sake,' Valerie said. 'What's wrong with you now? I'm your mother, you silly girl. Ssshhhh!' Bouncing her, she walked round the room. Briefly Daisy was comforted but she wasn't happy and soon began to cry again. 'Are you hungry then? Do you want a bottle?'

'Shouldn't think so,' Peter said. 'I fed her half an hour ago.'

'Does she need changing then?'

He shrugged and she felt the nappy, putting her nose down to sniff.

Peter left her to it. 'Better go and feed the sheep. Should have done it this morning but I kept thinking you'd be back.' He went into the hall to pull on his boots.

Matt followed him. 'Want a hand?'

'No thanks.' Peter would have welcomed the help but not from him. 'I can manage.'

'I don't mind, I'd like to.' Matt persisted. 'When your dad's away like Valerie says. It's a lot to do on your own.'

So she hadn't told him their dad was dead. 'It's OK, I'm used to it.' He took his jacket and went to the door. 'There's only room for one on the tractor anyway and I'm taking the dogs.'

He had prepared the hay and sheep nuts. All that remained was to hoist them onto the trailer. Matt stood watching as Ben and Meg jumped aboard and Peter set off up the track.

A chorus of *baas* rose from the sheep as the tractor came into view around the side of the hill. It didn't take long to fill the racks and troughs. Afterwards he stood for a while, filling his lungs with the wind that blew across the moor, watching the colours of the sunset, wondering what his dad would have said about Matt.

When he got home the house seemed empty apart from Daisy who lay sleeping, a dribble of milk running down her chin. He went into the hall and looked upstairs. Subdued voices came from Valerie's bedroom. The door was closed. For a minute he listened. There was a bump and a creak. The voices fell silent.

Peter didn't want to know. Noisily he went to the outside door, opened it a few centimetres and shut it again with a bang. He banged the living-room door also and went into the kitchen to make the dogs' food. Daisy woke and began to cry. He left her while the dog meat came to a boil in the big black saucepan. When Valerie did not come downstairs, he went through and picked the baby up, wiped her face and rocked her until she settled back to sleep.

Still Valerie did not appear. He drained off most of the simmering water and tipped the meat into the dogs' dishes, added a handful of biscuit and carried it out to the barn. Ben and Meg wolfed it down while Peter attended to his ferret. The second he heard the rattle of his door, Buster came running. He was eager to escape and go hunting, to root out rats and mice from their nests behind timbers, to go exploring through the drains. Peter draped him, lithe and fierce and pungent, round the back of his neck and carried him to a bed of hay in the byre. Lit by the yellow wall lights, he played with him, letting the ferret crawl through his jersey and squeeze up the legs of his jeans. Time and again Buster ran off, chittering and hump-backed like a weasel, and Peter chased after him, fetching him back and rewarding him with morsels of raw liver from the dog meat.

But his mind wasn't on the game. It was hard not to think about Matt and his sister; the berth in the lorry where they had spent the night; wondering what they were doing right then, up in his dad's bedroom. He hated it. Ginger Matt in his grubby jeans. Valerie going with him in a moment. Taking over the house without a thought to himself. Leaving him with Daisy.

After fifteen minutes he let Buster capture what remained of the liver, a bloody scrap the size of a golf ball, and returned him to his run.

Lights were switched on in the house and there was a sound of voices. Peter returned, accompanied by the dogs. Daisy was still asleep. As he went into the kitchen, Valerie was pushing Matt's clothes into the washing machine. He could smell them, sweat and cigarette smoke.

'Where is he?'

'Upstairs having a bath.'

'About time.'

She swung round. 'It's just his work clothes. When he's away he has to sleep in the lorry. Gets a wash and brush-up whenever he can.'

Peter thought about it. 'Will he be staying?'

'Tonight anyway.'

'Just tonight?'

'I'm not sure. Says he'd like to stay on a few days. Fancies it here but he's got the lorry to think of, they'll be looking for it back at the haulage yard in Glasgow. He's switched off his mobile so they can't reach him.' She filled the drawer with washing powder and fabric conditioner and turned on the machine. 'Maybe he'll go down and come back, have to see.'

'I thought you said his batteries were run down.'

'Eh?' It took her a moment to recall the lie. 'Well he charged them up overnight, didn't he.'

A voice came from the bathroom. Matt was singing. Peter felt sick. His dad used to sing in the bath.

Valerie was unperturbed. 'I hope you'll like him. He's a nice bloke when you get to know him.'

'When you get to know him? You haven't known him a day yet and you've spent most of the time in bed.'

She flushed and looked away then met his angry eyes. 'Yeah, I suppose. Sorry, Pete. But he is a nice bloke. Really.'

'He's a jailbird.'

'But he explained that. It's years ago and he only hotwired a few cars.'

'Oh, that's all right then.'

'Come on, don't spoil things. Give him a chance.'

Peter considered it and shut the door to the hall. The singing was muted.

'You making dinner?'

Valerie was hunting in the deep freeze. 'I thought we'd have pizza then one of them arctic rolls. That OK?'

'Up to you.' He returned to the living room. The dogs looked up hopefully. 'No chance, you've just had your dinner.' He switched on the TV.

A while later, the peat fire blazing, he was watching an old sitcom when the door opened and Matt appeared.

'That's better.' He rubbed his hair with the towel round his neck and lit a cigarette. Clouded in smoke, he watched the screen and laughed. 'I remember that. It's the one where he ends up on roller skates, isn't it?'

Meg sniffed his legs. He ruffled her head with the hand holding his fag.

Peter stared. Matt was wearing his dad's dressing gown, woollen checks with a thick brown cord. Beneath it he seemed to be naked. Bony red wrists protruded from the sleeves. Bare feet were pushed into his dad's slippers. He had shaved off the ginger stubble, leaving sideburns to the bottom of his ears. Peter recognised the aftershave. It was the one his dad liked. He'd bought him a bottle for his birthday.

Valerie came from the kitchen. 'That's an improvement. Had a good bath?'

'Yeah, great.' He took an ashtray and flopped into an armchair, arranging the dressing gown to cover his thighs. 'That you making dinner? Smells good.'

'Pizza,' she said briefly. 'Fancy a beer?'

'Got any whisky?'

She brought him the bottle and a glass, a small jug of water and a can of Export.

'Thanks.' As she turned away he caught her wrist and pulled her back, looking up into her face with a smile.

Her eyes went to Peter. In some embarrassment she smiled back and returned to the kitchen. Matt wasn't troubled. As if he had lived there all his life he poured a large whisky, added a drop of water and pulled the tab off the can. The beer foamed. He caught it with his mouth, leaving a white moustache. 'Ahhh!' He wiped it off with the towel and settled deeper into the armchair. 'Tastes good.' A corner of dressing gown fell from his white knee. He twitched it back and stretched his legs towards the fire. It fell again. He left it trailing.

Peter couldn't stand it and went up to the bathroom. A ring of scum circled the bath. A wet towel hung over the side. Matt had used whatever was to hand. His dad's razor was wet. And the can of shaving foam. And Peter's own toothbrush. He stifled a yell of rage. His heart thudded. Kneeling on the damp mat, he wiped the bath clean. The washbasin was speckled with stubble. He rinsed it away and mopped splashes from the floor. Then carefully he washed the razor and toothbrush under the hot tap, his dad's toothbrush too, and carried them to his bedroom. But even as he hid them between T-shirts in a drawer, he knew he would have to put them back. Matt would want to know where they had gone. Valerie would confront him. There would be a sickening row.

He switched off the light and threw himself on his bed. Hands behind his head, he thought about his dad and the life they had enjoyed until his ill-health took him away. In its place – he pictured Matt in his work clothes, now lounging there in his dad's dressing gown as if he owned the place. The look in his eyes when he smiled up at his sister.

Daylight had been gone for an hour. Beyond his window the stars were shining. For a while he watched them then closed his eyes and waited for a shout to tell him the pizzas were ready.

32

Cross My Heart

HE STAYED THREE days.

The worst time was the first night when Peter lay awake in bed and heard the muffled sounds of lovemaking from the far end of the landing. He tried to blot it out: pulled the pillow over his head, stuffed the duvet into his ears with both fists. 'Shut up!' he shouted. 'Shut up!' and lay shaking. When after a time he removed the pillow, the couple in his dad's bedroom had fallen silent.

On the nights that followed the noises were not repeated, though for a long time Peter lay listening in the darkness, praying that sleep would overtake him before they started. Perhaps, he thought, the lovers went upstairs during the day when he was out of the house, but at bedtime, to his great relief, all was quiet. He heard voices, tears from Daisy, a flush of the toilet, soft footsteps on the stairs – and that was all.

Matt tried to make himself agreeable, telling jokes, adjusting the tractor engine, hosing down the yard, but despite these overtures Peter could not like him. Jim was too recently dead for him to accept another man about the house, certainly one who used his dad's razor, wore his dressing gown, drank his whisky and slept in his bed, let alone with nineteen-year-old Valerie. After a few months, had Matt trodden very carefully, Peter might have come to tolerate him, perhaps even like him. Three days was not long enough. And to be fair, the fault lay not with Matt but with Valerie who had so eagerly invited him to share their lives.

But whoever was responsible, Peter wished to spend no more

time with them than necessary. So on the Sunday, when to his surprise Matt took the van and drove to Mass at St Mark's, the only Catholic church in the area, he packed sandwiches and a flask in his rucksack and rode his new bike down through the village to the harbour. There he spent the day pottering about the boat shed, fishing for dabs and exploring pools like multicoloured gardens in the rocks.

On the Monday and Tuesday, dark February days with gusty rain, Matt drove him to the road to catch the school bus and was there to pick him up again at quarter to four. Matt was starting a cold. His blue eyes watered and he blew his nose loudly into crumpled tissues.

That Tuesday evening, as Peter drove out to feed the sheep, he should have been happy because the next three days were half term, but the thought of spending three days with Matt and Valerie – five if he counted the weekend – filled him with dread. How would he pass the time? As the tractor approached, the ewes came bounding down the hillsides. It was the high moment of their day. He filled the feeders and stood watching as they jostled for the high-protein sheep nuts. They were strong and healthy, he had reason to be proud, but in another month lambing would start. How would he cope then? There was no answer. Apart from anything else, how much longer could Jim's death be covered up?

As he reached the house he was met by the savoury smell of cooking. He was surprised because most of Valerie's meals were ready-cooked, bought at the supermarket in Clashbay. Today, however, she was preparing one of his favourite meals, stir-fried chicken to be followed by a family-size tiramisu. 'What do you want to drink?' she said, surveying the top shelf of the fridge. 'Coke, lager, cider ...'

'Lager?'

'Can't do you much harm once in a while,' she said. 'Not as if it's going to turn you into an alkie. Matt says he used to drink it regular when he was your age.'

Peter remembered how Jim used to give him a little beer in

the bottom of a glass. 'OK,' he said.

'Lager, yeah?'

He thought about it. A whole can was a lot. Besides, if Matt used to drink it he'd rather have something different. 'No, cider.'

It tasted good. But Peter did not realise how much alcohol there was in cider and before the can was empty he felt a bit peculiar. When he rose to clear away the dishes, he had to grab a chair to keep his balance.

'You and Matt sit down,' Valerie said. 'I'll wash up and make the coffee. I've got a box of those chocolate truffles, the ones you like.'

'What's all this for?' He stifled a belch. 'It's not my birthday.'

'We've got a favour to ask you.'

'No,' he said.

'You don't know what it is yet.'

'Yes I do. You want me to look after Daisy again. The answer's no.' He shut his eyes and slouched back on the settee.

Valerie hesitated then returned to the kitchen.

He heard the murmur of voices and rattle of dishes. By the time coffee arrived his mood had mellowed.

Valerie sat beside him and tore the cellophane from the chocolates.

He chose a favourite and bit it in half. 'Come on then, what for?'

Her eyes flew to Matt. 'It's just the one night,' she said. 'You being on holiday and all. I mean, Daisy's better with you than she is with me and I'm her mother. You'll not have any trouble and I'll be back the next day.'

'Yeah? Where are you going?'

'It's Matt,' she said. 'If he doesn't get the lorry back to the yard they'll be having the police out looking for him. It's just to Glasgow. If we leave first thing tomorrow we'll be there by lunchtime.'

'I'll get my cards after this, sure as nuts.' Matt sat close to the fire. He scratched his forearms, tattoos blurred by the ginger hairs. 'But I know a few people so it'll give us a chance to look round.' He sneezed violently.

'You mean for another driving job?'

'Yeah, well that's what I do. There's a shortage of experienced HGV drivers. Say what they like, my licence is spotless. Get down early, go and see a couple of people I worked with before. Bit of luck I could be fixed up again by knocking-off time.' He took a mouthful of coffee. 'Tell them I'll be able to start in a week or so. Spend the night down there, hire a car next morning and we'll be back by teatime.'

'That easy?' Peter turned to Valerie. 'You said you wouldn't be late when you went to the dance – an' that was just in Brathy.'

'I know, love, but it'll be different this time, I promise.' She put a hand on his knee. 'Please, Pete.'

He searched for a way out. 'Why can't you take her with you?'

'I thought about that but she's better off here, really she is.' Valerie had her excuses ready. 'The lorry won't take a baby seat for one thing. And what do I do if Matt has to start going the rounds? We'll not have a car. It might be raining.' She crossed to the carrycot where Daisy lay sleeping.

'But I don't see why you have to go at all.' Peter was wriggling. 'Why not just stay here? It's not as if he's joining a ship. He's not going to be away for months.'

'Oh, you're right, but I just feel so cooped up. You know what I'm like.' Her brow furrowed, she looked at him with pleading eyes. 'It would be marvellous to get away, just for a couple of days. See some shops instead of these endless bloody moors. Go to a couple of clubs. A real life-saver. I'll bring you back a present.'

Peter didn't want a present, that was the last thing on his mind. What he wanted was life to return to the way it had been before. He loved Daisy, he was happy feeding her and didn't mind changing her nappies, but he didn't want to be left alone with her. He didn't want the responsibility. What if something went wrong? He looked at Valerie – could she be trusted to keep her word this time? But she was right about one thing, the baby was better off at home than being trailed around Glasgow in the rain. He drew a deep breath. 'All right,' he said reluctantly.

'Oh, Pete, you're a star!' She rushed across, kissing him on the hair, the cheek, the lips. 'There's plenty of food in the freezer, stuff you like. And I've bought some – '

'It's just the one night.' He pulled away. 'Don't get any ideas. I don't need feeding for a week, you'll be back the next day. You've promised.'

'Don't worry, we'll be here.' She licked her finger like a schoolgirl. 'Cross my heart and hope to die.'

'Well, don't forget.' Peter scrubbed his lips on his sleeve. 'This is my half term, I'm supposed to be on holiday. And I've got the sheep to look after as well. You've got to be back on Thursday.'

Matt winked. 'You got it,' he said.

33

The Blue Mondeo

THEY DIDN'T WAIT till morning. In the middle of the night, when Peter was fast asleep, Valerie carried Daisy into his room in her carrycot and slipped silently downstairs. He did not stir as they loaded two small holdalls into the van and drove out of the yard.

Matt thought there was a good chance the missing lorry had already been reported, so he planned to drive down to Glasgow under cover of darkness.

At two o'clock, with the moon appearing fitfully between clouds, he pulled out of the quarry at the end of the track, the deep roar of the eighteen-wheel juggernaut waking Bunny in her cottage a hundred metres away. Valerie shut the gate behind them and climbed back aboard. She loved it, loved the intimacy of the big cab of the lorry with Matt at her side, his strong hands on the wheel; loved the rough male smell of cigarette smoke and diesel; loved the huge radio speakers and the chat of the night-time DJs as the lorry's powerful headlights lit the road ahead and the black countryside sped by.

Matt's cold was no better. He hawked and opened the window to spit into the darkness.

A while before dawn they stopped at a motorway service station for breakfast, leaving the lorry in the remotest, darkest corner of the car park. Valerie freshened her make-up in the passenger mirror and took Matt's arm as they crossed the foyer to announce to the few people present that she was the driver's girl. The image was dented slightly when she had to fish out her purse in the shop, and a second time in the restaurant to pay for Matt's full Scottish breakfast and her own toast and coffee. But Valerie was too excited to be troubled for long. She had brought Jim's cash card with her and there was a cash machine in the service station, so she was able to withdraw a hundred pounds to keep them in funds.

Glasgow was awake and the high green gates of the depot had been open for an hour when Matt swung off the industrial dock road and parked in a bay close to the office. The boss, a fat man named Mr McReady, had just arrived and was in a bad mood that morning. The sight of Valerie repairing her lipstick and Matt swinging down from the driver's door as if he had not a care in the world roused him to a fury.

'Where the bloody hell do you think you've been?' He ran down the wooden steps and across the concrete. 'Saturday you were supposed to be back. I've got a load sitting in Dundee. Concrete for that new harbour up the coast. Contractors are doing their nuts, threatening to sue.'

'Not my fault.' Matt tucked in his shirt. 'Got a dose of Delhi belly. Had to go to a B&B. Felt like hell for a couple of days. Curried prawns, reckon they were off. Vomiting and the screaming squits. Wouldn't have been safe to drive.'

'Aye, an' I'm the Duke of Edinburgh.'

'It's the truth. Ask the lassie there if you don't believe me.'

'Give me a break, son. D'you think I came up the Clyde on a banana boat?'

'Well ring my landlady,' Matt bluffed.

'Why didn't you phone then? There's one in the cab.'

'On the blink,' said Matt, who had pulled a wire loose on the drive down.

'You've got a mobile.'

'Couldn't get a signal. Like I said, I was stuck in the bog so I asked my landlady to phone for me. You mean she didn't?'

'You know bloody fine. Just like I know bloody fine you've been shacked up with yon redhead for the past three days. Lorry parked away out of sight so the cops wouldn't spot it, right?'

'You've got it wrong, Mr McReady.'

'Have I? Well, I'll tell you what I haven't got wrong, you're sacked. It's not the first time you've come back late with some cock an' bull story. Get yourself up to the office there and pick up your cards. I'll pay you till last Saturday, think yourself lucky. Then shift your arse and your fancy woman out of here.'

He walked away.

'Bastard!' Matt called after his back.

Mr McReady turned. 'I'd button your lip if I were you. One phone call and I'll have the police round here. Wouldn't be the first time they've had the pleasure of your company. Now do yourself a favour and just get out. OK?'

Fifteen minutes later they found themselves standing on the dock road with their holdalls. Trucks and lorries roared past. 'What do we do now?' Valerie said.

Matt looked at his watch. 'Come on, there's a caff round the corner. Have a cup of tea while I ring round.'

It didn't take long. A mate in Sunderland gave him the names of a couple of long-distance hauliers who were a driver short. If Matt could make it there by lunchtime or early afternoon, there was a good chance he would be taken on.

'What about me?' Valerie said.

'Well I've got to get you back home. Like I said, I'll tell them I can't start till next week.'

'Thanks, Matt.' She pressed against his shoulder. 'Where's Sunderland anyway? Sounds a right dump.'

'Just south of Newcastle.'

'Newcastle! I went there with Tinker's Cuss one time. It's the other side of the country isn't it? How we going to get there by lunchtime?'

'No prob.' Matt smiled and hooked the phone on his belt.

'How do you know that? There might not be any trains.'

'Come on, sweetheart,' he said. 'This is Matt you're talking to remember.'

'What do you mean?' she said. 'Hire a car?'

'Well,' he shrugged. 'Hiring wasn't exactly what I had in mind. Borrow maybe?'

'Do you mean you've got a pal who could …?' She stared at him. 'No, that's not what you mean is it?'

He took her hand. 'Come on, let's see what's on offer.' They began walking.

Valerie was scared but soon she began to smile. She gave a little skip of excitement and looked at the cars parked nose to tail along the pavement. 'Do you mean you can start any of these?'

He shrugged. 'Not some of the new ones prob'ly, but most, yeah.'

'How?'

'You'll see in a minute.'

'No, I mean how'd you learn?'

'I told you, it's what I used to do. I done time for it.'

Her eyes sparkled. She hugged his arm more tightly.

They turned from the industrial roads into a commercial district. Matt looked up at the buildings. Office workers sat at the windows. 'Too open,' he said. 'Come on, we want somewhere quieter.'

They passed garages, carpet warehouses, the first shops, and soon were approaching the city centre.

The streets were busy. Parking was expensive. Free parking was hard to find.

Matt turned into a cobbled back lane. There was a stink of garbage from overflowing bins behind restaurants. A rat slid from a burst bag and disappeared into a hole. From one end of the lane to the other, city workers had parked their cars alongside the dirty brick wall.

'Look at them,' Matt said. 'Ten thousand quid sitting begging. And that's just the rubbish – thirty thousand some of them.'

Valerie said: 'Moses' car cost twenty – twenty quid, I mean.'

'Yeah? Who's Moses?'

'Guy I stayed with in Bristol. Got it out a scrap yard and done it up.'

'Good for him.' Matt shook his head. 'What do this lot expect? It's like letting a kid loose in a sweetshop.' He turned to Valerie, 'Come on, your choice. Which one do you fancy? Nothing too flashy.'

She giggled and stood back, trying to make her mind up.

'Come on, we haven't got all day,' he said. 'Don't want to hang about.'

She pointed to a shining blue Ford Mondeo.

Matt nodded. 'Good choice. Prob'ly got the alarm on though. Hang on.'

He gave the car a casual push. No klaxon shattered the quiet of the lane. He gave it a shove, rocking on the springs. Still no alarm. 'Silly bugger. Think he wanted someone to nick it.'

He crouched by the driver's door and took something from his holdall. 'Here, you keep a lookout. Let us know if anyone's coming.'

Valerie looked up and down the lane. 'Did you bring your stuff with you?'

'Sshhh,' he said concentrating. 'Had it in my locker at the depot.'

It took less than two minutes. The lock clicked. He pulled the door wide and thrust a lever into the housing beneath the steering wheel. It burst open revealing complicated circuits. He fiddled with the wiring. With a roar the engine sprang into life.

'Someone coming.' A man in a business suit had turned from the crowded road and came walking towards them down the lane.

Matt's heart beat faster. He prepared to hit him if necessary and flee. But the man, still several cars away, saw them standing by the open door and took no notice.

'Come on,' Matt said to Valerie. 'Get in. Throw your bag on the back seat. Act like it belongs to us.'

He glanced towards the approaching figure. His suit was striped. He carried a briefcase like a lawyer.

The car stood close to the wall. Valerie squeezed past the steering wheel into the passenger seat.

The man was passing. Matt stood in front of the hanging wires and gave an easy smile. 'Hello.'

'Good morning.' The man walked past.

Matt slid behind the wheel and pulled the door shut. The cars were parked bumper to bumper. It took a bit of manoeuvring before he could pull out into the lane. The lawyer, if lawyer he was, had stepped into a silver Mercedes. He waited for them to pass before following.

As they reached the road he was right behind. Traffic was heavy. Matt drew out ahead of a double-decker bus leaving the Mercedes behind. They never saw it again.

Valerie was on edge. 'That was close.'

'Not a bit. He had to get out same as us. You don't think he's going to hear about a nicked Mondeo, do you? There's dozens of cars stolen every day. He's forgotten about us already.' Matt grinned and squeezed her knee. 'Come on, darlin', stop worrying. Enjoy yourself. Here we are, nice car, heading out into the country. What more do you want?' He switched on the radio and flipped through the channels. Radio 1 blasted from the speakers.

In twenty minutes the city was left behind. Matt drove fast and well. He had travelled the road many times: south down the M74, the western motorway that leads to England, then east along the Tyne valley to Newcastle.

Shortly after eleven they stopped for a coffee at a service station among the hills. On the way out Matt pulled into the pumps to top up the petrol.

'What for?' Valerie pointed to the gauge with her cigarette. 'Tank's half full. That's enough to get us there.'

'Good car.' He thrust in the nozzle. 'Might as well keep it for the drive back north. I've got a mate with a body shop outside Newcastle. He'll rig us up a couple of new number plates.'

Valerie was getting anxious. 'Isn't that a bit risky? What if we get stopped?'

'Well that's the whole point, darling.' He stared at her. 'So we don't get stopped. If we had an accident maybe, but I've never had one yet. Not since I was nineteen. Anyway, it wouldn't affect you, not with a nipper up north.'

The pump cut out. Valerie reached for her purse but Matt pulled out his wage packet and went to pay the cashier.

The motorway was smooth and fast. In sweeping curves it stretched before them, winding through the hills. The engine purred. The speedometer needle was steady at seventy-five.

'Wonder what she'll do?' Matt pressed his toe lightly on the accelerator. The car surged, the blue leather seats pressed against their backs. Eighty-five in seconds. He trod a little harder. Ninety. Ninety-five.

Valerie touched his elbow. 'Matt, slow down.'

'Yeah, yeah. Just do the ton and I'll drop back to seventy.'

It wasn't Matt's lucky day. Too late he spotted the police car on its rise above the motorway. They were past in a flash. Instinctively he took his foot off the accelerator and stared in the driving mirror. The Mondeo had already slowed to eighty as the blue police lights came on and the white car slipped down the embankment into the stream of traffic. The unmistakable wail of the siren reached them above the noise of the engine.

'Oh, shit!' Far behind he saw the flashing lights in pursuit. The police had pulled out into the fast lane. Other traffic moved aside to give them a straight run. Matt put his foot down. The Mondeo picked up speed. The ton was gone in seconds. He went still faster. The needle hovered at a hundred and twenty. Other traffic seemed to be crawling.

'Matt! Slow down! I don't like it.'

'There's a turn-off in a bit over a mile.' His jaw was set, red with stubble. 'If we can get ahead of those lorries they mightn't spot us. With a bit of luck they'll get blocked out.'

'It's not worth it. It's only a car.' Valerie grabbed his arm. 'Slow down!'

He wrenched it away. 'Let go, you silly cow! You'll have us off the road.' The car swerved. He fought to control it.

At the same moment a muddy Land Rover, driven by a farmer who'd been up since four and had his mind on other things, pulled out into the fast lane to overtake a big refrigerated lorry.

Matt jammed his foot on the brake. They were travelling too fast. The Mondeo went into a skid, slewing sideways as it did so. Gravel flew like bullets from the central reservation. The bonnet crashed into the barrier and the car leaped high into the air, corkscrewing back across the road. The boot and one door flapped wide. With rending metal it struck the rear of the lorry in the middle lane, narrowly missed a lorry in the inside lane, and somersaulted over the barrier without so much as touching it. Beneath lay a deep ravine. The body crumpled on rocks. The petrol tank was torn open.

Valerie and Matt were killed outright.

Seconds later the car erupted in a ball of fire.

34

Wednesday – Scar Hill

DAISY WOKE UP. It was three o'clock on Wednesday morning. Her mother had been gone for an hour. For a while she lay peacefully staring into the dark, then her face crumpled and she began to cry.

Peter was dead to the world, locked in a dream about football in a sort of hell with pillars and fires and grotesque opponents who played so badly they made him laugh. Daisy's cries became part of the dream. He held her to his chest and ran towards fields that had appeared in the distance. The football had grown legs and chased after him. So did the players. They were angry now. His feet became tangled in long grass.

The dream faded and he found himself in bed. Dazed with sleep, it took him a moment to adjust. Daisy was in his room. How had that happened? He switched on the bedside light. The dazzle stabbed his eyes. Her carrycot was alongside his bed. If he had got up to go to the bathroom, he might have trodden on her.

She was yelling lustily, demanding attention. Cross that Valerie had moved the baby out of her own room, he went to the landing and switched on the light. Her door was ajar. He tapped and pushed it wide. The bedroom was empty. The covers were tumbled. The wardrobe stood open.

'Val?' He shouted downstairs. 'Val!'

There was no reply. They had gone. He went down to the hall to make sure. All was dark. The front door was unlocked. He looked out into the yard. In the light of a hazy moon he saw it had been raining. The van was gone. He switched on the yard light to make sure.

A single bark came from the outbuildings. Assailed by a pang of loneliness, he thrust his bare feet into boots and crossed to the shed. Ben stood waiting to greet him. Meg looked up from her bed.

'Come on then,' he said. 'Let's go into the house.'

Daisy was still yelling. He gave the dogs a digestive biscuit and went upstairs. Her face was scarlet.

'Poor Daisy.' He pushed back the blanket. 'What's wrong? Are you hungry then?'

But it wasn't hunger. She was wet – and worse.

He looked down the back of her nappy and made a face. 'Pooh! You are one dirty baby!' He took a towel from the banister and draped it beneath her to keep the ominously warm and heavy nappy off his pyjamas. 'Yes, you are,' he said without rancour. 'You're a dirty baby. And who's got to do something about it? Me, your poor Uncle Peter.' He shifted her to the other arm and carried her downstairs, holding the rail for safety. 'Still, it's not your fault is it? When you've got to poo, you've got to poo. Unfortunately.'

The peat fire had gone out. He switched on the electric and spread the towel on the living-room table. Changing her was messy but not too bad because she was still on milk, though he would rather have been smelling roses. He dropped the dirty nappy into a nappy sack and reached for the baby wipes. Soon she was fresh and clean and the crying stopped. He wrapped her in a warm towel and cuddled her against his chest.

'Do you want a bottle?' He looked down into her face and she smiled up at him. 'A little walk around then a nice bottle and back to bed. Is that right?' The smile became a tiny crow of pleasure. For a few minutes he carried her round the room then set her on the settee and went into the kitchen to make the bottle.

Before she had finished it her eyes were closing. Peter rocked the bottle and when for a whole minute she failed to suck he eased the teat from her lips. Instantly her eyes opened and prepared to fill with tears. Quickly he popped the bottle back. Having got what she wanted, Daisy gave a couple of half-hearted sucks and closed her eyes contentedly.

Peter's eyes were closing too. He was drifting on the edge of sleep when Daisy gave a little fart. His eyes snapped open. A faint but unmistakable smell drifted to his nostrils.

'Oh, no, Daisy,' he said. 'Not already.'

He had a look; the smell drifted away. Only wind. But how, he wondered, could a baby who looked so sweet have such a messy digestive system? He kissed her wispy hair. She smelled of milk, and baby shampoo, and just baby. He shifted her to a comfortable position in the crook of his arm and settled against the cushions to wait until she was fast asleep. Then he would carry her back upstairs and crawl into bed himself. He felt he could sleep for a week.

The room was still. Through slit eyes Ben regarded the pair on the settee. They did not stir. He gave a sigh and went back to sleep. The clock struck four. Then the quarters. And five. Peter did not hear it.

A wet patch on the leg of his pyjamas roused him at twenty to six. Daisy lay sleeping against his side. The hand holding the bottle had fallen into his lap. Drip by drip the milk, warm and then cold, had soaked into his trousers.

The room was warm. Surprised he had fallen asleep at all, let alone for two hours with Daisy on his arm, he eased her aside and stood up. His trousers felt horrible. He peeled them off, holding the wet patch away from his skin, and threw them into the wash, then wiped his leg with the dish cloth and found a clean pair in the drying cupboard.

Daisy was sound asleep. He made himself a cup of tea, took a couple of biscuits from the packet and ate them beside the electric fire. Where, he wondered, were Valerie and Matt at that moment? Why had they left in the middle of the night without waking him?

The clock struck six. His eyes were closing again. Daisy did not wake as he carried her upstairs and laid her in her carrycot.

Then Peter crawled into bed and pulled the duvet to his chin. The room was dark. The only sound was the soft rush of wind in the eaves. Gratefully he closed his eyes. Within a minute he was asleep.

But not for long. An hour later he was awakened by a familiar sound. Daisy was demanding attention.

The day passed slowly. There was a lot to do, though when he thought back he seemed to have done nothing at all.

First, second and third there was Daisy. She had to be fed, and changed, and walked, and amused, and comforted, and bathed, and picked up, and set down, and picked up again, and checked when she was sleeping. Her bottles had to be sterilised. Her clothes and towels and blankets had to be washed and hung out to dry, then brought in again when it started to rain and hung over the clothes horse.

He had to wash some of his own clothes too – though Valerie's washing and Matt's dirty socks and underwear, left strewn about the bedroom, he kicked into a corner. He had to clean out the fire and bring in peats and keep the house warm. He had to feed the dogs and let Buster loose to run about the living room, but make sure he went nowhere near the baby. He had to prepare his own meals, and get rid of the kitchen waste, and clean the house, which since Matt's arrival had got into a mess. He had to feed the sheep.

This created a problem. He could not take Daisy on the tractor or in the bumpy trailer, he needed the van. And the van, he supposed, was at the quarry where Matt and Valerie had left it. A baby, he knew, should never be left unattended but there seemed no alternative. So in the early afternoon, when she was sleeping soundly, he treble-checked that everything was safe – the fire low and the guard in place, the carrycot on the settee with no cushions above it, Daisy on her back with the blanket not too near her face, the cooker and electric fire switched off, the bathroom heater also switched off, and all the lights and taps – then he shut the door and drove quickly on the tractor to the end of the track.

As luck would have it, he reached the quarry just as Bunny was turning from the road in her new green Land Rover, instantly recognisable by the multicoloured dragon she had painted along one side and the flight of parrots on the other. She waved for him to stop.

It was the very last thing he wanted. Reluctantly he halted at the stony entrance.

'Hello there, Peter.' She drew up alongside. 'Fetching the van back?'

'Yeah.' He called down from his iron seat. 'Valerie's boyfriend went off in his lorry and we need it back at the house.'

'Didn't she go too? The lorry woke me up at some unearthly hour and I thought I saw her at the gate.' Bunny crossed to speak to him, thrusting her hands deeply into the pockets of a corduroy parka. 'What about the baby? Did Valerie take her along or is your dad looking after her? What's her name again?'

'Daisy.' He hesitated. 'Er – dad's looking after her.'

Her lively Jack Russell, with a patch over one eye, followed her to the tractor and lifted his leg against the big rear wheel.

'Get out of it, Jasper.' She waved a threatening arm and the dog, who knew he was perfectly safe, trotted away. 'Your dad's looking after her then. I'm sure she couldn't be in better hands.'

Peter searched for something to say. 'Yeah, he's good with her, feeds her and changes her and everything.'

'I'm sure he does. Well, he had to bring up you and your sister, didn't he. Long time ago now, of course.'

It wasn't something Peter had thought about. 'Yeah, I suppose so.'

'How's he keeping anyway?' she said. 'I haven't seen him for ever so long. Not since Christmas, I should think. Not since the heavy snow.'

'He's fine thanks. Just busy with the sheep. Some of last year's lambs still out on the hill.'

'So everything's all right? He's always been a private man, I realise that, not one to drop in, but I used to see him maybe a couple of times a week. You know, off and on. Just driving past or in the shop or somewhere. These days I never seem to see him at all.'

'You must have just missed him, he's around the same as always.' Peter had never been pressed like this, never told quite as many lies. His cheeks burned. 'We're all OK, really.'

She searched his face. 'I'm not one to poke my nose in, you know that, it's just that I've been a little worried about the three of you out there – the four of you, I suppose I should say. You driving up and down. Your sister having her baby in all that snow, and now going off with her boyfriend in his enormous lorry. Your dad never around. I mean,' she searched for the words, 'I do understand he has a little trouble from time to time with – well, you know. It's not his fault, I'm not criticising. Something like that's happened to so many of our young soldiers who were sent out there into the desert. All those pills and injections they had. I was just hoping things hadn't got any worse. Wondering if maybe there wasn't something I could do to help.'

He shook his head. 'No, honestly, Dad's fine. I'll tell him you were asking.'

Bunny wasn't happy about it, but when Peter and Valerie were so fiercely independent there was little she could do. 'Well, if I can help in any way, any way at all, you've just got to let me know.'

She stood back.

'Thanks very much.' The engine had been ticking over. Peter engaged first gear and eased the throttle forward. 'Bye.'

'You're my closest neighbours,' she called above the roar of the engine. 'That's what neighbours are for.'

He didn't reply and drove off into the quarry, avoiding fallen rocks and splashing through the puddles. The van stood beneath a crag, close to where Matt had parked his lorry, hidden from the road. Peter stopped in his usual spot and jumped down. The tractor was old and so well-known that no one would steal it, so he left the key in the ignition for Valerie and Matt when they returned.

Jasper was hunting the quarry for rabbits. Bunny called and he scampered back. The door of the Land Rover banged shut. Peter heard it turn and descend the track to Three Pines.

The van was unlocked. Daisy's pretty car seat, decorated with flowers and lambs, had been thrown into the back. He rescued it from the debris and dirt and dried-out spillage. Valerie had hidden the key under the mat although he'd brought the spare key just in case. He settled himself and pulled the door shut. It bounced back open. He slammed it hard. The door stayed shut.

The van rocked along the track which after the severe weather was in a worse state than ever. In ten minutes he was home. The dogs met him with swirling tails and they went into the house together.

Daisy lay as he had left her, only now she was awake. Contentedly she gazed up at the tasselled lampshade and a brightly-coloured picture of animals in the jungle which Peter had painted in school and Jim had pinned to the wall.

He washed his hands and bent to pick her up. As his face appeared before her, Daisy's eyes brightened and she gave a delighted gummy smile. Peter smiled back, it was impossible not to, and hoisted her to his shoulder.

35

Sick Baby

THEN IT WAS Thursday. Late afternoon, Valerie had said. What did that mean – four o'clock? Five? Eight? Maybe they wouldn't get back that night. At least, Peter thought, if that was going to happen she would phone this time.

The morning passed, a repeat of Wednesday. He made lunch. The afternoon drew on. The wind was rising and had got beneath a corner of the byre roof, making it rattle. He climbed a ladder and hammered a couple of nails through the rusted metal, knocking the ends over to grip. It wasn't a permanent job but with luck it should hold for the time being. At three he strapped Daisy into her car seat and went to feed the hungry sheep. When he returned he picked up the receiver and dialled 1571. There was still no message.

Should he make dinner for himself, he wondered, or wait a couple of hours so they could all eat together? Perhaps they would eat on the way up. There was no way of knowing. He took a family-size pizza from the deep freeze, grated extra cheese on top, decorated it with sardines cut lengthways and set it on a baking tray ready to put in the oven.

The hours passed. At six he gave Daisy her bath, holding her as Valerie had shown him and was described in *Baby's First Six Months*, the book he had bought in Clashbay. It was written for men as well as women. Peter had no hang-ups about looking after his little niece but it was reassuring to see the illustrations of dads with dark stubble and hairy forearms feeding and bathing their babies. His own hands were tanned and sported a couple of scabs from his work with the sheep.

He fastened the clean nappy and dressed her for the night in her vest and Babygro. Then he gave Daisy her evening feed and set her down to sleep.

When Valerie and Matt had not arrived by seven he was hungry and made some tea and toast. When they were not there by eight, he cut a large wedge from the pizza and put it in the oven.

At nine Daisy began to cry. He went to see what was wrong. Her nose was runny. She needed changing again.

'Sshhh!' he said comfortingly. 'That's all right. Who's a good little girl? Come on, let's go downstairs.'

It was soon done but Daisy continued crying and had started a little cough. He walked the carpet, talking to her softly, patted her on the back, sat at the table, sang 'Puff the Magic Dragon' and 'Morningtown Ride' which Jim used to sing to him, and slowly she was comforted. He returned to the bedroom. Her eyes were closed, she seemed to be asleep. Gently he lowered her into the carrycot. Abruptly her eyes opened and she began crying again.

'Oh, dear!' He was getting impatient. 'What's wrong with you tonight? You're not normally like this.'

He carried her back downstairs and made a bottle but she didn't want it. Where, he wondered, swearing aloud, was her *bloody* mother? *She* should be here caring for her baby, not him. Running out of ideas, he turned on the TV with the sound switched off, and sank into a corner of the settee. For another ten minutes, as he nursed her and murmured softly, the crying continued. Slowly it grew less. With flushed cheeks and tearful eyes she looked into his face and twisted aside. What was she feeling, he wondered, what terrible distress? 'Who's my best girl?' he murmured, much as he would talk to the dogs. 'Yes.' He wiped away drools with a tea towel. She gave a burp and milk spilled down her chin. He mopped it up and set the towel aside. Was this what had been troubling her all along? Just wind? Whatever it was, Daisy relaxed and within two or three minutes was asleep.

For a while, still holding her, Peter dared not move then crept forward to collect the TV control. He switched on the sound. Deafening gunfire blasted through the room. Frantically he lowered the volume and looked down into the baby's face. She had not stirred.

At eleven he made her comfortable in the carrycot and went to bed.

At three she woke him with her crying. He made her a bottle.

At six she needed changing.

At eight he was woken by Ben who came upstairs and nudged him because he needed to go outside.

'Oh, no, Ben. Go away.' He pulled the duvet over his head.

Ben raked at him with a big paw.

'Ohhh!' Peter pushed back the bedclothes. Ben's whiskery face was right beside him. Bright sunlight illuminated the curtains. 'All right, give me a second. I'm coming.'

Ben jumped up, both paws on the mattress, and nuzzled him with a wet nose. A slobbery tongue licked him on the jaw.

Peter pushed him off.

Abruptly he remembered – had they returned? In a moment he was across the cold floor. A glance told him they had not. The bedroom door stood as he had left it. He pushed it wide. The tumbled bed was unoccupied.

It struck him like a blow. For a third day he was being left to look after Daisy on his own. All Wednesday, all Thursday and now Friday. He could manage, somehow he would have to, but where were they? He didn't have Matt's mobile number. Didn't know the name of his employer. Didn't, when he came to think of it, even know his surname. There was no way, no way at all, to get in touch with them. All he could do was wait until they turned up, or at least made a phone call. Perhaps they had rung during the night. He ran downstairs but there was no message.

Disconsolately he let the dogs out and trailed back to the bedroom. Before the day had properly started he felt wretched.

The carrycot stood on his bedroom chair out of the draughts. Daisy stirred and made little baby sounds. She was about to start crying again and when he picked her up she did. He sat on the edge of the bed. The house was cold, he'd have to set the fire. He had tried to keep her warm but she was coughing and her nose was streaming. Her nappy needed changing yet again. Then she would want her morning feed. It was never-ending. He pulled his pyjama jacket to his throat. Where *were* they?

At that moment the charred remains of Valerie and Matt, what was left of them, lay three hundred and fifty miles away in the mortuary of the Royal Infirmary in Dumfries. Since that was the region in which the accident had occurred, that was where they had been taken. The car was completely burned out. The police had traced the owner through the number on the chassis. They knew the car had been stolen. No one had any idea who the occupants were.

Peter guessed that Daisy had caught Matt's cold. It developed quickly. The runny nose of Thursday had become a river of snot. He wiped it away but twenty minutes later there it was again, hanging from her nostrils. When she sniffed it disappeared back up, and when she coughed it shot down over her mouth. It made him feel sick.

The stiff breeze of Thursday had become a gale that rattled the windows and whirled stalks of hay around the yard. The forecast was for worse to come.

He was outside preparing the sheep feed when faintly above the noise of the wind he caught the sound of the telephone. He raced back to the house and snatched up the receiver. 'Yes?'

But it wasn't Valerie, it was Gerry, a good friend from school. 'Hi, Winnie. How's things?'

'Fine.' Peter masked his disappointment.

'Listen, Charlie just rang to say there's a game this afternoon. A bit windy but it'll be good fun. Are you coming?'

'Dunno if I can.'

'Ah, come on. It's that lot from Brathy. The team needs you.'

'I've got to give a hand with the sheep.'

'Can't you do it this morning? Without you we'll be a man short. We'll have to ask Fat Ally to stand in.'

'Sorry. I'll come if I can but I really can't promise.'

'Ah, mate.' Gerry was disappointed. 'Hey, what's that I can hear in the background? That your sister's baby?'

Daisy was crying at the top of her lungs in the living room.

'Yeah. I thought it was her on the phone – Valerie, I mean.'

'You looking after the kid on your own?'

'Course not, dad's here. That's why I've got to help.'

'Poor you, sounds a right pain. Our Morag – you know, my wee sister – she never stopped. Wah, wah, wah! Drove me nuts.'

The morning dragged and the afternoon was no better. When he tried to give Daisy her midday feed, she was fretful and cried. It was hard to suck because she couldn't breathe through her nose. After a while he gave up the struggle and nursed her until at last she fell asleep again. He snatched a quick lunch of baked beans then loaded the van and battled through the wind to feed the sheep. By the time he had done a couple of jobs about the yard, daylight was fading.

For the hundredth time he looked towards the road and listened for the sound of an engine. The track remained empty. 'Rotten bloody bastards!' he shouted above the gale.

In the mid-evening, after another slice of pizza, he felt so low he opened a can of lager. Far from cheering him up, it upset his stomach and gave him a headache.

At ten he went to bed and was woken an hour later by Daisy. She had been rubbing her face and her cheeks were shiny with snot. She had been sick, and when he changed her nappy he discovered she had diarrhoea as well.

No sooner had he set her down than he had to change her again. Her forehead and tummy felt hot.

It was a wild night. A northerly storm roared round the

house. Rain battered the windows. The corrugated iron on the byre roof had broken free and clattered up and down. He carried the baby into Valerie's room where it was quieter. While he cuddled her he read some pages about baby ailments in *Baby's First Six Months*. Daisy had a cold, that much was plain, and with sickness and diarrhoea it might be flu. To his horror, he read that the early symptoms of meningitis are similar to a cold – though at bath time there had been no sign of any rash, nor did she seem floppy or troubled by the light. All the same, the book advised parents to consult a doctor. Anxiously Peter rocked her, ensuring she was not too hot, and after a long time, worn out with crying, she fell asleep. He fetched the carrycot and covered her with a soft towel because her last blanket was dirty. Following instructions, he propped the head a little higher than the foot.

Sleep in his own room was impossible. He was debating whether to crawl into Valerie and Matt's bed which smelled of sleep and cigarettes, when there was a loud crash from outside. He ran to the window. Nothing was to be seen but raindrops lashing the glass. He hurried downstairs, tightening the cord of his dressing gown, and switched on the outside light. As he opened the door, the roaring of the storm filled his ears. Icy rain hit him in the face. It took a moment to realise what had happened. A huge sheet of corrugated iron had been torn from the byre roof and blown across the yard. Rusty and buckled, it stuck up like the wing of some enormous bird. A silver object lay on the concrete. The corrugated iron had hit the van and torn off a wing mirror.

He retreated indoors and looked from the window. Torrential rain lashed the puddles and poured through the hole in the byre roof. Directly beneath lay their store of hay. Wet hay went mouldy. When the weather improved he'd have to spread it out to dry, as much as he could anyway. There was no way he could repair the roof. When Matt came back he'd have to give him a hand.

More immediately, should he try to secure the sheet of tin?

It was doing no harm where it lay but if the gale flipped it back across the yard the van was vulnerable. So were the windows of the house. He pulled on boots, a baseball cap and a long coat of his dad's and ran out through the rain.

Soon he had manoeuvred the van to a safer spot. As he emerged, the wind plucked the cap from his head and whirled it away, high over the roofs. He never saw it again. The rain blurred his eyes, the coat flapped round him as he crossed to the sheet of corrugated iron. He grasped a rusty edge, taking care not to cut himself, and gave a tentative pull. It scarcely moved. He set his legs and heaved. The corrugated iron was heavy, difficult to shift in the best of conditions, impossible in the storm.

Peter left it and ran back to the house, relieved to be spared the struggle. His hair was plastered flat and the ice-cold pyjamas clung to his legs. He pulled them off. His other pyjama trousers were waiting to be washed. He rummaged in the drying cupboard and found a pair of Jim's with a hole in the knee. They trailed on the carpet. He hitched them high and rolled up the waist.

He was scrubbing his hair with the kitchen towel when the living-room clock struck the half hour. Half past what? Half past two. He hated going to bed with wet hair. A cup of tea by the electric fire would give it time to dry. Besides, he was chilled to the bone and shivering. He filled the kettle so there would be enough for a hot water bottle.

As he carried them to the settee his eyes were closing and before the tea was half drunk Peter was overcome by sleep. The hot water bottle grew cold. He did not hear the clock strike three and four. And Daisy in the bedroom above him had been crying for a full half hour before the sound woke him. Blearily he struggled to his feet and made his way upstairs.

Her eyes were gummed. The mucus streaming from her nose had turned thick and dirty yellow. She had vomited again and had diarrhoea. She was very hot.

Daisy was a sick baby.

36

Could You Come Over?

BUNNY WAS IN her dressing gown. In winter she liked to get up early and sit by the stove with a mug of fresh coffee and a good library book. When the phone rang shortly after seven she was surprised and a little alarmed. Who could be ringing at that hour? Was it bad news? Was one of the family ill?

'Hello.'

'Is that you, Mrs Mason?'

'Yes?'

'This is Peter Irwin.'

'Oh, hello, Peter. I thought I recognised your voice.'

He searched for the right words.

'What can I do for you?' she said.

'Could you come over?'

For a moment she was silent. 'But of course. Is there something wrong? Is it your dad?'

'No.' He gripped the receiver. 'If you could just come over.'

'Are you all right?'

'Yes, I'm fine.'

'Is it an emergency?'

'Sort of.'

'Is there anything you need this second, I mean over the phone?'

'No.'

'I'll be right there.' The line went dead.

Peter returned to the living room. When Daisy was ill he had no option, she had to see a doctor. It was as simple as that. His own problems no longer counted. The only question had been who he should ring: Dr Bryson himself? Constable Taylor? Mrs Harle, his head teacher? Billy Josh? Gerry's parents? In the end, the person he thought would be easiest to talk to was Bunny Mason. She had already offered to help and was right there at the end of the track.

Daisy lay sleeping. He wiped the runs from her nose with a handful of toilet paper. She gave a whimper and tossed a little but didn't wake up. Peter looked around and tidied the room, opened the curtains. When visitors came, he knew, they should be offered tea or coffee. He went into the kitchen and set out mugs and a packet of biscuits. Abruptly he realised he was still in pyjamas. Quickly he went upstairs and got dressed. He was buckling the belt of his jeans when he heard the Land Rover. Carrying his jersey, he hurried down and opened the door.

The worst of the storm had passed but the wind still gusted round the outbuildings and blew his hair.

The dogs ran past him to inspect the intruder. They knew Jasper, who always travelled in the passenger seat, and trotted alongside looking up.

Bunny swung in a circle and drew up outside. She spotted Peter and summoned a smile. The boy was alone. Where, she wondered, was his father? And his sister? Had she not returned yet? 'Stay there,' she told Jasper and stepped down into the yard.

'Hello, Peter. A wild night.' She eyed the sheet of corrugated iron in the corner. 'A bit of damage, I see.'

'Yes,' he said and led the way indoors. 'Daisy's not well.'

In the two years, or nearly two years, since she moved north, Bunny had visited Scar Hill only once. She liked Jim Irwin and liked his house too, a bit rough-and-ready but clean and comfortable. There had been a deterioration. This time she saw dust on the stairs, dog hairs on the carpet, stains on the settee. In the middle of the settee, in a carrycot with dirty handles, lay Valerie's baby. Bunny remembered her as a sturdy and pretty little girl. Now she was fevered and suffering from some baby ailment.

She looked around. 'Where's your dad?'

Peter knew he would have to confess everything but not right at that moment. 'He had to go to the sheep,' he said. 'There's been some dogs worrying them.'

Bunny was not happy about it. Why had it not been Jim who phoned her? Something was wrong. 'What about your sister?'

He shrugged. 'She hasn't come back yet.'

'So it's just you and the baby?'

He nodded. 'I tried to give her a bottle but she didn't want it.'

Bunny looked him in the eye then sat on the settee and felt Daisy's forehead. The mother of three children and grandmother of two, she had seen most illnesses and knew what was serious and what was not. The baby was very hot. A sudden sneeze and discharge of greeny-yellow snot told her that most likely Daisy was suffering from a feverish cold, maybe flu. She lifted the towel that covered her and saw the little girl was dressed in a clean top and leggings. Her nappy was clean too. She set the towel aside to let some of the heat escape.

Peter stood beside her, his face tight and anxious. Bunny looked up and smiled. 'Nothing too serious. She's got a cold and a bit of a temperature, that's all. Babies are like that. Get some little bug and you think they're going to die. At least you do when it's the first one. All the same, better get Dr Bryson to give her the once-over.' She glanced at the clock. 'Catch him before he sets off on his rounds. Do you want to ring him or shall I do it?'

'You,' Peter said.

They went into the hall. 'Hello? Dr Bryson? ... It's Bunny Mason here. Sorry to disturb you on a Saturday. Look, I'm up at Jim Irwin's place ... Not as far as I know. Peter tells me he's out with the sheep. It's his daughter's baby I'm ringing about ... that's right, Valerie ... Well, she's not here at the minute and they asked me to come over and look at the wee one. Nothing serious, I think, just one of those baby things ... That's right,

a bit scary when you've never seen it before … You too?'
Bunny laughed. 'What's that? … Running a temperature?
Yes, she is, that's why I'd like your professional opinion … A
thermometer?' She raised her eyes and Peter shook his head.
'No, I don't think so … I see. Well, we could take her along to
my house if that would be any easier.' She looked up again and
Peter nodded. 'What time would that be? … Three o'clock? I
don't suppose you could make it any earlier? … Eleven? That
would be perfect … What's that? … Well, Jim's not here right
now, as I said, but I'll leave him a message … That's splendid.
See you then … Bye.'

She put the phone down and turned to Peter. 'You got most
of that? We'll leave a note for your dad and take her along to
my house. Doctor says he'll look in around eleven. Oh, and
he wants your dad to arrange an appointment for himself. He
hasn't seen him for some time, apparently. Hasn't been picking
up his prescription.'

They returned to the living room.

'Well, I don't know about you,' she said, 'but I could do
with a cup of tea. Have you had your breakfast?'

Peter had not.

'Well look,' she said. 'If you don't think it's a bit cheeky of
me, why don't I rustle something up while you put on the fire?'
She rubbed her hands. 'A bit chilly for the baby.'

As he cleared away the ashes and brought in fresh peats,
Peter thought that perhaps the time had come. The firelighters
were kept in the cupboard beneath the sink. Bunny was busy
at the stove. He rose, holding the packet in a dirty hand, and
drew a shaky breath.

'Mrs Mason?'

She turned. 'Yes, Peter.'

He said, 'I've got something to tell you.'

37

Breakfasty Fingers

BUNNY GAZED AT Peter and didn't know what to say.

Breakfast was over and they sat at the table with empty mugs and their plates pushed back. He had told her everything: how his dad was sick because of the war and had to take pills for his heart; how he had found him dead on the hillside and buried him in the peat; how this was to give himself time because he didn't want to be sent away and was frightened for the dogs; how he had looked after the sheep; how Valerie had lived in Bristol, come home pregnant and given birth during the blizzard; how he had gone for help on the tractor and hurt his ankle; how they had lived on his dad's Social Security money; how Valerie had gone off with Matt and left him to look after Daisy; how they were two days overdue and he had no way of getting in touch; how he knew he was in serious trouble but now Daisy was ill it didn't matter.

'I don't know how you managed to keep going.' Bunny shook her head. 'How old are you now – thirteen? Second year in the high school and all this piling up on your shoulders? It should never have happened.' She tried to take his hand but Peter drew it away. 'One thing I *can* tell you,' she said, 'and I know what I'm talking about because in my life down south I was a magistrate for over ten years. You are *not* in any trouble. Believe me.'

Peter looked at her. A magistrate, yeah, right. In old joggers and an anorak. Surrounded by goats at the end of the track. She was trying to be kind but it just wasn't true. How could he conceal his dad's death and bury his body *without* being in trouble? All that money they'd taken, that was theft, it had to be. All the lies he had told. And never mind himself, what would happen to Daisy now? Would she be taken into care because Valerie had left her at Scar Hill with her young brother and not come back? A picture he'd seen on TV of a baby dragged from its screaming mother and carried off by a policewoman had given him nightmares.

'There'll be a lot of questions,' Bunny said. 'Can't be avoided, I'm afraid. But there's nothing to be frightened about.'

That was all very well to say. It terrified him. Sitting at a table to be questioned by strangers. Men in suits and women who'd pry into everything personal and private. People who'd strip his feelings bare. People who'd tell him he couldn't possibly stay on at Scar Hill and would have to be sent away.

'Who?' he said.

'Who what? Who'll want to talk to you?'

He nodded.

'A social worker, I expect. And the police. Maybe someone from the children's panel.'

Peter thought about it. Like a boy at school who had been breaking into houses and smashing car windows.

'They're not going to be hostile, Peter, it's not some sort of inquisition. They're here to help. It's their job. They want what's best for you.'

'Like what?' he said. 'Send me off to live with foster parents? Some boys' home in Glasgow? Or Manchester?'

'Where did you get all that from? Why should they send you to Glasgow or Manchester? You're not listening to me, Peter. These are kind people, they've got children of their own. They're going to be horrified. They don't want you to be miserable, they want you to be happy and secure.'

'I'm happy and secure here,' he mumbled.

'No you're not. And you know you can't live here by yourself. Anyway, there's Daisy to consider. And Valerie.' She thought for a moment. 'You're absolutely sure you don't know where she's gone?'

Moodily Peter picked up a smear of marmalade on the tip of his finger. 'Like I said, I don't think I ever heard his second name. She said they were going back to his depot in Glasgow.' He shrugged. 'Left in the middle of the night. I've got no idea.'

'I'm not sure anything can really be decided until she comes back. Obviously some arrangement has to be made about Daisy.'

'You mean right now?'

'Well yes, and for the future. See what the Social Services have to say. It's up to Valerie to persuade them she's a fit mother and nothing like this will ever happen again. Maybe she'll decide to stay on here. You could live with her. That would be all right, wouldn't it?'

'She's my only relative,' he said. 'Apart from my mother but you can forget her. I'd like it if Daisy stayed.'

'But not Valerie?'

After a long time he said, 'She hates it up here, she'll never stay on. At least, I don't think so. She's different from me. She likes the city and shops and hairdressers and things.'

'Yes, I can see that.' Bunny sighed.

'But living here's the only thing I want to do.'

'I realise that as well.'

'If they do send me away,' Peter said, 'I won't be able to take Ben, will I – or Meg?'

'It depends where you go.'

'But it's not likely is it? I mean, if they send me to a children's home or people in the town, they'll never let me keep a big dog like Ben, will they?'

Ben knew he was being talked about and crossed to the table.

'And if I can't, he'll get sent to a dogs' home, won't he? They both will.'

'I suppose they might.'

'Do you think they'd get put down?'

'Put down?' Bunny was startled. 'Why would they get put down?'

'That's what happens to dogs when nobody wants them.'

'I know that, but who wouldn't want two beautiful dogs like Meg and Ben?'

'I don't want them to go there. I don't want them to go anywhere. They're my dogs, I want them to stay with me.'

Ben smelled his breakfasty fingers and licked them. Peter rubbed his rough grey head. The tall dog rested his chin on the table, on the lookout for a titbit. Peter gave him a left-over corner of toast.

Daisy still lay on the settee in her carrycot. She gave a snotty sneeze. He took the paper towel he had been using as a napkin and wiped her clean. 'There, is that better?' He smiled and returned to the table.

'I don't want Daisy to go away either,' he said. 'I want us to stay together. I want to be there while she grows up, see she's OK.'

Bunny considered him across the table. 'She's lucky to have you for – well, I almost said a big brother but you're her uncle, of course. And when you talk to the social worker and whoever it is, I'm sure all these things will be taken into account.' She sat up and became more businesslike. 'But so far you and I are the only people who know anything about it – apart from Valerie and her boyfriend, of course. So maybe if we make a few plans here and now we'll have a better chance to influence what happens next.'

'You're taking Daisy home with you and the doctor's coming. Isn't that what's happening?'

'Yes, but I mean after that, for the next few days.'

'I thought you said I'd have to …' Peter's voice trailed away.

'But not right this minute. We'll talk to Dr Bryson and while he's there I'll give Constable Taylor a ring. If I can get him I have no doubt he'll be up straight away.' She thought for a moment. 'I think the best thing's for you to come home with Daisy and me and I'll get you settled into a bedroom at Three Pines. Maybe I can persuade Social Services to let the two of you stay with me until Valerie comes back. For the next few days anyway. Surely she'll be home by then.'

Peter hesitated. He wasn't used to getting help.

'I mean, if you'd be happy with that,' she said. 'What do you think?'

The possibility had never occurred to him. 'Thanks very much,' he said.

'I don't see why anyone should object. And if they do, well, I hope I've still got a *bit* of influence.' She stood and straightened her clothes. 'I know people up here think I'm a bit of an oddball, but when I lived down south – well, let's just say I didn't always drive a Land Rover with pictures on the side.' She gathered up the breakfast dishes. 'How if I wash up while you get a few things together. You won't need much, just your pyjamas, toothbrush, change of clothes.'

'OK.' He started towards the hall. 'What about the dogs?'

'They'll come with us, of course. Might have to keep Jasper and your Ben apart, but who knows, maybe they'll be great pals. Oh,' her voice pursued him up the stairs, 'and we'll need nappies and bottles and things.'

'I'll get them when I come down.'

There was a suitcase in the landing cupboard. Peter threw in underpants, T-shirts, a jersey. He remembered he had no clean pyjamas – maybe he could wash them at Bunny's. He'd need his school clothes too. And his rucksack. And the book he had to finish reading for Monday.

He sat on the bed for a minute and began to think about what he was doing. Did he really want to go to Three Pines? Everyone asking him questions: Dr Bryson, Constable Taylor, the person from child welfare. Of course he wanted to go, he told himself, what else could he do? But not just yet. Not, as Bunny had said, right that minute. It was too sudden. He needed a little time. Time to get used to the idea. Time to say goodbye. He couldn't simply walk out. The sheep hadn't been fed for a start. And there was all the dirty washing in the machine, not just his pyjamas but his socks and spare jeans and Daisy's clothes and the blankets she'd been sick on. And maybe if he had time, he could fork out the wet hay in the byre and cover the rest with a tarpaulin. Then there was …

He came halfway down the stairs. 'Mrs Mason?'

She emerged from the kitchen, drying her hands on a tea towel.

'I was wondering,' he said. 'Do you think maybe I could …?'

'You're not having second thoughts, Peter?'

'No, of course not.' As he tried to explain his cheeks grew hot. 'The beds aren't even made. If anyone comes to see the house, maybe I should tidy up a bit. I tried to keep it nice like dad, but with Valerie and Matt and the baby and everything …'

Bunny looked at him steadily.

'It's just a few little jobs, it won't take long.' He descended a few steps. 'An hour, an hour and a half. Then I'll drive over with the dogs – and Buster, he's my ferret.'

'You'll never do all that in an hour.'

'I can come back this afternoon.'

Peter was an unusual boy but all the same … 'You're not planning anything stupid are you?' she said.

'How do you mean?'

'Well, you're not planning to run away, for example?'

'Run away? Of course not,' he said.

'It's not a good idea.'

'I thought I was coming to you,' he said. 'Where could I go this time of year anyway? It's freezing, I'd die on the hills.'

Bunny heard alarm bells. 'Don't say that,' she said.

But Peter had no intention of dying on the hills, joining his dad out there. He knew exactly where he would go. It wasn't the first time he had thought of running away to avoid the stares and questions and being packed off somewhere like a stray dog. A dozen times he had lain in bed, hands behind his head, staring into the darkness and making plans he never really expected to carry out.

Bunny wasn't satisfied. 'You are telling me the truth, aren't you?'

'Yes,' he said and didn't feel guilty. 'You're being very kind.'

'Well, I'm just telling you,' she said. 'Don't.'

Peter wandered the house collecting baby wipes and teats and sterilised bottles and tubes of cream and everything else Daisy might need.

'I really can't stay any longer just now,' she said. 'When I got your call I came straight over. Some of the animals haven't been let out yet, and I think I left the front door open. If the goats get in the house they'll eat everything in sight, turn the place into a midden.' She suddenly remembered: 'Oh, my goodness! And I've left the illustrations for my new book spread out on the table. I really must run.' She picked up the carrycot. 'And you'll be along in an hour. No later than eleven because the doctor's coming and you've got to be there.'

He nodded.

'Promise?'

'I said so, didn't I?'

'And we'll come back this afternoon to finish tidying up. Make sure everything's the way you want to leave it.'

The way you want to leave it? How long was she thinking about?

'I'll have to come back to feed the sheep – every day, I mean.'

'I realise that, Peter, but you don't have to do everything yourself, you know. Maybe I can help with the sheep.' She smiled encouragingly. 'Don't worry, that's the main thing.'

Don't worry? How could he help worrying, Peter thought. Important matters were being decided, matters that could affect his whole life.

He followed Bunny into the yard. A gust of cold wind hit him in the face. Daisy sneezed, emitting a fresh flood from her nose.

Peter caught hold of the carrycot and wiped it away. Leaning over, he gave his tiny niece a kiss on the cheek.

Daisy stared back, her eyes wide and blue and serious, then

her face puckered and she began to wail.

Peter wanted to pick her up, comfort her, hold her, say goodbye. Instead he stood back, fearing Bunny might become suspicious.

'We'll fit the car seat later,' she said, stowing the carrycot on the rear seat. 'It's just along the track. I'll drive slowly.'

She shut the door. The crying was muted. Peter looked in through the window.

Bunny zipped her anorak and swung into the driving seat. 'Eleven o'clock, remember. Don't be late.'

He raised his hand and followed the Land Rover as it turned out of the yard.

Soon it was hidden behind a swelling of the moor. He felt the pang of separation and stood listening as the note of the engine faded.

But there was no time to be lost. He ran back to the house.

38

The Sheep Pen

PETER CHECKED HIS watch: half past nine. An hour and a half before they came looking for him. It was barely enough.

The sheep could not be left hungry. Luckily he had prepared the hay and nuts the night before. He heaved them into the van and drove fast up the track, bucking like a rally car as the wheels met rocks and flooded potholes. Normally the animals stood waiting at the gate but today, because he came early, they were scattered across the meadow and came bouncing and baaing at the sound of the engine. Roughly he pushed through them to fill the troughs and hay racks. By now their unborn lambs were heavy and they were permanently hungry. Feeding time was the high moment of their day. Eagerly they pressed round the troughs. Peter left them to it and sped back to the house. At once, lest he should forget, he scribbled a note about feeding them the next day and left it on the table.

His school rucksack was not big enough but Jim had held on to his army rucksack, a reminder of the days when he was a strong young soldier. For years it had been crushed into the back of a cupboard. Peter dragged it out and began filling it with what seemed the bare essentials: sleeping bag, a sheet of plastic, lightweight food, dry dog food, tinned meat for Buster, ferret nets, fishing line, spare clothes and waterproofs, mess-tins, firelighters, matches in a plastic bag. Jim, who at one time had dreamed of joining the SAS, liked to talk about living off the country, and Peter often caught fish and rabbits, so he was not wholly unprepared. He collected the tobacco tin which contained his hidden hoard of money and buckled it into a pocket. Buster went on the front seat of the van in his carrying box, the dogs and rucksack went in the back.

In thirty minutes Peter was ready. He checked all the doors and windows were fastened and hid the house keys in the byre. After a last look round the yard, he drew a deep breath and set off in the direction of the main road.

It was a time for action not regrets but how long, Peter wondered, would it be before he returned to Scar Hill? Had he slept there for the last time? He looked from the window and was just in time to glimpse a gable as the house vanished behind a rise. The swollen river surged alongside the track. He blinked hard and settled himself in the driving seat.

It was his plan, dreamed up long ago, to hide the van behind bushes at the Four Crowns and double back into the moors the way he had come. Whoever came looking for him would find the van quite quickly and assume he had taken the obvious route, down the long slope into Strath Teal where there were woods and barns and shelter. No one, he thought, would expect him to be heading in the opposite direction, up into the hills.

He drove faster than was safe, frightened Dr Bryson would arrive early and Bunny would return to fetch him. All went well. With fifteen minutes in hand, he reached the Four Crowns and turned up a grassy bank between two mounds. The wheels skidded, leaving deep scars, then gripped enough to climb twenty metres and turn behind an outcrop of rocks and whin bushes.

Peter left the keys in the ignition. Ben and Meg scrambled out to explore while he adjusted the straps of the heavy rucksack and hoisted it to his back.

He listened but there was no sound of pursuit, just the roar of a distant lorry on the road. All he needed was an hour to vanish into the moors. He looked down the grassy bank and was pleased at the tyre tracks. The torn black earth would soon lead his pursuers to the van. With luck it would start them on a wild goose chase down the long hillside into the glen. He buckled the waist strap of the rucksack and hung Buster's box over his shoulder. Then, dropping out of sight of the track, he headed back towards Scar Hill and the high moors that lay beyond.

It was hard walking but the life of a shepherd kept Peter fit. His stout boots gripped the earth and kept his feet dry as he tramped through bogs. But though the morning was fine, raindrops clung to the heather and soon his jeans were sodden. It was nothing new. He had dropped a handful of biscuits into his pocket and munched them as he tramped along.

At twenty to twelve a vehicle drove up the track, disturbing the birdsong and splash of hidden streams. Peter's route was parallel, quarter of a mile to one side. He stopped to listen. Who was it? The driver couldn't see him but he couldn't see the vehicle either. He wondered what was happening.

At that moment he was as close to Scar Hill as his route would take him, although the house was hidden behind a ridge. Quickly he hid the rucksack among some rocks and ran across.

'Ben! Meg!' He called the dogs to his side. 'Lie down. Lie down! Good dogs. Now stay. Stay!'

Cautiously he crept to the heathery summit.

The house was about two hundred metres away. Bunny's Land Rover swung round the byre and drew up in the yard. She got out, accompanied by Dr Bryson.

Who was caring for Daisy, Peter wondered.

He heard voices but from that distance could not make out the words. They would see the van was gone but apparently had not spotted the tyre tracks at the Four Crowns. Bunny went to the door and found it locked. She rapped loudly, several times, and peered through the windows.

'Peter? Are you there?' Her words reached him. She said something to Dr Bryson. Then called again, 'Peter!'

They searched the outbuildings. Scar Hill was deserted. Together they scanned the surrounding moors. Dr Bryson pointed up the track towards the pasture where the sheep were fed, and beyond it the waterfalls and rough hillside where the track came to an end. Beyond lay the high moors and Blae Fell, the way Peter was heading. It didn't trouble him because they would find no van. Obviously, it would appear, he had not gone that way.

He watched the Land Rover draw away. Bunny had been so kind, he felt bad at letting her down. At the same time, he had no regrets. He needed to be alone for a while.

Far off he could see the peat-brown gash of the falls, and the tiny specks of sheep gathered round the feeding troughs. He ducked back behind the ridge and continued his journey.

The rucksack was heavy but Peter had only a few miles to go. After an hour he pulled out the sheet of plastic and sat by some rocks on the slope of Blae Fell. The clean, cool wind blew round him. He imagined how his dad, who was buried on the far side of the hill, would have loved it there. What would he have said about Peter running away? Peter thought about it and came up with no answers – except for one thing. He would have understood.

The sky grew threatening and it looked as though he was in for a spell of heavy rain, then the clouds began to break up. By mid-afternoon, when he came in sight of his destination, the moors were dappled with sunshine as far as the eye could see.

The sheep pen stood in a fold of the hill. It was the spot where, in the autumn, Peter and Jim had driven a small flock of sheep to treat a scraggy ewe infested with maggots and another with footrot. At that moment it stood in a patch of sunshine, stone walls yellow with lichen and bracken broken to a ragged red carpet by the storms of winter. He tucked his thumbs under the straps of his rucksack and strode down the final stretch of hillside.

It stood exactly as they had left it, a centuries-old circle of stone, chest-high and above twelve metres across. Peter hitched open the broken gate and crossed to the lean-to which was to be his shelter. It was smaller than he remembered, a rust-red roof of corrugated iron supported by worm-eaten timbers. Half a bale of hay and another of mouldy straw were heaped against the back wall. A mat of ancient sheep droppings was covered by dead weeds and grass. He swung his rucksack to the ground.

The hay and straw would make a good base for his plastic sheet and sleeping bag. Not surprisingly it was damp. He dug it out in armfuls and slung it over the wall to dry. As he did so his hand struck something soft and furry. 'Aahh!' He jumped back. A huge rat, squeaking with fright, fled from the ruins of its home. Instantly Ben and Meg were in pursuit but the rat was too fast and disappeared into a gap between the stones. For a long time they searched, snuffling and scraping but the rat had gone to ground. Buster scratched eagerly at the wire of his box. Peter thought of loosing him. Buster would have pursued the rat right into its rocky labyrinth. He decided against it. What harm was the rat doing? Leaving the dogs to their excitement, he began unpacking the rucksack.

Purple shadow spread across the moors. Sunlight retreated up the fell. The puffy clouds turned flamingo and salmon, then grey.

As daylight faded the air grew damp and colder. Mist gathered in the hollows. Peter descended to the stream and filled a mess-tin and plastic bottle with water. He broke scraps of wood for a fire and prepared a base out of the wind and close to a wall where the flames were least likely to be spotted. Stones and straw provided him with a seat. He shivered and pulled his sleeping bag round his shoulders but dared not light the fire until the telltale column of smoke would be hidden by darkness.

Shortly before seven he set two firelighters in the middle of his rough hearth, surrounded them with a wigwam of twigs and struck a match. Soon he sat before a warming blaze with a mug of tea and a biscuit. The dogs lay nearby, well fed and blinking contentedly at the flickering flames. Buster, in a leather harness, roamed the sheep pen at the end of a cord. If the circumstances had been different, Peter would have been blissfully happy.

The evening passed slowly. After a while he fried three rashers of bacon in the larger of the mess-tins, mopped up the fat on slices of bread and made a sandwich. It was delicious but he was still hungry. Warming his hands round a second mug of tea, he leaned back against the wall. The stars were brilliant. An owl flew past on silent wings. Later he heard it, or a different owl, as it screeched on the hill. There were other sounds too: the far-off bellowing of a stag, the dry bark of a fox, a hundred rustlings from the little creatures that lived in the grass.

The rotten fence posts and other scraps of timber dry enough to burn were soon gone. He kicked a couple of slats off the gate and broke them by jumping on them. As the fire sank, the February cold fingered through his clothes. Long before he would have gone to bed at home, Peter spread his sleeping bag beneath the awning. Sleep was slow in coming. The setting was strange. He was uncomfortable. The night breeze fanned his face. No matter how he pulled his head down, it found a way through. After a time he gave up trying to sleep and lay watching the last glow of the embers and tiny spurts of flame that lit the walls.

A hundred thoughts came and went and returned to plague him: Daisy, his dad, Valerie, Bunny, Scar Hill, school, tomorrow. Not to mention his freezing feet and the big rat which might be watching nearby.

The dogs, too, were restless. They were not used to spending a night in the open air. Ben curled up against his legs. Peter pulled a hand from the sleeping bag and rubbed his ears.

He must have slept for a while because when he examined his watch again it was after eleven. But it was long past midnight and the stars had crossed the sky before he sank into a restless slumber that continued until six in the morning when he was wakened by the hammering of rain on the tin roof an arm's length above his head.

39

Reckitt's Mines

SHORTLY AFTER IT stopped raining a helicopter flew over.

Peter heard it before he saw it. 'Ben! Meg! Come here!' He dragged them beneath the awning.

The dogs were startled.

'All right. Settle down. Sit! Stay there.'

Crouching beneath the low roof, he scanned the sky. The helicopter, green with orange and white markings, appeared round the side of the hill. It was heading across the moors but changed direction to pass over the sheep pen. Peter ducked back out of sight. Nothing lay in the open to indicate his presence. The ashes of the fire were black. For what seemed a long time the helicopter hovered overhead then turned away. The noise of the rotors faded. Like a dragonfly it grew smaller against the clouds. He emerged and straightened his back.

RAF and forestry helicopters flew over the moors occasionally but this, a lighter aircraft with different markings, suggested they might be searching for him. He had decided already that it was impossible to spend another night in the sheep pen. It was too exposed; the shelter was inadequate. As he lay in his sleeping bag with the rain battering overhead, he had puzzled his brain for a better hideout. There were plenty of barns around the village and down in Strath Teal but he decided against it. People with barns had dogs which would sniff them out and raise the alarm. Before daybreak he had come up with an idea.

Six or seven miles away, half a day's walk across the rolling moor, a tributary stream ran from the hills to join the River Teal. It had carved out a valley where two centuries earlier mine shafts had been driven horizontally into the rock to extract the rich minerals. For decades it had been a major industry, attracting workers from as far away as Ireland and the continent. Tremendous mounds of rubble were still to be seen, rusted rail tracks, and the ruins of buildings which had housed planners, wage offices and the ragged workforce, a dozen to a tiny room.

It was known as Reckitt's Mines. Peter had cycled there several times to explore the buildings and hunt for unusual pieces of rock. Ignoring the warning notices, he had ventured deep into the flooded mine shafts until fear and the stygian dark forced him to beat a retreat. On one occasion, like Theseus in the Labyrinth, he had tied the end of a big ball of string to a boulder and unwound it as he went in case he got lost. The mines intrigued him and he had written a project about them for school. He knew, for example, which minerals were extracted and what they were used for. He knew that the stream which carved out the valley was called the Milky Burn because when the mines were in operation the water ran white from the crushed stone – though now it ran crystal clear, unlike most of the moorland streams which were red with peat. It was, he realised, a place where people might come looking for him, but it was a long way from the village and at that moment he could think of nowhere better.

It was impossible to remove every trace of his presence but he did his best and shortly before ten o'clock, having breakfasted on bread and butter, cold beans from the tin and water from the stream, he started out. Blue patches of sky had appeared, it promised to be a fine day. Meg and Ben loved the adventure, sniffing through the heather and rocks for whatever might be hiding there.

Ben took off, yelping excitedly, after a small herd of deer.

'Hey!' Peter shouted. 'Ben! Come here!'

The big dog took no notice. Twenty minutes later he returned, his eyes shining and muzzle lathered with foam. Peter examined it for deer hairs – there were none.

He felt very exposed, even though his jacket and rucksack merged into the colours of the moor. Constantly he scoured the land for signs of pursuit.

Shortly before midday he heard the helicopter again. He called the dogs to his side and sank to the boggy ground. The icy water saturated his jeans. As long as he did not move, Peter knew, he was unlikely to be seen. 'Stay there!' he said angrily and hid his white face in his clothes. The helicopter – the same machine or one with the same markings – came from an unexpected direction and passed half a mile off.

He rose, picking his wet jeans from his legs, and hugged the dogs to show he was not really angry. Briefly he wondered about changing and decided against it. His jeans would dry on him. When his dad got wet on manoeuvres he hadn't stopped to change his trousers. If he hadn't, Peter wouldn't either.

Trying to ignore the discomfort, he walked on. He found himself thinking about school friends. At that moment they would probably be at home. Soon they would be sitting down to Sunday lunch. Maybe in the afternoon they would watch TV. On Wednesday they would be going back to school. Football practice on Thursday and a match next Saturday. He pictured them: Gerry, Magnus, Cameron, Charlie. When, he wondered, would he see them again?

Reckitt's Mines, as he approached through a wilderness of stones, was a collection of a dozen grey buildings, some no more than an outline of walls, others with part of their roofs remaining. The windows were smashed. Beams lay rotting among the debris.

Four mine shafts had been driven into the hillsides. Two had collapsed, their entrances blocked, but the others, he remembered, led far underground. The roofs were so low that even a boy aged eleven, as Peter had been the last time he was there, had to walk stooped. Much of the way they were flooded, ice-cold water swirling to his knees. The roofs dripped. Crystals, the beginning of stalactites, glittered in the beam of his torch.

But that February afternoon the mine shafts were of little interest. He was looking for a spot among the ruins where he could lay his sleeping bag and be protected from the rain. Luck had stayed with him throughout the day, for the clouds which were opening as he left the sheep pen had gathered again until they hung purple and threatening above the moor. From the look of it there was going to be a downpour.

The buildings stood on both sides of the stream but those on the near bank were mostly rubble. Peter crossed over. As he wandered from ruin to ruin, the first peal of thunder grumbled about the valleys and a few fat raindrops hit him on the shoulders.

The shelter he chose was a two-storey building which might once have been a refectory or offices. The decaying walls were topped with ferns and self-seeded trees. Some had grown too large and been blown down in gales, ripping off sections of the wall as they fell. Much of the roof was gone and half the upper floor had collapsed, but adjoining the gable wall at ground level, a worm-eaten patch of floorboards had survived. It was dry and Peter saw that it would not take long to brush off the crumbling mortar, twigs and bird droppings that had accumulated over the years. Even better, there was a fireplace and a chimney with daylight at the top.

He dropped his rucksack and pulled it open. It was all very well trying to emulate his father but the insides of his legs were chafed raw. He peeled off his jeans and was just stepping into a dirty pair he had rescued from the washing machine when a flash of lightning lit the valley. It wasn't close but the crash of thunder that followed had a vicious, splitting sound, followed by a rumble that echoed around the sky for many seconds.

Meg was frightened by thunderstorms. She whined and crept to Peter's side, tail between her legs.

He fastened his jeans and put an arm round her. 'It's all right. There's a good girl.'

She wasn't comforted and pulled away. Restlessly she roamed the house, looking for a place to hide. She found it in a gap that led down to the foundations and slipped from sight. Ben was untroubled and stood looking from the doorway at the sheets of grey rain that came sweeping down the valley.

Peter joined him.

The afternoon was dim. A flash of forked lightning split into branches and fizzed to the ground somewhere on the moor. Peter counted under his breath: one, and ... two, and ... three, and ... At five the ripping thunder, like a sheet of torn tin, split the silence, followed by the long belly rumble.

Another terrific flash lit the buildings that stood like skeletons in the deserted valley. On its heels came a second flash, crossing the sky horizontally. For a dazzling split-second Peter saw the black entrance to a mine, the wilderness of stones, the bushes growing high above the ground. A standing wall was illuminated from behind, windows like blazing eyes and a door like a mouth. Gloom returned, still darker after the flash. The afternoon was rent by thunder. Then the hiss and drumming of torrential rain.

There were ghost stories about Reckitt's Mines. Peter had written them in his project: the spectres of a group of men who had suffocated underground; a manager found dead in the snow with a pickaxe through his brains; a Polish miner who had gone mad and strangled his friend. His dad had told him there were no such things as ghosts. Peter had no problem with that on a sunny day, but he was alone in that haunted place. It was not hard, as he looked out on the chaotic flashes and darkness, to imagine the mad miner picking his way through the ruins.

The storm passed overhead. The static made his scalp prickle and the little hairs on his body stand on end. Lightning struck the rim of the valley and the very building where he stood – or so it seemed, for the air turned blue for a moment and there was a smell of ozone. With a cry he sprang back from the doorway.

Peter loved thunderstorms. Sometimes at Scar Hill he had run out in his shirt, exulting in the thunder and lightning, lifting his face to the rain until he was soaked to the skin. The chance of being struck, he knew, was millions to one but this at Reckitt's Mines was too close for comfort. Thunder cracked on the heels of the flash, too fast to count the seconds. Water ran between the houses, washing drifts of pebbles downhill. For fifteen minutes he stood watching and was sorry when the storm moved away down the valley. The air, already pure, had a fresh smell, tingling to his nostrils. The clouds brightened and a scrap of blue sky appeared – big enough, as Jim had been fond of saying, to patch a pair of sailor's britches. Meg emerged from her place of hiding.

To his delight, the boards where he was planning to sleep had remained dry. If they could withstand that downpour, Peter thought, they could withstand anything – provided the roof did not collapse on his head.

In the daylight that remained he hung up his sleeping bag to air, explored the buildings and collected enough wood to keep the fire burning all night.

By an excellent piece of good luck he spotted the grate for the fireplace protruding from a pile of rubble. It was swollen with rust but enough to raise the bed of the fire and provide a good draught. As Peter lit it with firelighters and small pieces of wood, the sparks whirled away up the chimney. He zipped his jacket to the throat and sat close, holding his hands to the warmth. The dogs joined him, blinking in the firelight.

The Milky Burn, swollen by the rain, filled the air with an incessant roar.

For four days and three long nights Peter remained in his hideout. Upstream the valley was prettier, carpeted with moss, ferns and heather. Downstream, where it levelled and joined Strath Teal, the vegetation was bushy and lusher.

Prompted by boredom as much as the need for food, he carried Buster to a bank where there was a big warren. In no time a couple of fat rabbits were struggling in the ferret nets. He killed them with swift blows and carried them back to his shelter. It didn't take long to gut and skin them. Sharp-eyed crows had perched nearby and when he threw out the offal and heads, they fought to carry the treasures away. Buster, buckled into his harness and line, was given a liver and dragged it away to a hole he had made his own. The dogs had to wait until dark and stood drooling in the firelight as Peter boiled the gamey meat and mixed it with their dry food in the mess-tins. For his own meal, he cut the boiled meat into thin slices and fried it in fat. It took a lot of chewing but tasted not too bad with a sprinkling of salt and some ends of fried bread – a bit like chicken.

Nights began early. At dusk, when daylight had faded enough to hide the smoke, he lit the fire and cooked his dinner. By eight, even though he dawdled over his food, it was finished. And by nine, for there was nothing to do except talk to the dogs and keep the fire burning, he crawled into his sleeping bag and rested his head upon the rucksack. Mostly he faced the flames but sometimes he turned the other way where, beyond the fallen end of the building, the winter stars wheeled above the moor. Later in the night the moon, which was nearly full, swung into sight above the shattered valley. He loved those clear skies, but with the absence of cloud came the frost which nipped his nose so that he rolled back to the warmth of the fire and threw on more wood.

He slept long hours but his sleep was broken, not just by the creeping cold but by his troubled thoughts, to which was added the outcome of his running away. With helicopters out searching he could only be in more serious trouble. How long, he wondered, could he stay free? Would they catch him or should he give himself up? As he snuggled into his sleeping bag and listened to the tumbling water, he felt he didn't want to – ever.

Peter had brought with him a coil of fishing line and a small tin box of hooks. Downstream, where the peat gave way to soil, there were worms. A crooked branch served as a rod. The flood had subsided and in a couple of hours on the third day, which was Tuesday, he caught three small trout. A little further on, where the Milky Burn meandered between grassy banks, there was watercress. As far as food was concerned, he might have remained at the mines for weeks.

But people were looking for him.

Peter had no way of knowing that the helicopter which hovered over the sheep pen that first morning, had flown on to Reckitt's Mines and landed just a hundred metres from where he was now living. Two men, the pilot and a volunteer, had searched the buildings from end to end and even ventured up the flooded mine shafts with torches. They were bound to return sometime and on the fourth afternoon, as Peter wandered downstream with his crooked fishing rod, he heard the throb of the rotor blades. It was hard to make out what direction the sound was coming from but at once he called the dogs and scrambled down into a watery gully overhung by branches. His foot slipped and landed in the burn with a splash. As he struggled to keep his balance his second foot slipped also. Calf-deep he stood in the icy water. The dogs were alarmed. Hastily Peter clambered out and joined them on a rocky ledge.

The helicopter came into view, whirling up Strath Teal and turning up the Milky Burn towards the mines. It passed overhead, only fifty metres above the ground. The noise was deafening. The down-thrust tossed the branches wildly. It was there, it was gone. The walls of the gully prevented him from seeing. Cautiously Peter clambered out. From the grassy brink he could see the roofs of the mine buildings half a mile further up the valley. The helicopter was hovering. Slowly it sank from sight. The roaring ceased. Men's voices, faint as gnats, reached his ears.

He thought swiftly. There was no way he could return. A score of things advertised his presence: the swept boards, the trampled weeds, his sleeping bag, the rucksack, Buster's carrying box. They were bound to be seen.

What was he to do now?

He threw his rod into the water, called the dogs and set off running downstream.

40

Owl Cottage

PETER APPROACHED THE barn with caution.

Daylight was fading. An orange moon, rising and full, hung above the farm roofs. Already there was a touch of frost in the air.

Fortunately the barn was a distance from the house. Unfortunately the farmer, a fat, florid man named McKim, had not locked his dogs up for the night before eating his dinner. Peter kept Ben and Meg close beside him but something – the scratch of his jacket on a thorn, a snapped twig, a smell – alerted the farm dogs. Barking ferociously, they came racing from the yard.

There were two, a Doberman and a lean collie. With an answering snarl Ben bounded to meet them. In an instant the dusk was alive with twisting, snapping, savage bodies. First one had the upper hand, then another. Meg, perhaps sensing that Ben was outnumbered, joined in. The air was loud with snarls and yelps and barks. Peter waded in, shouting, trying to break it up. He grabbed Ben's collar and dragged him back. At the same moment he felt a fierce pain in his thigh. The Doberman had bitten him. He kicked out furiously and felt his boot thud into the animal's side. It yowled and backed away. Ben broke free, leaping back into the fray. Meg had the other collie by the skin of its neck and wouldn't let go. Peter grabbed Ben again and hauled him off. The Doberman lunged and shredded the sleeve of his jacket. Ben whirled round and made a slashing bite at its face. Teeth clashed. They drew back bristling.

Floodlights came on at the farm. Mr McKim began shouting:

'What the hell's going on down there?'

Peter responded. 'Your dogs have attacked us.'

'Who is it?'

'Never mind that,' Peter shouted back. 'Call them off. Murderous bloody animals. You should keep them tied up.'

The Doberman was kept as a guard dog, but hearing the boy's voice the farmer realised he might be in trouble. 'Max!' he called angrily. 'Bracken! Lay off! Come back here. Come 'ere, you brutes!'

He was a harsh man. Reluctantly the dogs ran off.

Peter had had a fright. Roughly he clapped his companions but they were too worked up to take notice. 'Come on.' He set off running the way they had come. 'Come on!' Unwillingly, with many backward looks, they followed.

'Who is it?' Mr McKim called again. 'Come here. Show yourself.'

Peter's fingers were slippery. He smelled them, touched them with his tongue and thought it was blood. Was it his own?

The muddy farm track crossed the river, broad and black and glinting in the moonlight. A hundred metres brought him to the road, single-track with passing places, that ran the length of Strath Teal. He turned towards the coast and Tarridale, ten miles to the north. More lights came on at the farm. Through the wintry trees that lined the river he saw Mr McKim making his rounds, ensuring the intruder had gone.

Peter's feet, in his wet socks and boots, had become blistered. He wanted to examine his thigh. It didn't hurt although it ached a bit, but a dog bite had to be attended to.

A car came along the road. He called the dogs into a thicket of birch trees. As the headlights swept past, he was horrified to see that Ben's neck and chest were covered with blood. 'Come here, boy. Ben.' He crouched beside him and explored the cold wet hair with his fingertips, searching for the wound.

He thought he found it and Ben gave a little yelp but didn't seem too troubled by it. Peter hugged him and Ben looked round to lick his face. Right then there was nothing Peter could do about it.

They walked on. The last dregs of sunset turned to night. As the sky darkened the moon grew brighter, reflecting on the windows of a cottage on the hillside above him, half hidden by trees. Were the owners merely out, Peter wondered, or was it a holiday cottage like so many in the area, used for a few weeks in the summer by people from the south? It was worth investigating. He needed a place to spend the night. Perhaps there would be a shed. Perhaps, if the owners were away, they had hidden a key.

The drive, which was precipitous and bordered by rhododendrons, joined the road at a bend. A convex mirror stood opposite to show the oncoming traffic. Peter did not see the name, Owl Cottage, painted on a board overgrown by ivy. He crossed a cattle grid at the foot of the drive and started to climb. The way was steep and twisting. Cautiously he approached the front porch. Was there a security light? The darkness remained unbroken. He looked all round. There were no neighbours, the cottage stood alone, separated from the wilderness by gravel and a small front garden. A big oil tank stood among the trees. Beneath him lay the road and moonlit river. On the far side and a short distance up the strath, the floodlights were still switched on at the farm.

Peter turned his attention to the cottage. It was a traditional stone Highland dwelling with two dormer windows and a little porch built on the front. The shelves in the porch had contained plants but were now bare and scattered with dead leaves. The downstairs curtains were drawn. The mat had blown aside. It suggested the owners were away from home. He tried the door. It was locked.

The back door of the house was at the side. It also was locked. So was the small stone outbuilding with a mossy roof that stood opposite.

Each side of the back door stood a row of plant pots and

small urns filled with dead flowers. A few broken slates were propped alongside. They gave him an idea. He tipped back the pots and felt beneath. The wall was in moon shadow so he could see little. His fingers encountered grit and wintering slugs. He was beginning to despair when all at once there it was – a key. In a small plastic bag to prevent it rusting.

It fitted the shed. At least he would have shelter for the night. But what shelter! A dirty stone floor among broken bikes, discarded furniture and other household debris. Why would anyone hide the key to a junk shed? Why not keep it in the kitchen? Unless a key to the house was hidden in the shed. In the pitch dark Peter explored ledges, rotting saddlebags, every hidey-hole he could find. No key was to be found.

It was colder in the shed than outside. He began to shiver and retreated into the moonlight. The bite in his leg was hurting a bit. And Ben needed attention. He patted Ben's chest and found the hair harsh and clotted. The blood was drying.

Peter turned his attention to the house. The back door was old and had a big keyhole. It appeared to lead directly to the kitchen. He wondered about breaking a window to see if the key was inside the lock, but it was too far away to reach.

He returned to the front. The porch door had a Yale lock. That could easily be opened from the inside. And if the door between the porch and the house were locked, he could spend the night in a rattan chair which stood in the moonlight. There was even a rug thrown over it.

Peter had never broken into a house or caused wilful damage in his life. With thudding heart he drew his sleeve tight and jerked his elbow into the small pane of glass nearest the lock. The glass didn't smash but the beading was rotten and gave way. Two panes fell inside and broke on the tiles with a shocking crash. The dogs were startled. Peter stared round, ready for flight. A minute passed. No doors banged, no lights came on, no angry voices disturbed the silence. He reached through and turned the lock. The door swung open. His boots crunched on the broken glass as he stepped in from the night.

The inner door was flimsy, glass panels from top to bottom to allow light into the hallway. It had no lock. He pushed it open and went through.

Peter was terrified. Until recently he had been an honest boy. Now he was breaking and entering.

Directly before him was a staircase. The air was warm. He rested his hand on a ghostly radiator. The owners, or someone who kept an eye on the cottage, had left the central heating on at low to keep it dry.

The downstairs rooms were in total darkness. He opened the curtains, allowing moonlight to flood through windows which faced across the strath. The rooms felt strange: strange smells, strange furniture. Like rooms in a black-and-white film. Like rooms in a troubled dream.

The electricity was switched on, he could hear the soft hum of the central heating pump. But what about the water, Peter wondered. Where would he find antiseptic to clean the bite on his leg and the wound on Ben's neck? And he was hungry. What food was there in the house?

Before he went searching he checked upstairs. Two bedrooms with sloping ceilings and the beds made up – a woman's dressing gown, a Paddington Bear. A small bathroom at the back. He pictured the steep, overgrown hillside above the house and risked the light: toothpaste, soap, towels, a cabinet which contained pills and insect repellent but no antiseptic. He returned to the hall.

Even with the curtains closed he dared not try the lights in the front rooms. They would advertise his presence. The kitchen was at the back, beneath the bathroom. He led Ben and Meg inside, shut the door to the hall and felt for the light switch. The strip light flash – flash – flashed and came on dazzling bright. There were no curtains. He switched off and collected a bedside lamp with a frilly apricot shade from upstairs.

The water was turned off but the stopcock was beside the door. He ran the tap into the sink, peat-brown water from some nearby stream, heavy with sediment. He left it running to clear. The cupboards were well stocked: cans of soup, tins of beef and mushy peas, unopened packets of biscuits, tea and coffee, dried milk, enough to make himself a decent meal. And as if that were not enough, a red switch by the oven operated the immersion heater. He turned it on. If no one came, he could have a bath and spend the night on the settee in the sitting room.

He tore open a packet of chocolate digestive biscuits and bit into two, like a sandwich. The dogs were drooling. He gave a handful to each and filled the kettle. But before making a hot drink or doing anything else he had to tend to their wounds, his own and Ben's. Meg seemed to be unhurt. He dropped his jeans to examine the bite.

It was on the muscle at the front of his thigh, bruised and a bit swollen with ragged scratches. At the end there were two black puncture marks where the Doberman's teeth had penetrated more deeply He wrung out the dishcloth and wiped away the dry blood. It looked better after that but dogs' teeth had germs. If he didn't clean it properly it might get infected. There was a big bottle of household Dettol in the cupboard under the sink. He slopped some into the washing-up bowl and added water, as hot as he could bear it. It didn't really hurt and he scratched at the punctures with a fingernail to force in the milky disinfectant. There was no more he could do. It had begun to bleed again. He mopped it with a kitchen towel and pulled up his jeans.

They were torn but had given him some protection. Ben's neck was much worse. Half his chest was matted with blood. Ben was unconcerned, he had enjoyed the fight, but Peter made him sit while he searched for the wound. It was a nasty tear fully five centimetres long, deep and dark, right through the skin to whatever lay beneath. Peter looked round the kitchen. Ben's injury was more important than the owner's towels. He mixed fresh disinfectant and soaked a hand towel, pressed it against the wound and did what he could to sponge away the blood. Ben hated it, hated the smell and tried to escape.

'Come here!' Peter pulled him back and smacked him lightly to show he meant it. 'Now stay still.'

At almost the same moment Meg jumped to her feet, staring towards the door. She gave a sharp bark.

Peter froze. Then he heard it too, the sound of an engine. Leaving the bloody cloth and bowl of red water, he jumped to the light switch and pulled open the door. Headlights were coming up the drive.

41

Full Moon

THERE WASN'T A key in the back door.

'Ben! Meg! Come on!'

Peter ran out through the hall. In the sudden darkness he crashed into the chair in the porch. It fell on top of him. The rug became tangled round his feet. He flung it aside and ran on, out into the moonlit night and round the end of the house. Icy steps ascended to the back garden. He trampled through wintry flower beds and crossed the lawn. A rotting fence divided the garden from the wilderness on the hillside. There seemed to be no gate. Peter kicked two, three, four times with the sole of his boot and the fence broke apart. He pushed through and was swallowed up by the shadows.

The vehicle was a muddy Land Rover and the driver was Mr McKim. The muzzle of his guard dog, Max, had been badly gashed in the fight and needed stitches. His collie was bitten around the neck. He had driven the two dogs to the vet he used on the outskirts of Tarridale. On his return, as he made his rounds and locked the dogs up for the night, he had spotted a dim glow of light on the hillside opposite. It came from the back of Owl Cottage. The owners, he knew, were not expected back before Easter. Something was not right. He remembered the intruder and thought he should take a look.

As he swung up the twisting drive all seemed normal, then from the corner of his eye he spotted a movement at the end of the house. A smallish figure and two dogs. The headlight was not on them and when he looked again they were gone.

'Hey! You!' He pulled up on the gravel and jumped out.

'Come back 'ere!'

There was no reply. He heard breaking wood and crashing footsteps in the undergrowth.

'Don't think you're going to get away.'

He stumbled on the slippery steps and crossed the lawn. The moon shadow beneath the trees was intense. The noise of flight continued.

'Bloody bastard!' He stood by the broken fence. 'I'm going to call the police.'

The sounds grew fainter. Panting from his exertions he returned to the house.

The door stood wide. His shoes crunched on broken glass. Switching on lights as he went, Mr McKim searched the rooms. Nothing appeared to have been touched. He entered the kitchen. His horrified gaze fell on the bloodstained towel and basin of red water. A packet of biscuits stood on the unit. The light of the immersion glowed red. The intruder had left his woollen hat behind.

But it was the blood that held his attention. He remembered the voice at the farm – a boy's voice. Maybe it was that boy everyone was talking about. The son of that drunkard – what was his name? The boy who'd buried his father and run away. Who'd been looking after his sister's little kid. He turned the bloodstained towel with his toe. Was Max responsible for this? It wouldn't be the first person he'd attacked. What kind of injury was it, for God's sake? The boy must be in a bad state. If the police found out he'd be in all sorts of trouble. The bloody dog might have to be destroyed – and he'd paid good money for Max. He did his job well. Too well on this occasion, it seemed. What was to be done? Mr McKim did not find the question difficult – do nothing. Turn off the lights and slip away fast, before anyone saw him. Leave the house as it stood. Tell nobody: not his wife, not his grown-up son, not his labourer. Most definitely *not* the police.

Two changes he made: he switched off the immersion and shut the front door. And next minute Mr McKim, with headlights dipped, drove quietly away and returned to his farm.

Owl Cottage stood empty in the moonlight.

The hillside was treacherous: a broken stump jabbed Peter in the ribs, brambles coiled round his legs, ditches tricked his feet, twigs whipped him in the face. For half an hour he hurried on, above the road and parallel to it, putting as much distance between himself and the cottage as possible. Dry-stone dykes barred his progress. He climbed them and crossed rough pasture where sheep scampered off with whirling tails and inquisitive cattle came trotting to investigate.

His legs were weary. He was weary all over. Peter longed for some place where he could lie down and sleep. It was not to be found on the frosty hillside. A tumble of stones beneath a wall provided a cold seat facing across the strath. He sank down and closed his eyes.

The night breeze stirred his hair. Occasionally the weeds rustled. Owls hooted in the wood.

As he fled, he had kept a constant lookout for police cars on the road below. There had been none. Looking back, he had seen the lights extinguished at the cottage and the Land Rover return to the farm. What did it mean? Did the man intend ringing the police from home? But an hour later no car with flashing blue lights had come speeding up the road. In fact, the only traffic had been two cars and a truck, none of which had stopped. The cottage remained in darkness.

He shifted to get better shelter, drew up his knees and pulled his collar to his ears. If only, he thought, he had brought the rug from the cottage, it would have been so easy.

Meg whined, she was trembling. He drew the dogs close.

For another hour he sat looking across the strath. Beneath him lay the road and fields and the winding River Teal. The night was so clear that stars shone right to the crest of the hillside opposite.

Briefly he must have dozed then woke with the cold. The

staring moon had moved across the sky. The northern lights flickered like curtains and sent up their shifting searchlights. The folds of his jacket were white with frost.

Some time around ten Peter realised that if he were to survive the night he must have shelter. Apprehensively he looked down the steep slope below him. Thorns and bushes grew chest-high. Slowly he straightened. He was so cold that his feet were clumsy and would not go where he wanted. The moonlight was deceptive. But grabbing branches, slipping and sliding, he made progress and in time found himself on the brink of a cliff above the road. It took a while to work around it but at last, with relief, he stepped out onto the level tarmac.

He thrust his fists into his pockets. Walking warmed him up. For a while he found new energy and a new sense of purpose. Perhaps, he thought, he could even walk on to Tarridale. The feeling did not last and within a couple of miles he found himself seeking, with increasing desperation, some place that would offer him shelter and a degree of warmth.

A house appeared on the left. There were lights behind the curtains. At the head of a short drive there was a garage. It was locked.

The owners had put out the wheelie bin for the morning. Peter lifted the lid, wondering if by chance they had discarded some old clothes, anything to keep out the cold. Shadows hid the contents. He tilted it towards the moon. Nothing but debris and bags of kitchen rubbish. He let the lid fall.

Beside the bin was a container for recycling newspapers. It was blue plastic, they were all blue plastic, though in the moonlight it was hard to tell one colour from another. It gave him an idea. Newspapers were warm. A layer of newspaper, Jim had told him many times, was as good as an extra jersey. Peter looked inside. The box was half full. He pulled some out but they were awkward to carry so he dumped them back and took the whole box.

A branch road led into the hills, linking a few scattered cottages. Opposite, beneath overhanging trees, stood a bus shelter. It was an ugly modern structure of perspex and steel. Intrusive though it was in that Highland glen, it seemed to be the only refuge Peter was going to find.

He went inside. A slatted bench ran along the inner wall. He dropped his box on the concrete and sat down heavily.

But before he thought about himself, even though he was so weary, Peter had to care for the dogs. He had brought them to this place. They also needed protection against the cold night air. The moon aided him. With his Swiss Army knife he cut armfuls of dead bracken and scattered them under the bench. Then he spread a thick layer of newspaper on top and ruffled it up to make a bed. The dogs would rake it around to their liking. It was the best he could do.

His own preparations took longer. It was awkward, wrapping newspaper round his legs and holding it in place while he pulled up his jeans; tucking it down his waist and up under his jersey; covering his arms and making a clumsy hood for his head. After a struggle it was done, not well but not badly for a first attempt. Then he stretched out on the bracken-covered bench above the dogs and tried to lie still, because every time he moved the newspaper rustled loudly and let in a draught of cold air. But it was warmer than he had expected, and after a restless hour Peter sank into the sleep his body was craving.

He woke before five and though he lay with his eyes closed, it became apparent that he would sleep no more that night. The moon had swung round the sky and now shone full upon the bus shelter. Children waiting for the school bus had scratched messages and jagged pictures in the perspex. They shone white in the moonlight and he read them as he lay with his head on his arm. Some of the names he recognised.

It was very peaceful. His breath clouded in the air.

And as he lay there that frosty morning, Peter realised that his flight was at an end. Without food, money and a sleeping bag there was no way he could continue. When he ran away he had simply wanted to be alone for a while. He had not envisaged helicopters and sleeping rough in a bus shelter. It was time to go home and face the music.

But how was this to be done? He did not like the thought of being reported after the events of yesterday and picked up by the police. Nor did he want to phone, as if in need of help, and have a car come to collect him. There was only one way: he would walk back to Scar Hill over the moors, the way he had come, and give himself up.

Peter leaned over and looked beneath the bench. Meg and Ben seemed warm and settled. Their eyes shone like points of light. He put down a hand and told them about going home. They couldn't understand, how could they, but in a way ... Meg turned her head and licked his wrist.

He lay back with a great rustling and watched the misshapen moon through the perspex. Not a single window was lit in the nearby houses.

42

Helicopter on the Hill

A PERIOD OF high pressure had settled over the country and the frosty night was followed by a brilliantly clear morning.

Peter stuffed the newspapers back into the bin, threw out the bracken and set off in the dark. By nine o'clock he had crossed the river, climbed from the valley and was high on the open moor. A cold wind blew in his face and the little lochs danced in the sunshine. A group of red deer hinds watched his approach and bounded away across the heather. Five miles to the north, the way he was heading, Blae Fell lifted its head above the wilderness.

The dogs seemed unaffected by their night in the bus shelter but Peter's back was stiff and his legs were weary. To add to the discomfort, his socks had not dried out and his blisters hurt, though the Doberman's bite seemed to be healing. Head lowered, he trudged on. Scar Hill seemed a long way off.

He had intended to walk all the way but when the helicopter appeared an hour later, he was relieved more than sorry. After a brief struggle with himself, he ran to the top of a rise and waved his arms. The pilot spotted him and altered course. With throbbing rotors the helicopter hovered and dropped to the moor as gently as a leaf.

The blades freewheeled to a halt as Peter walked to meet it. The doors slid back. The pilot and another man jumped down.

The pilot wore orange overalls and a helmet. He was young and blue-eyed with a pleasant, open face. His name was Davy.

'Peter Irwin?' he said.

Peter nodded.

'Thank God! Are you all right?'

'Yeah.'

'Where the hell have you been? Everyone's been worried to death about you.'

Worried? Peter was surprised. Who could be worried? Angry, more like.

'I was – ' he gestured vaguely. 'Spent a night at the sheep fanks. Then Reckitt's Mines.'

'Yes, we found your stuff.' The pilot took in his dirty face and hands, his ripped jacket, the half-wild expression in his eyes. 'You look as if you could do with a good hot meal and your bed.' He rummaged in a breast pocket and produced a bar of chocolate. 'Here.'

Peter shook his head.

'Don't be daft, take it.' The pilot pushed it into his hands and to Peter's surprise put an arm round his shoulders.

The other man said, 'The whole village has been out looking for you – police, mountain rescue.'

Peter recognised him. His name was Murdo Sutherland. He was a lean man with a craggy face. An old friend of his dad's. Gamekeeper on an estate the far side of Strath Teal. It was Murdo who'd been bitten by the conger eel and nearly bled to death.

'I'm sorry,' Peter said. 'I didn't mean to cause all this bother.'

'Dinna worry yourself, son. You've had a rough ride. Just so long as you're safe.' He patted his knee to make friends with Ben and Meg. They liked his smell and came up with wagging tails. 'What are their names?'

Peter told him and looked round at the pilot. 'Do you know if they picked up Buster?'

'Don't tell me, your ferret?'

He nodded.

'Yeah, he's fine. Murdo there's been looking after him.'

Murdo looked up. 'Great little fella. Put him in a run over at my place. Bring him back when you're ready.'

'Thanks very much.' Peter hesitated. 'Do you know anything about Daisy?'

'Daisy?'

'My sister's little girl. Just a baby. I was looking after her, then she got sick.' Now he'd stopped walking Peter began to feel cold. He gripped the neck of his jacket.

'You're freezing, boy. Here, I've got a couple of flasks in the chopper.' The pilot swung aboard and returned with a small rucksack and red survival blanket. 'Come on, get you warmed up, then we'll head home.'

'Home where?'

'Scar Hill – that's where you live, isn't it?'

A low cliff provided shelter from the wind. Peter draped the blanket round his shoulders. They made themselves comfortable on rocks.

The tea was hot and sweet. Davy produced sandwiches and a slice of cake.

'Go on,' he insisted when Peter tried to refuse. 'I had a fry-up for breakfast, what did you eat?' He pulled off his helmet, revealing a tangle of fair hair.

Peter squinted into the sun. Warmth began to radiate from his stomach.

'What about Daisy?' he said again. 'Have you heard anything?'

'Yeah, I saw her this morning as a matter of fact. Lady Crompton's looking after her. Said she'd been sick but it was only a forty-eight hour thing. Fine again now. Chuckling away there in her carrycot.'

'Lady Crompton?' Peter was puzzled.

'Lives the end of your road. Said she knew you. Didn't you phone her to tell her the baby was ill? She's the one found you were missing, got all this started.'

'No,' he said, 'I rang Bunny Mason. She's the one lives at the end of our road.'

'That's right, Lady Crompton. Used to be married to that man started all the supermarkets. You know, *Crompton's: the Shopper's Friend.* There's one in Clashbay.'

Peter was confused. 'I'm sorry, I don't follow you. D'you mean she's got her sister staying or something?'

'Not as far as I know. I've been to the house a few times and I've never seen anyone else. Lives there by herself, doesn't she?'

'Are you telling me she's the same person?'

'Well, yeah.'

'But I don't understand. If she's Bunny Mason, how can she be Lady Crompton?'

'No great mystery, she got divorced. You've seen her husband in the papers often enough. You know, fat little Billy Crompton with a big cigar and a bimbo on each arm. *Sir* Billy Crompton, I should say. Knighted for his services to industry.'

Peter shook his head.

'Prob'ly have done, just not been interested.'

The moors spread before them, mile upon mile. Meg rested her head on Murdo's knee.

'It's quite a story,' Davy went on. 'I don't know all the details but from what I can make out, Billy's wife – that's Lady Crompton – she had no taste for the high life. Not after the first few years anyway. Dinners and cocktail parties, having to play the charming hostess, everyone talking money and takeovers, knocking back the champers. Then her husband fooling around with these slappers half his age and getting into the gossip columns. Couldn't stand it. So she started putting all her energy into good works: you know, charities and fund-raising, that sort of thing. Travelled all over the place. But in the end she'd had enough. The children were grown up and she wanted out. So she gets a divorce and goes back to her maiden name, Bunny Mason. Comes up here for a bit of peace and quiet. Wants to try her hand at writing children's books – had one published too. Since the papers got hold of the story they've been having a field day.'

It took a while to digest. 'So it was true, what she told me, about being a magistrate and all that?'

'Don't know about magistrate, but yeah, if she said so. None of the people up here knew anything about it. But then you went AWOL and she was worried to death. So she used her influence and, well, here we are.'

A pair of chaffinches landed on a nearby rock. Peter threw a crust towards them. They were not used to being fed out there on the moor and flew away.

After a while Peter said, 'If she's still looking after Daisy, does that mean our Valerie never turned up?'

'Who's Valerie again?'

'My sister. Daisy's mother.'

''Fraid not, son,' Murdo said. 'Not for want of looking neither. Seems she's just disappeared. Her and that boyfriend of hers. Took the lorry back to Glasgow, right enough, but the boss give him his cards. Can't say he didn't deserve it. After that,' he shrugged, 'just vanished into thin air. Not a word.'

'Something must have happened,' Peter said.

Murdo hesitated. 'Gave your dad a bit of a run around, didn't she? Took off before.'

'But she wouldn't leave the baby,' he said. 'She'd never go off and leave Daisy behind.'

'No one's heard anything.'

'Could she be looking for a place to stay?' Davy said. 'A little flat maybe. Then come back and take the baby down with her.'

'Yeah, but she'd give me a ring wouldn't she. Far as she knows, I'm still there looking after Daisy by myself. I'd have to go and get food. They'd be asking about me at school. She knows that, she's not stupid.'

'Let's just hope we hear from her soon.' Davy looked round at his helicopter. The long blades drooped. 'First thing we've got to do is get you home. I'll give them a buzz, put everyone's mind at rest. ''Specially Lady Crompton, she's been very upset.'

'Because of me?' Peter said. 'It wasn't her fault.'

'It's not a question of whose fault.' Davy stood up and stretched. 'You ran away and she's upset. Think about it.'

He collected the flasks and crossed to the helicopter. Peter followed, still shawled in the red blanket. As he left the shelter of the rocks the cold wind hit him in the face.

Davy took a mike from the control panel: 'Hello? ZX1 to base. ZX1 to base.'

After a few moments a woman's voice crackled back.

'Hello,' he said. 'That you, Skip? ... Yes, Davy here. Look, great news, we've got the boy ... Flagged us down up here on the moor ... 'Bout a mile, mile and a half near side of Strath Teal ... No, he seems to be fine. Bit tired, looks like he needs a good meal and his bed. I've given him a hot drink and a sandwich ... Say again?... Well, if you want the doc to look him over. I'll take him back to Scar Hill then, that's his place ... Yeah, right. Murdo and I can knock up a bit of nosh while he has a bath.' He glanced at Peter and turned aside. 'Listen, I'll get him to show us where his dad's buried – if he's agreeable, that is. Save taking him out again later. What do you think?... OK, will do.' He turned back and saw Peter watching. 'Yeah, give you a call then ... Blue sky, couldn't be better ... Right, bye ... ZX1 to base, over and out.'

He replaced the handset. 'I don't know if you caught that, Peter. What do you say? Fly you back home and you can show us where your dad's buried on the way.'

Where your dad's buried – just like that. Peter hadn't dared to ask. He liked Davy – but if he knew, did that mean everyone else did? His friends? His teachers? The whole village?

He gave a small nod.

Murdo said, 'Nothing to feel bad about, son.' He rested a gnarled hand on Peter's shoulder.

'I didn't know what else – '

'Your dad thought the world of you. I'll tell you one thing: when my time comes, if they'd bury me out there on the slopes of Blae Fell, I'd die a happy man.'

'We'd best be getting along.' Davy climbed aboard and

passed Peter a spare helmet. 'You sit up front here beside me. Murdo can go in the back with the dogs. Be OK in the chopper, will they?'

'Yeah, they'll be fine,' he said.

'Have to tie them up close to the bulkhead, stop them falling around.'

'I'll do it.' He pulled off the blanket and called Ben. 'Come on then. Good boy. Up we go.' He clicked his tongue. Obediently the big dog, who would have died for Peter, jumped up and followed him to the rear of the aircraft. Davy handed him a rope and he tied Ben's collar to a strut.

Ben smelled of disinfectant. Peter hadn't finished washing out the blood and his breast was still matted. The bite was a thick scab.

'What happened to his neck?' Murdo said.

'Got in a fight but it's healing now.'

'Aye, I had a look. He'll be all right. Take him to the vet and get a jab, just to be on the safe side.'

Ben knew they were talking about him and looked up. Peter rubbed his ears.

Meg was reluctant, she did not like the helicopter. After a lot of coaxing Peter lifted her aboard. She was heavier than he expected. 'Hey, you're getting fat.' He set her on the deck and was struck by a sudden fear. She couldn't be … He ran a hand under her belly and felt the swollen teats. 'Ah, no!' he said. 'Don't tell me. That's all we need, pups. Come on, Meg, give me a break.'

When had she been in heat? With all that was happening he hadn't noticed. There was only one dog could be the father. Ben stood watching as if whatever was happening had nothing to do with him.

Peter tied her to an adjacent strut. 'All right, it's not your fault.' He cuddled her because she was frightened and thought she was in trouble. 'Good girl, yes! Good boy!' He gave them some little dog biscuits that Murdo carried in the pocket of his field jacket.

Davy showed him how to fasten the helmet and strap himself in. He slid the door shut. With a roar the engine started up. The rotor blades revolved – faster and faster until they were a blur.

'Ready?' Davy looked across.

'Yeah.'

The engine note picked up. At a speed that forced Peter down into his seat and made his head spin, they whirled up into the sky.

43

Return to Scar Hill

PETER LOOKED DOWN from the cockpit. At fifteen hundred feet the moor had flattened out. Mile upon mile, the land was brown and russet and green with outcrops of grey rock and patches of black peat. Little lochs, edged with ice, reflected the sky like mirrors. It was a land untouched by man. A dinosaur plodding beneath them, pausing to tear up bunches of vegetation, would not have seemed out of place.

Any other time Peter would have exulted in the ride but now, as he spied the shoulders of Blae Fell and tried to work out just where, on its lower slopes, his dad was buried, his heart was anxious.

Davy looked sideways. 'When all this has blown over we'll have to take you a trip somewhere,' he said. 'Where d'you fancy? Out to the islands? Down the country for a good nosh-up?'

'Thanks.' Peter smiled back.

But he thought, *When all this has blown over.* Yeah, neat. Come and look me up.

Davy said no more and Peter returned to searching the hillsides.

'Down there.' He pointed. 'A bit below them rocks.'

'Sure?'

'I think so. Looks different from up here.'

The helicopter dropped below the summit. Rabbits dashed for cover. Sheep bounded off with swirling tails.

'Yeah, that's it,' Peter said. 'I recognise that little cliff.

Davy needed a flat spot. With a gentle bump the helicopter

touched down, rocked and came to rest. He switched off the engine. The rotor blades freewheeled to a halt.

Peter got out first and pulled off his helmet. The silence of the moor, broken only by the whine of wind in the metal spars, clapped about his ears. He remembered the spot well, even though the grave was nowhere to be seen. He aligned the scatter of boulders with the cliff higher up the slope and started to climb. Soon he saw it, a rough black rectangle, well over to one side.

Snow had weakened his simple cross, the late winter gales had knocked it to the ground. It lay on its back, half-hidden by the heather. The wood was sodden but his dad's name, *James Allan Irwin,* and the years of his birth and death, were as fresh as the day he had painted them. In the five or six weeks since his last visit, the peat had settled. Little plumes of grass and weed had established themselves round the stark black edges of the scar.

Davy and Murdo joined him. They tried not to intrude but Peter didn't want them there, he wanted to be alone. Davy moved away but Murdo took off his cap, revealing a bald brown dome. He was looking down but his thoughts were elsewhere. Jim had been a drinking pal.

Peter tried to conjure up his dad's memory but only fragments would come. He said a silent sorry and gazed blankly at the grave. Like yesterday he remembered digging it, sweating in the icy wind, toppling in his dad's body, the spadefuls of peat thudding down, battering in the cross with his spade. It was a nightmare. And now, instead of picturing his dad as he had been in the past, all he could wonder was whether his body was being preserved, like the man in Denmark, or was starting to rot. He didn't want to think about it and moved away.

Davy produced a can of marker paint and sprayed a huge orange cross in the heather. 'Won't be me that comes back,' he explained. 'Probably a police chopper.'

'What'll they do?' Peter asked.

Davy hesitated: 'Dig him up and take him back.'

'Where to?'

'Clashbay Infirmary, I should think. Or maybe down to Inverness.'

'In a body bag?'

'You don't want to be thinking about these things,' Murdo said. 'Try to remember your dad as he was.'

But Peter wanted to know. 'They'll have to carry out a post-mortem won't they?'

'I expect so.'

'Like on TV, on a slab and everything?'

'I don't know. I've never seen a post-mortem.'

'I can tell them before they start,' Peter said. 'It was his heart. Doctor Bryson's been treating him. He was trying to reach his pills when he died. They were scattered all over the place.' The memory brought a lump into his chest. 'What about after? Will he have a funeral or will they just bury him?'

'For goodness sake, boy, what questions. Of course he'll have a funeral. He was your dad.' He glanced at Davy then back at the tense, scruffy boy who stood before them. 'Look, we don't want to be talking about all this here. Let's get you back home and into the warmth.'

They returned to the helicopter and Peter directed them to Scar Hill. The orange cross spun away beneath them, the moors fled past and in no time at all, it seemed, there was the track, there were the sheep, there was the rocky outcrop that gave the house its name. Davy hovered above the buildings and selected a spot for landing. Birds flew off in alarm and the heather tossed wildly in the down-draught. The helicopter touched down and came to rest.

Somehow, although he had only been away for a few days, the house looked abandoned. Two planks were nailed across the door which had been kicked in by the police when they were searching for him. Ben and Meg came scrambling from the helicopter, delighted to be home. He collected the keys from the byre, even though they were not needed, while Davy and Murdo tore off the planks. The lock was splintered; the door swung open at the touch of a hand.

Peter led the way into the familiar rooms, impregnated with the tingling scent of the peat fire. The air was cold, the grate full of ash. A fine film of dust lay on the furniture.

'Right.' Davy looked around him. 'Got an immersion?'

'In the kitchen.'

'Switch it on and get yourself into a hot bath. All right if I light the fire?'

Soon the first smoky flames were licking up the chimney. Peter gave the dogs a double ration of meaty chunks. Davy went into the hall and made some phone calls. Murdo explored the food cupboards and made coffee.

'Got a clean set of clothes?' he said. 'I'll put that lot in the wash while you have your bath.'

The water was about ready as the first car arrived. Whoever it was, Peter did not want to meet them. He gulped the last of his coffee, grabbed a biscuit and ran upstairs. There were voices in the hall. Surely they would not follow him into his bedroom. Quickly he pulled off his dirty clothes and threw them down to Murdo.

The cold gave him goose pimples. Standing by the electric fire, he examined himself in the wardrobe mirror. His face and neck, hands and feet, were black with dirt. Elsewhere he looked clean enough, though bruised and scratched in his flight from Owl Cottage. The dog bite, though it did not hurt, was still red and a bit puffy. Both heels showed ragged blisters. He smelled of sweat.

'Can you hear me, Peter?' A voice rang up the stairs. 'It's Bunny Mason.'

'Yeah,' he shouted back. 'I'm just getting into the bath. Not be long.'

But Peter planned to take his time. He did not look forward to meeting Bunny Mason (Lady Crompton, as Davy called her), or Constable Taylor, or social workers, or whoever else might turn up at Scar Hill in the next hour and fire questions at him. These were people who had reason to be angry with him;

people who had been out searching when he was safe all the time; people who would ask him about his dad; people whose job it was to decide his future. He flitted along the landing and locked himself in the bathroom.

For half an hour he lay with the water to his chin, topping it up as it cooled. More cars arrived. People called upstairs. 'Yes,' he shouted back and sank below the surface.

But Peter couldn't stay in the bath for ever. Reluctantly he emerged and rubbed himself dry. There was TCP in the bathroom cabinet. He dabbed some on cotton wool and scrubbed his assorted wounds. Then he dressed in his grey school trousers and best jersey, and went downstairs.

Mouth-watering smells rose to meet him.

For a minute he stood at the living-room door, trying to make out what was being said inside. The voices were not angry, on the contrary they sounded quite lively and at ease. There was laughter at some remark. Nervously he pushed the door open. All eyes turned in his direction. Everyone fell silent.

Six people were waiting to greet him. Four he knew: Bunny Mason, Constable Taylor, Davy the pilot and Murdo Sutherland. The others were a young policewoman and a man with a kindly face in his forties who turned out to be a youth worker named Mr Fyffe. All had cups of tea or coffee. A plate of biscuits stood on the table.

'Peter!' Bunny jumped to her feet and hugged him tightly. 'What a fright you gave us all, running away like that!'

He stood silent, not trusting himself to speak.

She let him go. 'Davy and Murdo said there wasn't much wrong with you. I must say you look all right to me.'

'Yes, I'm OK.' He wiped off a drop of water that ran from his hair.

'You smell of TCP.'

'It's nothing,' he said. 'I got bitten by a dog though.'

'A dog bite! Is it bad?'

'Not really, its teeth went in a bit.' He touched his thigh.

'When?'

'Just yesterday.'

'You'll have to let the doctor see it. We'll go this afternoon, get an anti-tetanus jab.'

'Ben too.'

'That's right, the pair of you.' She smiled. 'Murdo was telling us.'

'Where's Daisy?'

'I left her at home. Mary's looking after her – you know, my cleaning lady.'

'How is she?'

'Oh, Daisy's fine. Just a bit of a cold.'

'Can I go and see her?'

'Good gracious, of course you can.'

Ben didn't like so many strangers and touched him with a black nose. Peter put down his hand.

Mr Fyffe asked, 'Why did you run away, son?'

'Never mind that right now.' Murdo emerged from the kitchen with a big fry-up. 'The lad needs a hot meal inside him. Your questions can wait.'

Peter discovered he was hungry and soon was mopping the fat from his plate and reaching for a mug of tea. Then he found himself on the settee with Davy at his side, unburdening himself for the second time of everything that had happened that winter and trying to explain how he felt about it all: his dad's illness and death, burying him on the hill, the arrival of Valerie, spending Jim's Social Security money, Daisy's birth in the snowstorm, Valerie's disappearance, looking after the baby, her illness, running away, and finally his fears for the future, having to leave Scar Hill, and being separated from the faithful Ben and Meg who had never known any other home.

Constable Taylor said, 'You seem to think everyone's going to be angry with you. Why's that?'

'Well,' Peter looked from one to the other. 'All the things I've done. I did try to ring you when dad died, and Billy Josh, but there was nobody there. Then Valerie and me took all that money and everything.'

'So you're in big trouble?'

He nodded mutely.

The policewoman said gently, 'Don't you realise we've all been worried to death about you?'

'That's right,' Bunny said. 'Oh, Peter! I did try to tell you. Have you still been thinking everyone's furious? That we'll all think you're a bad boy? Going to end up in court? I should have realised!' She shook her head. 'It's the very opposite, love. People haven't been out searching because you're some sort of criminal. It's because we all *care* about you. Everyone's been terrified you'd had an accident, or got lost, or gone into the river, or frozen out there on the moors. The telephone's never stopped ringing. Do you know there were ten degrees of frost last night? And you didn't even have your sleeping bag, you left it behind at the mines.'

He shrugged. 'I was all right.'

'Yes, we can see that now, but we didn't know at the time.'

Constable Taylor said, 'The first job of the police isn't to punish people, Peter, it's to help them. Especially a boy that's looked after his dad like you have and never been in trouble in his life. In a village like this we know all these things.'

Peter couldn't believe it. 'Do you mean I'm *not* in trouble? After everything that's happened.'

'Of course not, love,' Bunny said.

'As far as the money's concerned,' Mr Fyffe said, 'you can forget about that because it's already been paid back. Lady Crompton here sorted it out. Mind, I think we'll have to have a little chat with your sister when she turns up.'

Peter looked towards Bunny who smiled reassuringly.

'Our Valerie,' he said. 'Have you heard nothing at all?'

'There has been one development,' said Constable Taylor, 'but it doesn't get us very far. We've tracked down the lorry. Routine police work, the owner had reported it overdue. Had a load for that big farm supplier just along the coast here. The driver's name was,' he flipped through his notebook, 'Matthew Ramage. That sound right to you?'

'He was called Matt,' Peter said.

'Is this him?' Constable Taylor unfolded a piece of paper.

It was a fax, a photo of Matt taken a few years earlier. His hair was cropped short. He wore a white T-shirt and leather jacket.

Peter nodded.

'Apparently he turned up at the depot with some cock-and-bull story about being sick. Wasn't the first time he'd tried it on and the boss give him his cards.'

'Did they say anything about Valerie?'

'He had a young woman with him; it sounds like your sister.'

Peter tried to imagine it. 'What happened to them?'

'I'm afraid that's it. He collected his wages, walked out the depot gates.' Constable Taylor shrugged. 'Just disappeared.'

Bunny said, 'Surely his employer had an address.'

'Just a flat he'd shared with some other lads. They hadn't seen him for six months.'

Peter said, 'Valerie used to live in Bristol.'

'That's useful.' The constable made a note. 'I don't suppose you've got an address?'

'Sorry.'

'Well, we'll let them know anyway. Who knows, they might come up with something.' He ran a hand through his hair. 'All we can do is wait.'

'Social Security have got them on the computer,' Mr Fyffe said. 'If Valerie or this Matt sign on anywhere in the country, we'll know about it.' He sat forward, nursing his mug of tea. 'Listen, Peter, I don't know what you've heard about people like me, but basically my job's to make sure children are safe and happy. We don't always succeed, but we do our best. The very last thing we'd want to do is take a boy away from his home or separate him from his dog. I've spoken to a lot of people about you over the past few days and had nothing but good reports. I think I can promise that – well, I'll let Lady Crompton tell you about it.'

Peter looked from one to the other.

'Well, Peter.' Bunny stood by the fire. 'I'm sure this must be a bit of an ordeal for you, so I'll get straight to the point. I've had some long talks with your teachers, and Mr Fyffe here and some other people, and if you'd like to, they'd be very happy for you to come and stay with me at Three Pines. There's plenty of room. So many animals already, your Ben and Meg won't make much difference. We'd both have to make a few adjustments, of course, but I think we'd get along pretty well. I've brought up two boys of my own, I know what boys are like. I'd be glad to have you there. You can help me with those damned goats for a start. Learn to milk Molly. We'd be able to pop along here and feed the sheep and keep an eye on the house. And you'd stay on at the same school, so you'd not be losing your friends.' She thrust her hands into her jacket pockets. 'So there's the offer – it's up to you.'

Live at Three Pines. Peter had never considered it – at least, not to stay there more than a few days.

'How long for?' he said, frightened he had misunderstood.

'Until we have news of your sister anyway,' Bunny replied. 'When she turns up you might like to go off and live with her, but we'll cross that bridge when we come to it. What I'm suggesting is you make Three Pines your home.' She smiled. 'You've got a choice of two bedrooms. What do you say, young man? Give it a go?'

Peter couldn't believe this was happening. 'Are you sure?'

'I wouldn't ask you if I wasn't sure.'

'Then yes,' he said. 'Thanks. It would be great.'

'Good,' she said. 'Then that's settled.'

'What about Daisy?'

'Daisy will come with you,' she said. 'For the moment anyway. Like I say, until we have news of her mother.'

Ben seemed to know that something important was taking place and pressed against him for reassurance.

Peter rested a hand on his back. The people who had gathered to meet him were all smiling. He tried to smile back although what he wanted, even though the occasion was momentous, was to escape into the open air.

'Go on then,' Bunny said briskly. 'Away out with you, make yourself useful. I haven't fed the sheep yet today. Why don't you do it.'

'Yeah, OK,' he said. 'Come on, Ben, Meg.'

He took two biscuits from the plate and ran off down the yard holding them high and the dogs bounding and leaping at his side.

44

Wild Daffodils and a Letter

IT WAS IMPOSSIBLE to keep things out of the papers and Peter's return caused much excitement, not just locally but in the national press and even on television. Three Pines was besieged by reporters. They drove up the track to photograph Scar Hill. When Jim was exhumed from his shallow grave they gathered on the hillside to report the activity – though the grave itself was hidden beneath a canvas tent. Pictures of the body bag being carried to a police helicopter, and the endless moors which surrounded the spot, appeared in every newspaper in the country.

To protect Peter from all this unwanted attention, Bunny arranged for the animals to be cared for and took him away for a short holiday. They stayed at a hotel in Glasgow, which to Peter's surprise turned out to be a wonderful city. The contrast to recent events could hardly have been greater and they had a happy time visiting restaurants, going to the cinema, ice-skating, sailing up Loch Lomond, and joining the crowds at Ibrox for a midweek Rangers–Celtic match.

While they were there, Bunny took him to buy a plain, charcoal-grey suit. Two days after they got back he wore it to his father's funeral. The morning was cold and misty. Peter refused to wear a black tie like the other mourners, but insisted on a red tie with a picture of a stag on it which Jim had bought him a few months earlier.

Before the funeral car arrived, he drove out to Scar Hill and picked a bunch of early daffodils from the clumps that grew wild near the house. Jim had loved the daffodils with their brave splash of yellow against the grey stone dykes and beaten grass of winter.

St Andrew's Church, which Peter had last attended with Valerie for the Watch Night service, stood on the edge of the village. He followed the ushers up the centre aisle. To his surprise the church was packed, partly with reporters and sightseers, but also because Jim Irwin, although a private man and given to periods of drunkenness, was popular in the village. Peter was the principal mourner, sitting with Bunny, Murdo Sutherland and another of Jim's friends in the front pew. His daffodils rested on the coffin. It was hard to believe that his dad lay in that polished box with the bright brass handles. He had been told the body was perfectly preserved and hoped that were true.

They sang Psalm 23 and the hymns 'By Cool Siloam's Shady Rill' and 'Onward Christian Soldiers' which, as a soldier who had fought in the desert, were two of Jim's favourites. In his eulogy the minister praised his dad's life and character and described what a loving father he had been to Peter.

A long line of cars followed the hearse to the graveyard. It stood above the shore with a dry stone dyke separating it from the dunes and tumbling blue sea beyond. Four men carried the coffin up the crunching gravel path and across the trim grass between the gravestones. Peter, walking with Bunny and Murdo, led the ragged procession that followed behind. In addition to his daffodils, held by an elastic band, a florist's wreath lay on the coffin lid. It was inscribed:

TO OUR DAD

WITH MUCH LOVE

PETER AND VALERIE

Jim's second burial was a very different affair from the first for the grave was deep and immaculate, the sun shone, and in place of trampled peat and heather, a dozen wreaths from friends and well-wishers brightened the grass nearby. Peter took a rope as the coffin was lowered and threw down a single daffodil from his bunch. Bright and brave, it landed beside the little brass plaque engraved with Jim's name and the dates of his birth and death. Cameras sparkled as the press photographers took pictures. The minister, his cassock and bands blowing in the breeze, performed the brief service of committal and indicated that as Jim's son Peter should be first to throw down a handful of earth. He did so, to the accompaniment of more flashes, and watched with a sad heart as others followed, the soil rattling onto the shiny lid.

The minister said the benediction and made the sign of the cross – and suddenly it was all over. People offered words of sympathy, the first chance they had had, and began drifting away. Peter read the cards on the wreaths. A reporter approached and tried to interview him; Bunny sent the man packing. It seemed wrong to walk off and leave his dad just lying there but there was nothing else to be done. As he looked back from the gate he saw the gravediggers busy with their shovels.

Everyone was invited for drinks and sandwiches at the Tarridale Hotel. Peter attended for half an hour because it was the right thing to do, then Bunny took him home to Three Pines.

He sat in an armchair with Daisy in his lap and told her about it. 'He was your granddad, you'd have liked him. He was a nice man. He'd have nursed you like I do and given you bottles. But he wasn't well. The army made him sick.'

Daisy looked into his face and blew happy bubbles. He gave her a squeeze and she crowed with laughter, showing her pink gums and smearing his suit with spit.

'When you're a big girl, I'll tell you all about him.' Peter nodded vigorously. 'Yes, I will.'

A letter had arrived from Messrs Simpson, Fraser and Cherriwick, a leading firm of solicitors, asking Peter and his guardian to call at their offices for the reading of his father's will. Two days after the funeral Bunny drove him to Clashbay in the Land Rover. She wore a smart green costume, earrings and a brooch. Peter wore his suit with a blue, open-necked shirt.

Mr Fraser ushered them into his room. He was a pleasant, balding man in a striped shirt, the sleeves gripped by red and silver armbands. An office junior brought coffee and cream with a plate of biscuits. Peter and Bunny sat facing Mr Fraser across his big polished desk as he pulled Jim's folder towards him and took out the will.

'I'll give you a copy to take away, of course, but the basic bequests are really quite simple. Everything, with one small exception, has been left to his son, Peter. That's you, young man. Your father had two bank accounts: a current account and a savings account. The figures have got to be finalised but together they come to about eleven thousand, two hundred pounds. There are a couple of policies to be cashed in, as well, which amount to a further eighteen thousand pounds, maybe a little more. In total it comes to a bit under thirty thousand pounds.'

'And all this goes to Peter,' Bunny said.

'No, there's the small exception I mentioned. Mr Irwin has left the sum of five thousand pounds to his daughter Valerie, in the event that she should contact him within,' he checked the document, 'the next three years.'

'And what about his wife, Peter's mother?' Bunny asked. 'She's still alive as far as we know.'

'Indeed she is, but they are divorced.'

'So she can have no claim on the estate?'

'That's correct.'

Peter said, 'Is it all right to ask? I don't want to see her again or anything but do you know what's happened to her? Dad never said.'

Mr Fraser smiled over the top of his glasses. 'Your father thought you might ask. He's left you a letter.' He slid an envelope across the table. 'I'm sure it won't answer all your questions but I believe it contains as much as he knew. I'm sorry you're not a little older but, well, there we are.'

Peter took it and read his name, *Peter Irwin*, in his dad's handwriting.

'You can read it when we get home,' Bunny said. 'That be all right?'

Peter nodded.

'Very good.' Mr Fraser steepled his fingers. 'Well, subtracting your sister's bequest, which will revert to you if she fails to appear within the given period, and taking into account the funeral expenses and our fee, your monetary inheritance will amount to something like twenty-three thousand pounds.'

Peter listened silently. It was unreal. This was his dad the solicitor was talking about. The words and numbers rolled through his head.

'I'm permitted to release some of this money now, to be placed in a bank account for your needs in the short term – clothes, holidays, education, that sort of thing. I'd suggest five thousand pounds. The remainder will, very wisely in my opinion, be invested at our discretion to be released to you on your twenty-first birthday.' Mr Fraser studied the documents before him. 'The most important and valuable item of the will, of course, is the house, Scar Hill, and the land and crofting rights that go with it. These, together with all the contents, have also been left to you. But like the money, your father's left them in trust until you reach the age of twenty-one.'

'What precisely does that mean?' Bunny asked.

'Well, they're his, but don't actually come into his possession until he's twenty-one. How old are you now, Peter?'

'Thirteen.'

'Well, for the next eight years we here, at Simpson, Fraser and Cherriwick, will manage the property for you. What's usual in these cases is that we lease it to a tenant, in your name, until you reach the required age. The income, of course, will go into your account – I'd suggest the investment account. On due date the property, including the land and crofting rights, come into your ownership. Then you'll be free to do whatever you like with it.'

Peter's heart was thumping. 'Does that mean I can go back and live there?'

'If you want to, yes. But in the meantime it leaves you free to concentrate on your schooling and go on to college knowing that when you're finished the house will be waiting for you. And the money too, of course. It may sound like a large sum now, but I assure you, if you intend to live at Scar Hill and need to restock and buy machinery it won't go very far.' Mr Fraser sat back. 'We've all heard a little about what you've gone through over the past few months. Nothing's going to compensate for the loss of your father, that goes without saying, but in other ways, once you've got used to the idea, I think you'll come to realise you're a very fortunate young man.'

'I'm sure he does.' Bunny finished her coffee and rose. 'I always liked Jim Irwin and never more than at this minute. You're right, Peter is lucky to have had a most excellent father. Thank you very much, Mr Fraser.'

Dear Pete,

If you are reading this I'm afraid I won't be around.

You're the best son any man could ask for and I love you very much. I'm sorry I haven't been the father I would have liked.

I never said much about your mum but I guess you have a right to know. Don't be hard on her, she's just different to you and me. In the early days, when we were first married and Valerie was a little girl, it was just great. Then I got sick and couldn't be the husband she wanted.

You were there the day she went off and I can never forgive her for putting you and Valerie through that. I didn't go after her or try to bring her back. After I left the army the marriage was really over and there was nothing either of us could do about it.

She never wrote but I heard bits from time to time. It wasn't much and not very reliable. She started calling herself Cynthia Talbot and got a job in a clothes shop in Brighton – she always liked clothes. I think she moved around a bit. One time she was supposed to have gone to Germany but it didn't work out. Last I heard was she'd married someone in the U.S. forces and gone to live in America. It might be right because she enjoyed army life, but it was illegal and very naughty because at that time she was still married to me. I tried to track her down but had no luck. That's when we got divorced.

I suppose she might come back sometime, or maybe when you're older you'll try to find her yourself.

I've just tried to be a good father and I think we're happy here at Scar Hill. Right now, as I write this letter, you're upstairs in bed. I don't know how much longer I'm going to be around. For ever if I had my way.

You're a grand honest boy and I couldn't be more proud of you.

God bless and have a good life,
Dad

The interest died down. Peter went to the shop with Bunny, met people from the village, kicked a ball about with friends.

A few days later he returned to school. He had always been a quiet, popular boy. In no time at all the other pupils, who had been warned by Mrs Harle and their teachers, stopped looking at him. They laughed and jostled as they trooped from lesson to lesson. Slowly life returned to normal.

But not quite yet.

45

A Visit From Constable Taylor

THEY WERE EATING breakfast when the phone rang. It was Davy, the young helicopter pilot. He had promised Peter a flight. Since it was Saturday and the sky was almost cloudless, would he be free to come that very morning? Peter certainly would and an hour later Davy landed on a stretch of moor close to the house. Bunny had prepared flasks of coffee and a lunch box for the two of them. Peter put on a helmet, strapped himself into the observer's seat, and off they whirled.

Peter loved it, they were the most exciting few hours of his life. First they hovered above the school playing fields where his friends broke off a game and stared up, shading their eyes to see who was waving. Peter saw them shouting and waving back crazily but their voices were drowned by the roar of the engine.

Davy had worked out a route. First they flew south-west, climbing above little puffs of cotton-wool clouds to ten thousand feet, higher than such a small helicopter had any need to go. Far beneath them the lochs and moors, white-capped mountains and deep sea inlets were spread out like a map. They flew out above the deep blue waters and fishing boats of the Minch, circled the Isle of Skye and returned to the mainland. Ben Nevis, the highest mountain in the country, lay directly ahead. Davy dropped to see hill walkers trudging through the snow and rock climbers clinging like spiders to tremendous cliffs sheathed in ice.

From Ben Nevis they turned up the Great Glen, skimming Loch Ness and searching for a glimpse of the humpy-backed monster. Bunny's coffee and sandwiches were finished and Davy had arranged lunch at a lochside hotel. It was a two-hundred-year-old Highland hotel with stags' heads on the wall. They ate looking out over the water and after a short break set off again.

Davy refuelled at an RAF station east of Inverness, then flew low across the Moray Firth where dolphins were leaping and a spouting whale, swimming on the surface, dived as they came close. They carried on north over castles and forests and in the late afternoon the well-known coast and islands – unfamiliar from that height – rose to meet them. There was the harbour at Clashbay, there was Tarridale, and all too soon they were touching down on the heather above Three Pines. Davy could not stay for coffee and cakes, he was on duty that night. Peter and Bunny stood watching, their hair and clothes tossed by the downdraught, as the helicopter took off and disappeared beyond the rolling summits of the moor.

A letter arrived from Mr Fraser, the solicitor, informing them that tenants had been found for Scar Hill, a shepherd and his wife with two children. They were renting the grazing rights too, and buying the flock, so needed to take possession within a few days, in time for the lambing. The house had to be cleared quickly.

Bunny in her Land Rover and Peter in the van were up and down the track constantly. Many of Jim's clothes were so worn that nobody would want them, but those that were tidy enough were washed and pressed and taken to a charity shop for the British Heart Foundation. A few pieces of furniture were to remain in the house but the shepherd's wife wanted a new suite and mattresses, a new cooker, a new fridge and many other items. So the saleable pieces were sent off to an auction room while the rest – the pots and pans and rugs and curtains and washing machine and electric fire and battered chairs they had used for as long as Peter could remember – had to be loaded onto the trailer and dragged away to the dump. Treasured and more valuable items, such as pictures and the old clock, were taken to Three Pines and stored in Bunny's loft.

At last it was all done and late one afternoon Bunny drove off with Jasper, leaving Peter to say goodbye to his old home – at least for the time being. Accompanied by the dogs, he walked through the empty rooms: here he had lain in bed and made patterns with the beams across the ceiling; here Jim had cooked their dinner; here Valerie had given birth to Daisy; here he had stood and watched his mother drive away with Morris Sinclair; here he had cuddled up beside his dad and listened to stories at the fireside.

He wandered into the outbuildings. Here was the bed where Ben and Meg had spent their nights; here was the crumbling, hay-filled stall where Jim had gone to escape his demons; here was the stain where he had spilled a bucket of sump oil from the tractor; here was the snowplough; and there were the sheep nuts that would last the tenant until well after lambing.

A small flock of jackdaws flew over the house and landed on the newly-repaired roof of the byre. It was late in the day, after roosting time, almost as if they had come to bid him farewell. There were always jackdaws at Scar Hill. There had been jackdaws the day they arrived, when he was three years old. Perhaps there would be jackdaws to greet him when he returned. But that was a long way ahead.

Peter let the dogs into the van, took a last look round and drove off down the track. The whins were in bloom, dappling the hillsides with gold. The stream reflected the last of the daylight. The house was hidden by the rising moors.

Every morning, as Peter set off for school, Ben accompanied him to the rickety gate. Every afternoon, as the bus came chugging up the long hill, he was there to meet it. Then Peter made a fuss of him and Ben jumped up, his big grey paws on Peter's shoulders, big black nose and tongue snuffling into his ear. A life without Ben, which Peter had feared, was something he could not bear to think about.

One afternoon in March, as they ran down the steep slope to the house, Peter stopped dead in his tracks. A police car was parked alongside the Land Rover. Peter liked Constable Taylor. Several times he had called at Three Pines, just friendly visits to see all was well, but on this occasion he felt a shiver of apprehension.

His intuition was confirmed when he went into the living room. Constable Taylor, who had three children of his own, was bouncing Daisy on his knee. Bunny stood watching him. As Peter appeared in the doorway their smiles faded. For several seconds no one spoke. The policeman returned Daisy to her cot.

At once Peter knew. 'It's Valerie, isn't it?'

'Come and sit down.' Bunny moved a magazine.

He dropped his schoolbag and sank onto the chair.

'I'm afraid so, son,' said Constable Taylor.

'She's dead, isn't she?'

The constable nodded. 'I'm sorry.'

Peter felt he had known for a long time. 'What happened?'

'Car crash.'

Constable Taylor tried to protect him from the most distressing details but Peter filled in the gaps for himself. As he understood it, Valerie and Matt had been travelling so fast they were almost certainly killed instantly. The fire that followed, stoked by the full tank of petrol and hemmed in by the walls of the gorge, had been very intense. To make matters worse, the location was far from the nearest town and by the time the fire engines arrived the car had been gutted. Cutting equipment was needed to remove the bodies. Valerie and Matt were burned beyond recognition – burned so badly that it took forensic examination to establish these were the remains of a man and a woman. The contents of the car – their holdalls and everything that might provide a clue to their identities – had been reduced to ash. The car was identified by serial numbers stamped into the chassis, but it had been stolen from the thronging centre of Glasgow and the identity of the thieves remained unknown.

Ever since, the bodies had lain on cold shelves in the hospital mortuary in Dumfries. But the police forensic department has a long arm. Several weeks later a computerised image of Matt's dental pattern was examined by a dentist who treated inmates at Barlinnie Prison in Glasgow. It matched the record of a young prisoner who had received treatment there several years earlier. His name was Matthew Ramage. The prison had his records. The police computer took only seconds to identify him as the lorry driver who had disappeared a few weeks earlier. They tracked down his distressed parents and his divorced wife who appeared neither sorry nor surprised. They already knew his National Insurance number and HGV licence number. They re-interviewed his last known employer, Mr McReady, who repeated that Matt had been absent for three days somewhere in the region of Tarridale. Yes, when he returned to Glasgow he had been accompanied by a young woman. A police officer drove north to confer with Constable Taylor. Constable Taylor was able to name Valerie Irwin. There was little doubt the body was Valerie and a swab taken from Daisy confirmed her identity by DNA analysis.

Peter's father dead. Now, after all he had been through, his sister too. Bunny saw that he brooded and did her best to distract him. For Peter had loved Valerie. Despite her careless and infuriating ways, she'd had a kind heart. She was a free spirit with a zest for life. And apart from little Daisy and his long-gone mother, she was his only relative.

Valerie's funeral took place a few days later. The sun shone through stained-glass windows into the church which was full of young people. With a heavy heart Peter followed her coffin to the graveyard to be buried just a few metres from their dad.

Now it was known Valerie would not be coming back, a decision had to be made. Peter loved living with Bunny Mason. In those few weeks she had become the mother he'd never known. He called her Bunny, and sometimes Auntie Bunny. Since his dad was gone and Scar Hill was occupied by tenants, he could not imagine a happier home than Three Pines.

'Well, Peter,' she said. 'What do you think?' It was the day of the funeral and they sat finishing supper at the kitchen table. 'I love having you here, I hope you know that. Nothing would make me happier than if you wanted to stay on. But the decision's got to be yours.'

'Do you mean for keeps?' He felt the blood rise into his cheeks.

'That's exactly what I mean. Now your sister won't be coming back. A final decision, stay here and help me look after the animals. Make Three Pines your home.'

In an alcove under the stairs, where the dogs had their beds, Ben sensed that something was afoot and trotted through to the big kitchen. He was followed by Jasper who had become his inseparable friend.

'Are you sure?' Peter said. 'It's what I'd like more than anything.'

'Of course I'm sure. I wouldn't have asked you otherwise.' She sat back, nursing her mug of hot chocolate. 'Good, that's settled then.'

'Thanks.' He didn't know what else to say.

The dogs stood watching. Peter's eye was caught by a squeaky rubber duck at the far side of the room. 'Hey, Ben,' he said urgently. 'Where's Quacks?'

Instantly alert, Ben stared around the kitchen, spotted his yellow toy and bounded across like a puppy. Jasper followed and they wrestled for it, snuffling and wuffing, tails flailing high in the air.

Meg came into the room. Calmly, as if she were too old for such games, she watched Ben and Jasper at their play. Her teats were pink and swollen. A week earlier, in a cardboard box lined with newspaper, she had given birth to six puppies in a cupboard at the end of the hall. Bunny woke Peter in the middle of the night and he came down to observe and help.

There was no doubt who the father was for two were grey, the image of Ben, two were a mixture and one was black and white like their mother. The sixth, a grey puppy twisted like a scarf, was born dead and Bunny took it away to bury in the pasture.

How much easier it was for dogs than people, Peter thought as he watched the pups slip out into the world enclosed in their little sacs, and saw how economically Meg bit through the umbilical cord and licked each puppy clean. So different from Valerie with her loud cries and long night of pain.

Bunny took Meg into the outer kitchen for a dish of Molly's rich milk with an egg beaten into it, and a helping of meaty chunks. Her babies, blind and helpless, spent half their time sleeping and the rest whimpering and snuffling into her belly for food. If they were to thrive she needed plenty of nourishment.

While Meg was absent, Peter went down the hall and looked into the cardboard box. The puppies were enchanting. Very gently, feeling how fat its belly was, he picked up the black and white one and held it close to his chest. The puppy did not like it and mewed to be returned. He held it a moment longer, stroking its soft fur with the back of a finger. The action reminded him of Daisy, sound asleep in her cot upstairs, and how he had stroked her new-born cheek in just the same way. Baby girl and puppies. Births and deaths. He replaced the pup among its brothers and sisters and picked up one of the grey ones. What would Ben make of them all, he wondered.

Leaving the cupboard door three-quarters shut, the way Meg liked it, he returned to the kitchen. On the way he paused and looked all round: at the paintings on the walls, up the well-carpeted stairs to the bedrooms, into the sitting room with its comfortable furniture. This was his home. He pinched the back of his leg to be sure it wasn't a dream and in a moment he would wake to find himself on the run again, hungry and hunted by the police.

46

Four Miles on the Bike

'YOU MUST KNOW Colin,' Bunny said. 'Colin McGregor, a lovely man. Lives down by the river. Drives the ambulance.'

'He plays keeper for Clashbay Rovers.' It was the Easter holiday. Peter sat on the sofa giving Daisy her midday bottle.

'That's him.'

'He's nice,' said Peter, picturing Colin in his green paramedic uniform.

'That's what I'm saying. And so's his wife. Used to be a staff nurse at the infirmary.'

'Mairi,' Peter said. 'Mrs McKendrick's daughter. 'We stayed with her – Mrs McKendrick, I mean – when we first came up here. While Scar Hill was being done up.'

'Yes, she told me.'

'She was still at school,' Peter said. 'I was only little but she used to play with me and take me down to the beach. She was lovely.'

'An absolute gem,' Bunny agreed. 'You'll not meet a nicer young woman this side of Christmas. Daisy couldn't have a more loving home. And they're so keen for her to come.'

Peter had known from the day he heard Valerie would not be returning that some time he would be having this conversation, or a conversation very like it. That didn't make it any easier.

'Mairi and Colin have both said – and they mean it – you're to look in to see her any time you want. After all, you're her uncle, the only relative she's got.'

'Yeah.' Daisy lay in the crook of his arm, nearly asleep. Peter rocked the bottle. 'And you're the only relative I've got, aren't you, Daisy?'

Bunny watched them. 'I'm really sorry, Peter. I know you want to stay together but I just don't see how it can be done. Not if you're going to stay in Tarridale.' She drew a deep breath, she wanted this conversation no more than Peter. 'I did say, right at the start, that I couldn't be a mother to Daisy for ever. I'm fifty-one years old, and that's just too old for a baby of what – nearly three months. By the time she's ten I'll be over sixty. She needs somebody younger. And Mairi's got a little boy of two – Angus. He's such a nice boy, he'll be like a big brother. They'll grow up together.' She hesitated. 'I don't know if I should really tell you this, but Mairi can't have any more children. That's why they'd love to have Daisy come to stay.'

Would Daisy be happy among strangers, Peter wondered, then realised they wouldn't be strangers at all. Colin would be her dad. Mairi would be her mum. Angus would be her brother. Mrs McKendrick would be her gran. He would be her Uncle Peter.

If Valerie hadn't been killed in the accident, he thought, she'd never have stayed on in Tarridale. Daisy would have been taken off to live somewhere down the country, some flat, maybe like the place they'd stayed in when he was little. He'd only have seen her a couple of times a year. Instead of a proper dad like Colin, there would have been a succession of Valerie's boyfriends – for why should Matt have lasted any longer than the others? When you balanced one against the other, Daisy would have a much happier and more settled life here with Mairi and Colin. It hurt to think of her going even that far, but it was only just beyond the village, he would see her all the time. When she was a bit older she could visit him at Three Pines and play with the animals.

'I know it sounds selfish,' Bunny said at length, 'but I've had three children of my own and brought them up. I've been a good wife and helped my husband's career. You can't imagine the years I've spent sitting on committees and the magistrate's bench. If I had a pound for every time I've sat at some ridiculously expensive dinner, or made polite conversation at a cocktail party and longed to be back home in a comfy sweater like this, I'd be – well, as rich as my *very* rich ex-husband. Now I want to do what *I* want. Which means living up here a million miles from London and getting on with my paintings and stories. I'm just delighted to have you here, Peter, we're going to get on like a house on fire, but I simply can't go all the way back to looking after babies.'

'Yeah, I know.' Peter nodded. 'I understand, really.'

The next morning he took some money to buy lunch and cycled down to the village to see friends and kick a ball around. The bike was a brilliant success. He was quite good at wheelies by this time, and the 'Hardrock' had so many gears that riding home up the long Sandy Brae was no problem.

Bunny had asked him to be back by four and when he arrived he found cakes on the table and Mairi and Colin McGregor visiting. Colin, a big sandy-haired man in jeans and an Aran sweater, held Daisy on his knee. She was tugging at his finger, fascinated by his wedding ring. Angus, their young son, lay on the floor and pushed his toy tractor around, making an engine noise with his lips. As Peter came into the room Daisy recognised him. Her face lit up in a smile. The others smiled too and Bunny made the tea.

They visited a second time, although Peter missed them, and a few days later Bunny drove Daisy and himself to their house by the river. Unlike Scar Hill and Three Pines, this was a new house built of brick. They called it Teal Sands. Colin had made a neat garden with lawns and flowerbeds and a fence to keep out wandering sheep, where daffodils bloomed beneath a twisted crab apple tree. A picture window gazed across Strath Teal; another faced down-river towards the broad white beach and the ocean. Peter knew the house although he had never paid it particular attention. It would, he saw, be a beautiful place for Daisy to grow up. A room had been made ready for her with nursery wallpaper, a white cot and a chest of drawers. Mairi prepared lunch while Peter made friends with Dixie, their young cocker spaniel, and went out with Angus to give Ben and Jasper a run.

Next afternoon they went again. Peter carried Daisy into the house, sound asleep and wrapped in a white blanket. He gave her a kiss and handed her carefully to Mairi. Colin stood behind. They came away after a few minutes, leaving Daisy in her new home.

The time had been chosen carefully because Peter had to go straight to school, where the changing rooms had been opened for a Sunday football match. He scored one goal, prevented another and went to a friend's house for tea. Bunny picked him up at nine o'clock.

In the days that followed he missed Daisy keenly. Bunny advised him not to visit too soon, to give her time to settle in. When he did call ten days later, cycling down after school with the April wind making his eyes water, the house smelled of baking and he found Daisy playing with a pretty rattle with flying ribbons. Already she looked bigger and somehow different in trousers and a baby-blue top he had not seen before. When he sat beside her she smiled up and gave a little gurgle, then transferred her attention to the rattle.

'She seems settled in,' he said.

'She was a bit restless the first day or two,' Mairi said, 'but she's fine now. Just a lovely little girl. And Angus is so good to her. We were afraid he might be a bit jealous but he's not at all. Keeps fetching her things to play with.' She nodded. 'Go on, pick her up. It's only a few weeks since you were looking after her all by yourself.'

So Peter hoisted her into his arms but Daisy struggled. She didn't want to be picked up. Her face crumpled. He recognised the signs, in a moment she was going to start wailing. Quickly he set her down again. At once her face cleared. She shook the plastic rattle.

The house was unusually peaceful. He looked around. 'Where's Angus?'

'Oh, he's out the back. Got some idea of digging a pond for

the frogs to come and lay their eggs.'

She went to the kitchen and returned with a Diet Coke and two new-baked currant scones spread with butter and jam. 'I'd give you a slice of fruit cake but it's just out the oven.'

'Thanks,' he said.

Mairi nibbled her lip. 'It's probably a bit soon to be talking about this, but Colin and I were thinking that sometime in the future the right thing would be for us to adopt Daisy. You know, so we'd really be her mum and dad.' She looked anxious. 'It wouldn't affect you or anything, you'd still be her Uncle Peter.'

He had talked to Bunny about it. It would give Daisy the security she needed. It was the right thing to do. He had one question:

'That means she'd take your name, doesn't it? She'd be called McGregor.'

'Yes.'

'Daisy May McGregor.'

'Not exactly,' Mairi said. 'We thought it would be nice to leave her family name in there as well.'

'You mean Irwin?'

'Well, that's what her mother was called, and her granddad, of course. We know how much he meant to you. So Colin and I thought we'd leave her name as it stands on the birth certificate and just add 'McGregor' at the end. Probably drop the 'May' because it would be such a mouthful. So she'd be called Daisy Irwin McGregor'

Peter could not keep the smile from his face.

'People will call her Daisy McGregor, of course, but the 'Irwin' will still be there. I don't think we should take it away, especially with you living just up the road.' She was relieved to see him so pleased. 'So is that all right?'

'Yeah, it's great.'

He took a bite of scone and looked down at the little girl beside him. She had abandoned the rattle and was playing with her toes. 'Come here, you,' he said and lifted her onto his knee.

'Daisy McGregor. Are you going to be a good little girl? Are you?'

A puzzled, concentrated look came into her face. Peter knew it well. 'Oh-oh,' he said.

Mairi laughed. 'Give her here. Go on, you finish your scones. I'll just be a minute.'

She disappeared into the kitchen and Peter heard her talking to the baby as she took off the nappy and wiped her clean.

'Oh, I forgot,' she called through. 'Look on the sideboard. Colin left you a couple of tickets for next Saturday's game. If you're not doing anything, he'll pick you up with one of your pals. About twelve o'clock.'

'Thanks, that's great!' Peter found them in a small brown envelope. 'I'll ask Gerry.'

He wandered into the kitchen.

Mairi fastened the fresh nappy and got rid of the dirty one. Happy to be clean, Daisy waved her arms and legs on the table.

'Oh, you are wicked.' Peter tickled her tummy. 'Just a wicked little girl.'

Daisy giggled with delight. A river of bubbles ran down her chin. He wiped it away and rubbed his fingers with a towel.

Angus came in from the garden. He wore rubber boots and was covered in mud.

'Don't you dare, Angus McGregor,' his mother said firmly. 'You stand right where you are until I get those boots off you. Are you going out again?'

He shook his head and dropped the old tablespoon with which he had been digging. Spatters of mud flew across the kitchen.

Mairi stripped him from his filthy clothes. In jersey and underpants he climbed on a chair to get a scone.

'No, you'll spoil your dinner.' His mother pushed them out of reach. 'What a child! Here, you can have an end of this lopsided one. And that's *all* you're getting.'

She swung Daisy to her shoulder. 'Sorry Colin's not here,'

she said to Peter. 'He had to go out just before you came. Young chap the far side of Brathy had an accident with the tractor. Nasty from the sound of it. Might lose his arm.'

Peter told her about his own accident, his twisted ankle and how nearly the back wheel had rolled over him.

'You were lucky.' Mairi had worked in Accident and Emergency. 'Terrible injuries with tractors. I remember a boy of sixteen …'

They chatted and soon it was time to go.

'Tell Colin thanks for the tickets.' Peter walked out the door into the sunshine. 'If he gives me a ring when he sets off, we'll meet him at the gate.'

Mairi stood holding Daisy. She had her rattle again and wasn't the least bit interested in her departing uncle. He planted a kiss on her cheek and pulled his bike from the wall. 'Thanks for the eats.'

'See you soon.' Mairi raised a hand. 'Bye, Peter.'

Angus appeared behind her clutching the rest of his scone. When he saw Peter had spotted him he smiled naughtily. Peter shook his fist. Delightedly Angus scampered back into the hall.

He rode away, wobbling as he found the right gear, and looked back from the road. Daisy had thrown her rattle into a flowerbed. Mairi was bending to retrieve it.

It was four miles home, mostly uphill – one mile to the village, three to the five-bar gate. Ben had waited for the school bus but no Peter had dismounted. Now Peter shouted and the big dog came galloping up the track from Three Pines. Doubly happy after his disappointment, Ben bounded around him.

'Who's my best pal?' Peter crouched and rubbed his whiskery grey head.

The sun had set. Far to the west, beyond Scar Hill, the after-glow shone above the mountains.

Peter remounted and freewheeled down the short track.

'Hello, there.' Bunny was shutting the hens up for the night. 'Just be a couple of minutes.'

The kitchen glowed golden. Through the window he saw paints and paper spread on the table. A smell of steak pie drifted to meet him. Peter pushed his bike round to the shed and went into the house.

Tales of the North Coast

Alan Temperley
ISBN 0 946487 18 9
PBK £8.99

Seals and shipwrecks, witches and fairies, curses and clearances, fact and fantasy – the authentic tales in this collection come straight from the heart of a small Highland community. Children and adults alike respond to their timeless appeal. The stories in *Tales of the North Coast* were collected in the early 1970s by Alan Temperley and young people at Farr Secondary School in Sutherland. All were gathered from the area between the Kyle of Tongue and Strath Halladale, in scattered communities wonderfully rich in lore that had been passed on by word of mouth down the generations. The selection provides a satisfying balance between intriguing tales of the supernatural and more everyday occurrences. The book also includes chilling eye-witness accounts of the notorious Strathnaver Clearances, when tenants were given a few hours to pack up and get out of their homes, which were then burned to the ground.

Tales of the North Coast is illustrated with vigorous linocut images produced by the young people under the guidance of their art teacher, Elliot Rudie.

The Bower Bird

Ann Kelley
ISBN 1 906307 98 9
(children's fiction)
PBK £6.99
ISBN 1 906307 45 8
(adult fiction)
PBK £6.99

I had open-heart surgery last year, when I was eleven, and the healing process hasn't finished yet. I now have an amazing scar that cuts me in half almost, as if I have survived a shark attack.

Gussie is twelve years old, loves animals and wants to be a photographer when she grows up. The only problem is that she's unlikely to ever grow up.

Gussie needs a heart and lung transplant, but the donor list is as long as her arm and she can't wait around that long. Gussie has things to do; finding her ancestors, coping with her parents' divorce, and keeping an eye out for the wildlife in her garden.

Winner of the 2007 Costa Children's Book Award.

It's a lovely book – lyrical, funny, full of wisdom. Gussie is such a dear – such a delight and a wonderful character, bright and sharp and strong, never to be pitied for an instant. HELEN DUNMORE

Inchworm
Ann Kelley
ISBN 1 906817 12 X
PBK £6.99

I ask for a mirror. My chest is covered in a wide tape, so I can't see the clips or incision but I want to see my face, to see if I've changed.

Gussie wants to go to school like every other teenage girl and find out what it's like to kiss a boy. But she's just had a heart and lung transplant and she's staying in London to recover from the operation.

Between managing her parents' love lives, waiting for her breasts to finally start growing, and trying to hide a destructive kitten in her dad's expensive bachelor pad, Gussie makes friends with another cardio patient in the hospital and finds out that she can't have everything her heart desires...

A great book. THE INDEPENDENT

This is definitely one of my top ten books. You have to read it, and it will stay with you forever! TEEN TITLES

The Burying Beetle
Ann Kelley
ISBN 1 84282 099 0
PBK £9.99
ISBN 1 905222 08 4
PBK £6.99

Meet Gussie. Twelve years old and settling into her new ramshackle home on a cliff top above St Ives, she has an irrepressible zest for life. She also has a life-threatening heart condition. But it's not in her nature to give up. Perhaps because she knows her time might be short, she values every passing moment, experiencing each day with humour and extraordinary courage.

Gussie's story of inspiration and hope is both heartwarming and heartrending. Once you've met her, you'll not forget her. And you'll never take life for granted again.

Gussie fairly fizzles with vitality, radiating fun and enjoyment into everything that comes her way. Her life may be predestined to be short but not short on wonder, glee, the love of things as they really are. It is rare to find such tragic circumstances written about without an ounce of self-pity. Rarer still to have the story of a circumscribed existence escaping its confines by sheer force of personality, zest for life.
MICHAEL BAYLEY

Me and Ma Gal
Des Dillon
ISBN 1 84282 054 0
PBK £5.99

If you never had to get married an that I really think that me an Gal'd be pals for ever. That's not to say that we never fought. Man we had some great fights so we did.

A story of boyhood friendship and irrepressible vitality told with the speed of trains and the understanding of the awkwardness, significance and fragility of that time. This is a day in the life of two boys as told by one of them, 'Derruck Danyul Riley'.

Dillon's book is arguably one of the most frenetic and kinetic, living and breathing of all Scottish novels... The whole novel crackles with this verbal energy.
THE LIST 100 Best Scottish Books of All Time – 2005

Singin I'm No a Billy He's a Tim
Des Dillon
ISBN 1 906307 46 6
PBK £6.99

What happens when you lock up a Celtic fan?

What happens when you lock up a Celtic fan with a Rangers fan?

What happens when you lock up a Celtic fan with a Rangers fan on the day of the Old Firm match?

Des Dillon watches the sparks fly as Billy and Tim clash in a rage of sectarianism and deep-seated hatred. When children have been steeped in bigotry since birth, is it possible for them to change their views?

Join Billy and Tim on their journey of discovery. Are you singing their tune?

Explosive. EVENING NEWS

Luath Storyteller: Tales of Loch Ness
Stuart McHardy
ISBN 1 906307 59 8
PBK £5.99

My Epileptic Lurcher
Des Dillon
ISBN 1 906307 74 1
PBK £8.99

We all know the Loch Ness Monster. Not personally, but we've definitely heard of it. Stuart McHardy knows a lot more stories about Loch Ness monsters, fairies and heroes than most folk, and he has more than a nodding acquaintance with Nessie, too.

From the lassie whose forgetfulness created the loch to St Columba's encounter with a rather familiar sea-monster nearly 1,500 years ago, from saints to hags to the terrible *each-uisge*, the waterhorse that carries unwitting riders away to drown and be eaten beneath the waters of the loch, these tales are by turns funny, enchanting, gruesome and cautionary. Derived from both history and legends, passed by word of mouth for untold generations, they give a glimpse of the romance and glamour, the danger and the magic of the history of Scotland's Great Glen.

That's when I saw them. The paw prints. Halfway along the ceiling they went. Evidence of a dog that could defy gravity.

The incredible story of Bailey, the dog who walked on the ceiling; and Manny, the guy who got kicked out of Alcoholics Anonymous for swearing.

Manny Riley is newly married, with a puppy and a wee flat by the sea, and the BBC are on the verge of greenlighting one of his projects. Everything sounds perfect. But Manny has always been an anger management casualty, and the idyllic village life is turning out to be more *League of Gentlemen* than *The Good Life*. The BBC have decided his script needs totally rewritten, the locals are conducting a campaign against his dog, and the village policeman is on the side of the neds. As his marriage suffers under the strain of his constant rages, a strange connection begins to emerge between Manny's temper and the health of his beloved Lurcher.

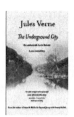

The Underground City
Jules Verne
ISBN 1 84282 080 X
PBK £7.99

Out of the Mists
John Barrington
ISBN 1 905222 33 5
PBK £8.99

Ten years after he left the exhausted Aberfoyle mine underneath Loch Katrine, the former manager – James Starr – receives an intriguing letter from the old overman – Simon Ford. It suggests that the mine isn't actually barren after all.

Despite also receiving an anonymous letter the same day contradicting this, James returns to Aberfoyle and discovers that there is indeed more coal to be excavated.

Strange events hint at a presence that does not wish to see the cave mined further. Could someone be out to sabotage their work? Someone with a grudge against them?
Or could it be something supernatural, something they cannot see or understand?

This is a new translation of *The Underground City*.

One of the strangest and most beautiful novels of the nineteenth century.
MICHEL TOURNIER

In the earliest hours of the morning shepherds gather, waiting for the mists that conceal the hillsides to clear. To pass the time they tell tales of roaming giants, marauding monks and weird witches. Enter this world of magic and wonder in *Out of the Mists*, a delightful collection of stories which will captivate and entertain you while answering your questions about Scottish history and folklore.

Why did St Andrew become the patron saint of Scotland?

How can you protect yourself from faerie magic?

What happened to Scotland's last dragon?

John Barrington uses wit and his encyclopaedic knowledge of Scottish folklore to create a compelling collection of stories that will capture the imaginations of readers of all ages.

Details of these and other Luath Press titles are to be found at www.luath.co.uk

Luath Press Limited

committed to publishing well written books worth reading

LUATH PRESS takes its name from Robert Burns, whose little collie Luath (*Gael.*, swift or nimble) tripped up Jean Armour at a wedding and gave him the chance to speak to the woman who was to be his wife and the abiding love of his life. Burns called one of the 'Twa Dogs' Luath after Cuchullin's hunting dog in Ossian's *Fingal*. Luath Press was established in 1981 in the heart of Burns country, and is now based a few steps up the road from Burns' first lodgings on Edinburgh's Royal Mile. Luath offers you distinctive writing with a hint of unexpected pleasures. Most bookshops in the UK, the US, Canada, Australia, New Zealand and parts of Europe, either carry our books in stock or can order them for you. To order direct from us, please send a £sterling cheque, postal order, international money order or your credit card details (number, address of cardholder and expiry date) to us at the address below. Please add post and packing as follows: UK – £1.00 per delivery address; overseas surface mail – £2.50 per delivery address; overseas airmail – £3.50 for the first book to each delivery address, plus £1.00 for each additional book by airmail to the same address. If your order is a gift, we will happily enclose your card or message at no extra charge.

Luath Press Limited
543/2 Castlehill
The Royal Mile
Edinburgh EH1 2ND
Scotland
Telephone: 0131 225 4326 (24 hours)
Fax: 0131 225 4324
email: sales@luath. co.uk
Website: www. luath.co.uk